10/08 . Sing 1400

ALSO BY KELLY LANGE

Trophy Wife

Gossip

A Novel

Kelly Lange

SIMON & SCHUSTER

SIMON & SCHUSTER
Rockefeller Center
1230 Avenue of the Americas
New York, NY 10020

SIMON AND SCHUSTER and colophon are
registered trademarks of Simon & Schuster Inc.

Designed by Barbara M. Bachman
Manufactured in the United States of America

1   3   5   7   9   10   8   6   4   2

Library of Congress Cataloging-in-Publication Data
Lange, Kelly.
Gossip : a novel / Kelly Lange.
p. cm.
I. Title.
PS3562.A48495G67   1998
813'.54—dc21   98-34221 CIP
ISBN 0-684-83263-1

FOR MY FABULOUS SISTER!

(who is also the spiritual sister

of my fictional "Maxi Poole"):

ELLIE POOLE—

You are kind, smart, savvy, fun,

and a woman who has definitely advanced

the interchange of gossip to

the level of an art form!

BRIARCLIFF, PENNSYLVANIA. It is midmorning on Sunday, June 12, graduation day for the class of '79. It promises to be a beautiful sunny day, warm but not hot, perfect for the exercises to be held on the massive, rolling quad at two o'clock this afternoon. Exclusive, expensive Briarcliff College for Women is backyard to strictly Main Line Philadelphia, and even the weather dares not disappoint on this day.

Inside Brooks Hall, one of the stately, ivy-covered quarrystone dormitories, four of the graduates are holding their own private goodbye party before the early afternoon commencement ceremonies. Suitcases, garment bags, totes, and boxes, all in varying stages of packing, are strewn about the room. Today, the four young women will be leaving this haven forever, each heading to a different state. They have been inseparable during these college years, and they will miss each other terribly. They are alternately hugging, sobbing, and laughing raucously.

Patricia Farnsworth Carroll, called Trisha by her friends, is a Philadelphia girl whose parents had planned to send her to Briarcliff even before she was born. Most of the Carroll women and all of the Farnsworth women had gone to Briarcliff, tracing back to when the college was founded in 1880.

Trisha was a golden girl, five foot seven and lean, with high cheekbones and clear, hazel eyes, a dazzling Grace Kelly smile, and a halo of blond hair cut just under her chin—thick, lustrous hair that always seemed to fall right back into place each time she tossed her elegant head.

In fact, everything that Trisha did seemed nothing short of perfect. Majoring in communications, she had tackled the work, as she did all areas of her life, with a no-nonsense efficiency that made it look easy. In her senior year she was class president, captain of the debate society, high scorer on the basketball team, and the lead actress in the drama guild, and still, she managed to place high on the dean's list.

Her goals included a wonderful husband, bright, healthy children, magnificent homes in several places like her parents had, and a glamorous career—Trisha wanted it all, and if anyone could manage to achieve that, she was the most likely candidate.

Trisha's roommate was *Lane Hurley*, a mischievous Boston girl with dewy pale complexion and a mass of dark Irish curls. Lane had transferred in as a second-semester freshman, after having been quietly invited to leave Smith College in Northampton when she and two other young women were caught smoking marijuana in her dorm room.

When the dean called the Hurley mansion in Boston's tony Louisburg Square with the news, Lane's mother fainted and her father was livid, and she was given one chance to reclaim her future. Just one, her father had emphasized—one more screw-up and she could go out and earn herself a living without any help from her mother and him. God knows what her brothers got away with over the years while he looked the other way, but no matter, Lane was practical, she had her father's business savvy, and she determined from the outset that it would be in her best interest to fly right at Briarcliff. And she never once veered off course. At least she never got caught.

Of the four, Lane was the adventuresome one, yet she navigated uncertain waters with a particularly level head—the perfect combination of qualities to make it in business, which had been her major, and was her dream.

Kathryn Blakely Spenser, of the New York publishing Spensers, had the kind of face that melted men's hearts even before she said hello. She was medium-dark complected with huge, smoky brown eyes, a finely sculpted cleft chin, lush, full, wine-tinted lips, and heavy, mahogany-brown hair with reddish glints, which she wore blunt-cut and cascading to her shoulders.

Dreamy, romantic Kate majored in English literature. She'd been content to immerse herself in the novels of Jane Austen and the love poems of the Brownings, while barely passing all of her courses with a C-minus average. Under her picture in the Briarcliff yearbook, class of '79, it was written that beautiful Kathryn Spenser would get anything she wanted in life. What she wanted was to marry the handsomest, most loving, most passionate man on earth, have a houseful of gorgeous children, and be treated like a princess.

All during their college years, men she hadn't even met, or certainly didn't remember meeting, would routinely send her mash notes, gifts, and flowers. Katie would usually shrug them off, while her roommate, Molly, would be unabashedly green with envy.

Fiery *Molly Adams* was small-boned and short in stature, but she made up for her diminutive size by a spirited feistiness that played perfectly with her dancing green eyes and wild mane of orange-red hair.

Molly was the only one of the four not born to wealth and privilege. A street-smart urban Southerner, Molly had come to the school on a fully funded scholarship, given each year to the top female student at Miami's Matignon High School, in memory of a departed Briarcliff alumna. The scholarship paid four years' tuition, provided the candidate kept her grades up, and Molly did.

In fact, except for her math classes, Molly earned straight A's. She was ambitious, driven, a tireless worker, and totally success oriented. She had actually scored lower on IQ testing than each of the other three, yet her grades had been consistently higher than all of theirs by far.

Along with her driven work ethic, Molly was a gifted artist. She had majored in fine arts, and she was leaving Briarcliff with the full confidence of youth that she would conquer the art world. She would start out working in galleries to pay the rent, while honing her painting skills in her off-hours. And she would, one day, create great art.

KATE AND MOLLY roomed directly across the hall from Lane and Trisha, on the third floor in the east wing at Brooks Hall. The prospect of leaving Briarcliff today and going their separate ways was bittersweet—exciting, but sad.

Molly had landed a job in a small art gallery at a summer resort on the New Jersey shore. When summer was over and she had a little experience on her résumé, she hoped to make a move to a big-time gallery in New York.

Trisha was going home, to her parents' estate in Philadelphia. With her dad's help, she would make the rounds of the city's top public relations firms, interviewing for the perfect job.

Beautiful Kate was madly in love with Elgin Horner, her blond, Nordic, football star steady from Brown University, who was also graduating this month. Kate would spend the summer at her family's place on the beach in New York's upscale East Hampton, relaxing and planning her wedding.

Lane was going back to Boston, which her friends knew she was dreading. As she put it, from the moment she got home tonight, she would spend all of her waking hours plotting her escape. Meantime, this symbolic pregraduation gathering of the four longtime college friends might be the last time for a long time that they would all be together.

ALRIGHT, I HAVE presents for everybody," Trisha was saying to the others now, taking a sip of the champagne they were sharing, even though it was still morning.

"Oh, no, we weren't going to do that!" Molly protested. While the other three never lacked for money, Molly never had an extra dime. "We agreed, no graduation presents all around—"

"This is different, Molly," Trisha cut her off. She dropped to her knees and fumbled about in the space beneath her bed, and came up with four large, unwrapped cardboard boxes.

"My dad sent these for each of us," she said, "after he heard me whining about how I'm going to miss you girls."

She handed up the boxes to each of her friends, then sat back on her bed and held the fourth one on her lap.

"Okay, do you know what these are?" she asked then, as the others studied the glossy green-and-white boxes with bold, black lettering that read ANSA-PHONE.

"Sure—those new answering machines that you hook up to your telephone," Lane chimed. "My brother has one."

"Exactly," Trisha smiled. "Daddy says to tell you all that they have detailed instruction pamphlets inside, and even a child can work them."

"What about somebody who can't do algebra?" Molly laughed.

"No excuses," Trisha decreed. "Kate, you are not allowed to toss this in the back of your closet for a decade!" Kate was known to procrastinate.

"I insist that we all take time out tomorrow, as soon as we're home, before we're even settled, to hook these things up, okay?" Trisha went on. "Then I expect three messages on *my* answering machine tomorrow, reporting that each one of you is up and running. Got it?"

"Got it," Molly laughed. The other two concurred. Trisha was the organizer among them.

"Your dad's a genius," Kate said reverently.

"Fabulous!" Lane whooped, as they all came together for a group hug before each had to hustle off to finish packing and get ready for the graduation ceremony.

"Thank you, Trisha," Lane spoke for all of them. "Now we will never, ever lose touch."

Book One

July 1998

Chapter 1

WHERE'S THE ARTIST? Isn't Aiden Jannus supposed to be here?" gorgeous British actress Debra DeAngeles asked as she scanned the faces of the crowd milling about the packed Beverly Hills gallery.

"Probably still in jail, after he took his clothes off in front of the Kennedy Center last week," her friend Maxi laughed. Television news reporter Maxi Poole was covering this art exhibit for Channel 6.

"Hmmm," Debra murmured with a beautifully wicked smile. "That's why I wanted to meet the guy. I think he's my kind of man— oozing sex appeal and raw talent, but a little kinky."

"A little kinky? You call being a wacked-out, totally fried hard-core drug addict *a little kinky?*" Maxi countered. "No question, though, Jannus is probably the most talented living artist in America. Certainly the most salable, at least at the moment. That's why we're doing this story."

The two women stood in the spacious main hall of the Feruzzi Gallery on tony Rodeo Drive. Maxi's camera crew was in the thick of the throng, shooting the action. And there was plenty of action—this was a major art showing, and the gallery was teeming with celebrities, art patrons, dealers, buyers, shoppers, curiosity seekers, groupies, and of course, the ubiquitous press. No rent-a-crowd here, because the artist was the brilliant but outrageous Aiden Jannus, and the walls of the gallery's several rooms were creatively hung with his jungle-wild, colorful oils.

Devin Bradshaw, owner of the giant clothing house L.A. Garb, was there with her husband, attorney John Tanner. Celebrity decorator Bailey Senn was examining the paintings, shopping the sought-after Jannus pieces for clients. Critics who scorned called Jannus's work "recycled Rousseaus," but they were few, and often their artistic disdain simply masked their pique because they couldn't get an interview with the recalcitrant artist.

Aiden Jannus himself was an oddly attractive man—mid-thirties, tall, rangy, with sunken, craggy features and unruly black Irish hair falling into dissipated-looking eyes—a Byronesque figure who, when he was not getting himself into trouble with the law, was committing stunning and much publicized social gaffes. Were he not the darling of the art world right now, he would be just obnoxious. An infamous abuser of alcohol and drugs, still he managed to turn out brilliant work, dazzling canvases of all sizes, and in great volume.

AUSTIN FERUZZI, the gallery owner—tanned, and dapper in Armani, with a full head of slicked-back dark hair and a face and demeanor that bespoke success—stood in a corner of the packed salon, looking a little nervous. Uncharacteristic for a man of his charm and guile, but he *was* a little nervous. Important press here, he was thinking, and he had no idea if the sonofabitch *star* of the show would even show up.

The Feruzzi Galleries had retained exclusive representation of the artwork of Aiden Jannus since the night that Austin Feruzzi ran into the artist in a bar in New York's SoHo district, well before he had emerged as a major talent. Feruzzi, who knew art and knew the art scene, saw Jannus as a comer, but a risky commodity, steeped as he was in the turbid world of alcohol and drugs. Still, Feruzzi had made a deal with him, signed that night on the back of a napkin while the two sat side by side on bar stools. Jannus had a good deal of trouble focusing during the negotiation, which went something like this:

"So what do you say, want me to represent you? Sell your stuff? I own major art galleries here in New York, in Beverly Hills, and in London—"

"Why not."

"Okay, then write your name on this."

"Whazzit say?"

"It says that you and I are going to make beautiful music together! Let's drink to it."

Jannus had scratched his name on the napkin, and promptly forgot that he did it. Until Feruzzi's lawyer paid a visit to his woodsy studio out in Sag Harbor a few days later and refreshed his memory, presenting the small, rumpled, rum-stained legal document. An excellent "get" with nothing to lose, Feruzzi had figured—when the man was on his game he was extremely good, and the galleries could always cut him loose if he didn't pay off, or if he became an embarrassment.

Aiden Jannus was just starting to be known in art circles then, just beginning to gain a reputation for being quite promising, albeit a reprobate of sorts. Perhaps the latter even added to his mystique back then, and it did still, Feruzzi knew. And since the Feruzzi Galleries had taken him on eight years before, Jannus had flourished—his artwork had become increasingly mature, and his reputation soared. His success, however, did not inspire him to clean up his act—not even a little. If anything, he was deeper into his addictions. Yet, his stellar work continued to pour onto the fine-art market in great volume.

What the hell, Feruzzi thought, eyeballing the gathered glitterati in his Beverly Hills gallery now, this bash was a no-brainer, whether Jannus showed up or not. The artist's finished pieces had been held back for months to present at this show. Collectors from around the country and abroad had eagerly awaited tonight's event. Scattered about the gallery now, wealthy buyers or their emissaries could be seen quietly negotiating with gallery reps, scrambling to purchase pieces of their choice.

Feruzzi's eyes settled on blond news reporter Maxi Poole. His first thought was, *Nice tits*; his second thought was, *Good, we're covered on Channel 6*. She was talking to Debra DeAngeles, the leggy, devastatingly sensuous star of a popular network prime-time television drama. Her tousled mane of hair was fiery red this season, and her tight, black silk slip dress hugged her curves like a second skin. One of these days, Feruzzi told himself—

He was distracted by the sight of his wife sweeping through the room—his tall, stunning socialite wife, Kathryn Spenser Feruzzi. He watched her tossing her lush, dark, shoulder-length hair as she moved her head from side to side, gracing one person then another with her greetings, lighting up the room with her brilliant smile, carelessly spilling champagne as she moved in understated Chanel and Cartier diamonds. Kate was easily the most beautiful woman in the room.

"Having a good time, darling?" he mouthed, as she slid into his orbit. Kate's job in life was to have a good time, he reflected ruefully. That's because it was basically *her* money. *His* brains, *his* skill, *his* business strategy, *his* salesmanship, *his* charisma, *his damn tail-busting dog-work seven days a week!* But it was *her money* that paid the bills.

Most of the gallery grosses went into interest payments on his huge loans. Feruzzi was up to his ass in debt on the business, but he made sure that the books didn't show it. He knew that astute Henry Spenser would cut off his cash flow in a heartbeat—one of the maxims the old man was tediously fond of reciting was, "I never throw good Spenser money after bad!"

Austin kept assuring Katie and his in-laws that the galleries' huge overhead, his pricey acquisitions, and the London expansion were worthwhile and necessary expenses, that the business was about to take off like a rocket, and that Aiden Jannus was the spark that would make that happen. And if this show tonight was any indication, he thought, he just might be right.

"Good time?" Kate called back to him over the heads of milling patrons. "Sure, good time, great time," she said, with just a hint of a slur to her words, and she continued on her overly cheerful, unsteady odyssey through the crowd.

Feruzzi noticed his New York gallery director, Molly Adams, at the far end of the salon, pensively perusing the canvases on the walls, seeming to take endless inventory. Molly had been a close friend of Feruzzi's wife Kate since the two had roomed together in their college days, and it was Katie who'd gotten Molly the top job in her husband's New York gallery back when it opened. With her trim figure and tousled rusty mane, Molly turned heads, but she was seemingly oblivious to her electric good looks. She was knowledgeable, diligent, and dedicated to fine art and the business of art—Austin Feruzzi knew that he was very lucky to have her.

Lane Hamilton, another member of the women's college clique, was arm-in-arm with her husband, Geoffrey Hamilton. The two had driven down for tonight's opening from Carmel-by-the-Sea, an exclusive, picturesque year-round resort up the California coast. Geoff Hamilton was Carmel's chief of police, and his wife Lane owned and operated Hamilton House, a popular antiques and bakery shop in the heart of town. Lane didn't deal in such pricey artists as Aiden Jannus in her boutique, but she appreciated his work, and this was an opportunity to be with "the group," her three very closest friends from college days.

Wealthy New York businessman Peter Newman was pacing the perimeters, shopping the artwork with his wife Trisha—Trisha Newman, network radio talk show host, was the other member of the tight Briarcliff College foursome. The Newmans were hosting a dinner at Morton's for the Feruzzis and a few friends after the showing tonight.

Tripp Kendrick, Feruzzi's Beverly Hills gallery manager, was working the room—shaking hands, chatting, all in the name of doing business. A social animal, Tripp knew all of the West Coast luminaries, as well as most of the others on the guest list tonight. Feruzzi lifted a glass of champagne from a passing waiter's tray. He had it covered, he knew. If this show was not a huge success, it wouldn't be because he had left anything undone.

LOOK, DARLING," Debra DeAngeles remarked to Maxi Poole in her melodic British accent, "Kate Spenser is positively pissed! Beautiful, but most decidedly drunk, don't you find?"

"You would be too if you were married to Austin Feruzzi," Maxi quipped, and the two women laughed aloud at their private joke. Maxi and Debra, as it happened, had been married to the same man, powerful, arrogant Hollywood film director Jack Nathanson. They were known to gibe that they had respectively "taken the course" on egomaniacal sociopaths, and in fact, they'd noted to each other a time or two, they could *teach* it.

"So what *is* that ferocious bruise on Kate's left cheekbone?" Debra queried.

"You see a bruise?"

"I miss nothing, you know that," Debra smiled. "Artfully covered up with makeup, yes, but it is quite definitely a bruise, and a wicked one at that."

"Wendy, who also misses nothing, says that the beautiful Mrs. Feruzzi is telling people that she tripped over a sprinkler head on her grounds and took a serious tumble," Maxi shrugged.

"I'm sure," Debra drawled. "More likely she tripped into a bottle of vodka and ran into a door. Where *is* Wendy, by the way?" Wendy Harris was Maxi's producer and close friend at Channel 6.

"Trolling for news right now, looking for something other than the obvious."

"Well, I'll catch the two of you later—I'm going trolling for men." With that Debra eased into the crowd, tossing Maxi a smile and a wink.

The star of the show was nowhere to be seen, true to his reputation for not showing up. We live in hope, Maxi thought. Aiden Jannus on tape could bump this piece from weather segment filler under the temperatures to a bona fide story. With Jannus, anything could happen. Or nothing, and that in itself would be news.

Maxi became aware of some sort of commotion going on near the door. Aiden Jannus had indeed arrived. Her crew got to him before she did. Maxi could see cameraman Pete Garrow moving with the artist, walking backward in front of him, the bulky Sony Betacam hoisted up on his right shoulder, rolling tape, producer Wendy Harris tight at his left shoulder. Business as usual, Maxi smiled, and now they were in business.

The rest of the press were fast closing ranks on Jannus, taping, filming, gathering audio, popping photos, taking notes. Maxi moved in next to Pete, who handed her a microphone without taking his eye away from the viewfinder. This was vintage Aiden Jannus, she observed. He was wearing a pair of navy-blue-and-white striped pajamas, a loose white T-shirt under the open pajama top, tennis shoes, no socks, and a three-day growth of beard.

He stumbled among the fairly startled but wildly intrigued guests, with the press closing in on all sides of him, calling out questions. Coming to a stop, he perched amid a sizable group of people who were standing in front of one of his larger canvases, discussing it, admiring it. When Jannus joined the group the conversation stopped for a beat, then people began pressing the artist with comments and questions about the piece. Jannus stood, staring at the painting stone-faced, ignoring them.

Suddenly, with the contingent of press continuing to flash and roll on him, he walked up to the painting, untied the fly on his pajamas, whipped out his penis, and aimed at the canvas.

"I'll show you what I think of this one," he said very quietly in his mild Irish brogue.

With that, he proceeded to urinate on the painting, producing a yellow stream that slid off the oils and dribbled down the wall. Then, tucking himself in, he turned and bolted for the door, and disappeared into the night.

Yes, vintage Jannus—the man never ceased to shock, Maxi considered. Pete dropped the camera from his shoulder and shut off the power. "I'd say we've got it, boss," he said to Maxi with a grin.

"Jesus, what do we do, pixelate his privates?" Wendy asked. "I mean, can we show this on the air?"

"Not at the dinner hour," Maxi laughed, "but it'll be everybody's lead at eleven!"

Chapter 2

"Lane, Katie, it's me, Trisha . . . I just got off the air . . . still recovering from our quick trip out there for the Aiden Jannus show. Jesus . . . Jannus! Crazy Irish degenerate—a latter-day Dylan Thomas. How long before he burns out or turns up dead under a bridge somewhere! L'enfant terrible, but his work is genius, yes? I can't wait for delivery of our triptych. Austin told Peter that the show was completely sold out, and the gallery took commissions on a ton of future work as well—no surprise.

"I'm conferencing just the two of you, by the way, because I want to throw out something about Molly . . . do either of you get strange vibes from her lately, or is it just me? She seemed so remote when we were all together out there. And when I asked about her love life at lunch today, she got defensive. Do you think she's uncomfortable that she's the only one of the four of us who never married? Let me know if you think her behavior has been odd lately.

"Everything's great here . . . my big news is Jason got accepted to Harvard today. So now he's accepted at both Stanford and Harvard, and Peter and I told him it was his choice . . . but I need you both to send up some heavy-duty good thoughts that he'll choose Harvard . . . I don't want him on the other side of the country. Yeah, yeah, I know he'd be right down the road from you, Lane, but Jason's my firstborn! At least at Harvard he'd be just an hour away from home on the shuttle. It's bad enough that Peter is away so much—I'm really going to be lonesome without Jason at home.

"By the way, Ivana was at Le Cirque today—she looks fabulous.

Who's her plastic surgeon? Does she go to someone in Beverly Hills, or to someone here in New York? I've got a wrinkle I'm not liking across my forehead, and maybe it's time. Okay, talk to me . . . Bye, gals." BEEP. TUESDAY, 3:12 P.M.

"Hi, Lane, it's Charlotte from the Antiques Exchange . . . I got a shipment today of the most incredibly divine oak-and-silver biscuit barrels! They are in perfect condition . . . the silver markings go back to the 1800s . . . they're still in their original boxes . . . never used. All handmade, each one is different. I have twenty-six of them, can you believe? Murray found them at an obscure estate sale outside of Birkenhead . . . that's a little township across the Mersey River from Liverpool . . . Murray was in England doing some buying at a big Antiques Convention in Manchester, and he saw the notice in the local paper . . . drove out there on a lark . . . anyway, these are perfect for Hamilton House! But you know I can't hold them, Lane, so get yourself or Lizzie down here! Call me. Bye, dear." BEEP. TUESDAY, 3:24 P.M.

Lane jotted notes on a spiral-bound pad as she listened to her messages. It was the midafternoon lull at Hamilton House, her combination antiques shop, bakery, and tearoom in Carmel-by-the-Sea.

Just one square mile in all, enchanting Carmel was a truly magic little English village on the Northern California coast, tucked into a forest of old oaks, variate pines, and historic cypress trees that grew right down to the most dazzling white sandy beach on earth. That pristine stretch of beach, the pounding surf, the salt air, the charming little brick-and-stone houses set in English gardens riotously ablaze with lavender, roses, impatiens, pansies, azaleas, and geraniums of every hue—everything about Carmel breathed continually renewing life into Lane's very soul.

True enough, stuffy Boston stifled her, had seemed to suck the life force out of her all during her growing-up years, so perhaps some of the Carmel mystique was, for Lane, simply the contrast. But the fact was, every day of her life here was heaven on earth, and she couldn't begin to imagine why Trisha and Molly preferred New York, and Kate actually enjoyed living in La-La Land. Different strokes, she guessed.

A customer had wandered into the shop. Lane watched as Liz, her assistant, approached the woman, who was quite obviously a tourist. Lizzie was young, black, and as efficient as she was beautiful. She smiled a greeting to let the visitor know that she was there for her, then left her to browse among the tasteful assortment of imported English teas, packaged scones and Scottish shortbread, gourmet Stilton cheeses and authentic British bangers, and HH's marvelous collection of antique porcelains and silver, mixed with treasures old and new, like fine Waterford crystal pieces, a rare old oak butter churn from Cornwall, or English bone china tea sets from Wedgwood and Royal Doulton.

Her eye fell on a small, much loved little oil painting that hung above an old pine hutch, a painting done especially for Hamilton House as a good luck gift back when Lane first opened the shop. It was done for her by Molly Adams, the artist of Lane's Briarcliff group. Now managing Kate and Austin Feruzzi's New York gallery, Molly still had time for her first love, painting.

Lane looked at this little canvas every day, and it never failed to evoke warm feelings. The subject was an impression of the pristine white chapel on the Briarcliff campus, its steeple proudly reaching toward the heavens. Bespeaking pride and purpose and goodness of spirit along with dignity and hope, for Lane, the painting conjured up delicious memories of the tight foursome during their college days. Over the years, countless customers had tried to purchase Molly's painting, but of course Lane would never let it go at any price.

Lane was proud of Hamilton House. She had been lucky to find the exquisite old strut-and-stone Tudor building in the heart of Carmel's colorful shopping center, right on Ocean Avenue between Lincoln and Dolores. Now thirteen years in business, she was competing effectively with wonderful Weinstein's Bakery, which had served Carmel since the early 1920s. And dear Mrs. Weinstein, who was on the Community and Cultural Commission with her, had several times assured Lane that there was more than enough business in the bustling little tourist town for both their excellent establishments.

Lane was proud of her husband, too. She had fallen in love with Geoffrey Alan Hamilton the moment she'd laid eyes on him. At first it was his tall, lean, muscular body and his rugged, sandy-haired drop-dead good looks that made her want to jump on his bones, on the spot. It wasn't until at least a week into their red-hot romance that she took note of the fact that Geoff was solid. A good man. He was a Carmel native. His father had been the city's chief of police for seventeen years, until he retired and Geoff succeeded him. That was fourteen years ago, when Lane was new in town.

She would never forget one second of that day. She'd looked at two properties that morning, prospective sites for the special shop she'd known she wanted to open since the day she moved here, down from San Francisco with her savings, her trust fund income, and a stake from her dad. The village was buzzing about a ceremony to be held at noon that day at Mission Ranch. It was to honor Gregory Hamilton, their outgoing police chief, and to watch him pin his badge on his son.

Lane was curious about Mission Ranch, the old farmhouse on what was once the grounds of Mission San Carlos Borromeo Del Rio Carmelo—lovely Mission Carmel, built in 1771, the second of Fra Junipero Serra's historic string of California missions.

Mission Ranch, now a restaurant and inn, was currently owned by Carmel's reigning celebrity, Clint Eastwood. The actor had fallen in love with Carmel during his Army years at Fort Ord. He visited often, filmed the cult movie *Play Misty for Me* there back in the early seventies, and, in fact, he'd gone on to serve a couple of salient years as Carmel's mayor. So Lane got into her yellow Volkswagen bug convertible, put the top down, and drove down Dolores to the old sheep ranch on Carmel River Beach, on the outside chance that Clint Eastwood would be there. That, and she didn't have anything better to do.

Standing shoulder-to-shoulder with half the town in one of the ancient dairy barns at Mission Ranch, Lane watched Chief Gregory Hamilton, a striking presence behind an old pine lectern, as he smiled broadly and gave his retirement speech. Retirement, hell, she thought as she checked out his long, lean frame, his handsome, well-tanned features, and his thick shock of salt-and-pepper hair, this man was definitely in his prime. To twenty-six-year-old, unattached, and admittedly horny Lane Hurley from proper Boston, the man looked to be as fit, as ruggedly good-looking, as charismatic and sexy as any movie star she'd ever seen. She made the silent observation that with this guy around, the town didn't need Clint Eastwood.

Then she saw his son! Her heart stopped as she watched the junior Officer Hamilton step up to the lectern and shake his father's hand, then hug him, then stand erect, even taller than his dad, as his father pinned his badge on him. Lane stood motionless while everyone applauded. She seriously thought that she was going to faint. As Geoffrey Hamilton took his place behind the microphone and began to speak, his words were completely drowned out in her own ears by the thunderous pounding of her heart.

As decorously as possible under the circumstances, she nudged her way through the crowd until she was standing right in front, about a foot away from the podium. She could have reached out and touched him. In fact, she had to restrain herself from doing exactly that. Not good form, she told herself, Carmelite civic leaders being a somewhat starchy bunch. But the second that Mr. Brand-New Police Chief Geoffrey Hamilton stopped speaking and turned to leave the platform, she pounced on him. Introduced herself, and offered her hand. And wouldn't let go of his. As the Carmel citizenry approached to congratulate its new chief, it had flashed crazily through Lane's mind that if she just hung on to him forever, they would never be apart.

That was the first day of her next fourteen years. Of her life! Now she and Geoff had two spirited boys and Beowulf, their big, wooly sheep dog, and they all lived happily in a lovely old English home on scenic Casanova Drive south of Ocean, with a breathtaking view of Carmel Bay. And still, to this day, her heart skipped a beat when Geoffrey Hamilton walked into the room.

Lane watched Lizzie ring up the woman's purchase, a hundred-year-old sterling silver trivet that she and Geoff had found earlier this year on a buying and sightseeing trip through the British Isles. Absently, she ran her fingers through her wealth of dark hair, a habit she had, an unconscious attempt to tame the shoulder-length ringlets that were made even curlier by Carmel's humid ocean air. Turning back to the telephone, she punched in the number for the Antiques Exchange, a wholesale antiques outlet in the city of Santa Ana, about thirty miles south of Los Angeles.

"Charlotte, it's Lane. Okay, yes! I mean, don't sell them, they sound great. I'll take them all, and I'll put just two or three of them out at a time. Give me until tomorrow . . . let me talk to Geoff tonight and see if I can manage a trip—we were just down there last weekend for the Aiden Jannus show. I'd like to come down, though, because I'm way overdue to shop your merchandise . . . you and Murray do find the most delicious old Brit items, and my inventory is disastrously low.

"God, business has been great, even in this economy. So yes, the British biscuit barrels have my name on them for sure . . . they sound perfect. Put a hold on them, and I'll call you tomorrow and let you know when I can get there. If I can't, I'll just have you deliver them sight unseen and bill me. Nobody knows better than you two what's good for Hamilton House. Besides me, of course. Talk to you tomorrow, hon . . . love to Murray and the kids . . . Bye-bye."

Lane depressed the phone switch, then punched in another number.

"Katie, hi, it's Lane. I think I'm going to make a quick trip south tomorrow. I need to pick up some pieces in Orange County. I'll know tonight if it's a definite . . . that is, if it squares with Geoff's plans . . . but I wanted to give you a heads-up, so you can pencil me on your dance card. Can we do dinner tomorrow night? Or if you're busy, tell me what night you have this week and I can put it off a couple of days. Call me as soon as you get this. Love ya!"

Lane hung up and glanced around the shop. A young couple were perusing the edibles, an older couple were looking at the porcelain figurines, and Maggie Carlson from the bookshop next door was seated at a table with her copies of the *San Francisco Chronicle* and the *Carmel Pine Cone*, taking her midafternoon tea and toasted crumpet break. Maggie had been in a deep depression since her husband was killed nearly two years ago. Two years, and nothing seemed capable of restoring the woman's sparkle, her *joie de vivre*. She was spooning imported British marmalade onto her muffin while peering through her rimless reading glasses at the newspapers, as she did every day at this time. Lane and Liz had learned the hard way that Maggie no longer welcomed chat, be it mundane Carmel gossip, or even quiet conversation about her loss, her ongoing grief, or her life now, so they respected that. After the usual brief pleasantries each day, the two made it a point to allow Maggie her privacy. Lane turned her attention back to the telephone and rang up another number.

"Trish, hi, it's me, darlin' . . . send me Jason and I'll send you my Robby . . . he could use a little New York polish . . . but not too much . . . he's absolutely delicious the way he is! I think he has his first major crush, by the way . . . he won't tell me about the girl, but he's walking around with this idiotic grin on his face. God, he looks more like Geoff every day.

"Whaddaya mean, Molly is acting defensive? Molly has always been defensive, and it's my observation that as we get older, we get even more so—of whatever we are. Molly was probably the only girl at Briarcliff who didn't come from tons of money, and she was defensive about that from the get-go, you know that. I think because she's so focused on her career, she's always put a lower priority on her love life. My feeling is she just never took the time to nourish a relationship, get married, and have a home life. Or children. But she thinks she's doing really great, and then she goes to lunch with you and she's reminded what really great is really like! I mean, do you have to take her to Le Cirque? You probably wore some understated Versace and your weight in gold and emeralds.

"And by the way, at thirty-nine you are not, not, not ready to have your face done. I'll slap you! And besides, you're on radio! Who sees you? Just kidding, I know you have a life. Oh, and yes, I do know who Ivana's doctor is. He's in Beverly Hills, his name is Dr. Steven Hoefflin, and he's the guy who did Michael Jackson. And right now he's embroiled in a huge scandal . . . he's being investigated by the California Medical Board on charges that he's done some weird things to patients while they were under anesthesia. For God's sake, Trish, don't you read The National Enquirer? Bye, sweetie . . . catch you later."

Lane was smiling as she replaced the receiver. Doing their phone-machine thing was always a kick. Since Trisha's dad had gifted the four young graduating pals with the first popular answering machine to come on the market, they had all moved up through state-of-the-art phone message technology over the years, and the four had kept on top of everything that happened, large and small, in each other's lives. Networking on the phone machines from coast to coast and from different parts of the world. Even while traveling, the four women checked in with each other. It had long since become second nature.

They did see each other as often as they could. Although Lane would only go kicking and screaming down to Los Angeles, unless it was business or something really special, Kate and her husband drove up the coast and vacationed at times in Carmel. And Lane had to admit that the two seemed happy, although she couldn't for the life of her understand what Katie ever saw in Austin Feruzzi. Handsome, yes, rich, yes, interesting, yes, if you liked that oh-so-smooth type, but there was something about him that didn't sit right with Lane. Gave her the creeps, in fact. She'd tried to discuss it with Geoff, but Geoffrey, God bless him, just would not stoop to gossip. Couldn't do it, he let her know every time, not by telling her that, but by stammering so uncomfortably that Lane would just laugh and let him off the hook.

So what was it about Austin? Austin Feruzzi, big-time art dealer with galleries in London, New York, and Beverly Hills—slick, bright, good looking in an oily way, charming, certainly. Kate had met him at a dinner party that Peter and Trisha gave one long-ago summer night at the trendy Bistro Gardens in Beverly Hills. Lane and Geoff were there that night, and they couldn't miss the sparks that ignited between Kate and Feruzzi. But Lane didn't trust him. The man had a high sleaze factor that set her bullshit detector jangling from the outset.

They'd never had children, just Kate's son from her first marriage. Right out of college she'd married Elgin Horner, her football star steady during senior year. They'd moved to Oakland when he was picked up by the Raiders, then down to Beverly Hills when the team became the L.A. Raiders in 1982. But Horner was never good enough for the Spensers, at least that was the way Lane read it, and their force-ful opinion had seemed to color Kate's. Three years into the marriage she filed for divorce, but to her parents' everlasting chagrin, she opted to stay in California with Shawn, her beautiful, golden-haired toddler. Soon she met wealthy Austin Feruzzi, who was older, divorced, and al-ready had his children, he'd told her. Didn't want any more. Wanted his life to be a playground with his beautiful Katie, he said. She never complained, and she was even more beautiful now than she was in col-lege, if that were possible, Lane sighed.

Then there was Trisha Newman of New York, East Hampton, and Gstaad. Trisha had to keep her wardrobe listed on computer so she'd know which ball gowns were at which estate. She'd met her husband while on a public relations assignment in New York for her firm— Peter Newman, now CEO and major stockholder of broadcasting gi-ant Global Enterprises, a man who commanded respect on Wall Street, who did business in most of the world markets, and who had friends across the country, and in the capitals of Europe and the Far East.

Peter got Trisha her syndicated radio show because he'd always been tickled by her gossip, as he called it, with her old college roomies on the phone machines. When he told the general manager of Global's radio station in New York that he wanted two hours, Monday through Friday, in prime afternoon drive time, for his wife to host a call-in talk show, the man agreed to it. Who was going to say no to the top boss? And to everyone's monumental surprise ex-cept Peter's, the gossip show was an immediate hit. And Trisha was having a ball.

Lane was distracted by a group of tourists trooping through the front doors. Had to be a busload of them, she figured. Lizzie had al-ready headed off the first tier up front, and Lane intercepted the rear guard that had spilled around to the aisles. Neither of the two stopped for the better part of the next hour, showing pieces, explain-ing their usage and histories, boxing gourmet delicacies, ringing up sales, wrapping parcels, running to the back for replacements, an-swering questions about Carmel village. When it was over and the doors closed behind the last of them, Lane and Lizzie looked at each other and sighed with relief.

"How'd we do?" Lizzie grinned.

"We did great!" Lane offered, glancing over the register tape. Then she heard Liz gasp in horror.

"What?" Lane demanded. Liz had rushed over to a shelf at the front of the store that held a collection of rare British carriage clocks.

"Did you sell the gold Edwardian miniature?" Liz gasped. "Or put it away?"

"Of course not," Lane said, her heart sinking. The small, turn-of-the-century gold-filled clock was a prize. She'd been meaning to separate it from the rest of the polished brass carriage clocks on the shelf and lock it up in one of the glass cases, but it had looked so adorable in with the larger ones that she just hadn't done it yet. Shoplifting had rarely been a problem in Carmel.

Until lately, Lane sighed to herself. Lately, her merchandise seemed to be sprouting wings and flying out of the doors and windows, unpaid for. She'd brought it up at a recent meeting of the Carmel Business Association, and though fellow shopkeepers commiserated, none seemed to have the problem. "Look to your display," one of her colleagues had advised.

Liz was frantically scouring the shelves and display tables. "Any sign of it?" Lane asked, without much hope.

"I'm sorry, Lane. I think it's gone."

"Shit!" Lane spit out. "Twenty-four hundred bucks out the door. And me, the wife of the police chief!"

Chapter 3

_____

"Kate, it's Trish. Peter and I just got home from dinner, and we had a message from Austin that he's coming in to New York tomorrow, but he didn't mention if you were coming with him. Are you? I'll get us tickets for Chicago, and there's a fantastic Lichtenstein retrospective at the Guggenheim. And Wendy Goldberg is doing a lunch for Madonna at her apartment on Thursday—that should be fun . . . we'll go together. Also, we're planning a small dinner on Saturday night. There's lot's going on.

"Now Katie, let me know before you get on the plane this time so I can make some plans, will you please? Last time you caught us completely by surprise. If I can have at least one day's notice, I can semi-graciously get out of any previous obligations. Call me immediately. Big kiss!" BEEP. TUESDAY, 7:02 P.M.

Kate erased her messages from the machine in her dressing room, picked up her glass of wine, and walked slowly into her expansive marble bathroom. Opening the glass-paneled medicine cabinet, she fished out a plastic container and downed a Valium. She hoped it wouldn't clash with the Prozac she'd taken earlier. It wasn't even eight o'clock yet, but she had a great urge to crawl into bed and black out for the night. But she knew she wouldn't be able to sleep, unless she took a Halcion. Little blue wonders, even though they got bad press. At least Prozac had been semi-redeemed. Like eggs. Four eggs a week were okay now, but popcorn was going to kill you. Who could keep up? She could feel the Valium starting to work.

She had managed to survive another knock-down, drag-out with

Austin, then he'd slammed out the door. For dinner. *Without her.*
That was what the argument was about. Austin was going to New
York tomorrow, without her. Why? she'd wanted to know. Hadn't he
wanted her *not* to work so she would always be available to be with
him? And hadn't he specifically wanted *not* to have children so they
could play together always? Her Shawn had taken to staying with his
father most of the time these days, sleeping on the battered couch in
Elgin Horner's tiny apartment in the San Fernando Valley. Shawn
had never warmed to Austin. She knew it was because Austin made it
obvious to both of them that he didn't really like having her son
around. And at fourteen, Shawn didn't bother to pretend he didn't
notice. He was at his dad's tonight, Austin was off somewhere, and
Kate was alone again.

She gulped down the rest of her wine, wishing the meds would
kick in faster so she wouldn't have to think about what went wrong
this time. Earlier tonight, when they were getting ready for dinner,
Austin casually mentioned that he was going to jump into New York
for a few days. He was taking a 9 A.M. flight in the morning, he'd
said. According to Trisha's message, Austin had given *her* advance
notice—so Trisha would book him on her radio show, Kate was
sure. But he'd just gotten around to telling his wife an hour ago.
Short notice, yes, but that was another issue. Kate had nothing on
her calendar that she couldn't get out of, and she would love to go
with him, she'd told her husband. But he wouldn't hear of it.

"I'm booked wall-to-wall with meetings," he'd said.

That was no problem, she'd countered, she'd have plenty to do
there. She would make a couple of phone calls, clear her decks here,
line up some New York fun, and throw a few things in a bag. She
never had to take much to New York—just about everything she
would need was already there, at their well-equipped midtown apartment.

"No!" he'd barked, and it had escalated into another screamfest.

They'd been having a lot of those lately. Austin kept trying to convince Kate that it was because of her drug abuse. *Drug abuse?* Her
doctor gave her some prescriptions to calm her down, and to help
her cope with Austin's craziness. The two were supposed to have
had dinner at the new Chasen's tonight with Viv and Ed Lewis, but
after their heated argument about the New York trip, Austin had

raged out the door, leaving Kate to call the other couple and make their apologies.

Too bad she couldn't use the excuse that a lot of her friends had to resort to now and then, Kate thought—they couldn't get a baby-sitter. She would love to be in *that* bind. But there were no little Fer-uzzi babies needing sitters. She didn't even have her son with her. She was bloody alone in a twenty-three-room house.

Dammit, it was her life, too. And it was her Fifth Avenue apart-ment, too. She was going to New York to see her friends, and her parents, period.

What the hell was Austin up to, anyway, that he didn't want her to go? Telling her that he wouldn't have any time for her. Was he having an affair? All the more reason why she damn well was going to go. Even if he wasn't having an affair, if he traveled without her like this it was going to *look* like he was having an affair, she groused to herself.

But he couldn't be having an affair, she thought. Their sex life was good. Men who were having extramarital affairs don't make passion-ate love with their wives. Do they? Maybe she should just go ahead and get pregnant. Lately she had been feeling the classic drumming beat of her biological clock as she pushed ever closer to the big *four-oh*. She'd always thought that she would have more children. Maybe she should just go in and have her IUD removed, and *que será será*.

The thought of it warmed her. She would love to have a baby. A sweet little sister for Shawn. Or another rambunctious baby boy. Or twins, even better. Her younger brother had twins. Austin's three kids were grown, in their twenties now and scattered around the country. They rarely visited, or even called.

In her heart of hearts, Kate was willing to bet that Austin would get all melty and protective if she told him that she was actually pregnant. And certainly they had enough help, so parenting wouldn't hamper their lifestyle. Women today went out, even worked, up to the day they delivered. They took care of themselves, they didn't gain a lot of weight. Heather Locklear had walked into the hospital, deliv-ered darling little Ava, then walked out looking radiant wearing her size 2 jeans.

Kate smiled. When they got back from New York, she was going to make an appointment with Dr. Greig, her ob-gyn. And if all her plumbing was intact, and there was no reason why it shouldn't be, by this time next year she would have a sweet-faced, delicious-smelling little bundle in her arms. She should have done it a long time ago.

She and Austin would make up when he got home. They always did. He'd be sorry, and they'd make love. She pulled a Louis Vuitton suitcase down from the high shelf in her dressing room, and opened it on her luggage stand. A few sets of undies, a pair of boots, some black high heels, jeans and shirts, and a couple of dinner outfits. She already had nightgowns and robes, slippers, running shoes, workout clothes, coats, sweaters, toothbrushes, cosmetics, and plenty of jewelry at the apartment in New York.

She was completely packed in less than fifteen minutes. With a satisfied smile, she closed up her suitcase—she was ready to go. They would purchase her ticket at the airport in the morning.

Kate sat down on the bed, leaned back against the plush, creamy Tappas silk headboard, and picked up the phone from her bedside table. She punched in Trisha's number. Not quite eleven-thirty in New York—maybe Trish was still up. If not, her phone call wouldn't wake anybody in the household. Kate knew that Trisha kept her answering machine on a separate phone line in her office off the family room, to which she always kept the doors closed. Trish didn't want anybody to overhear her messages. She had long ago assured her three women pals that their conversations were just between them, sacrosanct.

The answering machine picked up. Trisha must have gone to bed. As Kate spieled off her message, she could hear a great big smile in her own voice:

> "Hi, Trish . . . I'm coming, I am coming! By the time we get to the apartment tomorrow night it'll probably be too late to get to theater, especially if the plane is at all late . . . so why don't you get tickets for Chicago for Thursday night, and we'll do Wendy's lunch for Madonna. That sounds like great fun—do you think Madonna will have the baby with her? I hear she takes little Lourdes everywhere, and I'd love to see her. And yes, I definitely want to see the Lichtensteins, and do some shopping, and sit in with you during your radio show. And let's do a lunch at the Carlyle. Lobster salad. Yes! Molly too, if she can join us. Since I'll be

traveling, you set everything up, okay? And we'll be at your Saturday night dinner party—you'll let me know who's going to be there. I'll call you as soon as we get in.

"Oh, and I've got an absolutely delicious plan that I want to run past you both. You'll think I've lost my mind. Or finally got sane. See you very soon, can't wait! Bye, darling."

Chapter 4

"Hi Kate . . . hi Trisha . . . I'm conferencing you both . . . it's Molly. Got your message last night, Trish, but I got in late . . . had dinner with Tony after work . . . Tony Vandross, the dealer-from-hell I've been bitching about. He handles Charlie Otay, the brilliant Cuban sculptor. I'm trying to make this thing work for the gallery—but I would like very much to cut the man's balls off, and I don't mean figuratively. Of course I can't say that out loud, or I'd be hauled up on sexual harassment charges or something, but I can tell you girls.

"Anyway, Katie, I'm glad that you're coming in . . . and we're doing lobster salad at the Carlyle tomorrow . . . I'm up for it! And we'll all be together at Trisha's dinner on Saturday night. Wouldn't it be great if Lane could come in, too? What do you think, Trish, why don't you float it past her? I'll be at work when you get in tonight, Kate, so somebody leave me a message at home to confirm . . . and I'll meet the two of you at the hotel, in the dining room . . . the usual time, twelve-thirty tomorrow unless I hear different. Let my machine know for sure . . . I'll be checking. Bye, you two." BEEP. WEDNESDAY, 6:14 A.M.

"Katie . . . hi, it's Lane. I'm in my Explorer and heading to Los Angeles. Orange County, actually, where I'm going to pick up a shipment of authentic old British biscuit barrels for the shop. I'm still in Carmel, just got on the road, and I know it's ungodly early so you're probably not up yet, but I want to get this message to you before I lose the signal heading down the coast.

"So where are you? Trish says you're going in to New York today, but I haven't heard it from you. Are you dining with me in the Big Orange tonight, or with our other two sisters in the Big Apple? Of course, if you've already left for the airport, you won't get this message till you access from New York tonight.

"If you're not in town, I don't think I'll stay overnight . . . I'll just turn around and come right home . . . although Geoff doesn't like me to drive the trip twice in the same day. Maybe I'll go up as far as Pismo Beach and spend the night at the Whalers' Inn, my favorite little lodging house there right on the ocean . . . then I'll get an early start in the morning and drive the rest of the way, and get home by late morning. But if you are in town, and we are having dinner tonight, I'll stay over, if it's okay with you. In my favorite guest suite at the Villa Feruzzi!

"Anyway, you've got all my car phone numbers. I'm driving the SUV because I'll be shopping Charlotte's things—I'm sure she has plenty of wonderful goodies that Hamilton House can't survive without. It's about seven o'clock now, and I should be on the road for the next six hours or so, depending on any pit stops I make, so call me in the truck. I'm going to make a conscious effort to bypass all the interesting little shops along the way . . . I'll save my browsing for the trip home.

"I'll be at the Antiques Exchange most of the afternoon, and you have the number there. In fact, if I hear from you in the next few hours, why don't I stop by the house on my way through and pick you up . . . we can dish on the drive, and have a fun shopping afternoon together. Otherwise, I'll try you later, okay? Love you!" BEEP. WEDNESDAY, 6:57 A.M.

"Kathryn, dear, it's Mother. As I'm sure you've figured out, your father and I were asleep when you called last night, so we didn't get your message until this morning. We're delighted that you're coming in to New York for a few days. I took a chance that I might catch you before you left for the airport this morning, but I guess I've missed you.

"We'll be in the city through Friday, then we're driving out to East Hampton on Friday evening . . . if you and Austin can stay the weekend we would love to have you come out to the beach. The weather's perfect. Your father and I are giving a little brunch on Sunday. No business . . . just some of the Hamptons crowd . . . should be fun.

"Anyway, I'm stalling here to see if you'll pick up, but you've probably already left, so I'll leave a message with all the particulars at the apartment. We look forward to seeing you, dear. Much love . . . Bye-bye." BEEP. WEDNESDAY, 8:07 A.M.

"Mom . . . are you there? You said you'd call me at Dad's before you left for the airport. I'm going to work with Dad today. And I'm staying here again tonight. Okay? Bye, Mom." BEEP. WEDNESDAY, 8:17 A.M.

"Mrs. Feruzzi . . . this is Suzie at Dr. McQuinn's office. You had a ten o'clock appointment this morning for cleaning and a check-up. It's twenty after ten . . . we're waiting for you . . . are you there?

"Guess not . . . hopefully, you'll walk in the door any minute. We can still get you in, but the hygienist has a patient at eleven. If you just forgot, or for some reason you didn't get our reminder card, call me and we'll reschedule. Thanks . . . Bye." BEEP. WEDNESDAY, 10:21 A.M.

"Katie . . . where are you? I'm on the Ventura Freeway tooling through Woodland Hills, coming up on the 405 . . . need to know if I should go south on the 405 and come into Beverly Hills and pick you up. Wishful thinking, I guess . . . if you were home you would have called me in the truck . . . I'll give you another minute, see if you're there . . . Oh, Kaaaaaatie! If you're there, pick up . . . pick up.

"Well, guess not . . . guess you went in to New York after all. Just my luck, to miss you by a day. Okay, here I go past the 405

*and full speed ahead to the Hollywood Freeway and exotic Or-
ange County. Damn. You guys are going to have all the fun. I
haven't even seen* Rent. *I demand that all three of you call me
together tonight, from wherever. Call me late, around midnight
your time, at the Whalers' Inn in Pismo. If I'm not in my room,
have me paged in the restaurant.*

"*You know, I would love to drive right to LAX from Charlotte's
and get on an airplane and join you guys. Wouldn't that be a
hoot? We could all run around New York for a few days . . . do
our own brand of gossip on Trisha's radio show . . . shop . . . God,
shop! I guess so! I'm in sweats. You couldn't take me anywhere!
Also, how smart would it be to leave a sports utility vehicle full of
pricy British antiques in a parking structure at LAX? But it's fun
to dream. I'll catch you later, hon. You girls have a great
time . . . I am green with envy. Hugs and kisses . . . Bye now.*"
BEEP. WEDNESDAY, 12:34 P.M. END OF FINAL MESSAGE.

Chapter 5

"Miss Adams, this is Belinda Williams at Emporio Armani on Fifth Avenue. I found the suit you wanted in size two in another store . . . the gray silk with white piping that's on sale for half price. Call me at 727-3240 and let me know if you can come by for it, or if you want me to send it out. Thank you." BEEP. WEDNESDAY, 4:49 P.M.

"Molly, it's Trisha . . . I just got home from the station, and no word from Kate and Austin yet, but it's early . . . they could have stopped for a bite on the way to the apartment. Meantime, I've gone ahead and reserved a table for three at the Carlyle for lunch tomorrow, twelve-thirty . . . didn't want to wait, then be out of luck . . . you know how jammed up they get. Also, great idea to try to get Lane in here too. I left her a message demanding that she tear Geoff away from police business for a few days and come to New York and play with us. How much crime can they have in Carmel, anyway? I'll keep you posted, love . . . Bye-bye." BEEP. WEDNESDAY, 6:47 P.M.

"Trish . . . Molly . . . it's Lane. This is for both of you . . . I'm at the Gareys' Antiques Exchange down in Santa Ana. Believe me, I've thought about flying in. It's tempting, but getting my handsome and sexy but solid and very predictable husband to do something that spontaneous is out of the question, and I

couldn't just drop everything and pull it together that fast, either. But I'll be thinking about you girls.

"*Meantime, Charlotte has talked me into having an early dinner with her and Murray. It's about five-thirty here . . . I'll be at their house in Huntington Beach for the next couple of hours. Call me when Katie surfaces. The number at the Gareys' is 714-620-3321. I picked up some wonderful things . . . very productive trip! Bye for now . . . I'll check in later.*" BEEP. WEDNESDAY, 8:33 P.M. END OF FINAL MESSAGE.

Molly pressed the code number that would erase her messages at home, then hung up the phone. It was another late night at work—an after-hours customer who couldn't decide on a nondescript, not really very good watercolor. No sale was too small, that was their policy. You weren't making a sale, you were making a friend for the Feruzzi Galleries.

She looked at the notes she'd scribbled. Trisha and Lane, her sisters. Kate too. The four of them, so close for so long. For all of their adult lives, really. But now, for the first time in their long relationship, Molly felt a massive chasm between herself and them. For the first time she wouldn't, couldn't, confide in them. Not this time, and maybe not ever again. Because she had a new man in her life, this time it was a significant relationship that would work for her forever, and this time it would not sit well with her sisters. Which was a massive understatement.

Molly sighed. As she turned out the lights and locked up the gallery, she thought about the group, and the paths their lives had taken. Since the day she graduated from Briarcliff with a degree in fine arts and a passion for painting, her trek through the art world had not been easy. Her life was largely long hours in the workaday world of the gallery to support herself, all the while hoping someday to have enough time and enough money so that she could really focus on establishing herself as an artist who counted.

How lucky were the other three! For each of them, it had always been easy. Trish with her family money, her rich husband and her radio career. Trisha was having a fabulous time hosting her afternoon talk show, and being paid handsomely for doing it. Taking home hefty paychecks that she certainly didn't need, that she gave away to her charities, in fact. And even with her fascinating, high-profile job, Trisha still had time, invaluable time. She still had her mornings, her lunches, and dinners, and evenings and weekends free to enjoy. What luxury!

And Lane, launched with seed money from her wealthy Boston family to start her business. Life was heavenly for Lane, with her perfect husband and perfect kids in perfect Carmel-by-the-Sea, and the antiques shop she loved. And Dad Hurley always there for her should she ever have financial problems with Hamilton House.

Then there was Kate, who'd been called one of the top ten ravishing American beauties in a recent issue of *Vogue*. Katie made men stop dead in their tracks when they passed her on the street. And on top of that, she, too, was enormously wealthy. She could work, or not work, whatever her pleasure.

Yes, Molly's three "sisters" had always had the world by the tail, but Molly had to work her tail off just to come up with the rent on her tiny apartment in Chelsea, too expensive an area for her, but *de rigueur* for people ensconced in New York's art and fashion world. Any extra time she had, she painted, but it was precious little time, and she was almost always exhausted. Too tired to play. No energy to deal with dating. She had long since given up ironing the satin sheets, slipping into a black lace teddy, and lighting dozens of candles around the place for a man. That stuff was for great sex, she now knew, not for lasting love. And that *great sex* thing always burned out eventually, usually sooner than later, and in the harsh light of day you were left with nothing but rumpled sheets and gummy candle wax on the furniture.

Yes, Molly pondered, she was definitely maturing. Love meant something far different as she looked ahead to her middle years, something much more than just that red hot lovin' feeling. Love also meant someone to take care of her, finally. At the end of the day, she wanted a man who not only turned her on, but who could provide a lifestyle in which she could indulge her passion, hone her talent, and spend the bulk of her time doing what *she* loved, just as the other three did. And now she was going to have that. Now she had a man she was mad about, and who could give her the kind of life she needed—the kind that Kate, Lane, and Trisha enjoyed.

Bottom line, it was all about money—it always had been. If you had it, as her three best friends did, you dismissed it as not really important. But if you didn't have it, as she never had, you knew that it *could* buy you happiness—more precisely, it could buy you time, and buy you freedom to pursue your goals and be truly happy. It had always been about money, Molly Adams knew.

Now she had a significant shot at the good life for herself. Now she could look toward making her ever distant dreams actually come true. Marriage, a real home, someone to take care of her, entree into society, plenty of money, and the freedom to paint, to create. She would finally be able to explore the lengths to which her art could take her. She now had a man she adored, who held the key that would open those doors for her. This totally unexpected, unlikely hero in her life would define the rest of her life, and would finally, at forty, make life begin for her.

Funny, he had been coming on to her for years. And she'd resisted him for years. Hadn't even much liked him, really. Then suddenly, she felt the sparks, and the flickers quickly built to an inferno. This was her man! It wasn't that he had changed over all that time, not at all. *She* had changed. She had evolved. Her needs were totally different now. She no longer needed a man who would simply set her hormones raging. She needed a man who could also greatly enrich her life.

And no, she wouldn't, couldn't, confide her affair to anyone. Not even to her three Briarcliff sisters, who had always been closer to her than family. *Especially* not to them. As the only still-single member of their tightly knit quartet, the four had always liberally dished the latest man in Molly's life. Not this time. No one knew about this one. Molly basked in her delicious secret. And she relished, albeit uneasily, the knowledge that the rest of her world would know about him in time. And it would change the world as she knew it, forever.

The effervescent lights of the city reflected her mood as she hailed a taxi to take her downtown. She couldn't wait to get home. He was coming over tonight. But then came that nagging, creeping pain behind her eyes, presaging the black cloud that hovered over her ebullience.

Lunch with the girls tomorrow. She had half a mind to tell them at lunch, and be done with it.

Chapter 6

COOL, BRACING SALT air drifted in through the windows of the Explorer as Lane headed north on the old coast road toward home. As always, dinner and chat around the big pine table in the Gareys' country French kitchen was a luscious experience, down to Charlotte's sinful Grand Marnier profiteroles with chocolate sauce.

She had just talked with Geoff. The boys were actually doing homework, he'd said. Hard to believe! Lane had assured her husband that she would not attempt the seven-hour drive home from Huntington Beach tonight. She would stop halfway, at Pismo Beach. Charlotte and Murray had invited her to stay the night, but she was set on getting some of the driving behind her before she slept.

Besides, she intended to keep trying to reach Kate. Trisha had called the Gareys' house to let Lane know that she still hadn't heard from Kate and Austin, and it was nearly eleven o'clock in New York. Maybe Kate hadn't gone east after all, Lane reasoned. Maybe something had come up, which was certainly not unheard of in Austin's business. Perhaps they'd jumped on a plane to meet with an artist, or an artist's agent, or a client, in some other part of the country. Or the world. Many times in the past, Austin and Kate had seemingly disappeared, only to surface days later in some exotic locale where Austin had heard about a cache of artwork he simply had to explore. Kind of the rich man's version of a biscuit barrel expedition, Lane chuckled to herself.

And, there was always the possibility that they'd made a spur-of-the-moment day trip for the same reason. If that were the case, the Feruzzis could be rolling in later tonight, and Lane wanted to make one last try at connecting up with her friend, if only to share a half hour and a glass of wine on her way back up north. Or some girl talk into the wee hours, if she opted to spend the night at Kate's and leave for home in the morning.

Lane had gotten on the road just as darkness had begun to descend on the beach community. She groped around in the utility box between the seats, pulled out a CD, and popped it, sight unseen, into the CD player. She winced as raucous sound suddenly blasted out of the speakers. Pearl Jam. Seattle grunge rock. Obviously a musical selection made by one of her two sons on some Saturday afternoon trip to Tower Records with Geoff. Letting herself get into the slightly weirded-out, off-tempo, Generation X beat, she felt . . . well, younger. She felt good. It had been a good day. It was a great life.

She thought about her three friends in the simplistic, primal terms of the low-down music that flooded the big SUV. Trisha had been the richest of the four of them at school, and she was the richest now. Katie had always been the most beautiful, and she still was. Molly was the hardest worker, and certainly had never ceased to be. And Lane? She was the most adventuresome back then, she smiled, and she liked to think that she still was that. Or did being happily married and faithful to one man, the responsible mother of two children, and the proprietress of a well-run antiques shop in an upscale resort town disqualify her? Whatever, she wouldn't change places with any of the other three, or anyone else in the world.

The music, along with her euphoria, transported her swiftly and easily over the miles. As she rounded the south bay curve and headed north on the 405 freeway past the small, multicolored stucco houses of Hawthorne, the oil pumps of Carson, and the low-flying jetliners coming in to LAX, she punched in Kate's Beverly Hills number on the car phone. And still, the answering machine was picking up.

"Kate, Kate, Kate, where the hell are you, sweetie? You're not here, you're not in New York . . . the world is looking for you . . . especially me, because I'm about twenty minutes from your house! I'll lose the signal when I get closer to Sunset, so this is kind of Last Chance Cafe! Pick up, Katie, pick up . . . I wanna come-on-a-your-house! I want to see you!

"Oh, grrrrr . . . I give up. God knows, I tried. You'd better have a good excuse for not letting anybody know where you dis-

appeared to today. I guess I'll just swing right on by to the 101 and roll on up the coast to Pismo. Love you, darlin'... we'll catch each other next time, and I promise I'll plan it better. Ciao."

Well, too bad, Lane thought. She wouldn't get to see Katie, and it was much too late to do her usual grazing in any of the dozens of interesting shops along the way. Besides the inevitable few odd goodies, she never failed to pick up tips and pointers from her South Coast colleagues, even if it was simply a matter of display. Next time, she promised herself, she *would* plan it better. She would take *two* days, or more if Geoff could get away.

The thought of Geoffrey at home warmed her, as it always did, and she inadvertently stepped on the gas a little. He had made her promise to call as soon as she got to the Whalers' Inn, so he could stop worrying about her for the night, he'd said. What an angel! Then the mental picture of how her tough but only barely grizzled police chief husband would react if he heard that characterization made her laugh out loud.

She had just passed the Wilshire Boulevard turn-off, and was coming up on Sunset. Something made her veer onto the Sunset off ramp from the 405, and she found herself rumbling eastbound over the twists and curves of Sunset Boulevard. She made a left turn onto Benedict Canyon Drive, then a right onto Lexington, and she pulled up to the gate at Kate and Austin's huge, pink Mediterranean villa. What the hell, she thought, she was this close, she might as well just bang on Katie's door.

Lane reached out of the driver's window and pressed the doorbell. Within seconds, the familiar voice of the Feruzzis' housekeeper filtered through the intercom.

"Who is there, please?"

"Christina, hi, it's Lane Hamilton. Is Kate at home?"

After a pause, Christina said, "Mrs. Feruzzi is resting." My God, Lane thought, she *is* home. There's something wrong with this picture.

"Christina," Lane returned, choosing her words carefully. "Please tell Kate that I'm here, at the gate, and I need to see her. Will you do that?"

"She is asleep," Christina's tinny voice sounded on the speaker, registering a definite note of finality.

"Well, wake her up," Lane demanded then, projecting an authoritative tone of her own. In response she heard . . . nothing.

Lane waited for a couple of beats, then she reached outside the window and pushed the bell again. When still she got no response, she rang again, and again. Then she leaned on the bell, without letting up. Finally, Lane saw the big green-tinted double iron gates swing inward. Quickly, she maneuvered the Ford Explorer through the still-moving gates, and up the cobblestone drive to the estate's front portico.

Lane turned off the ignition and sat still behind the wheel for a minute, looking up at the massive front doors, not knowing what to expect. Then she saw one of the doors open a few inches, and a figure in what looked like a white bathrobe standing behind it in the half-light. Lane shouldered her purse, got out of the vehicle, and walked toward the door.

"Kate?" she asked tentatively, walking up the wide front steps.

"Yes," the weak but unmistakable voice of her longtime friend came back.

Lane approached the lighted doorway, and gasped. It was Kate alright, but her beautiful face was badly bruised, her lip was split, a still-raw wound had cracked open her cheek, and her right eye was black and red and closed to barely a slit. Lane stood motionless and stared at her friend, shock registering on her face. Kate opened the door wider.

"Come in, Lane," she said.

Chapter 7

---

*"Molly, darling . . . where are you? I just got in from the air-
port. I've got some business to take care of, then I'll grab a cab
and get down to your place a little after eleven. If you're in the
shower when I get there, I'll let myself in and chill down the
champagne I'm bringing . . . I love you, love you, love you!"*
BEEP. WEDNESDAY, 9:03 P.M.

*"Molly . . . it's Trisha. No word from Katie yet. We'll probably
hear from our missing gal-pal later tonight or tomorrow, but
even if she doesn't turn up for lunch, let's don't waste a perfectly
good reservation at the Carlyle, what do you say? Let's you and I
meet there at twelve-thirty, and if we don't drink with her, we'll
drink to her, yes? Call me and confirm. Big kiss!"* BEEP.
WEDNESDAY, 9:17 P.M. END OF FINAL MESSAGE.

Just as Molly pressed the ERASE button on her answering machine,
her doorbell sounded. Perfect timing, she smiled, as she rushed to
the intercom to buzz him upstairs. Knowing that he would be arriving late, she'd stopped on the way home to pick up a tin of caviar for
tonight, some fresh bagels, lox, and cream cheese for the morning in
case he could stay over, and a huge bundle of purple iris and bright
yellow daffodils for the apartment. That was another thing she loved
about New York: you could get anything you wanted at any hour of
the night.

Quickly, she appraised her image in the hall mirror. Amazing, she thought. Working a killer schedule at the gallery, painting as long as she could stay awake, averaging four or five hours sleep a night, and still, never had she looked this good. Her skin was glowing. Love was powerful stuff, she reflected, as she awaited his signature three raps on her door.

Removing the chain-lock, she swung the door wide, and he rushed in and swept her up in his arms. After a kiss that went on for days he stepped back, set the chilled bottle of Roederer Cristal he was holding on the entry table, and kissed her again.

"Quick, close the door," he grinned, when he finally pulled away. "We can't let any of this passion escape. If someone lights a match, it could blow up the building!"

"God, I can't believe you're really here," Molly breathed contentedly.

Pushing the door shut behind him, he double-locked it and inserted the safety chain in place. That done, he turned and took her in his arms again. "Can we go to bed now, and talk later?" he appealed to her emerald green eyes.

"My sentiments precisely," she smiled. "Want a drink?"

"Uh-huh . . . a big drink of you first, then some champagne," he responded, hungrily kissing her all over, running his tongue down the side of her neck and his hands up the front of her blouse.

Scooping her into his arms then, he carried her across the living room and into her spartan bedroom, and gently laid her down on her queen-sized bed. And began sensuously, albeit efficiently, undressing her. She helped him, wriggling this way and that until he exposed her small, perfect body in the low amber glow of the French Creole lamp on the chiffonier. Dropping to his knees beside the bed, for a long minute he remained perfectly still and appeared to drink her in with his eyes.

"You are so incredibly beautiful, Molly," he murmured finally.

"Get naked, stud," Molly laughed, and she pulled him up onto the bed with her.

Without ceremony, he stripped off his clothes and flung them to the floor, then fell upon her and proceeded to devour her with what seemed to Molly a young man's frenzy. Harder, faster, deeper, until he exploded inside of her.

Rolling over limp beside her then, he whispered, "Sorry to be so greedy. Couldn't help it. That one was for me, darling—the next one's for you."

"Mmmmm, I'll wait," she murmured. "Let's pour the champagne. By the way, are you staying over? Or did she come with you?"

He slid his arm under her slender waist and slowly drew her up on top of him.

"I'm here for the night," he said. "Kate decided to stay in Beverly Hills."

Chapter 8

"Kate . . . Kate . . . please pick up . . . are you awake yet, darling? I'm so sorry I lost control like that . . . it was all my fault. You know how much I've had on my mind lately, with the economy knocking the hell out of art sales, big problems with the London gallery, DeFarge pushing me for excess payments . . . and I guess I just went over the edge. It's no excuse, I know . . . I'm so sorry . . . I promise it will never happen again. When I finish up here, let's get away . . . take a little trip . . . Barbados . . . St. Bart's . . . wherever you'd like to go, darling. I love you, Katie. Please tell me you forgive me . . . I couldn't sleep last night . . . worried about you all night.

"It's ten o'clock . . . I'm still at the apartment . . . I'll be leaving for the gallery in about an hour . . . one of our Paris dealers is coming in with a couple of Hazen watercolors . . . then I'm going to have lunch with Peter Newman. He wants to talk about purchasing another Jannus. After lunch I'll be in the office for a while . . . then I'm going over to do Trisha's radio show. Please catch up with me, dear . . . and I'll keep trying you. I love you, Kate. Call me, darling." BEEP. THURSDAY, 7:04 A.M.

"Kate . . . are you up yet? It's me again. I'm leaving for the gallery now . . . it's almost eleven here. I miss you. I'm so sorry I flew off the handle . . . and you were right, there was no reason why you couldn't have come . . . I've just been overly pressured,

*not thinking clearly. Why don't you fly in tomorrow . . . spend
a few days in New York . . . we could have a nice weekend,
then leave from here on a short trip . . . down to the
Caribbean . . . just bring a few hot-weather things with you, a
couple of swim suits. We'll buy anything we need.*

*"Oh, darling, I feel so terrible about the other night . . . I was
wrong . . . I know that. I haven't heard from you . . . please call
me. I'll be at the gallery in about fifteen minutes . . . I'm going
to walk over there now . . . I love you so much, Katie . . . you
know that." BEEP. THURSDAY, 7:58* A.M.

*"Kate . . . it's noon . . . I'm going out to lunch with Peter
soon . . . are you there? I really need to talk to you, darling. I really need to hear your voice . . . to tell you how sorry I am . . . to
hear you say you forgive me. Katie? Please pick up. Well, I'll be
leaving for lunch at twelve-fifteen . . . nine-fifteen your time.
I'll be with Peter at Le Relais. You can call me there. Please,
sweetheart . . . I'm hurting. I need to know that you're
okay . . . that everything's okay . . . please call me. I love you.
Goodbye, dear." BEEP. THURSDAY, 9:03* A.M.

"Come on, Kate, get that bag packed . . . let's get out of here,"
Lane urged. Kate had stopped to listen to yet another message that
had come in on the answering machine from her husband.

"Maybe I should call him, talk to him—he sounds very sorry—"

"Katie, look at your face!" Lane broke in. "I think you should talk
to the *police!*"

"Oh, please, don't say that. He didn't mean it. He's been under
pressure—"

"Kate, you've got to get away from here, get some distance from
this, and from him, so you can think clearly," Lane countered, for at
least the tenth time since the night before, when she'd found her
friend so badly battered.

"I guess so . . ."

"And without any pills," Lane added pointedly.

"I need my medicine," Kate said.

"Fine, bring it with you, but after a few days breathing the fresh salt air in Carmel, I guarantee that you will not need tranquilizers. Until then, you're not in a position to make any decisions. About anything."

Sighing, Kate resumed putting clothes into her suitcase. "He's a very good husband," she offered in a small voice. "I have everything I want . . . he adores me—"

"Stop it, Kate," Lane demanded. "For God's sake, he beat the hell out of you. Tell me the truth, Katie . . . how many times has he done this to you before?"

"Never. I—"

"The *truth,* Kate—how often?"

"Never like this," Kate returned, her hand moving defensively to the angry cut on her lower lip.

"Of course never like this . . . they escalate. With wife beaters, every new incident is worse than the last. One of these times," Lane said quietly, "he could kill you."

"Oh, Lane, Austin would never—"

"Listen to me," Lane said, helping her friend put the last of the garments she'd set out into her suitcase. "He could kill you, Kate. Geoff will give you statistics on how many times domestic violence leads to homicide—"

"Oh God," Kate wailed, "you can't tell Geoff . . . or the children. Or anyone!"

"Kate, you need help—"

"No!" the other woman cried, pulling back from Lane. "You can't tell anyone. Promise me you won't tell a soul, Lane, or I won't go with you. You can say that I had a car accident—"

"You're making a mistake—"

"Promise," Kate demanded. "Not a soul. And that includes Molly and Trish."

"Alright," Lane conceded, "I promise. I won't tell anyone, until you say I can. Now hurry. You finish packing, and I'll make sure Christina has all my numbers in Carmel."

The phone in Kate's dressing room sounded again, and the answering machine clicked on. Kate stiffened. Both women stood and stared at the small slate-gray box as if it were a third person. A menacing third person.

*"Kate . . . Katie . . . can you hear me, darling? Please pick up.
We're at Le Relais . . . Jean François says hello—"*

Lane pounced on the machine and moved the volume lever on its side to MUTE, cutting off the sound of Austin Feruzzi's voice.

"Come on, Katie," she said then, closing up the suitcase and taking her friend's arm. "Get your purse, and let's get the hell out of here. We've got a lunch date in Pismo Beach."

Chapter 9

"Austin, it's Tripp. I've got good news and I've got bad news. We took delivery of a shipment from Delhi this morning . . . I figured it was more sun paintings since that's all we've been getting from DeFarge lately, but the crate was huge . . . and you know that Jonathan Valley has asked for a large Rhaji for his Malibu house, though DeFarge told us that the artist rarely does large-scale canvases.

"Now, I know that you've told me not to uncrate the sun shipments, just leave them back in your office for you to handle personally, but you're not back till next week, and I thought that this just might be the one for Valley after all . . . and sure enough, it is an enormous sun painting . . . about seven feet by five feet, with the sun a good twenty inches in diameter up in the top right corner . . . and the sun itself is treated differently than on the others. It's a big, concave, luminous yellow ball . . . it's wild looking . . . dramatic as hell! Looks like the build-up is done with resins over acrylic, but I can't tell for sure. Anyway, I put in a call to Valley and he happens to be in town today, so he's coming by to see it this afternoon—this one could be just the ticket for him.

"Now the bad news. Hate to tell you, but our star got himself in deepest doo-doo again this afternoon. Seems Jannus was getting on an airplane to go back to New York and they caught him packing heat! Christ, Austin, he carries a gun? Anyway, the airport police nailed him after he failed to make it through the metal detector. Evidently he made some kind of scene with the cops, big surprise, and they hauled him down to Men's Central Jail. I had *to get Jake to bail him out. He's scheduled to appear in court next Thursday. The press will be on it—they stake out the police blotter, as you know, and I'm sure it'll be all over the evening news. So now what?*

"By the way, I'm leaving this message at the apartment instead of at the gallery just to keep all of this absolutely private. I'll keep you posted. So long for now."

Tripp put the phone down. He wasn't too worried about Jannus. With the artist's bizarre track record, this latest peccadillo would probably just make him hotter. Pissing on his painting at the opening the other night actually shot the price of the piece way up. Go figure, Tripp thought, shaking his head.

Ten years ago, Tripp Kendrick had made a young man's decision to follow the sun—he left his low-paying job in a rare-book shop in Greenwich Village and hitchhiked to Los Angeles. His final ride was with three UCLA students who were coming home from a holiday at the Grand Canyon. Their last mile was to Santa Monica beach at sunset, and Tripp knew instantly that Southern California was home.

Answering an ad, he landed an entry-level job at Austin Feruzzi's small gallery in Santa Monica. Though he'd had no formal art training, he had an affinity for it, and he was a quick study, supplementing on-the-job training with books on art history, tours of other galleries, art openings in the area, and what he called personal learning trips to L.A. area museums—the Norton Simon in Pasadena, the stunning old Getty Museum on Pacific Coast Highway, the magnificent L.A. County Museum of Art on Wilshire Boulevard. From lowly clerk on Feruzzi's gallery floor, Tripp gradually assumed more responsibility over the years, and when Austin moved his growing business to upscale Beverly Hills, he made Tripp Kendrick his gallery director.

At thirty-six, Tripp was tall, trim, and strikingly attractive, with even features and sun-streaked hair. He was bright, inordinately savvy in art circles now, and New York–sophisticated despite his blond, tanned, California-surfer good looks. It was with an abundance of charm and an iron fist that Tripp Kendrick ran the tony Feruzzi Gallery in the heart of Beverly Hills.

Socially, he was much sought after—invited everywhere, written up in all the columns. Besides his sunny savoir-faire and his stunning good looks, a large part of his attraction was the unknown about him—Tripp kept his private life just that, private, which gave him a certain cachet. Westsiders, especially women, wanted clues to the Tripp Kendrick mystique, and that only added to his success in business. Many galleries had tried, thus far unsuccessfully, to lure him away from Feruzzi, but Tripp wasn't going anywhere. The Feruzzi Gallery was arguably the most prestigious in Southern California now, and he had the top job. Along with his considerable salary, he made a hefty commission on every piece he sold. And Feruzzi had promised him stock options when he took the company public.

Oh, he had some problems with his boss, but who didn't, he figured. Austin Feruzzi had a reputation for being slippery, borderline sleazy even, both in business and his personal life. But that did seem to be a sign of the nineties, men behaving badly. Never mind Aiden Jannus—with Hugh Grant busted on Hollywood Boulevard, Eddie Murphy caught with a transvestite hooker, Frank Gifford nailed on tape in a New York hotel room with a flight attendant right after having lunch with Kathie Lee, and Marv Albert indicted for forcible sodomy and *biting* a woman on the backside, for God's sake. Then there was hot Oscar-winner Billy Bob Thornton, charged with beating up his beautiful wife. And setting the national tone for indiscretions, our very leader, the president himself. Gennifer Flowers, Paula Jones, Monica Lewinsky, Kathleen Willey, and the list went on. Tripp never ceased to marvel that Austin Feruzzi was able to fly low, just beneath radar, with the worst of his opprobrious personal behavior undetected. At least so far.

In business, Austin Feruzzi was something else again. God only knew what scams he had going—Tripp didn't *want* to know. But he heard bits and pieces. And he ignored them, because they didn't really affect him. Austin took care of the big picture—acquisitions, expansion, signing artists, and the like—and Tripp took care of the day-to-day commerce.

Now he thought about the price of the Rhaji. The painting was more than twice the size of the others, so it would have to go for at least twice the price. Since the artist was a total unknown who had no market value on his merit, the gallery had been pricing the sun canvases by size. But the sun paintings had caught on; they were selling very well in New York and California, and in fact, the prices on the latest ones had actually been bid up by collectors. The paintings were bright, impressionistic primitives done in a riot of color, much more exuberant and vivid than the typical work that came out of India, and each one featuring an oversized, radiant, yellow-orange ball that represented the sun.

According to Austin Feruzzi, DeFarge had told him only that the artist's name was Rhaji Mentour, and that he was an exceedingly beautiful young Indian man from the village of Rampur that he, Charles DeFarge, had had the great good fortune to discover. Knowing what little he knew about DeFarge, Tripp was patently aware that no matter how many questions they asked of him, no matter how much valuable publicity the gallery proposed to put out on this gifted new artist, DeFarge would tell just what he wanted to tell, and no more. The one thing DeFarge did give to Austin Feruzzi was the assurance that the Feruzzi Galleries would have exclusive representation of the Rhaji paintings.

Charles DeFarge was unlike any other merchant with whom the gallery had ever done business. An international dealer in art, gemstones, and antiquity, he was headquartered in New Delhi, doing business under the banner CDF, Inc. Tripp had met DeFarge once, earlier in the year when the man was in the L.A. area. At that time, the gallery had been doing some limited business with DeFarge, and the dealer had come in to pay a courtesy call, as he'd explained it in his ultra-formal English, and to acquaint himself with the Feruzzi collections. That was before a division of DeFarge's operation, called URA, had started shipping the Rhaji canvases. Tripp had no idea what any of those initials stood for.

Austin had introduced the two back then, telling DeFarge that Mr. Kendrick was his indispensable West Coast gallery director and good friend. Tripp remembered, when they shook hands, how he'd been taken aback to find the man's grip at the same time sweaty, yet steely cold. DeFarge had struck Tripp as a slick operator, fluent in English, and handsome in an unsavory way, with expensive European designer clothes, gold jewelry, and dirty fingernails. On that one occasion when he'd met the dealer, albeit for just that short visit, Tripp had taken an instant dislike to Monsieur Charles DeFarge. And he remembered making a mental note that he and Austin Feruzzi seemed to have a lot in common.

Soon after his visit to the gallery, DeFarge had started shipping the sun paintings. When the volume of traffic between the gallery and DeFarge's URA had increased substantially, and the sun paintings had started selling briskly, Tripp did some checking on his own. He learned that DeFarge had a reputation in art circles as a not always reliable business connection, but one who had been known to make money for his clients with his creative but less than orthodox arrangements. But insiders whispered about sinister undertones. If you were known to cross Charles DeFarge, one of Tripp's New York contacts had told him, you could wind up dead.

Tripp shared that disturbing information with his employer, of course, but Feruzzi didn't want to hear it. Probably, Tripp thought at the time, because the sun paintings had taken off almost immediately, demand for them was increasing, and the price of the canvases was escalating. Tripp didn't really blame Austin for turning a deaf ear to his concerns. Dealing with DeFarge did seem to be good business, the Indian artist Rhaji Mentour looked to be a comer, and the Feruzzi Galleries had an exclusive on his work.

Despite the fact that little was known about the artist, buyers seemed satisfied with Indian provenance papers issued through the Feruzzi Galleries by URA. Tripp's considerable knowledge of art, combined with his intuition, told him that the artist was young, not seasoned, but more than moderately talented, as well as imaginative, creative, and exuberant.

After one of his stock boys uncrated the newest Rhaji, Tripp had stood in front of the brilliantly colored painting back in Austin's office and scrutinized it carefully. There was something different about this one, besides its size. It was lustier, more mature, better. He was sorry that he hadn't been able to reach Austin, but in the owner's absence, as Tripp always did, he would set a price for the piece.

Tripp felt certain that Jonathan Valley would love this painting, but he also knew that the actor's attention span was fragile when it came to toys, art, and women. Valley was going to New York the next day, he knew, to do some interviews with the Global television network, which was going to run a week's retrospective of his films, then he planned to scout locations for his next movie. He would be out of town for weeks. If Tripp were to tell him that he was going to have to wait until he got back to do business on this painting,

Jonathan would have all good intentions of getting back to it, but he would very likely forget all about it.

Tripp also knew the exact spot in Jon Valley's Malibu manse where this painting would work—on the wall above the creamy Velin leather sofa in the master suite that looked out on the ocean through floor-to-ceiling glass, and picked up the magic, red-golden light of the setting sun. Tripp knew better than Jon that he should have this painting, and he wanted it for him.

He got up and went into the back office, and studied the canvas to price it. A hundred thousand just by virtue of its size, added to which, this work was quite remarkable. A breakthrough for the primitive artist, in Tripp's educated view. A hundred and fifty thousand. He was comfortable with that figure.

He left the office, closed the door behind him, glanced around the gallery floor, and saw that all was well. He answered a couple of questions a customer had about a small de Kooning oil, then went back to his ledgers. Among his responsibilities, Tripp monitored with regularity the books and receipts. The profit margin on the sun paintings was well above the usual gallery percentage, and this particular one would shatter all previous records.

Tripp looked up from his desk, which was set in a niche on the back wall of the gallery. The glass entry doors had opened, and there was an inaudible but definite stir among the several patrons browsing through the canvases hung on the walls and the artifacts in the showcases.

Tripp was familiar with the commotion; it always accompanied the arrival anywhere of sizzling hot action-hero movie star Jonathan Valley. A commanding presence, Valley was tall and ruggedly handsome, with thick dark hair and a well-toned body which his fans had seen almost in its entirety, well-pumped and well-oiled, in most of his wildly popular genre films.

Valley was also an art collector, and one of the Feruzzi Galleries' best customers. The reason he patronized Feruzzi exclusively was known only to himself and to Tripp Kendrick. Although Jon Valley was seen around town with the requisite luscious, leggy females on his arm, his heart belonged to Tripp Kendrick, and had for years. Their affair was secret; knowledge of it would be a bombshell that would most certainly ruin Jonathan Valley's career. Even Austin

Feruzzi didn't know about it. No one did. Yes, it seemed that you could get caught doing almost anything these days, and you would be forgiven if you apologized and begged forgiveness on the television talk shows, but you could not be gay, and be accepted as a leading man in the movies.

Jon was alone. With a wide grin, he strode purposefully over to Tripp at the desk. Shaking hands, he said, "Hi, guy. Let's see it." Never was the slightest hint of their relationship exchanged between the two in public.

"It's in the back," Tripp smiled back at him. "You're going to love it, Jon."

The two men stepped into Austin Feruzzi's large workroom office. The new Rhaji painting stood on the floor along with several other canvases. Jon went right to it, looked at it for about a minute, then looked back at Tripp.

"How much?" he asked.

"A hundred and fifty thousand."

"Sold," Jon said, and he shook Tripp's hand again. "I'll have Duncan call you and get a check over here, and arrange for delivery this afternoon."

Chapter 10

"Welcome back . . . this is the Trisha Newman show . . . I'm Trisha, and my guest this hour is Austin Feruzzi, owner of the prestigious Feruzzi Galleries. We've been talking about the Edward Hopper show currently at the Metropolitan Museum of Art here in New York. Austin, you say Hopper's Tables for Ladies is a favorite of your wife's . . . why?"

"Well, because Kate says . . . and I think most of your listeners know by now that you and my wife Kate are old friends from college days—"

"Please watch whom you're calling old, Mr. Feruzzi!"

"I'm sorry, Trisha . . . I'd hate to have you and Katie on my case at once . . . the fact is, you two ladies are both young and beautiful . . . I'm old!" (laughter)

"That's true. Now, Austin, you were saying about Tables for Ladies—"

"Well, my wife thinks that Hopper was ahead of his time . . . that he was very much aware of the ambiguous and awkward position of a woman without a male escort back in nineteen thirty, when Tables was painted. Hence the title, suggesting that at this restaurant, unescorted ladies were indeed welcome—"

"Is that particular Hopper really one of your favorite paintings, Kate?" Lane asked.

"One of my favorites?" Kate hissed. "I've never even seen it. I have no idea what the hell he's talking about."

Lane's big Ford Explorer was hugging the curves of the coast highway approaching Big Sur, with its breathtaking cliffs overgrown with hoary, battered cypress trees jutting down to the roiling surf. It was a magnificent afternoon along the wide expanse of the Pacific, sunny, but with light breezes skittering up off the ocean, keeping the salt air fresh and cool.

They had stopped in Pismo and had lunch at the Spyglass, a favorite spot in the funky little beach town known for its seafood and its ocean view. Kate had barely touched her red snapper, but the pleasant beach ambiance, along with the comforting presence of her longtime friend, had managed to loosen her up a little.

She'd confessed to Lane that yes, Austin had a history of roughing her up, and yes, the intensity of the beatings had escalated over the years. And that many times when Kate had been a sudden no-show for an engagement they'd planned, or she had simply dropped out of sight for days, even weeks at a time, usually on an impromptu trip with Austin, it was because she was too banged up and bruised to appear in public. After each incident, Kate told Lane, Austin would always seem sincerely, genuinely sorry. And he would try to make it up to her with lavish presents, promises that he would never do it again, and earnest protestations of love.

"Kate," Lane had beseeched her friend, "why in God's name didn't you tell any of us? We could have helped you so much sooner. We would have—"

"I just couldn't," Kate had put in softly, cutting off Lane's objections. "I couldn't tell anyone," she'd said. "Not you girls, not my sister, not my parents—it was too humiliating. Oh, I came close at times. To leaving him, and confiding in all of you. Then he would do a complete turnaround, beg me to forgive him, and I'd give in again. And he would be so sweet, so good to me . . . for a while. Looking back, the pattern was eminently predictable. I should have seen it. But I wanted to believe him . . ."

"And where did Shawn figure in all this?" Lane had asked.

"Shawn hates Austin."

The finality with which Kate had made that definitive pronouncement had startled Lane. "Does he beat Shawn, too?" she'd asked.

"No—he doesn't hit Shawn. He wouldn't dare. Besides, he can't catch him. Shawn stays as far away from Austin as he can, and has from the minute he learned how to run. These days, he stays away from home as much as he can. I feel as if my son is slipping away from me—it breaks my heart."

"Yes, Shawn always does seem to be 'over at Elgin's—' "

"And I know he tells his father everything," Kate had put in bitterly. "Elgin is always giving me these knowing looks, these solicitous comments. I ignore them, but it's mortifying."

"And Elgin's influence—is it good for Shawn, do you think?"

"Shawn is fourteen. Elgin is his dad. And Elgin Horner was an L.A. Raider, for God's sake. Elgin could rob the Bank of America and he'd still be a hero in Shawn's eyes. And the man is in such desperate straits that he probably would, if he had a mask and a gun and he thought he could get away with it."

"But Elgin is basically a good man—"

"Come on, Lane," Kate had cut her off. "Elgin Horner is an aging loser who is going nowhere, and who never forgave me for leaving him. Who knows, he's probably secretly pleased that my husband has been beating me for years—he probably thinks I deserve it."

"Oh, Katie, how can you say that?" Lane had asked her. "Everyone knows that Elgin still loves you."

"And everyone knows that there's a thin line between love and hate, Lane. I don't *want* Elgin to love me. I want him to get on with his life, and stop poisoning my son's mind against my husband—"

"Katie, stop it! *Austin* is the bad guy here—he's doing his *own* poisoning!" Lane had tossed back at her. "You've *got* to face that."

Kate had breathed a baleful sigh. "You're right, Lane, of course—it's just so hard for me to come to grips with another failure, after twelve years. What the hell have I done with my life?"

"Oh, please, Katie—you're still young, you're beautiful, and you're a truly good person with a wonderful son and loving friends. But you've got to take *charge* of your life. *Now,* not ten years from now."

"I know you're right, but—"

"Kate, be honest with me, and with yourself—how do you feel about Austin right now, after he beat you nearly senseless this time?"

"How do I feel about him? I don't want to hear him, I don't want to talk to him, I . . . I don't ever want to see him again."

"Ever?" Lane had echoed hopefully.

Kate hesitated at that, and Lane had let it go. Katie needed time, she felt, and she intended to make sure that her friend had a quiet, relaxing, renewing respite in Carmel before being pressed to make any significant decisions about her life and her future.

To Lane, ever the outside observer, as impartial as she could be with a woman whom she truly loved, the picture was unmistakably clear. Many times she had listened to Geoff talk about domestic violence cases that his department handled, even in the serenity of beautiful Carmel, and always, the psychology was the same. Without help, the batterer's brutality invariably accelerated. And too often, by the time the police were called in, it was already too late.

"Do you want to listen to Austin?" Lane asked her now, waving a hand toward the radio in the dashboard, which was still dishing up art rap between Kate's husband and their friend Trisha Newman. Trish's talk show from New York came on three hours earlier in California, and Lane often put it on at Hamilton House for background listening during the usual lull after lunch time. She'd tuned in the show as they drove, thinking that it would be fun for the two of them to listen to Trisha together, not realizing that Austin Feruzzi was going to be a guest today.

"No," Kate insisted quite firmly, and she reached up and punched at the tuner buttons to change the station. "He's the last person I want to hear."

"You'll be hearing from him at my house, you know," Lane observed. "Christina knows where you'll be, and I'm sure that Austin will get to her when he doesn't hear from you."

"I know," Kate said.

"How do you feel about that?" Lane asked.

"Tired. I just wish it would disappear. Just all go away. You know, honestly, Lane, I wish he were dead. Dead would be easier than dealing with him. I could wear black and pretend I was sorry . . ." Spitting out the words, the usually tranquil Kathryn Spenser startled Lane with the quiet depth of her rage. Lane didn't respond, but kept her eyes trained on the road ahead, following the graceful, jagged line of the California coast.

Then Kate stunned her even more with her next pronouncement, spoken in a whisper, almost to herself: "But I love him. I hate him, I'd like to kill him—but I'm in love with him."

"Tripp . . . It's Austin. I just picked up your message. You said Jonathan Valley was coming in to look at the new Rhaji. Now listen to me, Tripp . . . DON'T, do NOT sell that Rhaji to Valley! Or to anyone! Just don't touch it at all until I get there. I can't believe you uncrated it . . . I've told you never to touch DeFarge's shipments, no matter what you think is in them, it doesn't matter where the hell I am. That's a hard-and-fast rule, Tripp—I thought I'd made myself crystal clear on that.

"Call me and let me know that you got this, and that you understand this. It's twenty to six here . . . call the apartment . . . I need your assurance that the new Rhaji stays covered up. No one is to even see it until I get back there. Okay? And I'll talk to Jake about Jannus. Bye."

"Christina, this is Mr. Feruzzi. Please pick up the phone if you can hear me. I'm calling on the kitchen line because I can't reach Mrs. Feruzzi. When you get this message, would you please call me immediately at the New York apartment? The number is up on the cork board, as you know. If I'm not in when you call, leave a message and let me know where Kathryn is, will you please? Thank you, Christina."

"Kate . . . it's me calling again, darling. I still haven't heard from you. I just finished doing Trisha's show, and I'm going over *to their place to have a drink with her and Peter after she gets off the air at six. Trish has some people coming she says I should meet, a couple who are doing a fourteen-room apartment on Park Avenue, and they're in the market for artwork. Then I'll run home and change. I'm going to a Knicks game with Jock Moranis . . . he has season tickets. Jock is interested in a pair of Charles Demuth gouaches that I have at the gallery here, and I've just about got him sold.*

"I'll keep checking in. Please, Kate, I'm worried about you. Call me at the apartment. I love you more than life. Goodbye, dear."

"Molly, hi, it's me, Austin. You're at the gallery, but I don't want to leave this message there. I'm sorry, dear, but I can't see you tonight after all. I just did Trisha's radio show, and I'm going to come by the gallery for just a few minutes to take care of a couple of things. Then I'm going to the Newmans' for drinks, and to meet some prospective clients . . . then another client is dragging me to a Knicks game. I'd rather take a stiff beating than go to a basketball game tonight, but I have to go . . . I'm real close to a good sale with this guy. I know he'll want to grab dinner and a few drinks afterward, so I won't be rolling in till well after midnight, and to tell you the truth, honey, I'm beat . . . so I'm going to try to get some sleep tonight. You sleep well, darling, and we'll have tomorrow night, okay? Good night, Molly. I love you."

"Hello, Traci? This is Austin Feruzzi. From the Feruzzi Galleries. I met you last month at Dottie and Skip Herrald's party in East Hampton. I know this is short notice, but I just got in from the coast and a friend of mine has two pairs of tickets to see the Knicks tonight. Would you and your friend Gillian like to join us? Or maybe another friend of yours, if she isn't available? Anyway, call me at the gallery and leave a message . . . 334-2900. If you can make it, we'll meet you at Madison Square Garden, the main entrance, just before 7:30 game time. We'll have a little

dinner afterward. I hope you can come, Traci—I look forward to seeing you again. Bye now."

"This message is for Enzo . . . this is Austin Feruzzi calling. Enzo, when you get this, would you please send three bottles of Dom Perignon over to my Fifth Avenue apartment? Leave them with Luis, the doorman. And send over a couple of nice cheeses, a good-sized slice of your best pâté, some crackers, maybe a tin of smoked oysters . . . a few goodies. You know what I like, Enzo. Thanks, buddy."

"Hello, Luis . . . this is Austin Feruzzi. Enzo from Del'Olios is sending some champagne over for me . . . would you please have it brought upstairs to my apartment? Have someone put the bottles in the fridge behind the bar, okay? Along with anything else that needs to be refrigerated. Thanks, Luis. I'll take care of you later. Bye now."

Austin hung up the phone. He was in the green room at Global's New York radio station on Broadway. It had been another good show with Trisha—hopefully it would bring in more business, he thought, as he walked out the door and down the hall toward the bank of elevators.

Free radio exposure on Trisha's network show was giving the Feruzzi Galleries name recognition all over the country. When tourists went to New York, Beverly Hills, or London, from Tennessee, Iowa, or wherever, chances were good that they would recognize the Feruzzi name in his ads and on his gallery doors, all of them on the most elegant streets in those cities.

Always humping, he thought. Even when he was playing, he was working. Yes, he was worth some money, but it wasn't serious money, it wasn't Peter Newman money. Peter was his idol—ultra cool, brilliant, witty, urbane, and rich. Very, very rich, and the money just kept rolling in without Peter's even taking notice, while Austin Feruzzi had to work every damn angle every which way from Sunday to turn over a buck. Peter Newman was *real* class, and Austin Feruzzi still felt like a pretender.

Oh well, at least he was better looking than Peter. He prided himself on his Mediterranean good looks. His father was Italian and his mother was Jewish—that made for sexy *and* smart, he told himself. They'd named him Augustine after his grandfather Feruzzi, and everybody had called him Gus. He hated the name Gus. So he changed Augustine to Austin when he went to Rutgers to study art. There, he was not nearly as successful at creating art as he was at creating himself. Like the legendary actor Cary Grant, Austin Feruzzi painted himself with a patina of class and charm, and he learned well how to use it. Only medium tall, he made up for that with a naturally toned body, even features, a matinee-idol smile, and a thick shock of medium-brown hair. Women noticed him. Now his still-full head of hair was just starting to gray at the temples—and women still noticed him. For him, women had always been easy. But money wasn't. Real money was hard.

Yes, ultra-rich Peter Newman was his idol, but they were very different. Peter Newman was the epitome of cool. But Austin Feruzzi was hot.

His driver was waiting for him in front of the building. On his way uptown to the Newmans' for drinks, he would stop by his gallery on Madison Avenue. He wanted to make sure that Molly had properly displayed the new Hazens in the window. Those should go, he thought. They were particularly good pieces, they made a marvelous pair, and he'd bought them well, so he'd been able to jack up their prices with impunity.

He also wanted to pick up the Demuths and bring them over to his apartment. He would replace the pair of Dalí lithographs over his living room fireplace with the two gouaches, and let Jock Moranis see them in a home setting. After the game and dinner at Elaine's, they would all go over to his place, and Austin was sure that the Dom Perignon and the two stylish young women from Sotheby's would inspire Moranis to pop for the Demuths. It should be a very productive night. And if he got laid later, all the better.

Damn, he thought, Kate was punishing him. He wanted to hear from her, and he wanted her to come in to New York tomorrow. He would gladly blow Molly off. Even if Kate had a few bruises, they could lie low in the apartment and have a quiet weekend, not tell anyone that she was in town, then on Monday the two of them could run down to the Caribbean for a few days. When they got back to the city Kate would be all tanned and gorgeous again, and they could see friends, and her family, and she could shop. Katie loved New York. He would buy her that yellow diamond dinner ring that she liked so much in Tiffany's window the last time they were here.

She would come around, she always did. If not today or tomorrow, he would take her down to Cabo for a few days when he got back to the coast. But tonight he was going to have some fun. He loved the Knicks, they could go all the way this season, this little Traci Landis was some hot dish, and he relished the idea of racking up a sizable sale to Jock Moranis at the same time. Always mix business with pleasure, another one of his maxims.

If someone were to see them out and about, the girls from Sotheby's could be explained away as business. Just as Molly Adams could. To a point. Of course, he didn't want to push that one. If he were to be seen too often around town with his cute little gallery director, it could make the gossip columns in the *New York Post*. Nobody would admit it, but everybody read "Page Six" in the *Post*.

He was sure that he would be able to explain away a few dinners with Molly, but he wasn't anxious to test it. And God knew, if Trisha found out about them it would be all over. Nothing got past that woman. Trisha Newman had none of Kate's sweetness or tolerance. If Trisha caught him anywhere alone with Molly, he'd be busted. The four charter members of Kate's group had a tight network—each knew when the others ate a sandwich! And what kind it was! If he were spotted with Molly in a nonbusiness setting, and Molly had not alerted the rest of the group in advance, Trisha would put it together.

So he hid out with Molly, and it was delectable. Yes, this little dalliance was very tricky. What the hell was it with him and danger? he chuckled. Thousands of magnificent women in New York, and he had to lust after one of his wife's closest friends. He had been trying to get a piece of delicious little Ms. Adams ever since she'd come to work for him, and finally she had come around, big time!

Of course he'd had to tell her that he intended to leave Kate one day and marry her. Married men always said that to the women they had affairs with, didn't they? Or at least suggested that they weren't happy in their marriages. But he was amazed that smart, independent Molly Adams had gone for that one. Whatever, finally he had nailed Molly, and she was fantastic forbidden fruit.

His limo pulled up in front of the Feruzzi Gallery on Madison. The gallery closed at six o'clock, but he could see that Molly was still inside with customers. His policy was never to throw patrons out at closing time, or to make them feel the least bit uncomfortable, no matter how late they kept the help. After closing, when there was just the slightest bit of pressure on a client, the likelihood of a sale increased tenfold.

Selling art was a balancing act, Feruzzi knew. The really heavy investors usually bought their art through private sales. People who picked up pieces in art galleries tended to make emotional buys. The trick was closing. If customers took a piece out the door with them, in most cases they would keep it. But if they said they would think it over and come back tomorrow, in most cases they did not. Much as he would rather not have to deal with Molly right now, Feruzzi liked seeing the lights on in his galleries after closing time.

Perusing the windows, he approved the way the Hazens were displayed, then went inside. Signaling him to join her, Molly introduced him to the clients, a European couple. They were considering a large, unique gelatin-silver print by Cocteau that was overlaid with whimsical brush strokes, and punctuated with a bold signature by the artist across the lower third of the piece.

He knew that East Coast clients were impressed when they met the owner of the worldwide Feruzzi Galleries, this busy man whom they were lucky enough to catch in New York. These customers would revel in special attention by the owner, and Molly would appreciate the sales help. She could use the commission.

Feruzzi did a little tap-dancing for the couple, who turned out to be a visiting businessman and his wife from Geneva. The better to close the Cocteau, he knew. Business was fun. So was life.

While the couple continued to deliberate, Austin eased Molly out of their earshot. After you did an appropriate song and dance routine from your repertoire, it was better to leave potential buyers alone to confer in private.

"You have some messages, Austin," Molly told him then. "I left them on the machine." That's when he saw that she had a little edge going.

"Oh?"

"You had a message from a woman," Molly went on, "who said that she and her friend would be able to join you tonight."

"Aah," Austin shrugged, "they're from Sotheby's, and I'm having them meet with me and Jock Moranis to help close the deal on the two Demuths. That pair came from Sotheby's, you know, and I need the girls to talk about the history and provenance, romance them a little."

Austin glanced at Molly to judge whether she'd bought that or not. The gouaches had *not* come from Sotheby's, but Molly didn't know that. It was a flimsy cover, but in Feruzzi's experience, most women believed what they wanted to believe.

Chapter 12

Darling, are you sure we want to sic Austin Feruzzi on the DeVorzons?" Trisha Newman put the question to her husband as he mixed a shaker of martinis at the polished hunter-green granite bar in their Park Avenue penthouse.

"Sweetheart," Peter smiled, "the DeVorzons are in the market to buy art, and they might as well buy it from the Feruzzi Galleries."

"Why?" Trisha sighed, accepting her cocktail.

"You know why. If Austin benefits," Peter laid out in exacting tones, "then Kate benefits. And you love Kate," he added unnecessarily.

"Of course I do, darling, but has it ever occurred to you that we might be aiding and abetting an unholy alliance?"

"What do you mean, dear?" Peter asked.

"I mean that maybe if Austin Feruzzi falls on his ass, Katie would open up her eyes and leave him, and find someone wonderful to spend her life with."

"Trisha," her husband said then, with just a hint of exasperation, "if Barbara and Adam like him, and if they want him to show them some artwork, don't say anything to jinx the deal, okay? I promised Austin this favor at lunch today."

"Well then, I'd best not say anything at all," Trisha countered with a mischievous grin, moving to one of the silk-covered couches.

She was teasing, of course. She would play the perfect lady when Adam and Barb DeVorzon and Austin Feruzzi arrived for drinks. Peter had often been instrumental in introducing Austin into situations where he was able to meet wealthy art clients, and to be fair, in the beginning, Trisha had asked her husband to do it. For Katie. And when Peter Newman took on an assignment, he gave it his all. It had been

Peter's idea for her to have Austin as a guest on the radio show when he was in town, to help the gallery business.

True, the man was a good guest, interesting, humorous, and glib. And true, he was married to one of her very dearest friends, and Trisha knew that when she helped Austin, she was helping Kate. Still, Austin Feruzzi always left her with something of an unpleasant aftertaste.

The doorbell rang, and Peter walked over to the intercom on the wall.

"Hello," he said into the mouthpiece, then he told the doorman to send the visitor up.

"It's Feruzzi," he said to Trisha. "Now you be good, do you hear? Austin is okay. He's just a little rough around the edges." Trisha rolled her eyes.

Gigi, their German housekeeper, opened the door of the penthouse to Feruzzi and ushered him into the room. Peter got up and shook his hand. And smiled affably, and asked him what he'd like to drink. The perfect host, her perfect husband, Trisha thought contentedly.

She sat back and watched the two men. Both in their late forties, both tall, tanned, powerful, wealthy—both charismatic, very much at ease, enormously good-looking men. Trisha mentally thanked God that she was married to the one with less hair and more soul.

Not that she ever in her life would have fallen for a man like Austin Feruzzi. He sold good art along with questionable art, all of it dispensed with liberal doses of snake oil. Also in the mix, ever obsequious, ever ingratiating, always he was selling himself as well. And for reasons Trisha had never been able to fathom, people were buying.

Including Kate. She'd bought Austin Feruzzi, hook, line, and more line. But as Trisha watched her friend's engaging husband banter with Peter at the bar, it occurred to her that perhaps that was no surprise after all. Kate was very wealthy and astoundingly beautiful, and she'd always had doubts that any man would love her for the good, sweet, smart, funny, and wonderful person that she was. Also, many really terrific men were intimidated by her beauty, would not go near her. It had always seemed to be the cocky guys who would dare ask Katie out. Elgin Horner, the flashy star running back who was her first husband. And Austin Feruzzi, whose ego was bigger than the room.

The doorbell sounded again. The DeVorzons. Trisha caught the intercom, and instructed the doorman to send them up. Then she joined the two men at the bar. Austin was regaling Peter with details on the latest scrape that Aiden Jannus had got himself into at the L.A. airport today. The two talked about how truly brilliant Jannus was, and how absolutely impossible he was at the same time.

"How can the man put out so much incredible work when he's such an undisciplined basket case?" Trisha threw out to Austin, looking up at the stunning Jannus triptych they had purchased at his recent Beverly Hills show, which now hung prominently above the massive limestone fireplace.

"Who knows?" Austin laughed. "Aiden Jannus is just some kind of evil genius."

"So," she said to Austin then, "I still haven't had a message from that little brat you married. Did you tell Katie that she missed some delicious lobster at the Carlyle today? Not to mention some delicious gossip."

"She still hasn't called you?" Austin asked, raising his eyebrows.

"Not a word—not a peep," Trisha groused. "Did you talk to her tonight?"

"Of course I did," Austin said. "She's fine. Just busy. She sends her love."

_____

Chapter 13

WOMEN ARTISTS JUST don't make it big like men do, it's that simple," Molly lamented aloud as she dipped her brush into a tube of brilliant sienna and dabbed at the canvas that was set up on her easel. The spare bedroom in Molly's apartment in the Chelsea district was fitted out as a makeshift artist's studio, inasmuch as it could be, given such small confines and poor light.

She looked around the tiny space, cluttered with canvases in various stages of completion, countless stacks of dog-eared preliminary renderings and line drawings, brushes soaking in jars of murky paint thinner, tubes of oils and acrylics spilling onto the floor, sketch pads, inks, soft pencils—and dust! Dust everywhere. She had no time to clean, and she certainly couldn't afford cleaning help.

The Swiss couple at the gallery had finally bought the Cocteau print, which earned Molly a much-needed ten percent commission, and she was able to close up shop. And Austin had gone off with clients. Now she sat at home alone with her painting. She loved it, and she was good. What chafed was that as good as she was, she couldn't make a living at it.

As she spread the sienna into vivid reds and yellows, the facts of life about this noble, creative would-be profession of hers continued to rankle—female artists just did not rise to the top in the world of fine art like male artists did. Other than Mary Cassatt, an American impressionist who had to sell in France, or Frida Kahlo, a Mexican woman who became known on the world markets only because she was the wife of brilliant artist Diego Rivera, or Georgia O'Keeffe, whose unorthodox lifestyle catapulted her into the public spotlight—other than a very few *unusual* women artists, who was there?

Her mind skittered to Aiden Jannus, as it so often did. Squandering his talent, denigrating his patrons and his collectors, disdaining his celebrity, debasing his work. The man did not deserve what he had, and what he had was the art world groveling at his feet. Though she took great pains not to let it show, she harbored tremendous resentment for Jannus. Artist Molly Adams sat in this dingy room, unknown, uncelebrated, paid next to nothing, and inescapably exhausted at the end of every sixteen-hour day, while artist Aiden Jannus had everything *she* wanted, heaped upon his head by an adoring world, and in return he gave the world the finger. Meantime, she had to spin her wheels, helping Austin and Tripp Kendrick mop up after Jannus's constant flagrancies, all the while indulging him like a spoiled, naughty child.

She thought about Austin Feruzzi—Austin had really *made* Aiden Jannus's career, and he could make hers as well. And then she thought about the inner conflict that she wrestled with—my God, she was sleeping with the husband of one of her closest friends on earth. And seriously planning to steal him away from her and marry him, and make a life with him.

She had been over this and over this in her mind. Yes, she had fallen in love with Austin Feruzzi, and wasn't all fair in love? Of course not, she knew. She *did* anguish over betraying her longtime friend and college roommate, whom she truly loved as well, and for so long. But Kathryn Spenser had always had every single thing she'd ever wanted handed to her on a golden pillow, including any man she chose to nod at. Kate brought Elgin Horner to his knees, the gorgeous football hero from Brown University whom every female at Briarcliff wanted, and Katie chewed him up and spit him out. She would have no trouble getting any other man on the planet that she happened to fancy—why would she?

Besides, Kate and Austin had no children, so there was no guilt on that score. In fact, she would actually be doing Kate a favor by coming between her and Austin—Kate had always wanted more children, and Austin was adamantly against it. Now Katie would be free to find a man who wanted babies too, and she could finally have siblings for Shawn before it was too late. Most important, Austin wasn't in love with Kate—he loved Molly now, he'd been very clear about that. He intended to divorce Kate and marry her.

This was a first for Molly, the first time in her life that she embraced the thought of marriage. Now, everything about the concept of being Mrs. Austin Feruzzi enticed her. The fiery sex, the wonderful leisure, respect, money, freedom from having to scrape by from paycheck to paycheck. She would finally have her piece of the pie, the good life that her three friends had always accepted as a given. Yes, it was unfortunate that Austin was married to Kate, but Molly didn't have another twenty years to find another man who could make her heart race, and who could also make her America's next Aiden Jannus.

It would all feel better after she told the other three, she told herself. She'd half intended to spill it all to Trisha and Kate at lunch today. Tell it to Katie at lunch, and if she fell apart, have solid, sensible Trisha there to pick up the pieces. What better place to do it than in the elegant setting of the crowded dining room at the Carlyle Hotel at midday? How perfectly civilized. No one would dream of making a scene there. It rather reminded Molly of vignettes from the classic movies of the forties, where sophisticated women in suits and hats sipped champagne and lunched together, and discussed such things. That's how Barbara Stanwyck, Lauren Bacall, or Katharine Hepburn would handle it.

But Kate didn't come after all; there was just Molly and Trisha. She could have used the opportunity to tell Trish, that was probably what she *should* have done, because after she absorbed the shock, Trisha Newman would probably have some practical advice on what she should do. Trisha dealt with situations like this on her radio show every day. But Molly lost her nerve.

Who was she kidding, Molly thought—none of the three would ever speak to her again. Back in college, it seemed that she was always on the periphery of the privileged world that the other three inhabited, always trying to find a place in it for herself. Now she would certainly be banished from their world forever. No matter, she would have her own world of privilege. A meaningful world, filled with art and beauty and creativity.

She allowed herself to fantasize about a gracious life, and long, lovely days painting in a *real* artist's studio, built just for her, spacious and sunny with proper light. She would no longer be working in Austin Feruzzi's gallery, serving the art-buying public for ten hours a day, six days a week. Instead, the important Feruzzi Galleries would be showcasing her art.

Besides, Austin had assured her that *he* would tell Kate, as soon as the time was right. When her conscience bit at her, she reminded herself that this was her life, after all, her chance at the American dream. And very significantly, probably her *last* chance.

She dipped her brush into a spot of brilliant magenta on her palette, mixed it with a fiery vermilion, and stabbed it onto the canvas. Life was a series of choices. She chose passion—her new passion for Austin Feruzzi, and her eternal passion for painting.

Chapter 14

MOM'S NOT ANSWERING the phone," Shawn Horner said to his father.

"So, maybe she's out," Horner answered his son, not looking up from the rumpled couch where he sat reading the sports section of the *San Gabriel Clarion*. He was reading his own column, about the controversy raging over the new sports arena proposed for Los Angeles to house the Lakers and the Kings.

"Something's wrong," Shawn said.

"What makes you think so?"

"Tuesday night she told me she was going to New York, and she'd call me when she got there. But she hasn't called for two days, and I can't get ahold of her."

"Did you leave messages?"

"Of course, Dad."

"Where?"

"Both places—here and at the apartment in New York."

Horner knew that his son had been punishing his mother for something, which was usually the case when the boy hung out at *his* humble pad for days at a time. And now he was feeling a little guilty.

"Maybe you ought to go home, Shawn. Even if your mom's not there, at least Christina will give you some clean clothes and a decent dinner."

"I don't want to eat there. I want to eat here, Dad. Why, do you have a date or something?" the boy asked mournfully.

"No, I don't have a date or something," Elgin said with his sideways grin. "It's just that I have low-rent meals and laundry service here."

"I don't care. I wanna stay over."

Horner looked at his watch. "Okay, pal—so what do you want to eat tonight?" he asked.

"Pizza."

"Again?"

"Why not?"

"Fine. Want to order?"

"Sure, Dad. Same ol'?"

"Same ol' for me—pepperoni and cheese."

Shawn went over to the Formica counter that divided the dingy living room and the small kitchenette. He sat on a plastic bar stool, picked up the battered Pizza Hut menu, and pondered the telephone. Maybe his dad shouldn't eat so much pizza. He still had a pro-football physique, Shawn thought. He just needed to work out more. And stop drinking so much beer. And lose some weight. Get rid of that gut. Elgin Horner could be a Raider again if he was in shape, Shawn was sure of it.

He picked up the phone and called his mother again. And again, the phone machine kicked in, and his mom's sweet voice came on, saying she was *sorry* she'd missed his call, she *did* want to talk to him, so *please* leave a message. When the beep sounded, Shawn hung up.

He got up and walked around the counter, went through the tiny kitchen and out the back screen door. His dad's place was on the ground floor of the sprawling Burbank apartment building, so they had a scruffy yard of sorts, and the two of them often tossed a football around. That's how he knew that his father could still be a Raider. All his friends thought so too. Elgin Horner still knew how to handle a football, and he was fast, and strong. And smart. But now he just *wrote* about sports. He'd had jobs at four or five different newspapers that Shawn could remember. And, although he never said so, Shawn knew that his dad was still in love with his mother.

Elgin Horner banged out the screen door and joined his son on the patchy expanse of grass, a scarred-up football in his hand. "So when's the last time you spoke to her?" he asked, tossing the ball to Shawn.

"Day before yesterday, like I said. She's pretty mad cuz I haven't been home since Monday."

He lobbed the ball back to his dad, who was now loping around the perimeter of the long, narrow backyard that stretched behind five ground-floor apartments. The two got into a rhythm and moved in synch.

"So what's the story?"

"Austin. What else? He hates me. I think he hates Mom, too, if you want to know the truth."

"Why do you say that?"

"Well, why does he hit her?"

"He needs help, I think. Maybe she oughta call the police. They'd get him some help, or put him in jail."

They'd had this talk before, many times. And they both knew that nobody was going to call the police, least of all Kathryn Blakely Spenser Horner Feruzzi. The story would be all over the news. In *her* mind, the scandal would be worse than any bruise he gave her.

"Maybe *you* ought to *intervene,* Shawn," Elgin called back, coming in closer.

Elgin Horner knew all about intervention and recovery, from his long and painful experiences with drug rehab. Cocaine was what finished his professional football career, and robbed him of a decade of his life. Sadly, it was that crucial decade between thirty and forty, the one that almost always determines whether a person is going to make it big or not. For most people, their twenties is for learning and working hard, and it all comes together in their thirties. Or not. After forty, it usually doesn't happen.

Elgin Horner, likable, great looking, college football hero, Ivy League graduate, star running back for the Los Angeles Raiders— Elgin Horner had great promise in his twenties, but he'd spent his thirties in a drug haze, wallowing in past glory and accomplishing nothing new. And hardly noticing that his old friends had all but disappeared, and the only guys partying with him now were neighborhood losers who slapped him on the back and drank the beers he paid for.

And still, he believed it was because Kate left him. Even after hours and hours of therapy designed to teach the recovering addict to take responsibility for his own life and the mess he'd made of it, deep down, Elgin Horner still believed that if Katie hadn't left him, he'd still be playing in the pros, and he'd have enough money by now to own a car dealership, or a restaurant, or a team. He'd *be* somebody. If Katie hadn't left him. Now he was writing a column three days a week for a raggedy-ass newspaper in the San Gabriel Valley for a lousy hundred bucks a column, and he was lucky to get that.

"So, you want me to drive you home to see if your mother's okay?" he asked his son now.

"Okay, Dad."

"Did you order that pizza?"

"No—"

"Then come on, let's go."

Chapter 15

"Austin . . . it's me, Tripp. Okay, yes, I know you told me not to uncrate the Rhajis, but you're going to be very glad I did . . . and by the way, this young artist is really maturing, Austin . . . this latest one is light-years ahead of the last few. Anyway, here's the good news . . . are you sitting down? I sold it! To Jon Valley! For a hundred and fifty thousand! Yep, I put our man Rhaji's price way up. The piece has already been delivered, and the check is already in the bank. So, a lucrative day for the gallery, and I'm going out to celebrate tonight! We've got a gold mine in this Indian kid, Austin, whoever he is! Have a nice night. Ciao."

Tripp was sailing! His ten percent of the sun painting sale was a hefty fifteen thousand—*that* would buy dinner! *That* was a pretty good twenty minutes' work! And yes, he was going to celebrate alright—he was going to celebrate with the buyer!

What made him feel especially good was that he really did believe the painting was terrific, and that it was an excellent buy for Jonathan. It would look fabulous in the immense master suite of his Malibu mansion, with its flat, European-white walls. Also, Tripp felt certain that Rhaji's worth would escalate, so it would also be a good investment for Jon. And he was sure that Austin would be more than pleased. All in all, it had been a very productive afternoon.

They were going to celebrate at Jon's beach house tonight, perhaps ceremoniously on the couch directly under the painting. Jonathan had called to invite him to dinner, and to tell him that by the time Tripp got out to Malibu, his carpenters would already have the Rhaji hung.

Speaking of hung, Tripp smiled to himself, he couldn't wait to be with Jon tonight. Even after five years, it was always sizzling with the two of them. Endless summer. Jon would give his chef the night off. Jonathan always made sure that it was cook's night out whenever Tripp was on his menu. Much as he trusted Armand, his longtime personal chef, Jonathan Valley saw no reason to put temptation in the path of any human being—the temptation to sell the salacious story of the mega-star's secret gay love life to the tabloids. Nobody knew about it. No one must *ever* know about it.

Tripp had offered to bring gourmet Italian take-out from Bice, but Jon said no, Armand would prepare something before he left, and leave it in the fridge—they would just have to heat it up. Jon and Tripp were not able to get together often, and when they did, food was never a priority.

Jon had told him that whenever he gave Armand an unscheduled night off, they always exchanged good-old-boy winks. The chef had to be aware that his very private boss would be substituting a superb meal, beautifully served, for an amorous adventure on his plate. But Armand, and all of America, surely thought that movie action hero Jonathan Valley scorched the sheets with models and starlets.

The stringent secrecy of their affair suited Tripp. He was just as private a person as Jonathan, and although Westside wags specu-lated, no one really knew for certain that Tripp Kendrick was gay. Tripp showed up all over town with the same brand of female beau-ties that Jonathan squired, and also like Jon, he sometimes slept with them as well. As they had frequently discussed, it served to deflect gossip about their sexual preference. But unlike Jon, Tripp really adored women, and he genuinely enjoyed having sex with them. He just much preferred having sex with men.

Like Jon, though, he considered his personal business his personal business, and no one else's. And tonight he was looking forward to diving headfirst into his personal business. He'd decided to take to-morrow off, let his assistant run the gallery. He would treat himself to a luxurious Friday. He would stay in bed until noon. With Jonathan. Jon would post Armand at the Beverly Hills house on Fri-day, so that they would not be disturbed at the beach.

Before he left the gallery, Tripp picked out a gift for Jon. A thank-you memento for his excellent sale today, but also just for being there, for enriching his life. He chose a gleaming, antique-looking brass letter opener, its magnificent handle encrusted with Moroccan rubies. Tripp knew that Austin Feruzzi had the ornate mini daggers reproduced, and had the blades imprinted with barely discernable Roman numerals that might be interpreted as dates—dates which would put the pieces into the antique category. Austin had instructed Tripp to put the handsome letter openers out on display just one at a time, each bearing a price tag of thirty-five hundred dollars.

Tripp never suggested to clients that the dates on the jeweled pieces were authentic, nor did the gallery put out papers on them. He had once watched Feruzzi smile and tell a customer that he'd priced them so low because he had never been able to *officially* authenticate them. Found four of the pieces in Marrakesh, Austin had told the intrigued client, each one slightly different.

In fact, the gallery had sold a couple of dozen of these exotic letter openers to date, and Tripp knew that the other galleries in the Feruzzi chain were selling them too. And yes, they were all slightly different, because they were handmade, and the old Moroccan rubies were set into the brass in a variation of designs. They were beautiful, they were unique, but they were definitely not old.

That little chicanery was okay with Tripp. It wasn't against the law, and everyone went away happy. The gallery got a whopping mark-up, and the customer got a magnificent piece that would long give him pleasure, along with the feeling that he just might have purchased an ancient dagger from the Byzantine Empire for a steal. It wasn't technically fraud; it was more like selling a dream.

Tripp was sophisticated enough to know that many such small subterfuges abounded in the art world. When Austin Feruzzi locked himself in the back storeroom for hours with the Rhajis, Tripp figured that he was busy doing *something* to them. Probably trying to improve the primitives with a blade and some oils or acrylics. Feruzzi was an artist of sorts himself, which had attracted the man to the art business in the first place. He had studied fine art for years at Rutgers University. It was only after he'd tried his hand at *creating* art that he became convinced that for him, buying and selling it would be much more lucrative.

Tripp had long felt certain that Austin Feruzzi had been clandestinely altering the Rhajis, and after seeing this latest one fresh out of its packing crate today, he now suspected that what he'd been doing was breaking down the slick resin sun symbols on the canvases and changing them to the orangy-golden acrylic images that Tripp saw when the Rhajis emerged from the back room. He didn't have a problem with that. Certainly Rhaji was not a known artist, and given Charles DeFarge's reputation, and the fact that he had not been forthcoming with biographical information about this Rhaji Mentour, Tripp speculated that the artist could actually be a bunch of Indian artisans working together in a cramped studio. They might never know for sure, and with the way the pieces were selling, it was probably better that they didn't know. Meantime, if Austin thought that he could improve the paintings, well, these were not signed masterworks, and it was Austin Feruzzi's candy store.

Tripp carefully removed the ruby-encrusted letter opener that was currently on display in a glass case. It was a beauty. He wrapped it in tissue, then in brown paper, and tied the package with string. He made a notation in the books that he'd purchased the piece, at his discount rate of forty percent off the selling price, and that the amount was to be deducted from his commission check. At nearly two thousand dollars, Tripp figured with a smile, Feruzzi would still be making a hefty profit on the piece, and his own commission on the Rhaji was still quite sizable.

He loved surprising Jon with interesting gifts, large and small, and indeed, he was on the receiving end of many such gifts himself. Tripp and Jonathan lavished goodies on each other like the early Liz and Dick. But never engraved. No clues, Jon would say—never leave tracks.

It was six o'clock, closing time. Tripp took a last look around, picked up his parcel, and locked up the gallery. He jumped into his black Ford Bronco and drove north into the hills toward his small, wonderful glass-and-limestone house high atop Coldwater Canyon. He would shower and throw a few things in an overnight bag, and head for the beach.

Chapter 16

"YOU'RE GOING TO come in and eat," Christina said sternly to Shawn, then, looking over at his father, she added, "both of you."

Father and son were standing uncomfortably in the immense marble entry of the Feruzzis' Beverly Hills mansion.

"Christina," Shawn blurted again, "where's Mom? She told me she was going to New York—"

"She went with your Aunt Lane, honey," Christina told him, softening when she saw how anxious he was. "To Carmel. This morning. They're probably just getting up there around now."

"To Auntie Lane's—?" Shawn started, puzzled.

"Lane Hamilton isn't your aunt," Elgin said to him.

"Well, I call her Auntie Lane," Shawn put in.

"Why?" his father asked. Elgin was very proprietary about his son's relationships.

"Because she's nice, and she said I can," Shawn returned with a hint of exasperation. He had spent many a vacation week in Carmel, playing on the beach with Lane and Geoff and their kids Robby and Jordan, and their big dog Beowulf.

"I'm sure your mother will be calling you, honey," Christina said then, looking at Shawn kindly. "And I have the Hamiltons' number—"

"I know their number," Shawn said, his voice cracking.

Christina could see that the boy was close to tears now. Putting a large arm around his shoulders, Kate's longtime housekeeper steered her son toward the big stainless steel kitchen.

Elgin followed, looking up and around the place as he walked, taking in the high ceilings, the splendid furnishings, the lavish decor. He was always awed by this house. Kate and Austin Feruzzi bought it right after they were married. Elgin remembered the very first time he'd come here to pick up Shawn—remembered feeling like such a loser, because he had never been able to provide Katie with anything remotely approaching this kind of luxury. It was only much later, when Shawn was old enough to understand such things, that his son had told him that the mansion was bought with Spenser money. His granddad's money.

"Now sit down," Christina ordered. "I'm going to feed you, then we'll talk about everything."

She settled Shawn and Elgin Horner at the big, round kitchen table, and set cheerful red-print place mats and silverware in front of both of them. Christina was a tall, big-boned Swedish woman with an abundance of faded blond hair that she pulled back into a bun at the nape of her neck, and held in place with two criss-crossed crochet needles. Her lined, no-nonsense visage betrayed love and concern for the boy she had watched over from the day he came home from the hospital in his mother's arms. Truth be told, she had a soft spot in her heart for the boy's daddy, too. In Christina's mind, Elgin Horner, for all his weaknesses, was not and never *had* been anywhere near the evil man that Austin Feruzzi was.

"I have some lovely little Cornish game hens already baked," she said then. "I'll just take two of them out and warm them up. Won't take but a few minutes. What will you be drinking?"

"Juice, please," Shawn said.

"Any wine?" Elgin asked hopefully.

"I thought you weren't supposed to be drinking wine, Mr. Horner," Christina scowled at him.

"Well . . . sometimes I do," Elgin said, smiling a little sheepishly.

"Not tonight—not in this house," Christina pronounced. "Coffee, tea, milk, juice, soft drinks, water—pick something else, Elgin." Christina had *been* there at the start of Elgin Horner's drug-and-alcohol-abuse days, and she wasn't about to brook any deviation from his Twelve Step program on *her* watch.

"Water will be fine, Christina," Elgin conceded. He knew better than to argue with her.

Christina bustled about, setting cold drinks and hot dishes in front of the two. Studying the small, crisp-roasted birds stuffed with exotic wild rice, the haricots verts, miniature carrots, and broccoli with cream sauce on his plate, Elgin glanced over at his son and said quietly, "Beats pizza, huh?"

Shawn dismissed the remark. Food wasn't on his mind. "So how come she didn't go to New York, Christina? She never said anything about going to Carmel—"

"You know, son, you have a lot of questions for a boy who doesn't bother to come home to see his mother—" Christina stopped herself. She saw the stricken look on Shawn's face, and was immediately sorry she'd started in on him. "Anyway," she shifted gears, "Miss Kate decided to take some time up north with Mrs. Hamilton."

Seeing that this didn't satisfy Shawn, that he was waiting for an answer to his questions, she put it out there. "She . . . wasn't looking so good," she said softly.

Shawn and Elgin looked at each other. They both knew that was code for *Austin beat her up again!*

"How bad?" Elgin demanded, his face tightening.

"Bad, Mr. Horner—"

"That *sonofabitch!*" Elgin exclaimed, pounding his fist on the table.

Shawn looked alarmed. Christina knew that the boy adored his mother, but had taken to staying away from home so much because of his stepfather. *She'd* never liked Austin Feruzzi either, and had never understood why a beautiful woman like Kathryn would put up with the man. As for Shawn, she could only hope that his father was behaving himself, and taking proper care of the boy. It was all a terrible mess, Christina had lamented inwardly for some time now.

"Look, you two eat while your dinner's hot, then you'll get on the phone and call Carmel. You'll feel better, Shawn. And when's the last time you had a bath, Mister?"

Shawn shrugged, and played with his food.

"Why don't you stay home tonight?" she asked him. "Make your mother happy."

"My mother's not here," Shawn muttered.

"Still, she'll like it when we tell her that you're sleeping in your own room, you're eating my food, you're wearing clean clothes—"

"Where is *he?*" Shawn put in sullenly.

"He went to New York, honey."

"So when's he coming back?"

"I never know. Any time, I guess—"

"Well I don't want to be here," Shawn scowled. "I . . . I wish he was dead, Christina."

Chapter 17

———————

"Lane, it's Lizzie. Got your message when I came in this morning. No problem, I'll steer the ship today . . . can't wait to see what you come back with. Franz woke up with a cold at two in the morning, so his son came in to bake. I tell you, the kid's a genius. He made some apple strudel that's been sailing out the doors since we opened. If any problems come up I'll try to reach you in the Explorer, since you'll be on the road most of the day. Don't worry about anything, Lane, and be careful, okay? Bye-bye." BEEP. THURSDAY, 10:17 A.M.

"Hi, Lane, Charlotte here . . . Murray and I adored seeing you yesterday. Next time, we hope Geoff and the boys can come down too, and you can stay for a weekend maybe . . . try out our southern beaches . . . but I know how busy you all are. Call and let me know that you had a safe trip home, dear, and I'll be interested in how our handsome biscuit barrels do at Hamilton House. How about filling them with Franz's incredible British scones? That's the way they were used in nineteenth-century England, you know. Love you!" BEEP. THURSDAY, 1:36 P.M.

"Lane, hi, darling, it's Trisha. Well, Kate never showed up in New York. Molly and I had lunch today. She's fine, but she seems totally distracted . . . I have no idea what's going on with her, and she's not telling.

"Now, my real concern is Katie. I just get the feeling that something's wrong. Austin is here in New York . . . he was on my show this afternoon, and he came for drinks tonight . . . he just left . . . but I still haven't heard from Kate. Austin says she's just busy . . . but you know it simply isn't like her not to call. I mean, we check in with each other when we burn the toast! She's not calling, and she's not answering. Any thoughts?

"Big kiss to Geoff and the boys. Bye-bye." BEEP. THURSDAY, 4:20 P.M.

"Sweetie, it's Geoff . . . I have to work late. Sorry, honey, but I'm going to miss dinner. It's our old friends, the Stallings brothers. Looks like they went way beyond drunk-and-disorderly tonight. I can't go into it, but we've got a dead body on our hands out on the truck route off Highway One. You and Kate have a nice visit, and I'll look over the guys' homework when I get home, okay? I'm hoping it won't be any later than eight, nine o'clock. Love you, Lanie. Say hello to Kate for me, and I'll be home as soon as I can." BEEP. THURSDAY, 4:52 P.M. END OF FINAL MESSAGE.

Lane pushed the ERASE button. She and Kate had just arrived at the house. Ordinarily she would have stopped off at the shop and unloaded the merchandise that filled the back of her SUV, but Kate was in no shape for a side trip of any sort. Lane had settled her in the cheerful guest suite upstairs, and ordered her to relax in a warm tub before dinner.

Dinner! She hated that Geoff wouldn't be here. Geoff's big-man strength, his aura of integrity, his warm congeniality made you feel that whatever the circumstances, everything was going to be okay. He would be able to ease the tension that clung to Kate as visibly as the nasty cuts and bruises on her face. Then again, perhaps Kate would actually be more at ease without Geoff at the table on her first night in Carmel.

Which gave Lane an idea. Why not send the boys out for dinner, too? Lord knows, they would leap at the chance to walk down to Ocean Avenue and scarf down junk food. It would give Lane a chance to be alone with Kate for a couple more hours, and continue the talk they'd been having while driving up the coast. Well, the talk *Lane* had been having. Kate was having none of it. Her initial resolve to never see Austin again, never talk to him again, had wavered over the miles.

Having listened to Geoff describe such cases for years, Lane was only too well versed in the typical course of domestic violence. After getting past her initial shock at seeing Kate bruised and bloodied, and after coming to grips with the fact that it was her husband who had beaten her, Lane had embarked on a program of persuasion to make her friend do something about it. Take charge of her life, instead of being a passive victim. It could only get worse with Austin, she'd told Kate, unless he got some help. And Lane added that in her opinion, Austin Feruzzi was not the kind who would admit there was anything wrong with him. She had resisted saying that he was not man enough.

"Lane, you just don't know him," Kate had insisted. "Other than that, he's really wonderful."

"Stop it, Kate," Lane had jumped on her. "Listen to yourself! You sound like a textbook battered wife. *He* is always sorry, and *she* always forgives him."

Lane went downstairs to the game room where the boys were ostensibly studying, to give them a few dollars and the good news that they were liberated until eight o'clock. She barely had time to instruct them to order salads with their burgers before their cute little eleven- and twelve-year-old butts disappeared gleefully out the doors and around the swimming pool, to the adventures of the great outdoors. More specifically, to the adventures of the Carmel Plaza mall.

Watching the boys scamper off, she wondered how long it would be before they would be borrowing the car. And going out with girls. And getting married and making her a grandmother. She shuddered. Maybe she should give serious thought to having one more baby while she still could. Hopefully, a sweet little girl, who would think it was actually fun to pick cabbage roses with Mom and help arrange them in a bowl. Lane smiled at the thought, and turned around and went back upstairs.

Dinner, she thought. Just her and Kate; keep it simple. She took a package of homemade linguine out of the fridge, and some fresh tomatoes, onions, and basil for pasta sauce. Halfway through the preparation, Kate appeared in the doorway of the kitchen, looking just a little better, and a little more composed. Amazing, Lane thought, how truly beautiful Katie was, even with a black eye, a badly bruised cheekbone, and a split lip. She poured two glasses of Chianti, and wordlessly handed one to Kate.

"A toast," Lane said then, raising her glass. "To you, and to better times. It's going to be okay, Katie."

"From your lips," her friend intoned, and they sipped the wine together. Kate went to work cutting up salad mixings then, while Lane made the sauce.

"Not too much, Kate," she told her then. "It'll be just us, you and me. Geoff's working late, and the boys went out for burgers. A rare treat on a school night, but summer school's almost over, and I wanted to give you one night of privacy before you're subjected to my all-male family."

"Your kids are adorable, and Geoff is wonderful," Kate smiled, but Lane could see relief flood her anxious face.

They had pasta and salad out on the enclosed redwood deck. The air was perfumed with the smell of wet grass and flowering lavender, narcissus, rosemary, and Belle Amour roses in full bloom. As the sun disappeared behind the cypress trees that lined the property, several pairs of lanterns mounted on each side of the open French doors came on automatically, casting a soft amber glow on the veranda. The salt air was bracing, and the rhythmic sound of the not-too-distant ocean waves crashing on shore was reassuring to Lane that all was right with the world. Well, with *her* world, at least. But what about Kate's world?

"Katie," she said again, "either he has to get therapy, or you have to leave him. You realize that, don't you?"

"Easier said," Katie returned, toying with her pasta. "We have twelve years together."

"That's not reason enough to stay with him."

Lane had no intention of asking if she loved the man. Kate had already protested that she did. She was sure that Katie was mistaking love for need, but that didn't matter, because having talked to her for hours today, she was equally certain that Katie didn't know the difference.

While they were lingering over coffee, the boys trooped out onto the deck. In a scramble of activity, the two gave their mom brief scuffles that passed for hugs, and bright hellos to their "Aunt Kate." Then the two of them stopped in their tracks and stared. Even on the dimly lit veranda, even though Kate had done a masterful job with makeup coverage, the boys couldn't miss the contusions and cuts on her beautiful face. And unlike Katie's Shawn, they hadn't yet reached ages when discretion took the place of brutal candor.

"Whoa! Who gave you the black eye?" Jordan blurted, while Robby just let out a low whistle. Out of the mouths of babes.

"She's taking karate lessons," Lane answered quickly, which her children knew was code for it was none of their business.

"Now run, finish up your homework, guys. Dad will be home momentarily to check it." The two lumbered off without further comment.

"So maybe they'll do homework," Lane sighed to Kate. "If Geoff doesn't get home soon, I'll have to check on them. I can't remember when I first realized that parenting was at least fifty percent police work. Enforcing the law . . ."

Lane could hear herself babbling on in the vain hope of minimizing the force of her sons' blunt reaction to Kate's injuries. She stopped when she saw that her monologue was completely lost on her friend.

"Geoff will be able to tell," Kate murmured dejectedly.

"Yes, Geoff will be able to tell, Katie, and I want you to talk to him about it. He'll listen, he'll understand, and he'll be able to help you. He's experienced—"

Kate got up from the table. "I'm going upstairs before he gets in," she stated with determination. "You said you wouldn't tell anyone unless I said you could, so don't tell him. I'll stay in my room until he leaves for work in the morning and the boys go to school. Then I'll get a taxi to the airport—"

"Kate, please, please, sit down," Lane implored, her eyes welling up with frustrated tears.

Kate lowered herself back into her chair with an air of defeat. Before Lane could begin to make a case for Kate staying in Carmel for a while and dealing with her problem, they heard footsteps approaching. They both turned to see Geoff materialize in the framework of a pair of double doors off the dining room. Lane looked up at her husband's tall, toned body and his ruggedly handsome face. Mentally comparing him to the man that Kate was married to, Geoffrey Hamilton loomed large as her storybook prince. He always did.

"Hi, darling," she said to him. "Join us for coffee."

Geoff approached the table and fixed his eyes on Kate, held them on her face as he sat down.

"You didn't tell me," he said simply, to Lane.

"No," Lane answered.

"Who did this to you, Kate?" he asked her, while his face registered that he already knew the answer.

Tears spilled over Kate's cheeks, and Geoff handed her his handkerchief. Carmel Police Chief Geoff Hamilton was one of the few men in the late twentieth century who still carried a clean linen handkerchief in his pocket every day, which he usually used to mop up women's tears, usually on the job. Lane's life with this man produced in her only infrequent tears, and they were almost always tears of joy.

"You know that he could be jailed for felony spousal abuse, don't you?" he asked Kate softly, as she sniffled into his handkerchief.

Geoff had zero sympathy for a man who would beat up a woman. Sensing that, Kate didn't even venture her homilies, about how he adored her, and what a good man he was *other than that*. Lane was relieved that Geoff was home.

"Listen to me, Kate," he was saying now, all business, no nonsense. "Family violence is the number-one cause of emergency-room visits by women. Domestic violence kills more than ten women in America every day. And the beatings escalate, Kate. It never gets better. It only gets worse."

He paused, letting his words sink in. Lane could see that Kate was actually listening. Geoff had the kind of dignified presence that compelled people to listen to him. Lane got up from the table and went inside to get her husband a mug for coffee. And to let the two be alone for a bit. Geoffrey was much more likely to talk some sense into Kate than she was.

Lane took longer than she needed to in the kitchen. She put on a fresh pot of coffee, and filled a plate with double-fudge cookies that Lizzie had brought by from the shop after closing up tonight. Lane knew that they would probably go untouched. Cookies were for happy chats, she reflected. This one was not.

By the time Lane went back out onto the deck, dutiful hostess with tray in hand, Geoff and Kate were sitting in silence. Attempting to break the tension, Lane busied herself with setting down the cookies, freshening Kate's coffee, pouring a cup for Geoff, offering cream. Still, no one spoke.

Then, Kate surprised the hell out of her. She reached for a double-fudge, and flashed her a glowing smile. "I'm leaving him," she said.

Chapter 18

STILL POISED AT her easel, Molly was putting final touches on her painting, and taking stock of the landscape of her life. She was plagued with doubt, fear that she had made a colossal mess of things. Trisha, Kate, and Lane had always been there for her, and they had no idea that she was about to cut herself off from all of them, and hurt them irreparably, besides.

Her reverie was abruptly interrupted by the telephone, ringing now in the adjoining bedroom. Letting the machine pick up, she listened.

"Hi, Molly, it's Trish. Lunch was great today. Is the lobster salad at the Carlyle just the best? Even better than in Maine, I swear. Loved seeing you, as usual, and you looked great, as always . . . though you did seem to be more than a little preoccupied today, Mol. Nervous or something. Maybe we could talk about that . . ."

Trisha. It was kind, cheerful, generous, loving, very perceptive Trisha. Molly did not have the heart to pick up the phone and carry on her deceptive charade. She listened while Trisha rambled on.

". . . speaking of nervous, I have to tell you I'm nervous about Katie. I told Lane the same thing. I still haven't heard from her, and this is not like her. Austin says she's fine, just busy, but I don't know. He was over for drinks tonight, then he left to go to a basketball game . . . with a client, he said.

"But listen to this, Molly . . . Peter was talking to his lawyer just now, Jay Arnstein . . . I think you've met him at dinner

here . . . well, Jay happened to be at the Knicks game tonight too. He called Peter from the car on the way home to catch him up on some early morning business they have, and he happened to mention that he saw his friend Austin Feruzzi at the game. With a woman! A young blond woman, very pretty. Jay said to Peter, 'I thought Feruzzi was married to a friend of your wife's.' Said he had his hands all over this woman . . . that they were laughing and kissing . . . looked like something was definitely going on there. You know how visible those seats on the floor at the Garden are . . . everybody can see you.

"So what do you think, Molly—should I tell Kate? My gut feeling is that I should. If I don't, who will? I mean, that's what our special friendship is all about, isn't it? Otherwise, Kate goes on blithely in the dark. Who knows, maybe this woman is why Austin didn't bring her to New York with him.

"Anyway, let me know what you think. I'll talk to you tomorrow, sweetie. And we'll do lunch at the Carlyle again soon. Bye, dear." BEEP. THURSDAY, 10:46 P.M. END OF FINAL MESSAGE.

Molly bolted into her bedroom and pounced on her answering machine. She rewound Trisha's message and played it again. Then she rolled the tape farther back and listened to the message that Austin had left her at home before he stopped in at the gallery tonight.

". . . another client is dragging me to a Knicks game. I'd rather take a stiff beating than go to a basketball game tonight, but I have to go . . . I'm real close to a good sale with this guy. I know he'll want to grab dinner and a few drinks afterward, so I won't be rolling in till well after midnight, and to tell you the truth, honey, I'm beat . . . so I'm going to try to get some sleep tonight. You sleep well, darling, and we'll have tomorrow night, okay? Good night, Molly. I love you." BEEP. THURSDAY, 5:17 P.M.

Close to a sale with this *guy*? A client? *He's* going to want to grab drinks and dinner? So I'll be too tired to sleep with *you* tonight? Could Austin possibly be cheating on Kate with her, and also cheating on her with some bimbo? She picked up the phone and dialed his apartment.

"Austin, this is Molly. It's almost eleven. Call me as soon as you get in. I don't care if it's three in the morning. I have to talk to you!"

Chapter 19

"Trisha, it's Lane, I've got news. It's late . . . it's after one o'clock in New York . . . I'm sure you're asleep, so you'll get this in the morning. You can stop worrying about Katie . . . she's with me.

"Well, we can't really stop worrying about her. Here's the situation . . . brace yourself . . . it turns out that Austin has been beating her. Are you still standing? I only found out because I showed up at her house unannounced yesterday, and I found her with a black eye, her face all cut and bruised and swollen . . . I am so upset and angry, Trish, I can't tell you. I don't know exactly what the fight was about . . . something about her going to New York or not . . . but it hardly matters. Apparently Austin has been using Kate as a punching bag for years.

"She's been keeping this terrible secret for so long . . . and she's not yet ready to tell the world. She wants you to know, Trisha, because you've been calling her every five minutes, but not anyone else. Not even Molly—Molly works for Austin, and that could be uncomfortable for her.

"I managed to get her out of the house and bring her up here to Carmel . . . she's asleep in the guest room right now. Geoff talked to her tonight, about domestic violence and what she could expect . . . he's going to get her into a concentrated spousal-abuse therapy program tomorrow. Kate doesn't know many people up here, so that's a plus. And in a couple of days, when her face looks better, we'll get Shawn up here. He'll have a great vacation, fun and beach time with Robby and Jordan.

"I think Carmel will do Kate a lot of good . . . help her start the healing process both mentally and physically . . . then in a few weeks, when she's ready, she's going back home to start divorce proceedings. She's leaving him, Trish! I am so relieved. Katie is sweet, and good, and she's so beautiful . . . she deserves much better . . . and now she'll have a chance at a new life . . . a chance to be happy.

"If you happen to see Austin, don't say a word to him, Trish. Just tell him that you haven't heard from Kate. God, we heard him on your show while we were driving back from L.A. I wanted to put my fist through the radio. Katie just couldn't listen . . . she switched stations. Lord, what a nightmare. Can you imagine, Trisha, she's been going through this for years? Never called the police . . . never reported the bastard, never told any of us . . .

"Kate said she's going to call you tomorrow . . . she'll tell you herself. Meantime, mum's the word, okay? I'll keep you posted—we've got to help her through this. I love you, sweetie. Bye-bye."

Lane put the phone down, rolled over, and snuggled under the down comforter on the king-sized bed in the master suite. From the time she'd found Kate so badly beaten last night, she had been vaguely nauseous. Further, she was beyond exhausted, but she didn't know how she was going to get to sleep. She had literally tucked Katie in, and kissed her forehead, then lowered her own tired body into a hot, swirling Jacuzzi bath while Geoff finished up some paperwork. Now he was in the shower, and she ached for his comforting arms around her.

She shivered in the warmth of the down bedding. Why hadn't Katie reached out, talked to her friends? Would Lane have talked about it had she been in the same situation? she asked herself. Talked, screamed, kicked him in the balls, bolted, had him locked up, divorced him, and sued the shorts off him, she answered herself. But that was the difference between her and Kate.

Geoff came into the bedroom, all steamy and sweet-smelling, with a towel tied around his waist. He was holding a glass of water in one hand, and something else in the other.

"Sweetheart, take this," he said to her.

"What is it?"

"An Excedrin PM," he returned, proffering the sky-blue tablet.

"A sleeping pill . . . ?"

"Over-the-counter."

"But you hate sleep aids. You always tell me to tough it out."

"Not tonight, honey. You're going to want to work tomorrow, and you have to be strong for Kate. Not to mention for two preteen masses of energy who will take advantage of any perceived weakness to get you to write out a check for unlimited video games, or something equally sinister."

Lane laughed and sat up, and accepted the tablet and the glass of water. She wasn't used to drugs of any kind, and she knew that just one of the pills would put her lights out.

"Better set the clock on my side," she said. "I've been known to sleep through a weekend on one of these."

"It's okay, Lane, you need it tonight," her husband said, sitting down on the bed. "I'll get you up. But now I'm going to soothe you to sleep."

She watched as he picked up a bottle of musk oil from the bedside table and twisted off the cap, then poured some of the smoky liquid into the palm of his hand.

"Mmmmm, I like the way you do that," she purred.

"Good," he said. "Now turn over . . . let me rub your back."

"How about rubbing my front a little, too?" she uttered weakly.

"I love it when you're drugged," he laughed, rubbing the oil into both his hands.

She wriggled out of her nightie; he slipped off his towel. Then he reached for her waist with his oily hands. He worked them slowly up to her breasts, then gently kneaded her nipples. She moaned. He took a second to flip off the bedside lamps, then slid into bed beside her.

Chapter 20

"Tripp, it's Austin. I just got in, just got your message. Now lis-
ten to me—get that fucking painting back! The London gallery
has just sold a Rhaji at nearly twice the asking because there was
a goddamn bidding war going on over there. So one the size you're
talking about has to go for a quarter of a million. Just get it back
from Valley, now!

"Look, I know he's a good client, but we can't take that kind of a
bath. There's a run on these canvases, and DeFarge is telling me
that he might not be able to ship us any more. He's probably trying
to get his price up, but as you know, dealing with DeFarge is always
a pig-fuck. So get it back, period, and cut Jon Valley a check for a
full refund. And call me at the apartment when you get in . . . I
don't give a damn what time it is in New York.

"And now that Jake got the court date continued, let me know
when you expect to get that fucking Jannus on a plane!"

Feruzzi slammed down the phone in his mahogany-paneled office in
the New York apartment. Disaster on all fronts. Jannus was a train
wreck waiting to happen. Tripp had let the Rhaji get out the door. De-
Farge was pushing him for more money. Molly had left a frosty message to call her no matter the time—she was obviously steamed. And
Kate still hadn't called at all.

Molly would have to wait. He had left his three guests out in the living room sucking up his Dom Perignon, while he'd come into the office to listen to his messages, see if maybe Kate had called. Now he
had to force a quick mood adjustment to go out and do a couple of sell

jobs: on Jock Moranis to buy the Demuth gouaches, and on Traci Landis to get her cute little ass into bed.

He screwed a smile onto his well-tanned features and went out to join the party. *His* party. Crossing the room to the bar, he poured a flute of champagne for himself, and raised his glass in toast.

"Here's to us," he said. "What a great night! And the Knicks even won!"

"Hear! Best night I've had in a long time," Jock Moranis said, smiling pointedly at his darkly exotic date, then drinking deeply.

Sonofabitch *should* be in a good mood, Feruzzi thought. Great looking, thirty-eight years old, beautiful wife and two kids tucked into bed in an English stone manor out in Bedford, and the stocks in his worldwide holdings splitting and multiplying like horny little bunnies even as he sat here with a drop-dead gorgeous chick draped all over him. Traci's leggy friend Gillian Brent from Sotheby's.

And why *wouldn't* the chick be clinging within an inch of her life to Mr. Moneybags Moranis? he thought further. She was no dummy. She'd been able to approximate the man's net worth before the Knicks were out of the first quarter. By dinner she was in *eyelash-batting* mode, and by now Moranis was a cinch to score. Well, Jock-o was going to say thank you for this gorgeous little snatch, compliments of Austin Feruzzi, by buying the fucking Demuths off his fucking wall.

Picking up his glass in one hand and the champagne bottle in the other, he walked around and freshened drinks. Then he sat next to Traci on one of the white-on-white silk couches, and slipped his arm around her. And smiled and winked at Jock Moranis.

"Life is good, isn't it," he said.

"Too good," his client rejoined.

"By the way, did you notice that pair of gouaches you had your eye on?" Austin tossed out then, waving his champagne glass toward the two companion pieces that now hung over his fireplace.

"Oh . . . no I didn't," Moranis said, turning his gaze up to the Demuths.

"I brought them up here so you could see them in a home setting. Ladies," Austin added then, addressing the two women friends, "I don't need to tell you that this man has excellent taste."

"They're marvelous," Moranis exclaimed. "Send them over to the office tomorrow, Austin, would you? With a bill."

"I want you to be sure, Jock," Feruzzi returned, frowning a little.

"Nonsense," Moranis smiled expansively, scoring even more points with the raven-haired Ms. Brent. "Get those babies down off your wall—they're sold."

Great, Austin congratulated himself. Now let's get the lovely couple out of here to a place where they can play each other for whatever they each need, then let's get little Traci into the bedroom and boffed in a hurry, then get her out the door and into a taxi, then deal with Molly, and try to reach Kate on the West Coast, and wait for Tripp to get his ass home from celebrating his goddamn nonsale.

Feruzzi smiled at his guests and drained his champagne glass. God, he was beat.

Chapter 21

T HE GUY IS a world-class asshole," Jonathan Valley muttered to Tripp, shaking his head.

They were sitting in the living room, enjoying after-dinner aperitifs of warmed Romana Sambuca floated with coffee beans, when Austin Feruzzi's frenetic message had suddenly blared from the answering machine in the den. It was being call-forwarded from Tripp's house in Coldwater Canyon to Jon's Malibu beach house. As Feruzzi's voice sputtered on, the two men exchanged puzzled looks. Feruzzi was calling back the painting, and boosting the price to a quarter of a million dollars.

"Fine," Jon said to Tripp when the message clicked off. "Call him back in a bit, and tell him that I'll have a check for the difference, plus tax, sent over to the gallery tomorrow."

"Maybe I should wait and call him in the morning," Tripp offered.

"Hell, no," Valley shot back. "The man is apoplectic. He's demanding that you call him back tonight. You heard him—no matter what time it is in New York, he said. So call him back tonight."

It was a little after ten o'clock in California. Tripp waited until eleven to make the call, and he got Feruzzi's machine.

"Austin . . . you there? Are you still up? Pick up if you hear this . . . it's late, about two o'clock your time . . . I just got in from dinner and got your message.

"I can't believe I was able to reach Jonathan Valley . . . just lucky he's still in town. I caught him at his beach house a few minutes ago . . . he said he was going to turn in pretty quick be-

cause he's flying in to New York tomorrow . . . he'll be working there for a while on his new movie . . .

"Anyway, I told him what you said, and would you believe, he said fine, he'll pay the extra hundred thousand on the painting! His take was it's exciting that the Rhajis are escalating so fast . . . says it looks like he'll actually have an investment, which he hadn't counted on at all . . . he just likes the painting. Anyway, he'll have Duncan Smith send a check over to the gallery tomorrow for the difference, plus tax.

"Great going, Austin . . . and that's another ten thou for me, so I'm a happy guy. I'm going to sleep now—I'll talk to you tomorrow. Good night."

"There, that ought to hold him," Tripp said, after he'd hung up the phone. "Now, are you absolutely sure that's what you want to do, Jon?"

"Of course," Valley said. "It's a nutty way to do business, but Feruzzi has always had a slightly fetid smell to him, in my book. But I'm in love with the painting, Tripp—and I don't want to get into a pissing contest with your boss. So it's done. Want to watch a flick?"

"Sure. But what time do you have to get up in the morning?"

"Noon," Jon grinned. "Got a late flight . . . leaves at three in the afternoon."

"Great, then let's watch something. What have you got?"

"What *haven't* I got!" Jon amended, as they walked into the game room together. With a move that was pure Gatsby, Valley pulled open six pairs of beechwood cabinet doors, one after another, displaying his enormous collection of videos.

"You could open a video store," Tripp observed.

"You're right. Tower Video routinely sends me nearly every new release. I've got them all—some here, some in Beverly Hills, some in New York—great old movies, new movies, and also plenty of dogs mixed in. Some hounds that I've actually been in myself," Jon laughed. "Or, if you're in the mood, we've got some classic pornos . . ."

Tripp chuckled as he perused the titles neatly lined up alphabetically. "By the way, tell me about *Dead Right*," he queried, referring to the next Jonathan Valley movie project.

"The usual," Jon smirked. "Blood and guts and shoot-outs, three colossal explosions and an impossible car chase, followed by an impossible foot chase, a shitload of spectacular special effects, and a lot of bitchin'-looking women."

"Perfect," Tripp laughed, looking up at Jon, who was absently fingering Tripp's gift, the ruby-encrusted letter opener.

"I love this piece," he said, continuing to stroke the jeweled markings.

"Hey, watch that blade," Tripp warned. "It's a lot sharper than it looks. It looks antique, but the dagger is new. The rubies are definitely old—they look like they're recycled from some ancient booty—but that blade is state-of-the-art, and it can cut your finger off."

Jon smiled and put the dagger back down on a table, and came over to the tape cabinet. Tripp had pulled out one of the videocassettes and was studying it.

"What did you find?"

"Call me crazy, but I'm in the mood to see *Citizen Kane* again . . . are you up for that?"

"Great idea," Jon said, taking the tape from Tripp's hand and setting it into the cassette player. "You know, I idolized Orson Welles. We had some wonderful dinners together at the old Ma Maison restaurant. I really treasure the times I spent with him . . . a genius, and an old rascal, besides. I can't believe he's gone."

"A lot of good people are gone, Jon. Goes by fast, doesn't it?" Tripp was obviously thinking about how many friends they'd lost to AIDS over the years.

"God, are we getting maudlin, or what? But you're right, Tripp," Valley said, "we have to enjoy every single day. Which gives me an idea—why don't you come in to New York for a little holiday? I'll be there for a few weeks, doing the interviews for Global, then some casting, and scouting locations for *Dead Right*."

"You know, maybe I can," Tripp commented. "I've just made a nice commission, thanks to you. Let me see if I can manage a few days off . . . can we take in *Ragtime*?"

"Not together, Tripp. We have to be very careful in public, as you know, even there. *Especially* there, because the New York papers have all the syndicated gossip columns."

"Of course you're right, Jon. And I'll take my usual room at the Pierre for appearances."

"Then you can see some plays with friends, and we can hole up in my apartment at night."

It was a stellar apartment, Tripp knew. Jonathan Valley owned a twelve-room co-op in one of the best buildings in Manhattan, a stately prewar jewel on East End Avenue, with a brilliant view of Gracie Mansion and the river.

Tripp loved New York. He had an army of old friends there, as well as family. And he was overdue to check out the New York gallery, to look over the display, and to compare notes with his counterpart, Molly Adams. Yes, he would treat himself to a short vacation. Not that it would be a vacation from his peripatetic boss—Austin Feruzzi was there right now, in full pomp and bluster!

Orson Welles flickered on the jumbo screen as Tripp settled back into the down cushions. God gave him a great life, he considered with a smile—but he also gave him Austin Feruzzi.

Chapter 22

GODAMMIT!" AUSTIN FERUZZI shouted to the empty room, simultaneously banging his palm down on the rock-hard travertine desktop in his office. Which hurt. "Damn!" he barked again. He had to get that painting back.

The phone rang. He listened. He heard his wife's voice finish the outgoing message, then Molly Adams's voice came on. Again.

"Austin . . . it's Molly. Are you in yet? I have to talk to you. I'll be waiting up until I hear from you." BEEP. FRIDAY, 2:17 A.M.

Jesus, Austin thought, the girl wouldn't stop. What *was* it with women? He'd been calling Kate all day and all night, and he hadn't heard a word from her, and this one wouldn't keep her fingers off the dial. When you want them, you can't get near them, and when you don't want them, you can't beat 'em off with a stick.

Austin sighed. His mind cycled back to the Rhaji. Since he couldn't seem to get Jon Valley to give the damn thing up, he had to come up with some other plan to get it back. And the more time that went by, he knew, the harder it would be. After all, Feruzzi had no legitimate claim to the painting—it was bought and paid for.

He tried to think it through. Tripp had said that the Rhaji had already been delivered to Jonathan Valley's beach house, and Valley was spending the night there. And that the actor would be flying to New York tomorrow, and business would keep him away for weeks, maybe months. Three thousand miles away from the Rhaji, up to his neck in movie business, and in no mood to deal with

Austin Feruzzi. He had to get that painting back before Jonathan Valley left L.A.

Feruzzi couldn't miss the fact that Valley never liked him. While most gallery customers were honored to deal with the owner, Jon Valley always made it a point to do his business with Tripp Kendrick, even if it meant waiting for days.

He came up with a plan. Bordering on desperate, he knew, but what choice did he have? He would fly to California tonight and just show up, unannounced, at Jonathan Valley's house in Malibu. He would charter a private plane to make the trip to the coast, and appeal to the man face-to-face before he left for the airport. Between now and then, Feruzzi would come up with some kind of plausible story about why he *absolutely had* to have that painting back, and *now*. And the fact that he would fly all the way across country in the middle of the night would underscore how extremely important it was to him. What the hell, to Jon Valley it was just another fucking painting. It *could* work, and what did he have to lose?

Checking his Rolodex, he called Fleetwood Aviation in New Jersey. It was a twenty-four-hour operation, catering to rich people who had to get somewhere right now.

"Fleetwood, Arch speaking, how can I help you?" Archie Ferguson answered in his signature monotone.

"Archie, it's Austin Feruzzi. Can you get me to L.A. right away? Tonight?"

"Well it's already morning, but yeah, we can get you out whenever you get here. You in the city?"

"Yes, and there's no traffic at this hour, so it should be a straight shot through the tunnel. I can grab a cab and be there in a half hour. Will that work?"

"We can get you up in forty-five minutes, an hour, depending how fast I can get a crew here. How ya gonna pay?"

"The usual. Bill me," Feruzzi returned.

"Cost you more that way than cash," Archie observed dryly.

"Right. And where the hell am I supposed to get that kind of cash at this hour of the morning, Arch?"

"Okay, okay, just lettin' ya know."

Fleetwood served a clientele that was liberally peppered with high rollers and shady characters who didn't want a record kept of their comings and goings, and who routinely paid for charter air trips with bags of cash.

"What kind of equipment you want?" Archie asked him then.

"What I always charter."

"What's that?"

"The smallest and the cheapest," Feruzzi answered. "It'll be just me."

"A Lear Twenty-four is eleven-fifty an hour plus tax, but it has to make a fuel stop. A Lear Thirty-six is sixteen hundred an hour, non-stop."

"I don't have time to stop."

"Okay. Teterboro to LAX?"

"Teterboro to LAX. And what if I book a round trip?" he asked. "Can I get a break on the price?"

"No, Mr. Feruzzi," Archie said with a hint of weariness. "I've told you before, the price goes by the hour, which takes in the cost of fuel, and the pilots' rates are set."

"Well, you have to get the plane back here anyway, don't you?"

"We account for that. But we have to pay pilots' expenses on lay-over—"

"What layover? I'm talking about an immediate turnaround."

"Immediate like touch down, refuel, and go back?"

"Yeah, right, I'm going joy-riding on a jet at three in the morning," Feruzzi shot back sarcastically. "I mean immediate like I'll get out, grab a car, do my business, and be back at the airport in a couple of hours. The pilots can eat breakfast in the Sky Lounge."

"If we get you out of here within the hour, you'll be in L.A. before six in the morning. What kind of business can you do at six in the morning?"

"Arch, I can do my business at six in the morning, okay? Now do you and I have business, or not?"

"Fifteen hundred off, you want to do it that way," Archie re-sponded laconically.

"Deal. Warm up a bird."

Feruzzi went into the master suite and pulled down a black canvas duffel from the top of the closet. He zipped it open and tossed in his dopp kit with toilet articles, a pair of jeans, a sweater, some deck shoes, and a change of socks and underwear. He closed the bag, picked up his wallet from the dresser, grabbed his jacket, and started for the door. And the phone rang again.

"It's Molly. Austin, I—"

Austin snatched up the phone.

"Hello, Molly. I just got in, and I'm beat. I've gotta get some sleep—"

"Austin, a friend of mine saw the woman you were with tonight," Molly cut him off in frostbitten tones.

"A friend of yours . . . *whaaaat?*" Austin sputtered.

"Young, blond, and you had your hands all over her, I'm told. At Madison Square Garden. The two of you were very cozy, laughing and kissing."

"Oh for chrissake, that's a load of crap, Molly," Austin threw back indignantly. "It's just not true."

"Well, what *is* true?" she demanded.

"What *is* true, is I went to see the Knicks, like I told you. Moranis took me, like I told you. And he also brought his daughters, who had just got home from college, because he has four season tickets on the floor and they wanted to see the game. Whoever told you *kissing* is a liar."

"You're the one who's lying, Austin," Molly hissed through the phone lines.

Austin bristled. "You know what?" he spat. "You can believe what you want to believe. I don't have time for this shit. I worked my ass off tonight, and I've gotta get some sleep." The best defense was a good offense.

"I don't think we should be together tomorrow night—" she started tremulously.

"Fine," he barked, and he slammed down the phone. Women! He shook his head in disgust. Picking up his bag, he flicked the lights off and slammed out of his apartment.

Chapter 23

"Hello, Lane, it's Trisha. It's early there, you're not up yet . . . neither is Katie, I'm sure. Peter just left for work, and I just got a chance to listen to your message.

"Lane, I am beyond shocked! That bastard! Thank God she's leaving him. And no, I won't confront him with this, but that's going to be hard, since I'd like to smash his face in. By the way, he's scheduled to come to dinner at our place tomorrow night. Now that he knows we know about this, he wouldn't dare show up, would he? Maybe I should call and uninvite him. No, then I would have to confront him, and I don't want to hear his bullshit version. Tell Katie to call me . . . we'll talk . . . I'll reinforce what you and Geoff have told her. She has my support one hundred percent.

"You know, Lane, it's typical that when a woman finally decides to leave a man, her friends can't wait to tell her that they could never stand the guy anyway, and then they supply all kinds of nasty little stories to illustrate their point. But it's true . . . I never liked Austin Feruzzi. And here's a nasty little story that just slid over my transom last night. One of Peter's attorneys casually mentioned to him that he saw Austin at the Knicks game with some young blonde last night, and they were more than cozy, right in public. I mean, good heavens, they televise those games . . . the world can see what's going on down in front right on the floor. The cameras constantly pan across those seats, looking for celebrities.

"At first I thought I wouldn't tell Kate. I ran it past Molly on *her machine, but I haven't heard back from her. But then I decided no, if I don't tell Katie, then I'm just like every other so-called friend who thinks she's doing you a favor by not hurting your feelings. Then you're a joke, because everybody knows what's going on except you. Our loyalty runs too deep for that. So I want her to know.*

"You can tell her, Lane, or when she calls me I'll tell her. Not that it much matters at this point, but she should know exactly what kind of vile, loathsome rat she's escaping from, don't you think? No, I never liked the man, and yes, I know exactly what you mean when you say that you and I tacitly agreed about Austin Feruzzi from the get-go. But beating her? My God, that's horrible! Thank heaven you and Geoff are there for her, and we'll do anything we can on this end, of course. Keep me posted. Bye for now . . . much love."

Trisha put the phone down and sat motionless at her writing desk. She was intensely disturbed at hearing that Kate had been putting up with physical battering from her husband all these years. It said everything about Austin, of course, but it also said something important about Kate. Something about her self-esteem.

But why? Katie was arguably the most beautiful woman she had ever known. Always, she had seemed to lead a charmed life. Had everything she could possibly want. All the material riches, all the men, all the attention any person could need. So what was it that made a woman who grew up in the age of liberation, who saw the women's movement born and flourish, who seemed so strong, as did each of their Briarcliff four-some—what made her put up with regular beatings at the hands of a husband who purported to love her? Hopefully, whatever it was would be exorcised in the course of the therapy she'd be getting now, and Kate would be able to change her life.

There was something that Trisha had not passed along to Lane in her message this morning. She would later. With a divorce pending, it was certainly something that Kate should know about. After the guests had left the Newmans' apartment last night, her husband told her that Austin Feruzzi had hit him up for money. He needed to borrow a million dollars, he said. And he told Peter, by way of explanation, that he had a temporary cash-flow problem.

Chapter 24

_____

AUSTIN WAS GLAD that he had driven himself to the airport
on Wednesday morning. Hard to believe it was less than forty-eight
hours ago that he'd had that blow-up with Kate.

On the night before, he'd let her know without question that he
did not want her traveling with him this trip. It was settled. In fact,
that's when he called and canceled the limo. No sense rubbing her
nose in it, he'd figured, having a car come to the house and a driver
ring the bell. He would just slip out quietly in the morning and drive
himself to LAX.

Joke was on him. Kate was up ahead of him, packed, dressed for
the trip, and ready to go.

"It's my life too," she'd said, smiling sweetly. "And it's my New York
apartment, and my friends and my family there. I'm going with you,
darling."

Well, no, dear, you're not, he'd let her know—albeit more forcefully than he'd meant to. She shouldn't have made him hit her. In
retrospect, of course, it would have been better had he just taken
her along. A couple of flying fucks with Molly Adams were hardly
worth the aggravation, even though Molly was a cute, feisty little
piece, and he'd lusted after her from the day Kate had sent her to his
office to interview for the job.

A wonderful artist and a smart businesswoman with gallery experience, Kate had told him. She had neglected to mention that Molly
Adams also had an adorable face, a tangled mane of fiery orange
hair, a spicy-hot temperament, and a sizzling little body. Took him a
decade to wear her down, but finally, a few months ago, who knows
why, she caved. But now she was getting clingy, and that was dan-

gerous. Oh sure, he said some things, made her some promises, but men do that in the heat of passion, don't they? Now he had to break it off completely with Molly, and he fervently hoped that she would keep her mouth shut. And stay on the job. She had become indispensable to his business.

The whole Molly thing had been a good lesson for him. *Much* too close to home!

It was ten after six. The sun had just come up in Los Angeles when the corporate Lear jet that was costing him eighteen grand minus his big-deal discount landed at Garrett Aviation, the private jet concourse on the south side of LAX. He'd hitched a ride on a courtesy van to the structure where he'd parked, and now he was tooling north up the 405 toward the Santa Monica Freeway and the beach. Good thing he'd driven his big County Land Rover. The way Tripp had described it, he could never fit this Rhaji into his BMW.

He had to get that painting back. Had to waltz out of Jon Valley's beach house with it this morning. Feruzzi knew the place; he'd been to a couple of parties there. Valley had often referred to the magnificent white Mediterranean villa on the sand as his hideaway. He had once jokingly said that he only sent the help out there to mop up after parties, and to shoot anyone who happened to be left.

The Rhaji was to be hung in Valley's master bedroom suite facing the ocean, Tripp had mentioned. Since it had just been delivered, it would probably be standing on the floor somewhere, leaning up against a wall, waiting to be installed. Waiting, actually, for Feruzzi to sweet-talk Jon Valley into giving it up.

It was all about the rubies. The damned antique Moroccan rubies. DeFarge was really on his ass—that's why he had to go through with this ridiculous, high-priced jaunt. Otherwise he might have decided to just eat the cost of this one shipment of gems—write it off, and offset the loss with the hefty mark-up on the painting.

He was amazed that Valley was willing to dish up a quarter of a million big ones for the work of some dabbler in a remote village in India whom nobody had ever heard of. He should have asked Valley for a million—that would have more than covered the price of the rubies, and Valley would never know what he had. What the hell, Jonathan Valley had money to burn. It was like he had a dump truck full of it, Austin mused, and the cost of this painting was like a few bills blowing off the top of the load.

Feruzzi was used to these movie multimillionaires who were richer than God and knew the value of nothing. The more something cost, the more they thought it was worth. Yup, he should have charged the guy a million bucks for it. The asshole would have paid the price without blinking, and this wacked-out trip wouldn't have been necessary.

Nice to dream, but he knew better. He knew that he had to get that damn painting back. DeFarge had been cranking up the tariff on his contraband, blackmailing Feruzzi to pay more and more, or threatening to blow the whistle on him.

The operation had started small, and in fact it had seemed like sort of a lark back then. He had met DeFarge through one of his dealers in Tokyo. Mr. Tokumatsu had told him in an aside that Charles De-Farge was "a quite interesting businessman, but one must indeed proceed with caution. However, if one enjoyed adventure, and was very careful, one might be able to make a great deal of money in partners with that particular Indian gentleman."

Feruzzi had started out ordering a few pieces from DeFarge in New Delhi, merchandise he took a chance on, since he was able to see the artwork in advance only in photographs. Some of the pieces were interesting, or tasteful, even quite good, others were pure dreck, and all of them were cheap. Austin would carefully weed out the rabid dogs to preserve the reputation of the Feruzzi Galleries, and send them off to charities for an inflated tax write-off. The rest he filtered into his collections in the three cities, and most of the pieces sold at very nice profits.

Early in the year, about six months into this trading, Feruzzi and DeFarge made plans to get together. They would meet for a drink at the annual International Art Fair in Malaga, which both were scheduled to attend. DeFarge departed the Art Fair a day before it closed, and headed off for what he'd told Feruzzi was a possibly advantageous deal to be made in Tangier, a city very close by, he'd noted, directly across the Straits of Gibraltar in Morocco. If he were to find the situation to be a potentially worthwhile venture, DeFarge had said, and if he thought it was something in which Mr. Feruzzi might be interested, he would ring him up at his lodging place that night.

When Feruzzi got back to his hotel from the convention hall in early evening, he'd had a message from DeFarge that he should meet him at noon the next day in a boîte in Tangier. Feruzzi was intrigued, and since he'd finished up his business in Spain, he made the six-hour trip, only to have the bartender in the saloon in Tangier hand him a note from DeFarge.

"Mr. Feruzzi, would you please meet me in Rabat tonight," the note read, and it indicated a small hotel in the Moroccan capital, and included directions.

When Feruzzi got to the Innis Kashaba that evening, he was greeted by yet another missive from his elusive host. He was to have a restful night's sleep, the note said, then he was to join Mr. DeFarge for breakfast at a restaurant in Fedala, which was just outside Casablanca, and just a short taxi ride from the hotel where Feruzzi was staying.

The note did not indicate a time that he should be in Fedala for breakfast. The "short taxi ride" from his hotel turned out to be eighty-five kilometers over a twisting, badly rutted coastal road. But when he finally rolled in, there in the dining room sat Mr. DeFarge, looking crisp and fresh in the middle morning in a lightweight tarpan Italian suit with an ivory-colored silk shirt accessorized with classic Cartier bow-knot cufflinks, and a printed silk cravat held in place at his neck by an extraordinary golden-brown tiger's-eye set in solid gold. DeFarge flashed a broad smile, displaying what seemed to be an overabundance of large, yellowed, very crooked teeth.

"Ah, Mr. Feruzzi, you have arrived," he'd said, extending his hand. No mention was made of how long he might have been sitting at that table, or what time this meeting was supposed to have taken place, or indeed, why the hell DeFarge had led Feruzzi on an uncivilized chase down the bumpy west coast of Africa.

"Will you join me for breakfast, sir?" he had asked quite cordially, as if they had just run into each other in the Palm Court at the Plaza Hotel in midtown Manhattan. Without waiting for an answer, he summoned a waiter and proceeded to order for both of them in French. Coffee arrived immediately, and DeFarge laid out his proposal.

He would be able, he'd told Feruzzi, to come by a rather sizable consignment of very rare, very old Moroccan rubies. It seemed he had connections who would be easily able to get these antique gemstones to his headquarters in Delhi, but from there, he'd said sadly, shaking his head and spreading his hands palms up, it was a problem. DeFarge went on to suggest, over delicious French croissants, an assortment of spiced meats, and strong Moroccan coffee, that he could efficiently secrete these lovely rubies within the buildup of paint on primitive pieces much like the ones he had been sending to Feruzzi in America.

He would charge in actuality much the same low prices, he explained, always with the smile, but his bills of sale for the paintings would, of course, be somewhat higher, because they would reflect the prices of the gemstones. Those magnificent rubies would then belong to Feruzzi at a fraction of their market value, because they would arrive without tax, without duty, and heavily discounted.

It seemed like a good idea at the time. And indeed, a succession of paintings had arrived at Feruzzi's Beverly Hills gallery, each with heavy applications of paint in the shapes of large, bright-yellow radiating suns placed in different spots on each of the canvases. Mixed into the buildup of materials that made up each of the sun symbols was a cache of the rare Moroccan rubies, as promised. Feruzzi had dared to have a small handful of the stones appraised; it turned out that their value was not in question.

In the privacy of the small anteroom off his office in the Beverly Hills gallery, the room where he stored very special pieces, and which he always kept locked, Feruzzi dug the rubies out of the sun symbols on the Rhajis. Then, having formally studied art, and being, he thought, at least proficient if not terribly creative, he would clandestinely repair the sun images on the canvases, forgoing the thick buildup which was now unnecessary, but adding a soft, orangy-golden acrylic glow with an overlay of oils to the sun symbols on each of the paintings. The result was quite good, he thought.

Further, he commissioned several jewelers at separate shops in L.A.'s teeming downtown jewelry mart district to set the Moroccan rubies into brooches, miniature picture frames, small hand mirrors, the handles of letter openers and such, all of which looked very old, but were actually reproductions. He then sold the sun paintings *and* the ruby-encrusted pieces for profits that usually amounted to ten times his cost, and more.

But now DeFarge was shaking him down and turning up the heat. His invoices for the Rhajis had been escalating by great leaps, and when Feruzzi had refused to pay such hefty overages, DeFarge threatened to tip off U.S. Customs. But DeFarge would be implicated too, Feruzzi had protested, and DeFarge had answered, "No, sir, only Rhaji, and Rhaji, alas, does not exist."

Looking back over the paperwork, Feruzzi noted that all shipments and correspondence having to do with the sun series had come from a postal box number in New Delhi. Payment had been sent to that same address, with all checks made out to URA. DeFarge informed Feruzzi that the initials URA stood for United Rhaji Associates, and that it was a company (not legitimate, Feruzzi now surmised) that dealt solely in the work of one Rhaji Mentour, whom the authorities would have great trouble locating, DeFarge had wryly pointed out. So the name Charles DeFarge was absent with regard to any of URA's transactions with Mr. Feruzzi. Meantime, Austin Feruzzi, of the Feruzzi Galleries in Beverly Hills, New York, and London, was substantially exposed.

No, even if Jonathan Valley wanted to pay *five* million for the Rhaji, Feruzzi had to get the damn thing back. With DeFarge threatening to tip off U.S. Customs, he could not have a painting that was chock-full of smuggled and very probably stolen gemstones out there that could be seized and traced directly back to the Feruzzi Galleries. It was a preposterous and untenable situation from which he had to extricate himself.

He would *have* to make a deal with Valley, no matter what it took, pick up the painting, and liberate the rubies—there must be hundreds of them hidden in that huge canvas, which had the largest sun symbol DeFarge had ever shipped, Tripp had said. He would recycle the Rhaji, pay DeFarge his ransom, then cut off all dealings with this dangerous Eastern rapscallion.

Feruzzi drove up to the gleaming Jonathan Valley estate that sprawled across four choice lots of pricy Malibu beachfront, and parked his white Land Rover. From the front gate at the road, the property looked deserted. Feruzzi rang the bell. He hoped that Valley was up. He was prepared to reason with him, even at this early hour in the morning. To beg if he had to. He would tell him that the painting had been promised, but Tripp hadn't known this. But there it was. Promised to Mafia, he would say, why not?—Mafia he'd borrowed money from, and the extra-large Rhaji had been specially ordered to be accepted for payment, and he couldn't afford to anger those guys. That ought to go down as credible to a rich, dumb, iron-pumping, testosterone-laden action-movie jock, Feruzzi figured.

There was no answer to his ring. He pressed the bell again and waited. Again, no answer, and no sounds at all coming from within. So he walked back down the street, past his white Rover, and over several blocks to a posted public beach accessway. He walked down the narrow path toward the ocean, and out onto the sand. Then he doubled back along the shore until he reached Valley's house on the beach side, all glass and deck and exotic flowering plants along a stone-lined lap pool that ran fully half the length of the massive villa.

This part of Malibu, far to the north near Dekker Canyon, was sparsely populated. Putting his hand to his forehead to shield his eyes against the morning sun, Feruzzi surveyed the line of jagged rocks and dense growth along Pacific Coast Highway on either side of Valley's mansion. Protracted expanses of terrain stretched between secluded estates, which Feruzzi knew were mostly weekend and summer homes.

On the long flight, he'd had plenty of time to think about how he would handle the painting. The Rhajis were meant to hang unframed—it wouldn't be heavy. Before going back to the airport, he would stop at his gallery in Beverly Hills, and lock it up in the private storeroom off his office. Later, when he got back in town, he would dig out the rubies, disguise this one thoroughly in the retouching, and ship it off to his London gallery to be sold.

Approaching Valley's house now, he peered warily through the expansive wall of glass that fronted on the ocean. And again, from the beachside vantage this time, he saw no signs of life inside; in fact, at this hour of the morning, there was nobody at all on this part of the beach, except for a lone jogger Feruzzi had seen running past when he'd first come down the path from the road.

Inside the house, the massive living room was itself a work of art, with its thirty-two-foot-high ceiling and stunning beach-facing wall of glass. At one of Valley's parties, Feruzzi had witnessed that astonishing glass wall hydraulically raised, like some fantastic movie special effect, exposing the massive room to the sights and sounds and the ocean spray of the pounding Malibu surf.

Now the giant manse appeared to be sleeping. He could hear no movement within, no sounds at all except for the rhythmic, low-level waves lapping gently on shore. By all indications, nobody inside the house was up. If he'd meant what he said about rarely having his help at the beach, Valley was probably alone inside—unless he was with a woman.

There were no really close neighbors. The complex alarm systems in these expensive homes were often tripped by mistake, he knew, and the laid-back Malibu sheriffs were not exactly the NYPD. The tall pair of doors on the west side of the glass wall were fashioned of beveled panes set into oxidized green copper door frames. Feruzzi could see the double-cylinder deadbolt lock behind them. For just a fleeting second or two, he fantasized himself deftly picking the lock with a credit card. He would jump inside, find the painting, toss the place a little on the romp, grab a couple of things to make it look like a burglary, and get out of there before Valley even woke up to respond to the ruckus.

Feruzzi had to smile. Obviously he had seen way too many Bruce Willis movies. He looked at his watch—6:37 A.M. He took a minute to quickly rehearse his story for Jon Valley yet again, then took a deep breath, straightened his shoulders, rang the beachside doorbell, and hoped for the best.

From inside the house, again he heard the euphonious tones of a vaguely melodic bell sounding in the quiet, stopping for a beat, then repeating the call. And again, there was no response. Feruzzi rang again.

"Whoizit?" demanded the sleepy but unmistakable voice of movie superhero Jonathan Valley over the intercom.

"It's Austin Feruzzi—I have to talk to you, Jon—"

"Wha . . . Where the hell *are* you?"

"I'm at your door . . . your *back* door—"

"Austin Feruzzi's in New York. Who the hell *are* you and what do you want?"

"No, I'm here, Jon, and I really have to speak with you," Feruzzi blurted.

He knew that he had to sound like a maniac. This was not going well. He'd figured that Valley would be up and about by now and getting ready to go to the airport. Obviously he'd rousted him out of bed, and the man was not happy about it. Feruzzi had an intense

urge to haul ass down the beach, jump into his Rover, and get the
hell out of there. But he had no choice. He had to suck it up and get
on with it.

"Look, Jon, it's about the painting—"

He was stopped in mid-sentence by the sudden raucous blare of
an alarm piercing the early morning serenity. Valley had apparently
tripped a panic button, which would summon Malibu's finest. Jesus
Christ, Feruzzi muttered, this dumbshit house call will probably
make the tabloids.

Then he was astounded by the sight of movie star Jonathan Valley
in the flesh, buff in a pair of tiny black silk briefs, moving quickly toward the tall glass doors, scowling into the sunlight reflecting off the
beach, both hands holding a gun in front of him which was pointed
directly at Feruzzi's chest.

In the instant when Valley realized that it was, indeed, Austin Feruzzi standing on his beachside doorstep, he dropped the gun to his
side and stared in astonishment. Then he shook his head slowly in
disbelief as the alarm continued to blare.

Feruzzi broke into an insipid grin and lifted his hands to his sides,
palms out, in a pleading gesture. "Let me in, Jon," he mouthed, "I
have to talk to you."

Holding the gun in his left hand, Jon Valley unlatched the door.
And said nothing, just looked disdainfully at Austin Feruzzi, waiting
for him to explain himself.

"Can I please come inside?" Feruzzi asked sheepishly.

Valley stood aside and allowed Feruzzi just enough room to come
past him through the doors. Feruzzi took three steps into the living
room, then turned around to face his reluctant host, who was still
standing at the door, still holding the gun, still looking at him as
though he had just descended on the place from the dark side of the
moon.

"Look, Jon, I know you must think I'm crazy—"

"How about phoning before you decide to drop in?" Valley spat
out, gesturing with the gun.

"Uhh . . . can you put that thing down? And turn the alarm off?"
Feruzzi managed.

"Austin, what the fuck do you want?" Valley roared over the din,
not moving from the door.

"I want the painting, Jon. I've gotta have the painting. It was commissioned by a another client, and Tripp didn't know—"

"So commission another one. What the hell are you doing here? Or are you just an ugly nightmare I'm having?"

Feruzzi laughed nervously. "Listen, Jon," he wailed, his voice at a desperate pitch over the tumult of the screeching alarm, "I'll pay you anything to get this one back. I'll ship you another one, right away . . . exactly like it, I swear. I chartered a plane to get here just to beg you to do me this favor. I need this. I'll refund your money, totally, and I'll ship you another Rhaji, same size, same picture, absolutely free . . . I'll put it in writing—"

"Feruzzi, what the hell is this really about?" Valley demanded then, grabbing him by the shoulder.

At that, Feruzzi broke from Valley's grasp and jerked away from him. Quickly, he moved across the living room, then out through a pair of French doors into the game room behind. Valley was right behind him.

"Stop, dammit! Where the hell do you think you're going?" he barked at Feruzzi's back.

"To see the painting. To show you why I need it . . . what the client asked for—"

"Are you fucking insane, Feruzzi?" Valley yelled after him.

"No, no, you'll understand when I show you . . ." Feruzzi kept moving, looking for the painting. He remembered that the master suite, where Tripp said it was going to be hung, was down the wide hall that led off to the left. He loped down the hallway, his footsteps on the marble floor muffled by the blare of the alarm.

"Uhh . . . can you *please* turn the alarm off?" he tossed back at Valley.

"No, asshole, I can't turn the alarm off," Valley bellowed, running after him. "If I turn it off, the cops won't come, and you need to be locked up—"

The door to the master-suite sitting room was open, and Feruzzi saw the brilliant Rhaji, already hung in all its sun-blazoned glory up on the wall above the sofa. Before Valley could stop him, he leaped up on the white leather couch, lifted the picture wire from the hangers, and snatched the Rhaji off the wall.

At that moment another man, in a pair of printed pajama bottoms, rubbing sleep from his eyes, appeared in the doorway to the adjoining bedroom. "What the hell's going on?" he asked.

Feruzzi lowered the painting to the floor and stared at the two men. One of them was the hottest male movie star in America. The other one, quite obviously his bed partner, was Feruzzi's own West Coast gallery director, Tripp Kendrick!

Chapter 25

"Lane . . . hello . . . this is Austin Feruzzi. Christina told me that Kate was up there in Carmel with you and Geoff. I've been frantic . . . I've been trying to reach her for three days. I'm sure she's told you what happened.

"Lane, please tell her to call me. I have to talk to her. I love her . . . please . . . tell her that. She'll listen to you. I need her more than life. Tell her I'm sorry . . . I'm really sorry . . . if I lost Kate, my life would be over. Please make her listen to this message, Lane.

"I'm in New York. I want her to come here and be with me. We'll go to Peter and Trisha's dinner together tomorrow night, and then we'll take a trip . . . we both need it.

"Tell her I . . . I'll get help, I promise. I never meant to hurt her. I've been under so much pressure. We have these fights, and I think we're both too hard on each other. But I'll take the blame . . . tell her I take all the blame . . . and I'm so sorry . . . I want her to call me . . . and come to New York . . . and we'll have another honeymoon, and a whole new life. We'll start fresh.

"We love each other. Tell her, Lane. You can make her understand . . . we have to be together . . . we're meant for each other . . . she's the love of my life . . . she always will be. Thank you from the bottom of my heart for helping us, Lane. She needs your help, and so do I.

"I'm here at the apartment . . . I'll be in all night. And even if she wants to stay up there with you for a while, get a change of scene . . . whatever she wants, I'll support. Please just have her call me . . . I miss her terribly.

"Thank you, Lane. You're a true friend to both of us. Give my very best to Geoff and your terrific boys, and a hug to that big, beautiful dog of yours. You have a wonderful family, Lane. Family is everything, I know that. Thank you for being there for us, Lane. Goodbye." BEEP. FRIDAY, 4:12 P.M.

The two women listened as Lane played Austin's message. Kate had tears rolling down her cheeks; Lane thought she was going to throw up.

They had just come home. Lane had left Hamilton House a little early so she could pick Kate up from her first day in therapy. They had stopped at Nelson Brothers on the way home for salad makings and fresh fish for bouillabaisse. Lane wanted to catch up on phone calls before she and Kate poured some wine and busied themselves with dinner.

On the drive home, Kate had seemed reluctant to talk about the program. Geoff had taken her to the Crisis Intervention Center early that morning, even before it opened. He'd called Lane to tell her that he'd left Kate in good hands. Later in the morning, Lane spoke to the director of the center, Kathey Delgado, a wonderful Carmel native whom Lane and Geoff both knew. Mrs. Delgado reassured her that Katie was doing fine. She had already taken orientation, and she was in her first session. Mrs. Feruzzi was a little ill at ease, the director had said, but that was understandable, and she was handling it like a champ. And Lane would be able to pick her up at four o'clock, she'd said.

Now Kate was sobbing. She sat with her head in her hands, tears streaming down her beautiful face, washing away the makeup, revealing the angry, blackened bruises. Lane put both arms around her and held her close, stroking her hair.

"Please don't cry, Katie," she soothed, "I know how hard it is . . ." Lane could feel the tears welling up in her own eyes as she felt Kate's shoulders heaving with anguish.

"Lane, I didn't belong there today," Kate blurted out. "Austin is not the monster those other women were talking about. He's good, and sensitive, and he loves me—"

"Kate, you have to give this a chance."

"No, I can't do it," Kate said, more forcefully now. "I can't leave him. It's been twelve years. He's the one who deserves a chance."

"Katie, think . . . how many chances have you given him already?" Lane implored.

"I've never left him before, and I can't do it now. I'm going to him, Lane. He's right, that's where I belong. And," she added, looking up at Lane now, her eyes shining through tears, "I'm going to have a baby."

"What?" Lane demanded, holding her at arm's length. "You're *pregnant?*"

"No," Kate laughed weakly, "not yet. But I'm going to *get* pregnant. I want a child. A child will bring us closer together. Everything will be wonderful."

"You always said Austin didn't want any more children . . . does he know that you want to have a baby?"

"No, but you heard him. He said he'll do anything to save our marriage. I'm sure he'll be thrilled when I tell him what I want. Shawn needs a sibling, he's so alone . . . I see you with Jordan and Robby . . . you and Geoff are so happy—"

"Kate, it's not the children that make our relationship work. Geoff and I have mutual love and respect . . . we really do have the basic fundamentals, and always have, long before the children came along."

"But Austin and I love and respect each other . . . you heard him—"

"Talk is cheap, Kate," Lane stopped her. "If a man hit me, any man, even Geoff, I'd leave."

Lane knew that she was being harsh, but Katie needed to hear it. She had to wake up and take a look at her husband's pattern of abuse before it was too late. She felt sure that if Kate stayed in Carmel for a while, and if she stayed with the program, she'd get it. She would see the light. But now Kate had broken down in tears again.

"No," she said between sobs. "I'm going to him. It's what I have to do. He's learned his lesson . . . he'll never do it again. I'm going to New York. Tonight."

Chapter 26

"Trisha . . . it's Lane. You're not going to believe this, but Kate's going back to Austin. Don't ask me why . . . I'm sick with worry for her . . . but there's no talking her out of it. She's insisting on taking the red-eye tonight directly from here to New York. Well, from San Francisco—Geoff is going to drive us to SFO . . . and yes, I said us. I'm coming in with her. Geoff can't get away, but Katie is definitely not up to this trip alone. She's hurting, physically and emotionally. She's eating tranquilizers like candy, she's crying off and on, and her face looks like she's gone a couple of rounds with Mike Tyson. But I can't talk her out of going, so I'm going with her.

"She's so sweet, Trisha. She's never been as ballsy as you and me, or Molly . . . and she's letting herself be walked on. Literally. I hoped therapy would help, but she won't give it a chance. Anyway, I'm on a dead run . . . have to throw some things in a bag. We'll get there early in the morning . . . and hopefully get some sleep. I'm going to stay at Kate's apartment for a few days . . . she wants me there for moral support, and that's fine, though I'm sure Austin will act like a saint. I suggested that she have Shawn join her now that school's out, but she shrugged it off. Shawn can't stand Austin, never could, and now he's old enough to figure out how to stay away from him. God, what a mess!

"Anyway, Saturday night we'll come to your dinner, I guess . . . is that alright with you? I am looking forward to seeing you, Trish . . . just wish it were in happier circumstances.

One good thing . . . maybe if we're all together we can talk some sense into Kate. Let's try. I've gotta get going . . . we'll talk tomorrow morning. Bye, sweetheart—love you." BEEP. FRIDAY, 9:54 P.M. END OF FINAL MESSAGE.

Trisha erased her messages. She and Peter and their two children had just come in from "21," Ali's selection for her birthday dinner. A pretty sophisticated choice for a fourteen-year-old, her parents had marveled, but their kids were New Yorkers, born and bred. Today was Alison's real birthday, but Sunday was her real party—a pool party at their East Hampton home for a hundred and twenty of her most intimate friends.

But she deserved it. Trisha had let her know that often while they were planning the party, and she was rewarded each time with a big, loving hug from her daughter. Both kids were everything a mother could want, and much more. They were a pair of good, sweet, industrious, bright, and loving youngsters. So Jason wore an earring—big deal. When Peter went ballistic over it, Trisha had jumped to her son's defense. The boy would probably grow out of it, she'd said, and if not, he could be a Harvard lawyer with an earring. If Gerry Spence could wear a fringed suede jacket, cowboy boots, a ten-gallon hat, and a ponytail in the courtroom and win every case, Jason Newman could wear an earring, she'd told her husband. And she'd actually sold him. That was three years ago. Trisha felt very blessed.

She hadn't realized it, but she had tears in her eyes when she closed the door to her office and went into the master suite. Peter was already propped up in bed, reading his new copy of *Forbes*. Looking up at her as she came into the room, he put the magazine down and took off his glasses.

"What's wrong, darling?" he asked.

"We're so lucky," she sniffed. "You're so wonderful, we're all so healthy, the kids are so good—"

"What's wrong, Trisha?" he asked again.

She climbed into bed next to him and moved into the comforting circle of his arms. "It's Katie," she sighed, laying her head against his chest. "She's going back to him."

"Honey, Kate's a big girl. She knows what she's doing."

"No, she doesn't," Trisha countered.

"Can we help?"

"I don't know. Lane and Geoff tried everything, but they couldn't change her mind. She's flying in tonight to be with him."

"Then there's nothing we can do, Trish, except be supportive."

"I always knew he was a creep, but *beating* her!" Trisha felt her face redden with anger.

"Don't think about it, dear. You'll be there for her if she needs you, but beyond that, you can't get into it."

"I guess not. Why do you suppose the bastard wanted to borrow money from us?"

"I have no idea. He didn't say, and I didn't ask."

Something about the way he said that made Trisha look closely at her husband. "Surely, you didn't *give* it to him, did you?" she asked incredulously.

Peter said nothing. And that said it all.

Chapter 27

"Austin, it's Molly . . . how could you hang up on me! Austin, I know you're there. Don't you think we should at least talk about this? Austin, for God's sake, think about me, will you? I mean, you're married, and to someone who happens to be one of my best friends . . . that puts me in a position I hate, to begin with . . . and then I hear that you were out with some other woman. Is she there with you now? Is that why you said you were too tired to see me tonight? I think I deserve an explanation, and not a hang-up, don't you? Please call me . . . I'm not going to bed for a while." BEEP. FRIDAY, 2:36 A.M.

"Austin, it's me again . . . I know you don't like me to leave messages at the apartment, but you leave me no choice. Dammit, Austin, don't treat me like this. You're the one who was out with somebody else, not me. And if you weren't, I would like a civil explanation of how someone happened to see you at the Knicks game with a blonde . . . whom you were kissing! I mean, what am I supposed to think? I want to settle this tonight. I know you haven't gone to sleep yet." BEEP. FRIDAY, 2:44 A.M.

"Austin, this isn't fair! Wednesday night you tell me you love me . . . you want to marry me . . . you want to spend the rest of your life with me . . . and now you refuse to discuss whether or not you had some woman with you at a basketball game

tonight, and I don't mean your client's daughter . . . some woman you were kissing right in fucking Madison Square Garden! I deserve to know what's going on, don't you think?" BEEP. FRIDAY, 2:58 A.M.

"Alright, I'm going to bed. Maybe you were so tired that you dropped off to sleep. I'm going to give you the benefit of the doubt. I'm also willing to give you the benefit of the doubt on whatever happened at the game tonight, too, so please call me before I leave for work in the morning so we can air this out. I'll talk to you tomorrow. Bye." BEEP. FRIDAY, 3:19 A.M.

"Hello, Austin . . . it's Molly. I really need to talk to you before I get to the gallery. I don't want to see you at the office without settling this first. Please call me, Austin, and let's fix this. You know I love you, dammit. Bye." BEEP. FRIDAY, 9:08 A.M.

"Mr. Feruzzi, if you're there, sir . . . this is Donaldo down in the lobby. There is a woman here to see you . . . a Miss Molly Adams . . . are you at home? I guess you're not there . . . I'll tell the lady." BEEP. FRIDAY, 9:44 A.M.

"Austin . . . it's me again. I'm at the gallery. I came by to see you on my way to work. The doorman called upstairs but you weren't answering. Anyway, I've changed my mind about tonight. I do want to see you. Maybe I was too hard on you. We need to talk. I want us to get past this nasty business. I want to apologize if I was wrong. Please call me at the gallery. Bye." BEEP. FRIDAY, 10:36 A.M.

"Hello, Austin, it's Jake. One of my paralegals just got Aiden Jannus on an airplane . . . left LAX at ten, gets into New York *sometime after six tonight . . . I'll have to have him back here on the twenty-fourth for his court date on the gun thing, which is Friday the twenty-fifth at nine* A.M. *Meantime, he has a couple of weeks to get some work done. Keep him on a short leash, Austin. Bye, buddy."* BEEP. FRIDAY, 1:26 P.M.

"Austin, please . . . I can't think about anything except us. I haven't heard from you all day. Please don't do this to me . . . you're being passive-aggressive, and it's not fair.

"I know that you love me, and I love you. I'm sorry, honestly. I'm really sorry. I guess I jumped down your throat. I'm asking you to forgive me. What do you want me to do? Come over there? Sit in the hallway in front of your door? I'll do it if I have to. I love you, Austin, you know that . . . for good and forever . . . and that's what counts here, isn't it?

"I know we agreed that I would never come to the apartment, but Kate's not in New York, and if I don't hear from you tonight, I'm coming over there in the morning, I swear it. I love you more than anything on earth. Please call and tell me that everything is okay. I love you." BEEP. FRIDAY, 9:42 P.M.

"Austin . . . hello, it's Kate. I got your message. I listened to it three times. Yes, I do love you . . . yes, I know we belong together . . . and yes, I want to save our marriage. I know you didn't mean to hurt me . . . and I believe you when you say that you'll never do it again. I think we've both had a very big scare, and I'm willing to start new if you are. In fact, I have a wonderful, delicious plan for us, and I can't wait to tell you about it.

"I'm coming to New York, as you've asked . . . and I do want to go on a trip to the Caribbean with you . . . on a mini honeymoon. We need it, and it's a perfect time to just be together. I'm taking a ten o'clock flight out of San Francisco tonight, and Lane is coming too. She's been wonderful, and I need her with me. I know you can understand that I'm a little wobbly.

"I'm not sure about Trisha's dinner tomorrow night. I . . . I don't look very good. I'll see how I look and feel tomorrow. But

the main thing is that I want to be with you. I love you too, darling.

"I'll call Mort and have him order a car to meet our flight. When you get this, you might call him too, just to confirm . . . it's United Airlines, Flight 305, arriving at JFK at six-thirteen A.M. Lane and I should be at the apartment sometime after seven. I'll settle her in the blue suite, then I'll crawl into bed with you. Sound good?

"If you get this in the next few minutes, call me at Lane's. Otherwise, we'll be on our way to the airport . . . Geoff is going to drive us. I'll see you in the morning. I can't wait . . . and I know that everything is going to be alright with us from now on. I love you. Bye, darling." BEEP. FRIDAY, 10:06 P.M.

Austin erased his messages. He was so exhausted he could barely stand. Back and forth across the country in sixteen hours, and he'd been too wired to sleep on the plane. He'd forgotten to order food put on board. He'd grabbed a quick bite at the snack bar at Teterboro because he was famished, and because he was too beat to stop for dinner in the city. Now he was back in his apartment, and crisis loomed—Kate and Molly on a collision course. Picking up the phone, he dialed the number at Molly's Chelsea apartment. He reached her machine.

"Hello, Molly . . . it's Austin. Look, this isn't working . . . it can't work. I got all your messages, and I'm sorry to put you through that, but I've thought things over carefully. I'm sorry to tell you like this . . . on the phone. But maybe it's best this way. I don't want to get into it with you . . . I don't want to argue with you . . . I don't want to discuss it—you can't come here. It's over! It was a mistake. I'm sorry, Molly. I'm in love with my wife, and I'm going to make my marriage work.

"Kate is coming in tonight—she'll be here at the apartment early in the morning . . . and we're planning a trip together. And we'll be at Trisha and Peter's dinner tomorrow night. It would be better if you didn't come . . . I think that would make it easier, especially on you.

"I don't want to hurt you, Molly, but we never should have gotten into this. It's probably my fault. I'll take all the blame. I don't know what the hell I was thinking of, except that I just flipped over you, but it has to be over.

"I'm sorry to tell you this way, but it's better to cut it off clean. Believe me, you're better off without me. In time, you'll forget this ever happened . . . and Kate must never know. I know you love her, and if she knew about us it would kill her. So please, let's be grown up about this . . . let's work together as we always have, and act as if nothing ever happened between us.

"Thank you, Molly. I know you understand. A part of me will always love you. Good night, Molly."

Austin put the phone down in his den and walked into the master suite. In the gleaming, black marble bathroom, he ran cold water over his face and brushed his teeth. Then he went into his bedroom and fell into bed. Molly was out of the picture. Kate would be here in the morning. The Rhaji was locked up in his private storage room in Beverly Hills. Aiden Jannus was on his way back to New York. Everything was under control.

And, he was in possession of some hot, volatile, potentially lethal information! He had long suspected that Tripp Kendrick was gay, which mattered not at all to him, but here was America's most popular and highest-paid movie action hero, a faggot! That would be a shock heard 'round the world! A mega career-buster!

Yes, he had the goods on Mr. Jonathan Valley, Mr. Big Shot Movie Star, Mr. Deep Pockets with his well-kept, dirty little secret, and the first installment on his silence was that casual walk out the door of the superstar's mansion on the beach this morning with the fucking Rhaji under his arm!

He had known full well that he would not be challenged. Nor did he intend to even offer Jonathan Valley his money back now. He was quite certain that Valley would not protest.

Feruzzi was asleep in minutes.

Chapter 28

"Jon . . . it's Tripp. God, I'm in shock . . . I know that you are too. By the time you get to the apartment, I'll probably have left for the airport. I managed to book myself on a flight at ten . . . gets into JFK at six-forty in the morning . . . should put me in the city around eight. Don't get up . . . just leave my name with the doorman, and he can let me in.

"I told Austin I was taking a week off . . . he said that was fine. He flew right back to New York yesterday . . . he's there. He laid his whole itinerary on me . . . he's going to Martinique with his wife on Sunday. Not a mention of his insanity at the beach . . . or finding us together. I'll see you in the morning, Jon, and I hope the hell we can figure out what to do for damage control. Ciao." BEEP. FRIDAY, 10:14 P.M. END OF FINAL MESSAGE.

Jonathan Valley erased his messages, then slumped back in the chair behind his desk. Looking out at the New York skyline from the floor-to-ceiling windows in his comfortable, wood-paneled office, he had never felt more uncomfortable in his life.

He and Tripp had always been so careful. Even when they traveled together, they flew separately. Jonathan had just arrived at his midtown apartment from an afternoon flight; Tripp was coming in on a red-eye in the morning. The two had talked a little after Austin Feruzzi had bolted from the Malibu house that morning, but mostly, they were stunned.

Valley had since been over the bizarre scenario in his mind a hundred times. In the most outlandish of circumstances, Feruzzi had caught them. "Well! This is cozy, gentlemen," he'd said with a leer. "Jonathan, I've changed my mind about giving you a free Rhaji. In fact, the price just doubled. And, Tripp, I'll call you from the plane in a couple of hours and let you know where I'm going to be."

With that, Feruzzi had smiled wickedly and picked up the painting from where he'd dropped it on the floor. At that point, the phone rang. All three had stopped to listen. Over the still-persistent wail of the burglar alarm, they could hear the answering machine click on, then the outgoing message, then a man from the home-security company:

> *"Mr. Valley . . . this is Westec . . . we have a tripped alarm at your Malibu residence. If you're there, please pick up the phone. If everything's alright, we need your code. If we don't hear from you in the next sixty seconds, we'll be sending a police response—"*

"Better jump on it and tell him everything's okay, pal," Feruzzi had said. Jonathan had pounced on the phone and snatched up the receiver.

"This is Jonathan Valley," he'd heard himself responding calmly. "Everything's fine. I set off the alarm myself, by mistake. My code word is hopscotch. But I'm going to call you later today," he'd added, looking pointedly at Feruzzi, "and change it."

Replacing the receiver then, Jonathan had walked over to the security-system keypad on the wall, and punched in the digits that shut off the alarm. He'd turned then to see Feruzzi walking out of the sitting room, carrying the huge Rhaji canvas with both hands. Jonathan had followed him out into the hall and through the living room, and watched the man exit through the same beachside glass doors that he'd come in. Once outside, Feruzzi shot back a look.

"We'll all be fine with this," he'd tossed out, almost jovially. "You'll see." Then he trudged off down the beach with the painting.

From that time to this, Jonathan had flirted with at least a dozen scenarios to put out the fire, to keep Feruzzi quiet, but he'd summarily dismissed each one. He had to find a way to put a muzzle on the man. Only a few people knew that actor Jonathan Valley was gay, all of them were in Jon's very limited private orbit, and all of them were trustworthy. But now there was Austin Feruzzi. Feruzzi could ruin him, and he had a sinking feeling that he was dealing with a snake who would bust him in a heartbeat if he could make a dollar doing it.

Jonathan picked up the phone, dialed the lobby, and asked for a wake-up call at seven. He intended to be up in the morning and waiting for Tripp when he got in. The two of them had to come up with a plan, and fast.

Chapter 29

AUSTIN FERUZZI was standing in the open doorway to the apartment, his arms outstretched, his face aglow as Kate and Lane approached. Donaldo, the daytime doorman, came down the hall behind the women, steering their luggage on a brass-framed trolley. It was Saturday morning, not yet eight o'clock. Lane was nervous, Kate was disoriented, and both women were exhausted.

"Darling Kate!" Feruzzi sang, wrapping his arms around his wife. "Oh, my sweet Katie, I've missed you so . . ."

Lane stood behind her friend, an involuntary shudder coursing through her body. Neither woman had slept much on the plane, and Lane had spent a good part of the flight trying to talk Kate *out* of going back to Austin. She had heard about so many wife-beating cases from Geoff, she kept telling her, and the pattern was invariably, relentlessly the same.

Unfortunately, Lane also knew, battered women almost always stayed with their batterers. Until they saw the light. And too often, that was too late.

"Come in, come in," Austin was saying to them now, smiling effusively. "How wonderful to see you, Lane."

For a split second, Lane feared that Austin was going to hug her too, but he must have sensed her resistance, because he settled for offering his hand. Lane instinctively pulled back, immediately busying herself with the open latch on her purse. Seeming not to notice the rebuff, Austin positioned himself behind the women and ushered them into the entry.

Donaldo removed the suitcases and garment bags from the trolley, and set them inside on the marble floor. Austin handed him a ten-dollar bill, and saw the doorman off, then he turned his attention to the luggage.

"Okay, ladies, whose is what?" he asked congenially. Strange, the man didn't seem to know his wife's luggage, Lane thought. She pointed out her own bags, and he picked them up.

"Let's get you into your rooms," he directed at Lane, "so you can freshen up and get some rest." Lane numbly followed him down the hall to the guest suite, a smiling Kate tagging behind.

The guest rooms were beautiful. Lane hadn't seen them since Kate had redecorated, attending meticulously to every detail. The sitting room furniture was upholstered in a nubby silk that suggested the hue and texture of sand. The walls and ceilings were painted in the same ivory-verging-on-taupe. Silk Aubusson rugs softened the hardwood floors.

Austin took Lane's bags into the adjoining bedroom. He set her suitcase on top of a brightly painted trunk at the foot of the bed, and hung her garment bag in the spacious closet. His wife stood behind him, inspecting the rods.

"Good, there are plenty of hangers," Kate murmured.

"You get Lane settled in, darling," Austin bustled, "and I'll be waiting for you in our room."

With that, he gave his wife a peck on the cheek and left the suite. Immediately, Lane could see Kate visibly letting down, the tension draining from her face. Their eyes met then, and Lane scrutinized her friend, noticing now that most of Kate's careful makeup from the night before was gone. Her bruises stood out in angry relief, and her features mirrored a gamut of emotions. One of them, Lane sensed, was fear.

The moment between them passed. Kate turned down the bed covers, revealing crisp Dani linen, winter-white with borders embroidered in navy stripes. She smoothed the duvet spread, a St. Remy in navy with a field of cheerful white persimmon blooms. Then she glanced up at the matching drapes, as if to assure herself that everything was good enough, perfect, in fact.

"I'm going to check the bathroom," Kate said then, "make sure the towels are right, and there's enough soap and lotion—"

"Katie, relax . . . please!" Lane beseeched, taking her friend's hand, searching for the intimacy they had shared over the past few troubled days. "Think about yourself. I'm so afraid for you."

"I'm fine," Kate returned, with a cursory smile and a note of finality, signaling that there would be no more conversation about her "unpleasantness," as she'd referred to Austin's beatings several times before. She disappeared into the bathroom, then emerged smiling, rubbing her hands together.

"You're all set," she said. "Will you be comfortable here, Lane?"

Not in *this* lifetime, Lane thought. "Of course," she said aloud, and forced a smile.

"Good. Let's have a nap. We'll talk at lunch," Kate said. But Lane had gotten the message that any real talking was over. She had successfully escorted Katie here; now Kate was letting her know that she was back in a shrouded world that was off-limits to outsiders. Lane was no longer her confidante. Kate had switched into hostess mode, and Lane was now her houseguest.

Kate brushed her forehead with a perfunctory kiss and left the suite, closing the doors behind her. Not even a thank you for trying to get her through, Lane thought. But she understood. Kate didn't even want to acknowledge what she'd been through. Her friend was pretending, desperately, Lane thought, that life was nothing short of normal.

Dispirited, Lane unpacked her things and tucked them into drawers and closets. She, too, could do nothing more than pretend that she was just a visitor, she realized. Finishing, she closed up her bags and stowed them in the closet. She went into the tawny-grained marble bath and took a quick shower, then slipped into a nightgown and climbed between the sheets.

As tired as she was, sleep wouldn't come. She propped herself up against the cushy down pillows and stared up at the ceiling. After a minute, she leaned over to the bedside table and picked up the phone. She dialed, then spoke quietly.

> "Geoff, darling, we're here. It's just after eight o'clock in New York . . . I know you're not up yet . . . but I need so much to be close to you. I'm so afraid for Katie, Geoff . . . she has blinders on. She's a different person around him . . . a robot, going through the motions. A 'Stepford Wife' . . .
>
> "Oh darling, I want so much to get right back on an airplane, but I don't dare leave her. Please call me as soon as you get up, before you take the boys to soccer. I love you . . . I need to hear

your voice. I want to talk to the kids, too. I want to hear the ocean. I want to come home."

Lane hung up the phone, and scrunched down under the covers. She felt a little better now, as if she had reached out and plugged into reality for a minute. Still, she couldn't shake her profound feelings of foreboding.

She flashed back to a domestic violence case that had greatly troubled Geoff. The woman had been so badly beaten about the face and head that she had become totally deaf. But she'd stayed with the man who beat her. Now that she had lost her hearing, she'd said, she really needed her husband to take care of her.

Chapter 30

O KAY, WHAT THE hell do we do about Feruzzi?" Jonathan Valley asked Tripp, before he even said hello.

"I don't know, Jon," Tripp returned tersely. "I've been thinking about nothing else."

It was eleven minutes after eight on Saturday morning in New York, and Tripp had just arrived at the door of Valley's upscale East End Avenue apartment. Taking his suitcases, Jonathan led him through the entry and up the stairs to the guest quarters. Tripp felt fatigue like a pair of leaden weights pulling down on his eyelids.

"How you holding up?" Jonathan asked him. "Want to catch some sleep?"

"Let's talk first," Tripp said, tossing his carry-on bag and leather jacket on the couch in his room. "Got any coffee?"

"Of course," Jon said. "Come on, we'll go down to the kitchen. I have to be at Global at nine. We'll have coffee, then I'll get out of here and you can grab a shower and sleep for a few hours. You look beat, Tripp."

"I know," Tripp grimaced. "Jesus, I just can't believe Austin showing up like that. I have no idea what it was about, Jon."

"I don't give a good goddamn what it was about," Jonathan said grimly. Though the actor appeared outwardly controlled, Tripp recognized something he rarely saw, white-hot anger raging behind his eyes.

"Something crazy—" Tripp started.

"Whatever the nature of that madman's dementia, the fact is, he's blown our cover, Tripp. That's what matters here. And don't try to tell me that the man can be trusted—I wouldn't trust Feruzzi to spit on me if I were on fire."

"I'm not going to argue with you," Tripp responded disconsolately. He slid into the round leather banquette in Jonathan's kitchen.

"How long have you known him?"

"I've known him, worked for him, for nearly ten years. I don't dislike him, I can't let myself, really—but you're right, Jon, he'd piss on his grandmother if he thought he could make a couple of bucks."

"So what should we do?"

"Fix it so he'll never tell anyone—ever."

"What does that mean? Kill him?"

"Sure," Tripp chuckled gloomily. "Kill him. Jesus, you've seen too many movies, Jon."

"I've been *in* too many movies. If this were one of my movies, I'd kill him."

"Yeah, well, unfortunately, this is real life."

Jonathan poured two steaming mugs of coffee and brought them over to the table, then he took a seat on the leather bench opposite Tripp. Taking a packet of sugar substitute from a bowl on the table-top, he tore it open methodically, poured the contents into his coffee, stirred carefully, then looked up at Tripp.

"I'm going to kill him," he said.

"Really," Tripp laughed again, but this time a little nervously.

"Think about it. This dirt-bag opportunist will bide his time, and when I least expect it, he'll expose me. Lay me out there. Probably sell the story to the tabloids anonymously. That's exactly what he'll do. Then I'll never work as a leading man again. Or maybe as anything. God knows—*you* know—that I've been so careful. But that fucking sleaze king will ruin me, Tripp, and I can't let that happen."

"It's the nineties, Jon—don't you think the public is much more tolerant than they were in Rock Hudson's day?"

"Get real," Jonathan dismissed him. "What if they found out that Schwarzenegger was gay? Or Stallone? Or Harrison Ford? Think those guys would still get the big pictures?"

Tripp had no answer.

"I've got to go," Jonathan said then, draining the last of his coffee. "By the way, I have dinner tonight at Peter Newman's, with some of the execs from Global."

"Really?" Tripp raised his eyebrows. "Do you know that Austin Feruzzi is a friend of the Newmans?"

"Great. You think he'll be there?"

"He could very well be. Peter Newman is the guy who introduced Austin Feruzzi to his wife. Kate Feruzzi went to college with Trisha Newman. Austin is a regular guest on her radio show."

"I guess I've heard something like that. So he might be there tonight."

"He didn't mention it to me, but sure, it's possible."

"Then maybe I *won't* be," Jonathan declared. Then, after a beat, he exploded, "No! Jesus, I refuse to tailor my plans around that snake!"

"That snake is my boss," Tripp said quietly, as if reminding himself more than Jonathan.

"Dammit, I've got to think this through, Tripp," Jon responded. "But I'm due at Global for interviews. You get some rest—I'll see you later this afternoon. Maybe we can brainstorm this land mine, figure out a way to diffuse it."

"Look, I could quit," Tripp offered.

"Christ, no," Jon flipped back, throwing his arms in the air. "Feruzzi certainly doesn't give a shit if he buries *me*. But you've been his right hand for a decade—he *needs* you. If you quit over this, he wouldn't owe you anything."

"You know, Jon," Tripp said thoughtfully, "I don't think there's a person who really knows me who doesn't suspect that I'm gay. They just respect my right to be private about my personal life. If I'm yanked out, it really wouldn't matter."

"Of course it wouldn't, your career doesn't depend on it," Jonathan bellowed. "Mine does. Even a hint of homosexuality and I'm finished. We've talked about this many times, Tripp."

"I know, I know. I'm too whipped to make any sense. You go, and we'll dope it out when you get back."

"Okay—get some rest, buddy."

"I'm really sorry, Jon—"

"Hey," Jonathan cut him off, "it's not your fault. Who the hell would believe that goon would come banging on my door?"

"The painting—"

"Yeah . . . why was he so desperate to have that damn painting? He rushed all the way across country to beg me for it. It can't be money—I offered him his asking price."

"I haven't got a clue."

"Find out, Tripp," Jonathan said resolutely, getting up from the table. "You're close to him . . . you're plugged in to his world. Find out what the hell is up with that fucking painting! If I knew the answer to that, maybe I'd have something on him that would give me some leverage, level out the playing field."

"I know him, Jon," Tripp countered. "Austin is a loose cannon. Whatever it is, it won't be good enough."

Jonathan strode out of the kitchen. He crossed the broad living room toward the front door, with Tripp following. He grabbed a jacket out of the entryway closet and shrugged into it. Then he turned back with a look of ferocious anger that Tripp had never seen before.

"When I had him inside my house, and I had a goddamn gun in my hand, I should have shot the bastard," he said.

Chapter 31
─────────────────────

"Trisha . . . it's Lane. We're coming to dinner tonight after all . . . the three of us . . . me, Kate, and Austin. I need to talk to you, but of course it won't be possible at your dinner party . . . so I'll talk the way we usually do, on the answering machine where I know it's private.

"It's awful here, Trish . . . the tension is so thick it sucks the oxygen right out of the room. Austin is relentlessly cheerful, and Katie tries valiantly to act as if nothing's wrong. I've wanted to flee from the second I got here, but I've been afraid to leave her.

"Geoff called me four times today . . . he's an enormous help. He says the typical wife beater has bouts of intense remorse after each episode, and Austin almost certainly won't hit her again while he's in this period. Until the next time, that is. Until he works himself into a rage again. Problem is, the intervals during which these creeps are deeply sorry and they overcompensate usually shorten, and the beating episodes come faster and more furiously.

"Also, Geoff says, four out of five battered women do not leave their batterers, and many of the other twenty percent leave because they're carried out. A lot of the women end up in the hospital, once, twice, several times before they find the strength to leave. And some of them get killed, Trisha—their final escape is death.

"I'm so depressed. I feel so helpless. I can't stay here forever like some kind of guard dog, and Geoff said even if I did, it wouldn't deter a batterer if he'd reached that point in the cycle where he *was compelled to strike. So I guess I'll go home after they leave for the Caribbean tomorrow. Thanks for your offer to stay on with you for a few days, but I need to get home.*

"*Anyway, we'll all see you tonight. Austin keeps telling Kate not to worry, she looks fine . . . but Trisha . . . try not to look shocked when you see her. Her beautiful face is still quite bruised and puffy, and she's trying to hide it behind tons of makeup.*

"*I wish we could help her, Trish, but I just don't know what else to do. Do you? I love you. See you at eight. Bye.*" BEEP. 3:43 P.M. *END OF FINAL MESSAGE.*

Trisha clicked off the answering machine with a sigh. When the three of them had arrived just a while ago, she was so taken aback at the sight of Katie's face that after the preliminary hellos, she'd ducked inside her darkened office and locked the door.

She needed to pull herself together. Kate's injuries were still painfully visible, even, as Lane had warned, under a heavy layer of skillfully applied makeup. It broke Trisha's heart to watch Kate gamely cheating her face to one side, trying vainly to avoid notice.

Sitting at her desk in the semi-darkness now, hot tears welled up and spilled over Trisha's cheeks. To think that Kate's husband, the man darling Katie trusted to love her and take care of her—to think that the bastard *did* this to her! And that this was not the first time; he'd been beating her for years! Trisha was livid.

She'd listened to the tape again, Lane's mournful message that had come in earlier that afternoon. Listened again, and tried to understand why a bright, wealthy, stunningly beautiful woman like Kathryn Blakely Spenser of the New York publishing Spensers would stay with a sick, violent, dangerous man like Austin Feruzzi. Trisha had decided not to erase the tape—she would keep it, file it away somewhere in case it was ever needed down the road. In court.

She went into her office powder room, flipped on the light, and peered into the mirror. Mascara was puddling under her eyes. Quickly she patched, and powdered, and freshened her lips, then she straightened up, and headed back toward the sounds of music and voices down the hall.

Standing apart for a few moments under the arched doorway to the spacious family room and bar, Trisha observed her husband and ten dinner guests standing about, most of them chatting in hushed tones. Something was off. The room seemed to be shot through with an anxious edge. But perhaps it was her imagination. She was so monumentally disturbed about Kate, she reasoned, that she might be magnifying the demons in the room, projecting her own anxiety onto the rest of her guests.

Austin was standing at his wife's side, demonstrably oversolicitous, Trisha thought. He was smiling at Kate indulgently, caressing her back, talking and laughing, trying too hard. And Kate was painfully ill at ease. Trisha watched as Katie smiled self-consciously and responded to the others, trying all the while to hide her bruises behind her hands.

Molly had called earlier and left a message that she wasn't coming tonight. Just that. She'd offered no reason for canceling at the last minute, and she'd sounded upset on the phone machine. When Trisha had tried to reach her to talk about it, Molly wasn't answering. But tonight, she just showed up, again with no explanation, and it seemed to Trisha that she was acting very odd. Making no attempts to mingle or even talk to anyone, Molly hadn't moved away from the bar since the moment she'd arrived. Alone now, sipping what looked to be a triple vodka over ice, she looked singularly remote and profoundly unhappy.

Even Lane seemed downcast, which was rare for her, but Trisha could certainly understand that, given what Lane had been going through with Kate. Lane, too, stood apart, and she seemed to be looking daggers at Austin Feruzzi. Subtlety had never been Lane Hamilton's strong suit. Trisha knew Lane was convinced that Austin would hurt Kate again, and that maybe next time, the damage would be irreparable.

Ironic and strange, Trisha mused. The four longtime best friends together in the same room, but tonight there seemed to be great gulfs dividing them.

Jonathan Valley had arrived late, and without the usual model-actress date on his arm. Jon had done projects with Global before, and Trish and Peter had been in his company many times. The popular actor was usually outgoing and genial, but tonight he seemed somehow preoccupied. And she could be wrong, but Valley appeared to be deliberately avoiding Austin Feruzzi, which was not easy in a group this small. This was a concern, because she had them seated next to each other at dinner, knowing that Valley was an art collector, and in fact had purchased several acquisitions from the Feruzzi Galleries.

At the moment, Valley was standing in a corner with Peter, who looked to be doing all the talking, probably about the publicity campaign for the upcoming retrospective of Jonathan Valley films on Global. Funny, Trisha thought, Peter seemed to be oblivious to the strange ambience in the room—could he possibly be missing it? Jon Valley kept looking away, glancing nervously around the room.

A disheveled Aiden Jannus had seemed to be drunk when he arrived, and was fast getting drunker. Austin Feruzzi had invited the artist, and Peter thought it was a great coup to get the man here to dinner tonight. Jannus was looking at his own marvelous three-panel triptych that was newly installed on the Newmans' wall. The subject was a field of brilliantly hued California wildflowers that skipped across the three riotously colorful canvases hung side by side.

The tipsy artist was mumbling—babbling something to the effect that he didn't even remember painting this piece of shit. He was proclaiming to anyone who would listen that he had never even *seen* a goddamn poppy.

"What the hell is a poppy supposed to look like? Is it supposed to be orange?" he was asking now, in the general direction of two Global executives and their wives, who stood huddled together in a group, trying to placate the great artist, and looking decidedly uncomfortable.

Tension! It was in the air, Trisha thought forlornly, there was no escaping it. Her festive dinner for twelve was a severely endangered species. Standing tall, she brushed a hand through her short crop of golden hair and steeled herself. Into the breach, she determined—it was her responsibility as hostess to save this dinner from consummate disaster.

First Molly. Because she wasn't quite ready to face Kate. She was afraid she would tear up again, or worse, say something nasty to Austin. The bastard should be in jail, she groused to herself, not in her home, drinking her scotch. She walked gamely up to the bar and stood next to Molly. "How are you?" she asked her, looking dubiously at Molly's gloomy face.

"Fine," Molly said.

"Everything okay?"

"Wonderful."

"Molly, what the hell's wrong?" Trisha blurted out. "Did I do something? Say something?"

"Of course not, Trisha," Molly responded with a touch of exasperation. "Why do you and Lane and Kate always think that everything is about *you?*"

Trisha glanced around, checking to see if anyone else was listening to this outlandish exchange. No one. The rest seemed absorbed in their own individual miasma. She felt completely out of control.

"Molly, I don't deserve this, and you know it," she said evenly. "You called and said you weren't coming tonight, gave me no reason, you showed up anyway, and now you're being rude. And you're half in the bag—what are you drinking, straight vodka? We've known each other too long for you to treat me like this—it's not acceptable."

"Then why don't I just leave?" Molly shot back, reaching for her purse on the bar. Trisha reached up and grabbed her hand.

"Why don't you *not* leave," she said, feeling her cheeks redden. "And why don't you tell me what the hell this is about?"

"Listen," Molly said stonily, turning to look squarely at Trisha, "our friendship was a teenage thing. Now that we're all grown up, don't you think it's time that we lived our own lives? Isn't it a little immature at this point to be laying bare among the four of us every move we make, every single goddamn thought we have?"

Trisha had no answer. Molly had been acting increasingly defensive and removed over the past weeks, and now she was being downright hostile, for no reason that Trisha could determine. Anything she said right now could only make it worse, she felt. She turned and moved to safer haven—to Lane, who was still sitting alone, looking very small on the big down-filled couch. Trisha sat beside her.

"Well," she said, "this is a convivial crowd, isn't it?"

"Dismal," Lane allowed. "Those poor Global people who work for Peter must think that they've dropped down the rabbit hole."

"They're the least of my concerns. Molly is irascible, and I have no idea why. Do you?"

"No, but she's been looking at Austin like she could kill."

"Did something happen at work, do you think?"

"Who knows. She hasn't told any of us."

"That's another thing. She just more or less informed me that she has no intention of confiding in any of us anymore about anything. Something to the effect that our four-way friendship was kid stuff, and it was time to cut the cords."

"She's glowering at Austin again, look—"

"Does she know he's been beating Kate?"

"No—we all agreed not to let her know, not yet," Lane reminded her.

"Well, it's pretty obvious that Katie's been beaten," Trisha responded tartly, "and, *hello*! It wouldn't take a genius to figure out that her husband was the creep who did it. Look at him, Lane—Satan in a Saville Row suit, oozing congeniality."

The two women looked toward Austin and Kate. The couple were standing with Peter now in the far corner of the room. Austin, his arm around Kate, a drink in his other hand, was regaling the other two with some kind of story. Peter was laughing heartily, obviously entertained.

"Jesus, Trisha," Lane said then, her open Irish face registering supreme annoyance, "doesn't Peter know that Austin is a batterer? That he could have killed his wife? That he still might?"

"Yes, of course he knows. I told him."

"Well, what does he find so damn fascinating about the man, can you please tell me that?"

"Um . . . obviously he's trying to be a good host," Trisha returned, taken aback by Lane's angry attack on her husband.

"Peter's the reason that bastard is in our lives," Lane shot back. "He introduced him to Katie. Look at him, Trisha—he loves the guy, always has. Explain it to me."

"For God's sake, Lane, are you blaming my husband for what's happened to Kate?"

"Sorry, Trish, but it infuriates me that Peter always treats Austin like he's some kind of graven image. I mean, would a good host swap football stories with O.J.?"

Trisha looked at Lane in disbelief. "Lane, I know that you've been very close to Kate all through this, and I know that you're angry . . . so am I. And you're away from your family, and you've been getting no sleep, I know all of that . . . but really, why take it out on me? Or my husband?"

Not waiting for a reply, Trisha excused herself and got up. She felt as if *she* were down the rabbit hole. First Molly, now Lane. What the hell did Lane want from her? Were she and Peter supposed to be rude to Austin in their own home? She had always put up with the man for Katie's sake. Isn't that what friends did? And yes, Peter seemed to genuinely like Austin, Lane was right about that. She didn't have a clue what that was about—probably a "guy" thing, she guessed. She walked over to Peter, who was still laughing at Austin's jokes.

"Trisha," Austin said as she joined the three of them, "don't you have a drink?"

"Ahh . . . no."

"Let me get you one," Austin offered, smiling jovially.

"A champagne cocktail would be nice," she told him.

Trisha watched Austin amble off toward the bar. That gets rid of him for three minutes, she thought. Her mind was doing a chaotic scramble.

"How are you doing, Katie?" Trisha said then.

"Couldn't be better," Kate pronounced, managing a smile. "We're going to Martinique tomorrow."

"Bring us back a bottle of Olde Christo," Peter put in. "It's the best rum on the planet, and we can't get it here."

"Sure," Kate said. "If we can, we'll send you a case."

"Katie," Trisha said, glancing toward Austin at the bar, "Austin's got to get some help—"

"Trisha, Austin's fine," Kate cut her off, looking pointedly at Peter. "I really don't want to talk about this."

"Honey, it's only Peter," Trisha tried to recoup. "He knows everything—"

"Stop it, please, Trisha."

"Excuse me, ladies, I'm going to talk to the Jennings," Peter offered, and he made a hasty move over to the Global executives and their wives.

Trisha pulled closer to Kate. "Katie, listen to me," she pleaded. "You're going away in the morning, we won't get a chance to talk, and I'm terribly afraid that—"

"Look, Trisha, I appreciate your concern, Lane's too, but really, this is *my* business, mine and Austin's. Please just drop it."

Trisha felt as if she'd had her face slapped. Two decades of the closest possible friendship between the four of them, and now they were at each other's throats. They hadn't tiffed since college, and back then it was usually about borrowed clothes or borrowed boyfriends. This was different. This was now, this was serious, and as far as Trisha could tell, all of it was about Austin Feruzzi.

She looked over at the man, standing next to Molly at the bar now, waiting for the bartender to pour the champagne for her cocktail. Molly was talking to him. Austin wasn't looking at her. He mouthed something.

Suddenly, Molly let fire in a high-pitched shriek, *"Liar! You're a frigging liar!"*

All conversation stopped in the room; all eyes were riveted toward the bar. Trisha was aghast. She heard Austin muttering noises like, *Come on, Molly . . . stop this now—*

"No, *you* come on," Molly screeched, and with that she reared back, and with a mighty heave, she tossed her drink in Austin's face.

The guests let out a collective gasp. Even Aiden Jannus was paying attention. Trisha looked frantically at Kate, who stood frozen, her mouth dropped open in horror. In the space of a few seconds that seemed an eternity, Peter flew between Molly and Austin. Austin was wiping alcohol out of his eyes with cocktail napkins, and Molly was trying to hit him again, this time with her fists. Peter was holding her off with restraining arms and some words that Trisha was sure were meant to placate, but they only seemed to inflame her more.

Finding her legs, Trisha rushed over to the bar. Kate got there at the same time, with Lane right behind.

"Bastard!" Molly was shouting at Austin. "Who the hell do you think you're treating like one of your little dimwit bimbos?" she demanded. Then her eyes sought Kate's.

"He was sleeping with me, Kate. He was cheating on you with me," she spat, "and cheating on both of us with some other woman. Loads of women. You can have him, Katie, but if I were you, I'd dump him."

"I don't believe this—" Kate whispered.

"Oh, believe it, Kate," Molly snapped at her. Then, scrutinizing Kate's damaged face, she said, "And by the way, when he would tell me that he'd 'argued' with you again, even *I* had no idea that it was code for 'he'd beaten you to a bloody pulp'!"

Instinctively raising a protective hand to her face, Kate let out a little gasp. Both Trisha and Lane reached out to put an arm around her. And still, there was no stopping Molly. "Listen to this, Mrs. Feruzzi," she said evenly, her gaze still leveled sourly at Kate, "on Wednesday night he swore to me that he loved me and he wanted to marry me, and on Thursday night he was out fucking some little twit from Sotheby's!"

"It's not true, none of it," Austin uttered to Kate, while the rest of the dinner guests looked on in shock. "She's making it all up. She's crazy—"

"Oh, really!" Molly narrowed her blazing green eyes, wearing her toughness like a suit of armor on her ninety-six-pound frame. "Then tell me if I'm making *this* up, asshole . . . you have a large, flat, brown mole on your groin, just above the hairline to the left of your dick—"

"Bitch—" Austin started.

"Which, by the way, is not very big," Molly added disdainfully, cutting him off. And with that, she snatched her purse off the bar, turned on her heel, strode across the room, and slammed out the door.

Chapter 32

PETER NEWMAN sat alone in his den, trying to figure out what the hell had happened in his home in the last hour. It seemed Molly informed Kate that she'd been sleeping with Austin. But the affair was over now, because Feruzzi has been sleeping with the world. Molly proceeded to attack Austin, and for some reason, Jonathan Valley joined the fight—he kept calling Feruzzi *fucking pond scum*. In the aftermath, Kate was hysterical, her tears making her already battered face look even more raw. At some point, Lane and Trisha guided her into one of the Newmans' guest rooms, and got her into bed.

And just a footnote to the catastrophic evening now, his guest of honor, Aiden Jannus, turned out to be a drunken embarrassment, first having insulted his own painting that was hung on the Newmans' wall, then moving on to insult everyone in the room.

Dinner was abruptly canceled, of course. He had sent about twenty pounds of beautifully prepared beef Wellington engorged with pâté de foie gras home with his chef and the four servers. Peter was abashed that this lunacy had gone down in front of two of his top executives at Global and their wives.

As for Feruzzi, whom he had known since college, Peter had always been amused by his antics and eccentricities. Austin Feruzzi was a character, he had long told his wife, an American original. And Peter had always tried to hang a mantle of respectability on the man, at least for public consumption. He was the one who was responsible for introducing Feruzzi into his own social circle, after all, and ultimately introducing him to his wife's longtime friend, Kate Spenser.

Why? Because he owed him, Peter knew. And now, of course, Austin Feruzzi owed *him*. Another goddamn million dollars, and that was just the tip of the iceberg.

TRISHA HAD LEFT her husband muttering in his den, and padded quietly down the hall. She tapped on the door of the guest suite where Kate was ensconced. Lane was with her, holding Katie's hand while she drifted in and out of sleep.

"Is she out?" Trisha whispered.

"Fitfully," Lane returned. "God, she took so many tranquilizers it scared me. By the time I realized that she had a cache of them in her purse, it was too late to stop her—she downed a handful in front of my eyes."

"What a nightmare," Trisha intoned, easing down onto the bed next to Lane. The two sat quietly for a while, watching Kate's labored breathing. Finally, Trisha broke the silence. "Lane, did you have any clue that Molly was . . . was—"

"Sleeping with Austin?" Lane finished for her. "It's almost too painful to talk about, isn't it. Believe me, I had no idea. None at all."

"Think back," Trisha said. "Were we all blind?"

"No . . . I don't think so. Austin is slime, nothing he does would surprise me anymore, but who would ever dream that Molly could betray Kate, could betray *all* of us like that?"

"Twenty years of friendship evidently meant nothing to her."

"But . . . why? What on earth could have made her do it? I'm never going to understand this—"

"I can't help, Lane. I have no answers either. All I know is, I no longer want Molly Adams in my life."

"It feels like . . . like a death in the family," Lane managed, squeezing her eyes shut. Tears slid over her cheeks.

Trisha reached down and covered Lane's hand that was holding Kate's. "Poor Katie," she sighed. "She didn't need this bombshell after being physically brutalized by that . . . that . . . what did Jonathan Valley call Austin?"

"Pond scum," Lane offered weakly.

"Right. *Fucking* pond scum. What do you suppose Jonathan's got against him?"

"Who knows?" Lane breathed, dabbing at her eyes with the back of her hand. "I guess he's just another member of the Hate Austin Feruzzi club. It's very popular. Trish, do you think Katie will really, *finally*, leave Austin now?"

"If this doesn't do it," Trisha pronounced in hushed tones between firmly clenched teeth, "I'm telling you, we're going to have to kill him."

MOLLY SAT ON a wooden stool in the spare bedroom that was her studio, furiously stabbing paint onto the canvas set up before her. Black paint, overlaid with frenzied slashes of angry, blazing red. Screw Austin Feruzzi, screw the job, and to hell with Trisha, Lane, and Kate.

She had always felt like an alley cat among Persians, never really able to hold her own with those three, and now she had come full circle. From pressing her nose against the windows at Briarcliff, fervently seeking entree back then to their rich-girls' circle, to forcing the three of them out of her life now by her innate alley cat behavior. Fine. She was going to paint, dammit, and she was going to make it or not on her own hook, with her own talent, her own name, and her own artwork.

And she would like to see Austin Feruzzi dead.

DAMN! ANOTHER GIANT pig-screw!" Austin Feruzzi groaned aloud, cradling a martini and rubbing his throbbing head. He sat alone in the living room of his and Kate's upscale apartment in midtown. After the debacle at the Newmans tonight, he had gracelessly slipped out of their Park Avenue penthouse and walked home. *Slouched* home. How could so much go so wrong! Molly freaking out, Kate breaking down, and perfect strangers looking at him as if he were a hydra-headed monster.

He would repair all the damage, he assured himself, but there was nothing he could do tonight. Molly had stormed out of there, and Kate and Lane had left the room without a word—the two women would be spending the night at the Newmans', Trisha had let him know in frosty tones.

He needed Kate. He had to pull it all back together somehow. Humpty Dumpty time! He had done it before, and he would do it again. He would get Kate back in his life, in his home, and in his bed.

He needed to repair things with the rest of them as well. He had to keep Molly in the gallery, where she was indispensable. He would reel Trisha and Peter Newman back into his periphery, and they would continue to support him and his business as they always had. Lane Hamilton would go the way of her friends in the end—they were all four joined at the hip.

Then there was big, pumped-up, macho-man movie star Jonathan Valley. Hah! A faggot under the skin. And the man had the balls to give him the superiority treatment tonight in the form of a stone-cold snub. I'll get you, pretty boy, Feruzzi thought to himself with a bitter smile—your secret is *not* safe with me. If you don't ante up, big time, I will hit you with a neutron bomb, the one that kills all the people but leaves the buildings intact. The impact will leave you career-dead, Mr. Superstar, but your lover Tripp Kendrick will be left standing to run my Beverly Hills gallery, as he always has.

This screw-up was going to take a monumental effort on his part, Feruzzi knew. He would have to kiss up to Peter and Trisha. He couldn't afford to alienate the Newmans, either of them. *He* was invaluable with referrals to wealthy clients, *she* with regular promotion on her radio show. And Trisha Newman was very close to Kate.

God, he *had* to smooth it over with Kate. He would make her believe that Molly had come on to him repeatedly, and that she was furious because he simply wasn't having any of it.

But how to explain that she knew about the damn mole? He could tell Kate that it was her interminable gossip with the other three on the phone machines. Sometime over the years, Kate must have let that bit of information out to her sisters—she wouldn't remember now, but Molly had never forgotten. Not bad, he thought. Still, he wasn't sure he could make that one fly.

Maybe he should just throw himself on the mercy of the court, tell Kate that he'd made a terrible mistake with Molly. Tell her that Molly had set out to get him because she was deep-down jealous of her old college roommate, and always had been. Jealous of Katie's beauty, her money, and her marriage. He'd say that Molly had been relentless, and that he, only human, had stumbled into her trap. Once. Then he'd told Molly that it was wrong, that he was sorry, that it could never happen again, and that had made Molly go crazy.

That tack could accomplish two things. It might appease Kate. It would also get Molly banished from Kate's life forever, which would certainly uncomplicate things. Kate was too much of a lady to ever again speak to a woman who had slept with her husband, no matter how close the chums had been.

And he wasn't above begging. If he lost her, he'd die, he would tell his wife. And after all, he was not with Molly, was he? He was with Kate. Wasn't that proof positive that his wife was the woman he loved?

He was still exhausted from his frenzied trip back and forth across the country yesterday. He would have to think this through, sleep on it, decide tomorrow which way to go. It was obvious that Kate wanted him, and wanted their marriage to survive. Her coming to New York today proved that, didn't it? She wanted to believe him, he reasoned—therefore he could *make* her believe him.

Divorce was not an option, and not just because Kate stood to inherit a fortune. Besides that, Kathryn Spenser Feruzzi was the perfect wife. She was rich, gorgeous, smart, socially plugged in, and God knows she was supportive of him. And she gave him plenty of freedom.

He would fix everything tomorrow, talk her into taking the trip they'd planned. Then he would be a very good boy for a while.

J ON . . . WHAT ARE you doing home?" Tripp threw out, surprised to see Jonathan Valley back so early from the Newmans' dinner. It was just after nine-thirty.

"The smug little sonofabitch actually tried to get me to commission a Jannus," Jon spit out to Tripp before he got inside the apartment.

"Who—?"

"He's gesturing over at Aiden Jannus," Valley continued without stopping, "who happens to be at the party, dead drunk, and he's saying, with that ugly smirk of his, 'Who knows how long Jannus is going to be productive? Or even among the living?' and on and on—and he's serious, Tripp. Kidding on the square. He's telling me in no uncertain terms that I have to fork over a million dollars to commission—"

"Hold on a second," Tripp interjected. "A Jannus? Who are we talking about, Austin—?"

"Of course, Austin. The point is," Jon fired back, "at a fucking *dinner party* for chrissake, Feruzzi tries to extort money out of me. You have to know that an overpriced Jannus is just the beginning. He's going to escalate, and in the end he will *still* probably ruin me. I *have* to stop that viper!"

"So you left early—"

"Sit down, Tripp—it's a preposterous story," Jon tossed back, dropping his lanky frame into one of the big, overstuffed couches. "If we did this scene in a movie, they wouldn't believe a frame of it."

He proceeded to lay out the evening's events for Tripp, and by the end of it, he was actually laughing.

". . . Molly Adams was a demoness enraged, Feruzzi's wife said he would hear from her lawyer, her two women pals closed ranks and steered her out of there, and Aiden Jannus was swigging from a bottle of champagne and laughing his ass off during the whole thing. Peter Newman was totally flummoxed, and the Global brass and their wives thought they were in the Twilight Zone—"

"And what about Austin?" Tripp put in.

"Feruzzi flew out the door, trying to duck all the stones they were hurling at him, banished from the realm by all the people in his world who count."

"But he's still *our* problem, right?"

That observation sobered Jonathan Valley. "Right, he's still *our* problem," he said. "You know the man—what am I going to do, Tripp?"

"I don't know, but for the time being, I think you *should* commission a Jannus. That will buy us some time to come up with something."

"Fine. I'll commission a Jannus. You order it, Tripp—I don't give a damn what it is. I'll buy some silence from the prick. I'll be Austin Feruzzi's latest cash cow. But not for long. I swear to you, I'm going to find a way to kill him."

Book Two

SEPTEMBER 1998

Chapter 33

_____

*"Molly, it's Austin. As you know, I'm leaving for California in
the morning. I'll be back in two weeks for the Paul Sierra opening, unless something comes up and I need to be here sooner. Be
sure to look over those small pieces from Nancy Staat very carefully before you display them—in her last shipment to California she slipped in two pastels by her brother. They're signed just
'Staat'—it's her little plan to get his stuff out there. Actually
they're not bad, but they're not her. So if she does that again,
talk to her agent and send them back.*

*"Oh, and Aiden called me at the apartment tonight—he's
coming in to the gallery tomorrow. To look over his pieces on the
floor, he says. Handle him, Molly. Call me if you need me."*
BEEP. FRIDAY, 5:57 P.M. END OF FINAL MESSAGE.

It had been nearly two months ago that Molly had stormed out of
Trisha's dinner party. Since then, it had been strictly business with
Austin Feruzzi. Initially, she'd quit her job. But not for long. After
barely a week away from the gallery she went right back, for reasons
that they both knew well.

Now she sat at her desk in the rear of the Madison Avenue gallery,
checking her messages before closing up. Austin was going to California. Kate was taking him back. Why should that surprise her? she
asked herself. How she loathed the man.

She had never heard a word from any of her three erstwhile
friends. No surprise there, either. Her best friends, her lifelong
friends. Her real family. The closest human beings to her in all the

world. Nothing. Nor had she tried to contact any of them. It was finished. The ties with her three Briarcliff sisters were completely severed, she knew, and she was the one who'd wielded the knife.

With each passing day, Molly's sense of loss deepened. The closeness of her friends had always been like a second skin. She had taken their presence in her world for granted—never could she have remotely realized how empty she would feel without those women in her life. Or how frightened. And most of all, how alone.

She was also dealing with the loss, not of Austin Feruzzi, but of what she'd *thought* she had with him. She had *thought* that he was her key to a whole new life. As for the man, himself, she truly abhorred him now. Hated him for using her the way he did. He'd treated her like just another one of his uptown chippies, but because he needed Molly in the business, *really* needed her, he couldn't just toss her away like he did them.

Women were always calling the gallery, leaving messages for Austin. And calling and calling. Until finally, they got the tacit message that he was never going to call them back. He was done. After a night, or maybe two or three nights, or sometimes even weeks or months, he was done, and they would be left to find that out the hard way.

God, she'd *known* all that. She was just dumb enough to think that she was different. She despised Austin Feruzzi, who was nothing more to her than her boss now, and he was still that only for purely pragmatic reasons. Yes, she'd been stupid to fall for him, to believe the things he told her. Of all people, she should have known better. She *knew* the man, she *knew* what he was. She had given in to raging hormones that had surged through her body on a sea of false promises. Never again, she vowed.

She erased the messages, picked up her purse, closed up her office, and made a final check of the gallery. It was empty. She stepped outside onto busy Madison Avenue, and locked the doors behind her.

It was still daylight. One of those rare evenings when she'd actually got out of work on time. Plenty of time to go somewhere, do something. She glanced about at the bustling street traffic before starting down the sidewalk. Her New York. It was always exciting.

But she had nowhere exciting to go, nothing exciting to do. No matter, she needed to paint. So much work to get to. She would pick up a salad, take it home, and call it dinner. Eat it in her tiny kitchen while she quickly scanned the newspapers. She walked briskly to the subway station, ignoring the crowds. Ignoring the couples. And most of all, trying hard to ignore the friends.

And again, she reran the tape in her mind, as she had every spare minute of every single day since everything blew up. She had thought it over, and over, and over again, backward and forward, and again she fervently wished that she could turn back the clock, roll back the tape, and change everything.

Now and then the alien thought crept furtively in behind her eyes that she would have been so much better for Austin Feruzzi than Kate. She was of his world, in his world. Maybe with her, buoyed by their mutual love of art, she would have kept him interested, stimulated. Maybe if they had started off together, he never would have needed to cheat.

Hah! A wry smile turned her lips as she ducked down the steps to the subway station—even *she* knew better. In fact, who knew Austin Feruzzi better than she did? Not foolish Kate, who saw her husband through a pair of extravagant, ultra-fashionable rose-colored glasses. When it came to Austin, Kate had an acute case of blurred vision, exacerbated by pills and alcohol.

Molly had a clear view, educated insights into the man. She was up close and personal, had worked with him for eleven years. And she'd slept with him. She'd been privy to his every facet, inside and out. Bright, charming, handsome, witty, sexy—and greedy, self-absorbed, egotistical, deceitful, and evil. That was the package. So why was she still running his gallery, and pretending to everyone except herself that she wouldn't like to see him dead?

The fact was, Molly Adams was tied to Austin Feruzzi by an iniquitous secret, which, if it got out, could send them both to prison. He'd reminded her of that, of course, though he hadn't really had to. And he had appeased her with promises. Come back to work, he'd cajoled, and he would make her the next Aiden Jannus. Magic words.

"But why in hell should I believe you?" she'd thrown in his face.

"Because," he'd replied noxiously, "you don't really have a choice, do you, little girl?"

She knew he was right.

"And because," he'd gone on, trying to soften the pernicious truth, "it just makes good business sense, I've told you that."

He explained again that Molly Adams's success would be good for sales, good for the gallery. And *very* good for Molly. And, he'd reiterated, he was the only person on earth who could do it for her, who was truly in a position to establish her as an important contemporary artist, who actually *could* make her the next Aiden Jannus.

Aiden Jannus! A wretched piece of work. Hauled up before a Los Angeles judge on a gun-possession charge, he'd been ordered into locked-down rehab. The marshals had led him away to a county facility, without even allowing him to come home to New York to pack up his things. The judge probably figured he didn't need any things, since the artist had shown up in his courtroom in cut-off jeans and bare feet.

That was seven weeks ago, and Aiden Jannus, in his small cell at Saint Catherine of Tours Drug Rehabilitation Center in San Diego County, had had a major epiphany. He had endured detox, gone with the program, seen the light, got himself straight, and cleaned up his act. Now he was on the outside, and talking.

Jannus's drug rehabilitation, like everything the artist did, had become national news. He was interviewed all over the press and on the television talk shows, an uncharacteristically humbled, grateful Aiden Jannus who repeatedly vowed never to sully his bodily temple with abusive substances again. He wanted only to live for his work, he said on all the shows, and he would be eternally thankful that he had been given this chance to reclaim his life. He even thanked the judge who'd sent him to the slam, as he put it.

Molly rolled her eyes. Men! All of them. She sorely missed her women friends, her Briarcliff group who had always been closer to her than any man. And ensconced so in their love, loyalty, and closeness over the years, she had never cultivated any other real friends. She'd never needed to. And so she had none. She was emotionally devastated, with no one even to talk to about it. And now there was the threat of Aiden Jannus, back to earth with a frenzy, and bound to create even more chaos in her life.

Her train came roaring into the station. For just a fraction of a second she understood why people had been known to leap down onto the mesmerizing stretch of tracks. She shook it off, and got on board.

A FEW BLOCKS AWAY, in his apartment on Fifth Avenue, Austin Feruzzi was busy packing some things for his trip to Beverly Hills the next day. His trip home. Finally. He had Molly back in his gallery, and now he would have Kate back in his bed.

But there were some loose ends still out there. Dangerous loose ends. Not the least of which was a sober Aiden Jannus.

Chapter 34

"Lane, hello, it's Trish . . . I just had a heart-to-heart with Katie. She told me that she talked to you this afternoon, too. So she's going back to Austin! There was no way I could persuade her to change her mind, or even to wait awhile . . . and I know that you've been trying to talk her out of it, too. But I guess it's a done deal—he's moving back into the house tomorrow.

"Well, we saw it coming, didn't we? There's nothing more we can do now but support her, and love her. God, I'm depressed. Talk to me, Lane. I'll be home tonight. Bye, dear." BEEP. WEDNESDAY, 2:14 P.M.

Lane pressed the ERASE button and shook her head sadly. It was midafternoon on a beautiful day in Carmel. Just a few customers were browsing about in Hamilton House, normal for the after-lunch lull on weekdays.

Yes, she and Trisha had seen it coming. Kate had blinders on when it came to Austin Feruzzi, and it didn't help that she was living in a hazy cocoon of tranquilizers and martinis. Lane and Trisha, ever practical, had been able to do nothing to dissuade Kate from going back to her husband, and now the boat had sailed.

Depressing, yes. And then there was Molly. None of the three had heard from her, nor did they care to. Still, Molly's betrayal was inordinately painful. It was an amputation. The group had lost a "limb" without benefit of anesthetic, and it hurt.

The natural reaction was for the other three to draw even closer together, and they had. Still, Molly's betrayal, hitting them smack in the face as it did, served to make the others just the slightest bit wary, even somewhat distrustful of their longtime friendship. If Molly could carry on a clandestine affair with Kate's husband, what were the others capable of? Did they really know each other after all? It turned out that they hadn't really known Molly.

Was Molly right? Had their close connection, born simply of circumstances two decades ago, outlived its relevance? Was it time to sever their intense dependency upon each other? They had long known that their extremely tight four-way friendship was unique. Perhaps they *should* ease up on the fervid day-to-day communication whereby they knew, cared about, commented on, and often acted upon nearly every thought each other had, and every move each other made. Perhaps each had been too dependent on the mutual caring, the reciprocal comfort of their exclusive group. If they pulled away from it somewhat, then at the very least, betrayal wouldn't hurt so much.

Certainly, what was left of the group could not save Kate, and it was not for lack of trying. Katie appeared to have all her levers directly set on SELF-DESTRUCT. Going back to Austin, setting herself up for more of the same with him, and all the while existing in denial in the iron grip of her continuing substance abuse. And the group that had always been so close, so caring, so wise, the now truncated group that had always cleaved together through the best and the worst of times, had fallen apart—it couldn't save itself, or any one of them.

Lane reminded herself that she didn't need saving—her life was solidly on track and enormously rewarding. Still, she couldn't shake her profound feelings of disillusionment, sadness, and loss.

Chapter 35

"Y OU HAVE YOUR key, Austin—why didn't you just come in?" Kate asked her husband, who was standing meekly on the front doorstep with his luggage at his feet. Meek for Austin Feruzzi, anyway.

"I'm a little nervous, darling—"

"Nonsense. Come in. I'll call Tony to get your bags."

"Can I have a kiss first?"

"Of course," Kate said, braving a smile for the man she'd been separated from for the better part of two months. Truth be told, she was nervous too.

She had been virtually negotiating with Austin, working out the terms of his return. At the top of her list: the physical abuse. She'd made it clear that he had to get therapy. And if ever he raised a hand to her again, she would immediately file for divorce. After that came the cheating, the neglect, the recurrent nastiness, and all the rest of it. It had taken Feruzzi longer this time to turn his wife around, and he'd had to throw a lot more charm, sweet-talk, and humble pie into the mix. Still, Kate was wary, and Austin was very much cognizant of that.

And she was still seething over Molly. Austin had made a monumental case for keeping Molly Adams on as director of their New York gallery. He had managed to convince Kate that their business *needed* Molly in New York, that the woman was irreplaceable.

About his extramarital fling with Molly, he'd told his wife that Molly had been coming on to him for years. She was a lonely, unmarried woman who had never been able to make it in a real relationship with a man, Austin claimed. Molly was a game player, he said. She was flirtatious, seductive. And in a weak moment, at a time when he and Kate were arguing, he'd strayed. He hated himself for it, he told Kate. It had meant nothing to him. But like the classic fatal attraction, when he came to his senses and broke it off with her, Molly got crazy. She became demanding, threatening. And, of course, it all came to a head at the Newmans' hapless dinner party.

However, he'd insisted, firing Molly Adams was simply not an option. He'd had long, carefully deliberated talks with his wife to spell out the reasons. It would take ages to train a new gallery director, if in fact he could find someone one-tenth as qualified for the job as Molly, and Austin had too many balls in the air right now to have to deal with that, too. Since Molly had been there from the day the gallery opened its Madison Avenue doors, she not only *knew* the systems, she'd *set up* the systems, and she was the one who made them work, he said. She knew intimately every piece of artwork in the place, not to mention each one that they had on order, as well as every single item that had been sold in the past.

Molly knew the clients, the art patrons, she even made it her business to get to know the casual customer who dropped in off the street, and most of the time she was able to convert them to loyal Feruzzi clients with her follow-up phone calls, mailings, and invitations to gallery showings. She made it a point to remember names and faces. Molly made each and every customer feel special, Austin had told Kate. She kept meticulous records, and knew what artwork each one had, and in which homes, whether or not the pieces had come from the Feruzzi Galleries. More, she was on a quasi-friendship basis with every living artist the galleries dealt with. And she knew exactly how much leeway the gallery had on the prices of every piece, down to the least of the inventory.

Yes, Molly Adams had made herself indispensable to the Feruzzi Galleries for more than a decade. She was counterpart to Tripp Kendrick in every way. Feruzzi reminded Kate that he'd often said he would like to clone Tripp and Molly into another person exactly like the two of them, for their London gallery. Keeping Molly was absolutely crucial for the business, he assured his wife, and what was good for the business was good for Kate as well. And as always, Kate wanted to believe him.

He had settled back into a purely business relationship with Molly, he said. And when Kate insisted that she never could, never would forgive Molly, he'd said of course he understood that, and it wouldn't matter, because the two women were three thousand miles apart, and would rarely need to cross paths again, if ever. He would see to it, he'd said.

Austin followed his wife into their splendid Mediterranean manse now. His castle. Glancing around, he was gratified that nothing seemed to have changed. He steered Kate upstairs, down the hall, and into their master suite. Closing and locking the big double doors behind them, Austin took her into his arms then, and pulled her close.

"My beautiful Kate," he murmured.

"I'm . . . glad you're home," she said tentatively.

Bending to kiss her then, Austin felt his wife stiffen slightly. "What's wrong, darling?" he asked.

"Nothing . . . I need a little time," she breathed.

"You're my wife," he said, tightening his hold on her. He gently massaged her back as he guided her toward the big four-poster bed.

"Please, Austin," Kate protested weakly.

"Please, *Kate*," he returned. "It's important—"

He didn't hear her reluctant sigh as he kissed her neck, then gently lifted her up onto the bed, while spilling pillows onto the floor. As he unbuttoned her creamy silk blouse, she whispered, "Please . . . get me a glass of wine first, would you?"

"Of course, darling," he said, and he walked over to the small bar area in the master suite. He opened the refrigerator and took out a chilled bottle of Pinot Grigio. He reached into a drawer for a corkscrew, then into a cabinet for a pair of wineglasses. It felt good being in his house, in his bedroom, with all his familiar things around him. And his wife.

He carried the opened bottle and the glasses over to the bedside table, and poured the wine. Handing one of the flutes to Kate, he touched his glass to hers.

"To the future," he said. "To you and me, and to our new life."

Kate closed her eyes and took a long pull at the wine. Relaxing perceptibly, she settled back on the pillows and drained her glass.

"More!" she smiled, offering up the empty goblet. "And come to bed," she said.

———————————

Chapter 36

Bᴜᴛ, Pᴇᴛᴇʀ, it's wonderful that Aiden Jannus has got himself straight. Wonderful for him, and for the Feruzzi Galleries, too—Jannus is practically the franchise. And now that Kate is back with Austin, we have to root for their business, don't we?"

It was pouring in New York, so the midtown streets were even more crowded than usual at early evening rush hour. Trisha and Peter Newman had ducked into Cipriani's on Fifth Avenue for a quiet dinner.

"Jannus won't make it," Peter offered, as he signaled for a waiter in the crowded restaurant.

"But he seems to be doing well—"

"They almost never make it," her husband interrupted, looking squarely at her now.

"But some do—"

"Very few. More than likely it's just a matter of time before Aiden Jannus will be right back out there, boozing and doing drugs."

"Why so cynical, Peter? Maybe Jannus will be among the few who *do* stay sober after rehab. Can't we hope?"

"You can *dream*, darling."

"Well, your pal Austin Feruzzi is certainly no help. I told you I caught him asking Aiden if he wanted a drink the other night."

"Oh, you know Austin—it probably didn't occur to him that there was anything wrong with offering the man a drink."

"*Please*, Peter. Austin has to be more aware than anyone that it's crucial to keep Aiden Jannus away from alcohol."

"Darling, Austin had had a few himself, we talked about that. I'm sure he just wasn't thinking."

"Well, I told Kate that she'd better have words with Austin. Good Lord, he could sabotage the man's recovery!"

"You think one drink would do it?"

"Of course one drink could do it! Jannus is an addict. He needs a support group around him that will help him stay *off* alcohol. And drugs. I even told Jules to leave the brandy out of the soufflé that night."

"I think you're overreacting, dear."

"Peter, I don't understand you on this issue. You've just said yourself that keeping an addict straight after rehab is a huge challenge—"

"It's *his* challenge, Trish. It's the *addict's* challenge. Aiden Jannus has to be responsible for himself, not dependent on others to pull him through this. And as I said, unfortunately they usually fail. And Aiden Jannus is very deep into it—he has spent most of his *life* abusing drugs and alcohol—it's become a part of his *personality*."

"You're right, it's up to him," Trisha said thoughtfully. "Still, we should do what we can to help, don't you think?"

"To a point. We can't be anybody's keepers. But to be candid, *I* don't have much faith in Jannus's recovery because *Austin* doesn't. Austin says the man is already dipping into the stuff, and Austin knows Aiden Jannus better than we do."

Trisha was perplexed. On the subject of Austin Feruzzi, she and her husband had never been anywhere near agreement. She loathed Feruzzi, but she tolerated him because he was back with Kate. Peter seemed to actually enjoy him. Seemed to *like* him, even. And always, he found a way to excuse Feruzzi's behavior, no matter how heinous. Even the wife beating. "Austin needs help," was all that he would say.

But the issue of Aiden Jannus was basic. If you had a friend who was a recovering addict, you didn't encourage him to drink. She couldn't imagine why Peter couldn't see it that way.

"Alright, one more question," she ventured. "Shouldn't Austin *especially* want Jannus healthy and productive?"

"Sweetheart, Austin never sees the big picture. But he's an okay guy. I'm sure he isn't consciously trying to hurl his top artist back into the abyss. He just doesn't think."

Trisha let it go. Austin Feruzzi was back in their lives, because he was back in Kate's life. But it was different now. Where before, Trisha simply disliked the man, now she privately loathed him. But her husband continued to be more than tolerant, more than friendly with Austin, as he'd always been.

Shrugging, she picked up her menu. Years of marriage had taught her that a husband and wife couldn't possibly agree on everything. Maybe it was that *good old boy* thing, she mused, an attitude that seemed still to prevail among prominent, wealthy businessmen, and it died hard.

Chapter 37

I DON'T BELIEVE WHAT I'm seeing," Gregory Hamilton said, *sotto voce,* to his dinner companion. His eyes had settled on a party of three seated several tables away.

"Someone we know?" Maggie Carlson asked a bit anxiously. The two had been making a conscious effort to keep their relationship quiet, at least for now. Carmel was a very small community, and its people took a proprietary interest in their year-round neighbors. Maggie and Greg did not want to promulgate their new relationship until they were sure that it would stick.

They had come over to Pebble Beach tonight for dinner at the famous Inn at Spanish Bay. Now they were sitting in the dimly lit bar, listening to the popular Brazilian trio that played there regularly.

"No, nobody we know," Greg responded absently. "What I'm seeing is a drug deal going down right under my nose."

"Good heavens, are you sure?"

"Oh, yes. Once a cop . . ." Gregory Hamilton had been on the police force in Carmel for thirty years, seventeen of them as its chief.

"But why would they do it *here?*" Maggie asked.

"Why *not* here?" Greg responded, his gaze continuing to peruse the three men who were trading envelopes at a corner table.

"Well, it's so *visible—*"

Greg turned his attention back to Maggie. "They do it *everywhere,*" he told her. "Casual observers just don't *know* what they're observing, and the lowlifes count on that. Besides, there's a particular kind of arrogance that goes with dealing drugs."

"My goodness, should you *do* something about it?"

"No," he smiled, "I'm a civilian now. By the time I could call it in and get some officers over here, they'll be gone. And if I jumped to make a citizen's arrest every time I saw something suspicious going on, people would be saying, 'Poor Greg, he can't let go.' "

Maggie threw back her head and laughed, which delighted him. She was a handsome woman, tall, trim, with angular features and rich sable-brown hair pulled back into a thick, lustrous dancer's braid. Gregory and his wife Marta had known Maggie and Whit Carlson for many years. They hadn't been close, but they'd considered themselves neighbors, as did nearly every year-round resident of tiny Carmel. And nearly everyone in town knew Chief Hamilton, of course, as now they knew his son.

In the two years since Whitney Carlson was killed by a drunk driver in a head-on crash on his way home from a business meeting in Monterey, Carmelites rarely saw Maggie Carlson laugh. Or even go anywhere. She'd kept mostly to her home and her bookstore. Carmel tourists likely thought her cold, aloof, but those who knew her knew that she was a woman changed by grief. Watching her eyes twinkle and her face light up with laughter brought a wide grin to Greg Hamilton's tanned, craggy features, and warmed his heart. They were good for each other, he was sure of that.

"We've been keeping company for seven weeks, Maggie," he said now. "Do you think we could chance a walk on the beach in town?"

"I think so," Maggie smiled, looking pointedly into his clear blue eyes. Gregory read her meaning—she was willing to take a chance on this relationship too.

"Tell you what," he said. "Let's drive back to Carmel and have a nightcap at the Red Lion Tavern."

"Really?"

"Definitely! We'll walk in arm-in-arm, what do you say?"

"Have you told anybody? About us, I mean?"

"No. We agreed not to. I haven't even told Geoff and Lane. Have *you* told anybody?"

"Of course not."

"Then let's go tell the whole darn town!" he said, standing up and offering his hand.

"We won't have to," Maggie beamed mischievously, taking his arm. "If we do walk arm-in-arm, the whole town will be talking about us over coffee at The Tuck Box in the morning!"

Chapter 38

So NICE TO SEE you both," said Victor Drai, proprietor of Drai's romantic French restaurant on La Cienega Boulevard in Los Angeles. It was currently the hottest eatery in town.

"Thanks, Victor," Austin responded, taking Kate's hand across the table.

Victor traveled in the "in" circles from here to New York to Paris and back, and of course he'd known that the Feruzzis had been separated. The *world* knew. Cindy Adams had done a whole column on it, for chrissake. Now that he was back on the inside, Austin was determined that it wouldn't happen again. Kate had finally stopped handing him veiled reminders that one slip, and he was gone. Well, he wouldn't slip. Couldn't afford to. The next time she might really tear up his ticket.

"I'm sending you something special tonight," Victor smiled. Yes, Austin thought, he was definitely back. When Victor Drai sent complimentary appetizers to your table, you were in.

"Why, thank you, Victor," Kate said, gracing him with her dazzling smile. As usual, Austin noted with satisfaction, his wife was easily the most beautiful woman in the room, and this was a tough room.

As Victor walked off to greet other diners, Kate turned her attention to her husband.

"I wanted tonight to be special," she purred. "I have something wonderful to tell you."

"What, darling?"

"Something that is really going to mean a whole new life for us," she teased, sipping her Perrier.

"Being with you again means a whole new life for me, Katie," he rejoined.

"This is something that will guarantee it, I'm sure," she said, smiling mysteriously now.

"What, you've found us a place in Cabo?" They both loved Cabo San Lucas, a gleaming little fishing resort on the Mexican coast, and they'd talked about buying a vacation home there.

"Oh, better," she said dreamily. "Much, much better."

"Come on, sweetheart, tell me—"

"Alright, here goes—I'm pregnant!"

"You're . . . you're *what?*"

"Pregnant, darling. We're going to have a baby. Finally! Dr. Grieg confirmed it yesterday."

"Lloyd Grieg? When . . . when did you suspect—?"

"A few weeks ago, but I wanted to be certain. I'm sure that it happened in New York, on that night that I flew to you from Carmel. You were so loving, so tender—oh, Austin, this is truly a love child."

Austin was stunned. "You're sure . . . ?"

"I'm loving your reaction," Kate laughed. "It's like a Doris Day movie. I'm fine, darling. Dr. Grieg says there's no reason why this shouldn't be a normal, healthy pregnancy."

Austin glanced around, checking whether anyone else in this trendy bistro was tuned in to their conversation. Kate pregnant! Was this a joke? Hadn't he always made it clear to her that he didn't want any more children? She did this to him deliberately, he realized. She knew about birth control, for chrissakes.

". . . and the baby is going to bring all of us, you, me, and Shawn, closer together," she was saying now. Kate looked positively luminous as she prattled on.

He tried not to panic, or worse, to yell at her.

". . . but what do *you* want, darling?" she questioned, looking up at him for a response.

"What—?" he managed.

"I said, I'd love a little girl, but of course another boy would be wonderful, too. A gorgeous Feruzzi boy. We'll know soon. But what do *you* hope it is, a boy or a girl?"

Jesus, Austin thought, good thing they were in a public restaurant—he felt like strangling her. She was killing him with this. He didn't want a girl *or* a boy! He didn't want a *baby!* They had been over this *ad nauseam* for the first five years of their marriage. But then she dropped it. He thought she'd long since gotten over it. Where the hell did this come from now? And without asking him this time, without even goddamn *informing* him that she intended to get pregnant!

He was furious. He wanted his glamorous wife beautiful and fashionable and looking like a million bucks on his arm. He did *not* want her fat and pregnant, then spending all her time skidding around a diaper pail or however they did it now, and mothering a wet, screaming baby who would turn into a bothersome, demanding child. Who would drain him of energy and money for the next twenty years! He'd been there, he'd raised his kids, and so what? He rarely heard from them unless they wanted something from him. To be honest with himself, he didn't even much like them, really, and they certainly never gave a damn about him.

Their smiling waiter came to the table bearing steaming plates of French appetizers. Kate was radiant. Austin had all he could do to rein in the urge to yank her up by the hair and drag her out of there. Give *that* to the columnists! He pulled himself together.

"It's wonderful, darling," he said. Their waiter was arranging dishes on the table.

"This one is for the lady, Victor says—and this for you, monsieur."

"Thank you," Kate said sweetly. And then, also to the waiter, "I'm announcing tonight that I'm pregnant!"

Oh Jesus, Austin thought. Now she's going to tell the fucking world.

"Fabulous, madame," the waiter beamed. "Then you are dining for two, you will enjoy this," he said, setting more dishes on the table before them. "And congratulations to you, Mr. Feruzzi."

"Thank you, Jacques," Katie smiled. "And thank Victor for us, please."

Austin felt like he'd been blindsided. "How soon . . . aah . . . how far are you along?" he managed to get out.

"Ten weeks," she said. "I'm hoping we can take a trip, a little mini honeymoon before I start showing . . ."

Ten weeks, he thought. Still early enough to have an abortion. He had always been able to sweet-talk his wife into anything. Now he had to talk her into getting rid of this damned baby.

He had more than enough crises in his life right now. The whole flap with Tripp Kendrick. His West Coast gallery director was professional, but wary and on his guard. He and his covert lover, Jonathan Valley, *had* to be racking their brains trying to figure out how to keep Feruzzi quiet about the actor's sleazy secret. Easy, Austin thought— just keep the cash coming. God knows, he needed it. Charles DeFarge had been escalating his prices outrageously, billing, overbilling, and dunning the Feruzzi Galleries, all with overtones of tacit threats. And then there was Aiden Jannus, sober now, and talking. Kate's pregnancy was just one more big frigging disaster.

"I have totally given up everything alcoholic, and no more tranquilizers," she was saying now, as she dug heartily into one of Victor Drai's specialties, the creamy veal pastiche. "I like Jo. Just Jo. Or Jo Ellen. Or Joe, for Joseph. What do you think?"

Did she not notice that he was livid? he wondered. Did she not remember that he had ruled this out a long time ago? Hadn't they had an understanding about this? Was she trying to get back at him? Or maybe she was kidding about being pregnant, testing him. Floating a trial balloon to see how it would fly. If it was okay with him, she really *would* get pregnant.

"You haven't touched your food," she offered now. "It's truly luscious. Victor is a genius. It's no wonder this place is packed every night . . ."

Victor, Austin thought. The waiter would mention it to Victor, of course, and the whole Westside would know about it by tomorrow. Then the papers would print it. "Beautiful Kathryn Spenser Feruzzi is pregnant at forty . . ." They never printed Kate's name without putting "beautiful" in front of it. Right now he felt like wringing her beautiful neck.

"... like, look at this one, Leeza, this piece of shit on the screen—I don't even remember painting that damn thing!"

"Mr. Jannus, we have to bleep out any profanity, so if you would please watch that—"

"Sorry, darlin'."

"Thank you. Do you mean you might have been so drugged out that you can't remember doing that painting?"

"Well, at first I thought I just didn't remember—I mean, I've been more or less stoned for about twenty years. But then I have to wonder, how come I know most of my paintings down to the last detail, yet some of them look like I never even did them?"

"Are you saying you think somebody else did them?"

"Maybe."

"But who would do them, and how? And why?"

"Who the hell knows, Leeza. You're really pretty. Are you married?"

"Mr. Jannus, please ... look at the painting up on the monitor now—it's one of your very famous ones—called Twilight. Do you remember doing that one?"

"Well, of course I remember doing that one—it's huge—it practically took up my whole barn, my studio in Sag Harbor. But y'know ... there are some parts of it that I couldn't have done. Like that tree down in the lower left corner. This is a nighttime, starry sky piece, right? So why the hell would I put a big ol' green leafy tree in it? Huh?"

"So you're telling us that you did parts of Twilight, *but not all of it?"*

"You think I'm nuts, don't you, honey. Well, maybe I am nuts. Maybe two decades of toot and shit fried half my brain cells, I don't know. What do you think?"

"I have no idea, Mr. Jannus—let's hear what our studio audience thinks—"

"Call me Aiden—wanna have dinner with me tonight?"

"Mr. Jannus, if you'll just remain seated right there, I'm going to walk into our studio audience and let them ask you some questions."

"Sure thing, honey."

"We are talking to brilliant American contemporary artist Aiden Jannus, and first off, I want to apologize to·you at home because we are having to bleep out so many of his words and phrases, but I'm sure that you are very likely familiar with Mr. Jannus's . . . uh . . . colorful language.

"Also, my apologies to all of you here in studio today, because you have to hear it. I hope no one is terribly offended by it.

"Aiden Jannus came on the program today to discuss his recent successful drug rehabilitation treatment, and he has been making some startling statements—you just heard him say that he thinks there's a lot of artwork out there with his signature on it that he didn't paint! Or didn't paint in its entirety.

"Is Aiden Jannus just being his old, mischievous self with us, or is this a real scandal in the art world? Let's hear from you, audience . . ."

Austin Feruzzi sat in front of the large-screen television set in his den in the mansion on Lexington, watching the morning *Leeza* show and quietly seething. Kate had told him she'd caught some promos on NBC saying that artist Aiden Jannus would be on today, discussing his drug and alcohol recovery. Jannus had always been hot copy, and now he was showing up all over the press, sober and talking about his rehab.

Austin sat with his eyes trained on the set. He couldn't believe what he was hearing now. Jannus was telling Leeza Gibbons and her huge television audience that there seemed to be much too much Aiden Jannus artwork out there, and in fact some of the stuff didn't even look to him like he painted it.

Kate walked into the den. "Oh good, you found the show that Jannus is on," she said.

"The sonofabitch is either still doing drugs, or he's gone completely off his rocker," Austin muttered.

"What do you mean?"

"He's talking some fucking nonsense about not doing some of the artwork that has his name on it. Fact is, he was just too out of it to remember."

"Oh, everybody knows that Aiden Jannus is outlandish," Kate said. "He always has been. Just because he's sober doesn't mean that he's not still eccentric. It's part of his charm."

"What about my clients who paid big bucks for his stuff, and now they're hearing him say that he never painted it!"

"Nobody's going to believe him—he's just being Jannus. His shenanigans just help to keep him in the public eye, and keep his artwork selling. I've always suspected that he knows exactly what he's doing."

"But this is *outrageous*," Austin fumed. "I have to get to him—tell him to knock this shit off!"

"Oh, it's just his latest craziness," Kate repeated dismissively. "If this turns into the current controversy swirling around Aiden Jannus, it'll just make him an even hotter commodity, it always has. I wouldn't worry about it."

"What do *you* know," he hurled at her. "I'm his rep. My company stands behind him—"

"*Our* company," she corrected him. "Austin, I came by to tell you that I'm having lunch with some friends," Kate said then.

"Oh? What friends?" he asked, without taking his eyes off the television show still in progress. People from Leeza Gibbons's studio audience were gushing over Jannus. Nobody seemed to be taking his charges seriously, his careless accusations that somebody else could have painted his masterworks.

"Nobody you know—members of the committee on the dinner

dance for MOCA. I'll be back later this afternoon." With that, Kate turned and left the den.

Austin was riveted to the *Leeza* show and her capricious guest. Aiden Jannus was still ranting on, still saying that he didn't paint this, and he didn't paint that. People from the audience were paying homage to him, loving him, and laughing at his antics. They got the artist laughing too. And Leeza was laughing. It was all one big silly joke. Austin Feruzzi felt a blazing headache coming on.

Chapter 40

"HI, LANE—NOTICE ANYTHING?" Liz asked. She had just come back into the shop from lunch.

"Umm . . . new haircut!"

"Had a trim on my lunch hour—but I don't mean that."

"New skirt? No, I've seen that one before—"

"The British pub table!" Liz exclaimed. Lane's eyes immediately jumped to where the small, ornate three-legged table had stood for the past year.

"Where is it?" she asked grimly.

"I *sold* it!" Liz whooped. "You know that Mrs. Twombley was in three times this week, looking at it for her daughter's entryway. Well, she came this morning with her Range Rover and hauled it away!"

Lane let out a mighty sigh of relief. "Oh Lord," she managed, "I thought you were going to tell me it got stolen!"

The shoplifting at Hamilton House had stopped several weeks before, as abruptly as it had begun. Lane and Liz dared to hope that the perpetrator had perhaps left the area, and it was over.

"Please," Liz laughed, "I don't think our *perp,* as Geoff would call him, could have made off with a heavy cast-iron table without our noticing, do you?"

"Who knows?" Lane groused. "That turn-of-the-century wall hutch disappeared, and that was no easy feat. And the little painting that Molly Adams did was snatched right off the wall." Actually, when that painting disappeared, Lane had found it symbolic. Molly was out of her life. Now this daily reminder of her former friend was gone too.

"You're right," Liz was saying. "How long has it been now?"

"Since we haven't lost any merchandise? Let's see," Lane said, opening a ledger book. "The last item that vanished was my beloved little sterling silver 'Bacchus' flask, and that was on August nineteenth, a Tuesday. At least that's when we noticed that it was gone."

Liz rapped her knuckles on an old oak display cabinet. "The shoplifting's stopped," she said. "Knock wood."

The phone rang. It was the private line on Lane's desk. She picked it up.

"Lane, hi, it's Trisha. Got a minute, or should I call back and talk to the machine?"

"Hi darling—no, I'm fine. Lizzie just got back from lunch."

"It's about Kate—"

"Now what?" Lane demanded, expecting the worst.

"Has she mentioned someone named Byron Lassen to you?"

"Yes . . . an art patron, I think—owner of that big frame manufacturing company, Crystal Artworks."

"Right. Well, I think our Katie has eyes for this Mr. Lassen, Lane."

"Oh, come on, Trish! We couldn't *pry* her away from Austin, and God knows we tried. And now she's having his baby!"

"Yes, but . . . I'm getting major vibes that she's interested in this man for reasons other than their mutual passion for art."

"Has she said something?"

"No, but as you know, with Katie, you always have to read the subtext."

"And . . . ?"

"And she gets all dreamy and girlish when she talks about him, like she used to get in college when she was interested in a new man, remember? And she mentions him much too often."

"Wishful thinking, Trish. Kate will never leave Austin. I've given up on that. Is this man single?"

"Oh, yes. She's managed to let me know that. I'm telling you, Lane, she's got a schoolgirl crush on this Byron Lassen. Next time you talk to her, listen with your third eye." Lane laughed. Trisha loved mixing metaphors.

"Good, let her have a crush. She deserves a pleasant diversion. If I were married to Austin Feruzzi, I'd probably kill him. A crush is healthier."

Liz had come over to Lane's desk with some invoice sheets in her hand.

"Trisha, I've got to go now—but I will definitely have my antenna up when I talk to Katie."

"You'll see," Trisha promised. "Love you, darling. Bye now."

Lane hung up the phone and thought about Kate for a minute. Since she'd found out that she was pregnant, instead of being ecstatic, she seemed to Lane to be somewhat distracted, unhappy even. Lane made a mental note to give her a call, as soon as she finished up with Liz.

Chapter 41

Y OU HAVE NO IDEA how beautiful you are, do you?" Byron Lassen wondered aloud, smiling across the table at Kate.

"I never much think about it—"

"Then let me tell you, as an avid admirer of art and all things exquisite, you are the most beautiful woman I have ever known in my life."

Kate had visibly blushed at that. Now, replaying the conversation over in her mind, she felt herself reddening again.

She and Byron had lunched downtown at Café Pinot today, a popular garden spot with outdoor dining on the grounds of the landmark Los Angeles Public Library. The library and restaurant were across the street from MOCA, L.A.'s extraordinary Museum of Contemporary Art, where the two had spent some time browsing before lunch.

For Kate, it had been an altogether enjoyable few hours. She had felt particularly lighthearted and cheerful at lunch, and the mood lingered. True, she didn't know him well, but Byron Lassen seemed to be a man who *did* listen, who *did* actually seem to care about what she had to say. Whatever it was about him, he made her feel good about herself.

He also just happened to be bright, witty, charming, tall, well-built, and extremely good looking, with his angular features and wheat-colored hair, and the most incredible deep azure-blue eyes. And *sexy.* she noted to herself. And he certainly seemed to be attracted to *her.* Was she being really silly? Of course she was, she knew that. But still, Byron Lassen was something lovely for her to think about these days, and she needed that.

Now, as she maneuvered her black Mercedes coupe westbound on the Santa Monica Freeway toward Beverly Hills and home, reality set in. Even though she knew that Austin wasn't there, that he had gone to New York the night before, still, the persistent dark cloud overhead that had been dogging her of late returned as she got closer to their house, her world.

Since that night a little more than a week ago when she had told Austin that he was going to be a father, he had reverted to being uncommunicative and churlish again. Clearly, he did not want this baby, and the prospect of an unwanted child seemed to have propelled him completely out of the peaceful, loving period that they'd been enjoying since she had taken him back this time.

Well, loving in the *early* weeks, she allowed to herself. Still, *peaceful* was a quality she had come to be grateful for over the years with Austin. A quality she would *settle* for.

Today, though, she had to wonder if she and Austin would ever reach peaceful terrain again. Even more self-revelatory, she wondered if she even *wanted* that. Wondered if she even *wanted* to continue on this roller-coaster ride with Austin Feruzzi, from loving, to peaceful, to sullen, to angry and violent—and then back to loving again, and so on.

Though she had paid little attention at the time, now some of what she'd learned in her concentrated therapy in Carmel had begun to raise its disquieting head—basic things, like the profile of the typical batterer: for most of them, the therapist had intoned, it was not a matter of *if,* it was a matter of *when* he reverted to type. It was as if, now that Austin had his wife back, he didn't have to be nice to her anymore. And, she had to admit to herself, it had been ever thus.

Worse, Austin seemed actually resentful of the baby inside her, this baby that she dearly loved and had been pinning her hopes on. Her "delicious plan" had apparently backfired with her husband.

Austin had always played her emotions like a yo-yo. After his last period of distancing, culminating with the devastating beating, came their recent closeness—down, up, and now she was dashed down again. At a time that should be one of the happiest of her life, she'd been feeling vulnerable, weepy, devastated of late. Her obstetrician attributed her low moods to the normal hormonal changes in pregnancy. She knew better. Her doctor said that she needed vitamins and rest. *She* knew that she needed to be appreciated and loved.

Ironic, her husband flew in to New York last night, and she'd had no desire to go with him. She remembered that night back in July when she'd so wanted to make the trip with him, and he didn't want her there. Didn't want her to get in the way of his base little trysts with Molly, she knew now. Well, he had invited her to go with him this time, but she'd declined. The fact was, she was enormously excited about her lunch date with Byron Lassen today, which she had planned, knowing that Austin would be out of town.

Her thoughts drifted back to the fascinating Mr. Lassen. She had met him at a museum fund-raiser at MOCA, which was why they both thought it would be fun to wander back there today. They had definitely connected back then. There was no denying the strong chemistry between the two. She wanted him to be her friend, she thought. She wanted him in her life.

But she found herself thinking about him too much, realizing that she wanted something more than friendship from him. She told herself that she was being ridiculous. It was her unhappiness with Austin that was making her dream up something between her and Byron Lassen that simply wasn't there.

They'd had some phone conversations, she and Byron, and a couple of lunches together since. His wife had died three years ago, of breast cancer, and he hadn't yet been able to even think about another woman, he said. So he didn't date. Kate decided that their attraction to each other was very probably mutual loneliness.

Still, since her relationship with her husband had taken its latest steep spiral downward, she couldn't seem to get Byron Lassen off her mind. *She* had called *him* to make this lunch date today. This *friendly* lunch date. Only to find out, today, that Byron Lassen stirred up a raging sexual surge in her that she had truly thought was long dead. She smiled. Dormant, maybe, but certainly not dead, she'd realized today.

And although she didn't know him well, she was somehow comforted by his reputation. By all accounts, Byron Lassen was different from Austin Feruzzi. He was well-respected. He was known as a good man. Generous. Caring. He had *integrity,* people said.

Suddenly, driving through tony Beverly Hills toward home, Kate was hit with another pivotal self-realization. After twelve years with Austin Feruzzi, *character issues* were extremely important to her now.

Chapter 42

"Hi," Maggie said with a sunny smile, greeting Greg at her front door. "Come on into the kitchen—I'm cooking."

As always when he set foot inside a place for the first time, Gregory Hamilton made an instant assessment. Maggie's lovely little English house in Carmel's main grid was orderly, comfortable-looking, tasteful, very clean—

He caught himself. Reminded himself that he was not here to make a report. Once a cop, he thought. It was just a habit, held too long.

He followed her into her cheerful kitchen. This was the first time that she had invited him into her home, the home that she had shared for many years with Whitney Carlson, her deceased husband. He couldn't shake the vague awareness that tonight was some kind of test, for both of them.

"You said white, didn't you?" he asked then, holding out a bottle of Boulay Macon-Villages white burgundy. "They told me at the Cornucopia that this was terrific."

"*You* are terrific," she smiled up at him, accepting the bottle of wine. "I'll keep it chilled until we're ready for it. How about a cocktail first?"

She seemed comfortable. He couldn't believe how nervous he was. Silly, he thought. But definitely nervous, like a schoolboy out on his very first date. Actually, it was an interesting feeling.

"I'm going to have a Kir Royale," she said, taking a bottle of champagne out of the refrigerator.

"Sounds great," he returned, with perhaps a little too much enthusiasm, given the fact that he had no idea what a Kir Royale was.

Maggie poured the drinks, handed one to him, touched his glass with hers in welcome, and went over to the oven to check on dinner.

"What smells so good?" he asked her now.

"Beef Stroganoff," she answered, peering through the lighted glass window at the bubbling casserole inside. "One of my specialties."

Greg dropped his lanky frame onto a bar stool at the end of the chopping-block island, and took a welcome sip of his drink.

"What's in this?" he asked, just a little sheepishly.

"Champagne and cassis, with a twist of lemon. Don't worry, most men never heard of it."

"Including me," he laughed.

He was beginning to relax a little. He could see that she had gone to a lot of trouble for him, and that made him feel a little embarrassed and at the same time awfully good. It occurred to him that he had lived alone for a long time. He'd almost forgotten what a woman's attention in a home was like. Nice. Maggie set an appetizing plate of hors d'oeuvres on the bar, and settled on a stool beside him.

Their chat was easy, as it always was. They finished their drinks, and she led him into the small dining room. A round maple table was set for two, with British bone china, creamy linen, and gleaming crystal. He knew about a beautifully set table, because Marta had taught him. And candles. Maggie picked up a small box of matches from the sideboard and lit the candles.

"Sit down," she said, with a flourish toward his place, then she disappeared back into the kitchen.

This was going well, he thought. Then he shook his head, laughing at himself. When was the last time he'd behaved like an adolescent? And suffered this kind of insecurity? That tonight should go well was very important to him, he guessed.

Maggie came back into the dining room with a basket of warm dinner rolls and two chilled salads. Perfect. The Stroganoff was delicious. His wine was everything it was promised to be.

But something was wrong. Greg had no idea what it was, but his instincts told him that something was wrong.

"Let's have dessert in the living room," Maggie said.

"Dessert?"

"Of course, dessert," she laughed. "I made it. It's light. You'll love it. Come with me, then I'll get coffee."

He followed her into the combination living room and study. She settled him on one of the couches, and went back into the kitchen to get the dessert.

Alone in the room, Gregory looked around. Suddenly, he realized with a sharp jolt what was so terribly wrong. Shock waves rolled through his body, and he thought for a minute that he was going to be sick. When Maggie came back into the room, he was on his feet.

"I have to leave," he said. And before Maggie could put down the tray of dessert and coffee that she was carrying, he was out the door.

Chapter 43

"CONTROVERSIAL AMERICAN ARTIST FOUND DEAD
TONIGHT—DETAILS ON THE NEWS AT ELEVEN."

Molly couldn't believe what she was seeing and hearing on television. It was a news "tease," one of those four-second blurbs that the anchors do to get you to watch the newscast coming up. She closed her eyes tight, and tried to get her head to stop reeling. It couldn't be, could it? It must be somebody else.

It was ten minutes to eleven. She'd come home from work and spent the last four hours painting in her small makeshift studio. And the work had gone well tonight, so she'd been feeling good. Well, as good as she ever felt these days, which in reality was barely okay, but better than miserable. Due for a break, she'd flicked on the television set to catch the news.

"WORLD-FAMOUS ARTIST FOUND DEAD IN HIS STUDIO
IN SAG HARBOR—DETAILS AT ELEVEN."

There it was again. And Sag Harbor! It *had* to be him. Molly felt paralyzed, her eyes riveted to the small television screen perched up on a cluttered shelf in her studio. Now the news "open" started, with pictures of the program's personalities floating across a glittering nightscape of New York. Then one of the anchors came on full-screen, a box over his left shoulder depicting Aiden Jannus, and he began the lead story:

"AMERICA'S GENIUS BUT OFTEN TROUBLED POSTMOD-
ERN IMPRESSIONIST ARTIST AIDEN JANNUS, THIRTY-
EIGHT YEARS OLD, WAS FOUND DEAD IN HIS STUDIO
EARLIER TONIGHT BY TWO FRIENDS WHO SAY THAT
THEY WERE CONCERNED BECAUSE HE HAD FAILED TO
MEET THEM FOR A DINNER ENGAGEMENT. OUR RE-
PORTER, PATRICK NOLAN, IS LIVE AT THE ARTIST'S
SAG HARBOR STUDIO . . . WHAT HAVE YOU LEARNED,
PATRICK?"

Now the live shot widened out to show yellow crime scene tape strung
around the periphery of Aiden Jannus's property in Sag Harbor. Molly
could see the side of his rambling gray-green clapboard house, and the
familiar rustic unpainted wood barn that was Jannus's beachfront studio. Various officials were milling around within the cordoned-off
area, and crowds had gathered outside the yellow tape, many standing
quietly, some pushing to get a better look, several being interviewed by
reporters. Aiden's scruffy, ancient golden retriever, Vincent, favoring
an arthritic hind leg, was pacing around slowly near the front door of
the studio. Molly couldn't breathe.

Backing away from the television set, doubling over, and wrapping
her arms around her stomach, she sank weakly down onto the stool
that was perched in front of her easel. She could feel herself close to
becoming physically sick. The reporter was droning on:

". . . AFTER SUCCESSFULLY COMPLETING A THIRTY-FIVE-
DAY COURT-ORDERED DRUG-REHABILITATION PROGRAM
IN SOUTHERN CALIFORNIA, JANNUS HAD PROCLAIMED
HIMSELF DRUG- AND ALCOHOL-FREE, AND GRATEFUL
FOR HIS NEW LEASE ON LIFE, AN IMMENSELY TALENTED
AND PRODUCTIVE LIFE THAT HAD EARNED HIM, BY SOME
REPORTS, AN ESTIMATED . . ."

My God, what happened to him? Molly screamed aloud at the television set. When did this happen? Why hadn't anyone called her? Did
anyone know? Did Austin know?

Now the reporter was interviewing two men, purportedly the two
friends with whom Jannus was scheduled to meet at Borelli's

Seafood House in town at eight o'clock. One was saying that they waited for him, called his house, called his studio, then went ahead and had dinner without him. His companion said that he had tried calling Jannus at home again at about 9:45, before the two men left the restaurant.

"I kept thinking, 'Oh, it's only Aiden being Aiden. Who knows what he's up to. He probably forgot all about our dinner . . .'" the other man was telling the reporter.

"No," insisted his friend, "I'd talked to him late this afternoon, and he said he wanted to talk to us, Jules and me—we've both known Aiden for years, you see, through thick and thin. He was as sober as you and me, and he seemed to be upset . . . so we made a plan to meet at Borelli's at eight—"

Molly tried frantically to come up with a plan of action of her own. It was three hours earlier in California, just after eight o'clock. The gallery would be closed. Getting up, she snatched up the phone on her small drafting table, and punched in Feruzzi's number at home in Beverly Hills. Kate's number, the one she knew as well as her own, but hadn't dialed for months. The ringing blared in her ear. Then a voice answered, sending her heart bouncing crazily in her chest. Kate!

"Hello?" Katie's sweet, musical voice.

"Hello, Kate," Molly began tentatively. "This is Molly . . . I . . . is Austin—" *Click!*

Kate had hung up. My God, this was a nightmare. She pressed RE-DIAL. This time the line kept ringing until the answering machine picked up. Molly listened to Kate's familiar outgoing message. She hadn't changed it:

> *"Hello, this is the Feruzzi residence . . . please leave your message at the sound of the tone."*

At the beep, Molly began to talk, choked up a little, then went on:

> *". . . just this minute heard about Aiden Jannus's death . . . they're saying the cause is not known, or not being revealed . . . I need to talk to Austin . . . please, are you there, Austin?"*

She hung up the phone, stumbled around the spare bedroom that doubled as her studio and office, and booted up her computer. Called up her Rolodex. Found Tripp Kendrick's file. Then dialed his number at home. After a few rings and beeps, an unfamiliar male voice came on the line.

"Hello."

"Hello, is Tripp Kendrick there?"

"Who's calling?"

"It's Molly Adams in New York—"

"Hold on."

Molly could hear voices and music in the background. After a couple of minutes, she heard Tripp's voice.

"Molly . . . hi . . . is this you?"

"Yes, Tripp . . . I just heard about Jannus! What—?"

"Jannus? Oh Jesus, *now* what?" Tripp asked wearily.

"He's dead, Tripp—"

"Dead!"

There was silence on the line. Tripp was obviously stunned. After a beat, he said, "Molly, where are you?"

"I'm at home—"

"What time is it there?"

"It's after eleven . . ."

"Look, Molly, I'm at a friend's house . . . at a party. My calls are being forwarded here. It's noisy—I can barely hear you. I'm going to find someplace quiet and call you back, okay?"

"Sure."

"Give me your number."

Molly recited her number, then heard him hang up the phone. As soon as she set the receiver down, her line began ringing. She picked up again.

"Hello, is this Molly Adams?"

"Uh . . . yes—"

"Miss Adams, this is John Ruiz of *The Washington Post*—we understand that you are the director of the New York gallery that represents Aiden Jannus, and—"

Molly hung up the phone. She was terrified. It rang again. Trembling, she picked it up.

"Who is it?" she demanded. Listening, she let out a breath. It was Tripp.

"Tell me everything," he said.

She heard herself babbling what she knew. ". . . He was supposed to meet two men for dinner in town . . . when he didn't show up, they went out to his studio. They went inside—you know Aiden never locked his door. And they found him . . . dead . . . They're not saying what, or how . . . of course there's a police investigation—"

"Do you know what time it . . . it happened?"

"No. Tripp, can you find Austin, please? Make sure he knows? I called his house, but . . ."

"Austin is *there*. He's in New York—"

"What? He didn't tell me he was coming . . . he hasn't checked in—"

"He went in last night," Tripp said. "He took a red-eye."

"Did he have business—?"

"In fact," Tripp said quietly, "he said he had to talk to Aiden."

Chapter 44

TRIPP KENDRICK HADN'T slept all night. Once the news broke, his phone never stopped ringing, legions of people wanting to know anything he could tell them about Aiden Jannus. Including press from around the world. He had no idea how they got his private home number, but he supposed that they had their ways. He wouldn't tell them anything. Also among the many callers were two NYPD detectives. He *couldn't* tell *them* anything.

It was after seven o'clock in the morning now, after ten in New York, and he still had not been able to reach Austin Feruzzi. Feruzzi would let him know how he wanted the press handled.

Unconfirmed reports said that Aiden Jannus had more than likely died of a drug overdose. Probably drugs combined with alcohol, was the rumor. Final toxicology results would take weeks, but witnesses leaked out that the death scene had the look and smell of a person who had OD'd.

Funny, Tripp thought, he had always half-expected this day to come, in the past. But not now. Not now when Jannus had just completed rehab, and had been heralding to all who would listen that he was clean and sober, and intended to stay that way. Tripp knew Aiden to be an oddly disciplined man, even though he did not present that way to the world at large. And that he seemed fiercely and publicly committed to his sobriety. In his own self-absorbed style, Aiden Jannus had appeared dedicated to this latest avowed tear that he was on, this crusade to change his life. It seemed unlikely to Tripp that the man would just fall off the wagon willy-nilly.

Meantime, the coterie of people who inhabited Aiden Jannus's world were stepping up to tell their stories. There were the two men who were supposed to meet the artist for dinner last night—one said that when he had talked with Jannus late that afternoon, the man was definitely sober. Having known Aiden for ten years, he certainly knew the difference, he'd insisted. Others had come forward, saying that they had spoken to him too. His housekeeper had left at around five o'clock, and he was fine then, she said. He was in his studio, working.

The details surrounding Aiden Jannus's death were being trumpeted on all the network morning shows. ABC's *Good Morning, America* had a psychologist on who worked with recovering addicts. He explained what could happen if someone had a big heroin habit, and abruptly stopped using the drug. Went into rehab. Got sober. Then weakened and fell off the program, shot some heroin. His body is no longer used to it, is not acclimated to accept it, and the amount that used to just get him high could kill him now. He could, this mythical drug addict, go into immediate pulmonary edema and die instantly, said the television doctor.

He told a story about a recovering addict he knew who had been drug-free for eleven years, and in fact, had become a drug addiction counselor. One of the dictums that addicts in a Twelve Step program are given is to go home, round up all the drugs in the house, and flush them down the toilet. And usually they will send a counselor home with the addict, to provide moral support, and to make sure that he does it. Well, this counselor, eleven years clean and sober, went home with an addict, helped him gather up his stash of drugs, and then they both caved. Shot some heroin. For the counselor, his body couldn't tolerate it. For him, the fix was an overdose. He died instantly.

Tripp was monumentally depressed. He went through the motions—shaved, showered, had coffee, scanned the morning papers, all of which headlined the story. He pulled clothes out of his closet, while his phone continued to ring, and the television shows droned on in the background. Now there was a talk show on, and the topic was Aiden Jannus's death, and the tragedy of drugs in America. A war we were losing, the host assured the audience, and losing some of our best and brightest in the process.

Tripp could hear the answering machine in his den picking up one call after another. People he had no stomach for right now. He had to open the gallery at ten. That was going to be another ordeal. Those who had not been able to get ahold of his home number would be calling the gallery. Or worse, converging there. Most likely there were press camped out in front of the place right now, stopping traffic, clogging up Rodeo Drive. Tripp shuddered. Then he heard the voice of Austin Feruzzi blaring from the answering machine:

> *"It's me, Tripp—it's Austin—pick up, Tripp. Jesus Christ, pick up the phone—"*

Tripp grabbed the phone in his bedroom and sank into a chair. He could hear his own heart pounding, feel beads of sweat rolling off his forehead.

"Yeah, Austin. What the hell happened?"

"What *happened*! The asshole is dead, that's what happened."

"Drugs?"

"Of course, drugs. What the hell else would it be? Listen, Tripp, don't talk to anybody, anybody at all."

"Two New York detectives called. Last night. I *had* to talk to them. Didn't I?"

"So what did you say?"

"Well . . . nothing, really. I don't *know* anything, Austin."

"Did you tell them I went to New York to talk to him?"

"No—it didn't come up. It seems a *bunch* of people talked to Aiden yesterday. Did *you?*"

"No. I was going to see him today. Too late."

Chapter 45

KATE HAD NO IDEA that her husband was even in the house until she heard his voice drifting out from his den, talking on the telephone. She thought she'd heard him mention Jonathan Valley's name. He hung up the phone just as she got to the room.

"Austin," she said to him, "I thought you weren't coming home until tonight."

"I came home early," he answered, without looking up at her standing in the doorway.

It was not yet nine in the morning. She was still dressed in a creamy white nightgown and peignoir, her face glowing with no makeup, her dark auburn hair tied up in a satin ribbon.

"I'm so sorry about Aiden," she said softly. "So much life, so much talent gone—"

"How about so much *money* gone! *My* money. *That's* what's gone!"

"Oh, Austin . . . he was thirty-eight years old. And he had finally straightened up, seemed to be doing so well . . . it's so terribly tragic. Surely you must—"

"Surely I must *jack-shit*!" Austin snarled.

Kate recoiled. Austin had become very nearly unbearable to live with ever since she'd told him of her pregnancy. And evidently today, even after the sad death of a longtime friend, was to be no exception.

"I thought that you'd have to stay in New York and help with arrangements—"

"Why? I'm his gallery rep. I'm not his family."

"Does he *have* family?

"How the hell do *I* know?"

Kate had heard as much as she cared to brook at this hour of the morning. Or at any time. She'd been telling herself lately that if it weren't for the baby, she would be very near the point of leaving him for good. She turned on her heel and left the room.

"Just a minute, Kate," he called after her. "I want to ask you something."

Kate came back into the doorway and looked squarely at him, her face registering a distinct look of disdain. "What?" she asked.

"Don't give me that look like I'm some kind of gutter trash," he barked at her.

"Austin, what do you want to know?" she leveled at him.

"I want to know *this,*" he roared at her, raising an arm in a defiant gesture. "I want to know who the hell is *Byron Lassen?*"

"He's . . . he's a friend of mine. From the museum group. We're working together on the childhood leukemia dinner."

Austin said nothing. His phone was ringing. He grabbed it off the hook, and in the same movement, slammed it back down on its cradle. And continued to glare stonily at his wife.

"Why?" Kate asked.

"Why? Because people are telling me that you're fucking some guy named Byron Lassen, that's why."

"Austin, stop this right now. Shawn's in the kitchen having breakfast . . . he'll hear you, for God's sake—"

"Oh, the kid came home? Must've heard I was out of town, huh?" Feruzzi's voice had risen to a yell. "Well, let's get him in here. Maybe *he* can tell me if this Byron Lassen has been sleeping in my bed!"

Kate turned and left the room again, and hurried down the hall. In high-heeled satin slippers, she rushed up the stairs toward their bedroom. Feruzzi leaped out of his chair and loped down the long corridor and up the stairs after her.

"Don't you come near me," Kate threw back at him.

"You're my wife! I want some damn answers," he demanded.

Shawn had come out of the kitchen and was standing at the bottom of the winding marble staircase, school backpack in one hand, staring at the two of them, looking terrified.

"Shawn, darling, please go on to school," Kate said to her son, her voice cracking. She knew that this would send him right back to his father's apartment tonight.

Christina came out of the kitchen and put a hand on the boy's shoulder. "Here's your lunch, Shawn," she said. Tucking a brown bag into his backpack, she steered him toward the front door. "Do you want me to walk with you to the bus stop?" she asked him, a little helplessly.

Shawn broke from her grasp and fled out the double doors. Christina followed the boy out, closing the big front doors behind her. *Christina doesn't want to hear it either,* Kate thought. Tears started rolling down her cheeks as she turned and continued making her way up the staircase. Her husband was right on her heels.

"You're screwing him, right?" he screamed at her now. Kate put both hands over her ears and cried, *"Stop it! Stop it, Austin!"*

He reached for her, his hands grasping at the slippery satin fabric of her gown. Kate shrugged him off with her body, slapped at his hands with hers, all the while continuing to climb the stairs. He grabbed at her hair then, ripping the ribbon off, getting a solid grip on her long, heavy tresses. Kate screeched. She whirled around and landed a sharp elbow in his eye, hard.

"Bitch!" he bellowed. "Who else are you fucking? Byron Lassen and who else?"

With that, Feruzzi hooked a brawny arm around her neck and yanked her down toward him. With his other hand he started to choke her. As Kate tried to beat him off with both hands and all the strength she could muster, one of her heels caught in the slats of the wrought-iron handrail. Trying to yank it out and hold Austin off at the same time, she felt her other foot going out from under her. With terrible force, she hurtled down the long flight of stone steps, rolling over and over again, until she landed in a crumpled heap, motionless, at the bottom.

Chapter 46

"Hello, Jonathan . . . this is Austin Feruzzi. Your Jannus is ready. The Aiden Jannus painting that you commissioned was finished by the artist. But the thing is, this was the last painting that Jannus did before he died. So it's going to cost you a hell of a lot more than we agreed on. A hell of a lot more. I can't let you have it for a million—it's three million now. You don't have to take it, of course, but if you don't want it, you'll forfeit your deposit. Up to you. Call me, and we'll discuss." BEEP. TUESDAY, 8:53 A.M.

"Can you believe this motherfucker?" Jonathan Valley pronounced with a low, angry snarl.

"I'd believe anything, Jon," Tripp said, albeit astonished at the call. He'd had no idea that Aiden Jannus had even *started* Valley's huge commission, let alone finished it.

The two were sitting in the actor's mahogany-paneled office in his Beverly Hills house on Summit Drive. It was the middle of the day, but Jon had summoned Tripp from the gallery to come over and listen to Austin Feruzzi's message. He'd called Tripp on his cell phone. The snake probably had a tap on the gallery phone lines, Jon had said. To see what kind of dirt he could pick up in conversations between Tripp and him. Just to flesh out his story for the tabloids.

"What the hell kind of man is he, Tripp?" he asked now. "His good friend Aiden Jannus is dead, and he's squeezing more money out of the poor sonofabitch before the body is cold. His wife is in the hospital, and from everything I hear, Feruzzi is the one who put her there. And now he's letting me know that I'd better come up with three million dollars on a Tuesday afternoon, or he'll ruin my life—"

"You already paid him half a million up front—"

"Yeah, and you heard him. If I don't take the painting at his newly inflated price, he'll keep my deposit."

"That's not legal. You two agreed on a price, it's in *writing*—"

"Legal! What a joke! What am I going to do? Sue his ass?"

"It's extortion—"

"No shit," Jonathan spit out. "It's not the half a mil, Tripp. The man will never stop gouging me, and if someday the trough runs dry, he'll kill me. I'll be as dead as if he cut me up in bloody bits and fed me to the sharks. He intends to keep me working for *him* for the rest of my productive life."

"You know, this *will* be a very valuable painting—"

"Not the point, Tripp," Jon cut him off. "After this painting, there'll be something else. Or there won't *have* to be something else. He'll just start dunning me outright."

"What do you want to do, Jon?"

"About *him*?"

"No, about the painting."

"That's easy. I'll take it. The big question is, what do I want to do about *him*?"

Chapter 47

PLEASE STOP CRYING, Kate," Elgin Horner implored. "It'll be okay . . . don't cry, my sweet Katie."

"My baby," she whimpered. "My little baby . . ."

"Shhh," Elgin soothed. "You have to rest."

"I have no one," Kate murmured then. "Nobody—"

"You have Shawn," Elgin said. "Shawn is outside in the waiting room. They said that I can bring him in when you're ready—"

"Shawn . . ."

"And you have me, Katie. You'll always have me—you know that, don't you?"

Kate lay in the narrow ICU hospital bed, looking small and weak and desolate, sobbing quietly now. She had undergone five hours of surgery for internal injuries, including three broken ribs, a cracked pelvis, and a badly bruised and bleeding kidney. Her head was swathed in bandages, large patches of blood and yellow serum seeping through the gauze in places. Her left arm had bent completely backward in the violent fall down the staircase, and it was set in a cast from hand to shoulder.

Under heavy sedation now, she had been drifting in and out of consciousness since coming out of the anesthesia earlier this afternoon. In her short stretches of wakefulness, over and over Kate had asked about her baby. The two surgeons had told her that they had not been able to save the baby. Still, Kate kept asking, and Elgin hadn't the heart to keep telling her that the baby was dead.

Her baby girl. After she'd had the CVS test last week, she told Shawn that it was a girl, and he'd told his father the news. Elgin knew how happy she'd been then, how much she wanted that baby girl. Now she kept whimpering that she had nobody, and that broke his heart. He so much wanted to be that *somebody* for Kate. He'd wanted that since the day he met her.

Surely now she would leave the bastard for good, he thought, watching her fitful breathing and her aching tears. Katie was in pain, and so was he.

Christina had called him with the news this morning. That Kate was in the hospital, in surgery, after a bad spill down the full flight of marble entry stairs. Elgin had better get the message to Shawn at school, Christina had told him, that his mother had had a terrible accident.

It was no accident, as far as Horner was concerned. He'd got it out of Christina that Katie had been having a fervid argument with Austin on the staircase when it happened. No accident. The man was going to kill her yet. She *had* to leave him now. She would, he was sure of it.

Elgin went to Beverly Hills High School and picked up his son, and the two had driven in silence to Cedars-Sinai Medical Center. They'd sat on benches in the small waiting room until the surgery was finished. When the doctors came out, they had asked to have a word with Elgin alone. He sent Shawn to the cafeteria to get a Coke, and a coffee for him.

One of the doctors asked Elgin about his relationship to Katie. "Next of kin?" he'd asked. "Yes," Elgin had responded. "And Shawn is our son." He'd left it at that. The two explained to him the extent of Kate's injuries, and told him that he could go in to see her then—but the boy couldn't. Too young, they'd said. Later, for a little bit, when she had herself more pulled together. It wouldn't be good for the youngster to see his mother this way, they said. The staff would let them know when it was okay.

That was twenty minutes ago. Elgin had been shuttling back and forth between Katie and Shawn, trying to comfort both of them, and not really succeeding on either front. Suddenly, Austin Feruzzi appeared in the doorway of the hospital room, and strode over to Kate's bedside. Ignoring Elgin, he looked down at his wife.

"Darling," he whispered, "you're going to be fine. You took a nasty fall. The doctors say that you're going to recover a hundred percent. Kate . . . can you hear me, darling?"

With a great deal of effort, Kate shifted her position so that she faced away from Austin. Elgin, on the other side of the bed, could see Katie's eyes flutter open and closed. She responded to her husband by not responding at all.

Feruzzi looked up angrily at Elgin. "You'd better leave, Horner," he said. "And take the kid with you."

He turned back to Kate then. Reached down and touched her shoulder. Katie visibly recoiled, Elgin saw. Feruzzi stiffened and looked up at him again, this time with fury in his eyes.

"Did you hear me, Horner?" he barked. "Get the hell out of here! Now, or I'll have you thrown out."

Elgin seethed. Feruzzi had the right of way. He stood up and shuffled out of the room. Stopping in the waiting area, he put an arm around his son and wordlessly steered him out of the hospital, and down to the parking structure across the street.

"I saw him," Shawn finally said to his dad.

"Yeah," Horner shrugged, and he took his boy home.

Chapter 48

A JUMPY GREGORY HAMILTON sat idling in his big white Chevy Suburban, with the windows up and the air-conditioning on. It was 6:30 on Tuesday evening. He was parked at the curb on Carmel's Monte Verde, three doors down and across the street from Maggie Carlson's house.

He hadn't talked to her since he had abruptly bolted out of her house before the two had even finished dinner last night. The lovely dinner that she had taken a great deal of care and trouble to cook for him. His first dinner at her house, and probably his last. He hadn't slept since then, and he'd been off and on sick to his stomach all day. Now he was back in Maggie Carlson's neighborhood, waiting. Watching and waiting for her to come home from work.

She'd called him several times today, left messages asking what in the world was wrong. He hadn't responded. He had been thinking nonstop about how he should handle this situation. The answer, of course, was simple and unavoidable. There was only one way to handle it. He had to confront her.

He saw her vintage red Thunderbird coming toward him up the street now. She pulled into her driveway, parked, got out of the car, then reached back into the front seat to pick up her jacket and a couple of packages. He watched her lock up the car, then walk across the grass and up the four wooden steps onto her small front porch.

She was dressed in a well-cut raspberry-red linen skirt that matched her jacket, a crisp white cotton blouse, tasteful gold jewelry, medium heels, her glossy dark hair pulled back in a loose French knot at the back of her neck. Lovely, and looking every bit the proper Carmel businesswoman. As Gregory observed her, he found his heart doing the familiar little flip it often did when he saw Maggie. He continued to watch as, keys in hand, she opened her front door and disappeared inside.

Sighing heavily, Gregory pushed open the door of his SUV and swung his lanky frame out of it and onto the sidewalk. There were no other people in sight. Resignedly, he traced Maggie's footsteps up her walkway and to her front door, and he rang her doorbell.

After a beat, she came to the door, saw that it was him, and opened it. And stood there, facing him.

"Hello, Maggie," he said.

"What is it, Greg?" she asked. "What happened?"

"Can I come in?"

"Why don't you tell me what on earth is wrong," she said quietly.

"Please, Maggie, let me come in. I have to talk to you," he returned, clearly uncomfortable.

She swung the arched front door open, then pushed the screen door out to let him in. Moving past her, he went into her tastefully decorated living room, and dropped down onto the same flower-print couch on which he'd had his revelation the night before. Maggie continued to stand at the front door, turned squarely toward him now, no expression at all on her face.

"Sit down, Maggie," Greg said somberly. "Please."

She walked studiedly over to the couch opposite him, smoothed her skirt, and sat down. And said nothing. Waiting for him to start, to let her know what this was all about.

"I . . . thank you for dinner last night," he stumbled.

"Stop it, Gregory, and tell me what's on your mind."

Looking into her eyes, Greg suddenly got the feeling that she knew what had catapulted him out of her house last night, and had brought him, in great discomfort, back here today. If she *did* know, she wasn't about to initiate the conversation. She wasn't going to make this any easier for him.

He leveled his gaze on her now, then shifted his eyes across the room to a spot just above her rolltop desk.

"What's on my mind," he answered her finally, gesturing with his hand in the direction of his gaze, "what is very much on my mind, is that painting on the wall."

Chapter 49

Don't cry," Lane said into the phone again. "Please, Shawn, don't cry. I'm going to come down there and take care of your mom, and take care of you . . ."

The school year had just started, and the boys were downstairs in the game room doing homework. Geoff was in the den looking over some paperwork, and Lane was in the kitchen working on dinner when the call had come in.

Lane squeezed her eyes shut and tried to keep the panic out of her voice, for Shawn's sake.

"Now, honey, try to tell me again what happened."

In a faltering voice, Shawn told Lane as much as he knew about his mother's fall and her injuries, ending with his trip to the hospital with his father that afternoon.

"Did you see your mom?"

"They wouldn't let me."

"I'm sorry. Where's Austin?" Lane asked him.

"I don't know. Home, I guess."

"And you're at your dad's?"

"Yes."

"Okay, darling, I'm going to call your mother right now and find out if she can talk to me. She might be asleep, I'll have to see. So give me your dad's number, and I'll call you right back, I promise, and I'll let you know if I reached her or not."

Shawn gave Lane his father's number, which she scribbled on a notepad by the telephone. She could see that her hands were trembling.

"And you'll tell me what she says?" Shawn asked.

"Of course I will."

"Will you ask her to call me? At Dad's?"

"Yes, and I'll get the number at the hospital for you, with her room number and everything, and you'll be able to phone her yourself, okay?"

There was silence now. Lane thought about her own boys. She knew exactly what was going on with Shawn. He was fighting back tears, and he didn't want Lane to hear that. Shawn was fourteen—too old to cry, he would think. But too young not to, she knew.

"Now listen to me, Shawn," she went on, to fill up the quiet. "I'm going to hang up now, and I'm going to try to reach your mom. I want you to stay right there by the phone, and I'm going to call you back in a few minutes, okay? I'm going to call you and let you know everything I find out. Okay?"

"Okay," Shawn managed in a very small voice.

"Good. Now let's make sure I have your dad's number exactly right." She knew she did, but she read it back to reassure him.

"It's right," he said.

"Alright, bye, darling. Now don't go anywhere. Okay?"

"Okay. Bye."

Lane hung up the phone. Her heart was breaking for him. Her first thought was to call Austin, but she decided against it. She would try to get through to Kate instead. Or at least to the hospital staff. That way maybe she would get the truth, instead of some jack-story from Austin Feruzzi.

She called the number for Los Angeles information. Got Cedars-Sinai. Asked for a patient named Mrs. Austin Feruzzi. Not listed. Kathryn Feruzzi? No, no one by that name, either.

"How about Kathryn Spenser?" she asked.

"Yes, we have Kathryn Spenser."

Of course, Lane thought to herself. Austin wouldn't want the press to get ahold of this.

"She's in Intensive Care," the woman's voice said now. "I'm sorry, but this patient cannot take any calls."

"Well, I need to talk to the intern or the resident on duty, to find out about her condition."

"Are you family?"

"Ah . . . yes."

"And your relationship?"

"I'm her sister."

"Your name, please?"

"Lane Hamilton. Spelled L-A-N-E, Hamilton."

"Hold on, please."

Lane's heart was pounding. Intensive Care! Why should she be surprised? Of course, Intensive Care. Geoff said unless it's stopped, it almost always escalates to this.

She was about to call out to her husband, have him come into the kitchen and give her moral support while she tried to get to the bottom of this, when a male voice came on the line.

"Hello, Lane Hamilton?"

"Yes, yes, who is this?"

"This is Dr. Ian Armstrong. Your sister is my patient."

"I just found out about her fall. Tell me everything, Doctor. What are her injuries? How is she?"

The doctor read off a long list of injuries. Lane's heart sank. "And the baby?" she asked. "What about the baby—"

"I'm sorry . . ."

"Dear God," Lane whispered.

"We did everything—"

"I'm sure. Is there anything else . . . really serious?" she asked.

"Do you mean life-threatening? No. But all of it is quite serious," he said. "Mrs. Spenser is a very badly injured woman. It's going to take some time for her to heal . . ."

He stopped then, as if he were gathering his thoughts.

"Yes, Doctor," Lane urged, "please go on."

"Well, besides everything I told you, she also has severe bruises on her neck. They couldn't have happened from the fall she took. Can you tell me anything about that, Mrs. Hamilton?"

"No. No, I can't. What did Kate say?"

"She's in no condition to talk about it. She's still heavily sedated after the surgery. I don't want to risk upsetting her tonight."

"Does she know about . . . the baby?"

"I don't know. I told her. A couple of hours ago. But I'm not sure if it registered."

"Dr. Armstrong," Lane said then, "I'm up here in Carmel. In

Northern California. I'm going to drive down there in the morning to be with her. I'll talk to her."

"We need to find out about those bruises on her neck, Mrs. Hamilton. It's the law—"

"I'll ask her."

"Alright. Take my number." He recited the digits and Lane wrote them down, beside his name, which she had already made note of on the pad. And she gave the doctor *her* number, in case anything happened overnight, she said.

They both knew without saying it that Lane had just assumed the role of responsible adult in Kate's care. Yes, there was a husband—but there were those bruises on her neck.

"Now, please . . . is it possible for me to talk to her?" Lane asked hopefully. "Even if Katie can't talk to me, Doctor, I'd like to say some soothing words in her ear. I want to tell her that I'm coming down there, that I'm going to take care of everything. She has a young son—"

"Hold on, Mrs. Hamilton. I'll see."

Lane waited for what seemed an eternity. Geoff wandered into the kitchen, and looked at her quizzically. "What's wrong, darling?" he asked.

"It's Kate. She's in the hospital. It's really bad this time, Geoff."

Her husband dropped into a chair at the kitchen table, facing her, listening. His tanned, lined face was etched with concern. Lane felt stronger for his proximity. She felt safer. Dr. Armstrong's voice on the line brought her back to the moment.

"Mrs. Hamilton?"

"Yes, Doctor—"

"I'm putting your call through to your sister's ICU room. The nurse has plugged in a phone there, and she's going to pick up and let Mrs. Spenser hear you. I don't know if she'll respond."

"Okay—"

A woman came on the line. She told Lane that she was holding the phone to the patient's ear, so she could go ahead and talk to her.

"Thank you," Lane said. "Kate . . . Katie, darling, it's Lane . . . can you hear me?"

Nothing.

"Kate, I'm coming down there," Lane went on. "Tomorrow morning. I'll stay at your house, and I'll pick Shawn up at school and take care of him. It's just going to have to be all right with Austin. I'll take care of everything, Katie—"

"Lane . . ." She could hear Kate say her name, barely above a whisper. "Lane—"

"Yes, darling, it's me. Everything is going to be alright, Katie—"

"My baby—" Kate whispered. Lane watched her own tears splash off the phone receiver.

"My baby," Kate said again, even weaker.

Then more silence.

"She's had enough, Miss," the voice of the nurse piped up.

"I understand," Lane said. "Please tell her again that I'm coming down to take care of her."

"I'll tell her."

Lane hung up the phone, and Geoff came over to her. She fell into his arms.

"Forget about making dinner," he said. "We'll go out for a bite."

"I have to call Shawn first," she said.

"Go ahead. I'll round up the boys."

"And Geoff . . . I have to go to her."

"I know, darling," her husband said.

Chapter 50

"Trisha, it's Lane. Trish, if you can hear me, please pick up. It's a little after ten, your time—maybe you and Peter are out to dinner . . . Trisha, the most horrible—"

"Yes, hello, Lane, I thought that was your voice. No, we had dinner at home tonight . . . Lane, are you alright?"

"It's not me, Trish—it's Kate."

"Oh God. Now what?"

Lane told Trisha as much as she knew, and that she was going to drive down to Los Angeles in the morning, and she was prepared to stay there for a while.

"Shawn is desolate. And angry. And most of all, terrified. He's with his father, but Elgin is a disaster, as you know. Shawn shouldn't stay there indefinitely."

"What will you do? Get Kate's permission to take him home with you for a few weeks?" Trisha asked.

"Maybe. Or more likely, I'll have to stay *there* for a while. There's school to consider. It depends on how long it's going to take for Kate to recover. They don't know yet, Trish."

"Bruises on her neck," Trisha said, trying to make sense of what Lane was telling her. "Austin—?"

"What do *you* think?"

"Of *course*, Austin. We can get him put away for this," Trisha said, her anger palpable over the phone lines.

"Katie would have to agree—"

"The baby, Lane. A little girl. It's murder. She'll leave him this time, Lane."

"I think you're right."

"We can't just think. We've got to see to it. Or *Kate* will be murdered next."

"That's exactly what Geoff said."

"Lane, do you need me there?" Trisha asked her then.

"I don't know. That's generous of you, Trish—you're on the other coast, and you have your show—"

"This is much more important. If you need me, I'll be there. Just let me know. And by the way, Lane, that reminds me . . . we got a very odd phone call earlier tonight."

"Oh?"

"From Tripp Kendrick at the Feruzzi Gallery in Beverly Hills."

"Yes, what did he want?"

"Well, in light of what you've just told me, Lane, it's beyond strange. He invited us to a party. On behalf of Austin Feruzzi."

"What kind of party?"

"A party to be held at Jonathan Valley's house in Malibu, he said, for the unveiling of what was evidently Aiden Jannus's last completed painting. Tripp said that it was commissioned by Jon Valley, and Aiden finished it before he died."

"And Austin wants to give a *party?*" Lane shrieked incredulously. "Did Tripp know that the man put his wife in the hospital today?"

"I don't think so. At least he didn't say anything about it to me, and I'm sure he would have. He knows how close we are, and Tripp is a decent guy."

"Maybe Austin told him yesterday to get the party going, or even earlier, before Kate was hurt—"

"No, he said Austin just told him this afternoon. When did Kate take this fall?"

"Early this morning. Before nine o'clock, Shawn said. He was just leaving for school."

"Then Austin set up this party *after* he nearly killed his wife? Not to mention the very day after his friend Aiden Jannus was found dead—what kind of a man does that, Lane?"

"A cold-hearted bastard," Lane spit out. "And why would Jonathan

Valley even agree to a party at his home that involved Austin Feruzzi? Do you remember what he called him at your house that night, Trish?"

"Ahh . . . pond scum."

"Right. More to the point, you couldn't miss noticing that he hated the man. So why would he do a party with him, or for him, or whatever it is?" Lane wondered aloud.

"Wait, there's more," Trisha tossed back. "Talk about rushing things inappropriately—the reason Tripp *called*, he said, was because there wasn't enough time to send out invitations."

"Why not? When *is* this party?" Lane asked.

"A week from Saturday," Trisha said. "Eleven days from now—count 'em!"

Chapter 51

FUCKING SENT PACKING again," Austin Feruzzi muttered to
himself. "Like it was my fault that she fell down the stairs."

"Did you say something, Mr. Feruzzi?" the flight attendant asked.
She was handing out newspapers to passengers in the first-class section.

"No, just thinking out loud," he responded, looking up at her.
Beautiful in an off-beat way, she was supermodel leggy, with a short,
shaggy mop of hair that was a chunky mixture of brown and blond,
and huge, tortoiseshell-framed glasses over saucer-shaped brown
eyes.

"Actually, I could use a vodka with ice," he said.

"We'll be serving cocktails right after take-off, sir."

"How about slipping me a vodka without all the attendant goodies, and we'll both pretend it's water," Feruzzi suggested with a smile.

"Ahh," she purred, and moved on up the aisle with her copies of
the L.A. *Times*, *USA Today*, and *The Wall Street Journal*.

Shrugging, he went back to lamenting his fate. He was banished
again. Moving to New York again. This was getting old. Kate
wouldn't even talk to him. When he would show up in her hospital
room, she'd just turn her back and give him the silent treatment.
Once he even tried sitting in a chair facing her and waiting it out until she woke up, but as soon as she became aware that he was in the
room, she blatantly turned away and ignored him.

Finally, Lane Hamilton, the iceberg, had a message for him. Kate
wanted him out of the house by the time she got home from the hospital, Lane said. Furthermore, he was not to come back to Cedars,
because Kate didn't want to see him. The woman had looked him

straight in the eye and told him that. Actually intercepted him down the hall from Kate's room. The two of them must have had the staff doing lookout duty, he groused to himself, that Lane Hamilton could cut him off at the pass like that.

Still, he'd been nice to Lane. Told her he was grateful that she took time from her busy life to come down here. Glad that she was taking such good care of his wife. Said he knew that Katie would rethink this when she was feeling stronger. And when she was ready, he would be there for her. He had offered his hand to Lane in friendship. She'd just nodded and turned back down the hall.

The bitch of it was, Lane was actually living in his house. Taking care of Shawn between trips to the hospital. Auntie Lane, Shawn called her. Austin never could warm up to the boy. It wasn't that he was such a bad kid, he just didn't have the energy for it. He'd done his own kids. Didn't want to do any more kids. Didn't want to go fishing, play catch, or go to one more damn soccer game. Let the real father do it.

Feruzzi had counted it a blessing in disguise that Kate fell down the stairs. No permanent harm done, and she'd lost the baby. Best thing that could've happened. No wonder he'd been so irritable lately. He'd been looking at two decades with yet another kid strapped to his back. Literally and figuratively.

Kate was being released from the hospital tomorrow, so he got himself out of the house today. The better part of valor, he figured. A convalescent Kate and a reproachful Lane was way too much for him to deal with. And now Trisha Newman was coming out, ostensibly for the unveiling party at Jonathan Valley's, but he knew that she would be nosing around the house, hanging with Lane and ministering to Kate. Ever since the night she found out about his affair with Molly, Trisha Newman had been treating him like he smelled bad.

On top of that, since Jannus died, Molly was threatening to bolt again. Just when he needed her the most. Molly hated him too, actively and quite perceptibly hated him. He never should have had an affair with Molly. She was Kate's age, for God's sake—he'd thought that she was mature enough to take it for what it was. Who knew that she would get it in her head that he should *marry* her? She laid *that* on him right at the peak of their affair, so he humored her, of course. And she *believed* him! At this stage in her life, shouldn't she know what the male animal was about?

He had to start the damn back-pedaling again. Had to get them all back in the fold. Flex his muscles for the exercise of buttering them all up with the old Feruzzi charm. Actually, Kate was always the easiest. The other three were hard.

The rangy, multicolored blond flight attendant was standing over him now, handing him a plastic cup. "Your water, Mr. Feruzzi," she said with a twinkle. Very cute.

"Why, thank you," he said, flashing her a smile. "What's your name?"

"Ricki."

"You *look* like a Ricki."

"I do?"

"It suits you. What does it stand for?"

"Veronica. But I don't like Ronnie."

"You're not a Ronnie."

"No?"

"Nope. You're definitely a Ricki."

"Can I ask you something, Mr. Feruzzi?"

"Of course you can, Ricki. What is it?"

"I know your art galleries, of course. Everybody does."

"Yes?"

"Well, I would be the envy of the absolute world if I could get an invitation to that big party at Jonathan Valley's estate on Saturday night—the party in honor of the last painting Aiden Jannus did. It's been written up everywhere. I know that every star in the world will be there—"

"Will you be in L.A. on Saturday night?"

"I live there."

"And you won't be off flying somewhere?"

"Are you kidding? I'd call in *dead* if I could be at that party."

"I might be able to arrange it," Feruzzi said with an impish grin. "Do you want to come with a date, or with a girlfriend?"

"It doesn't matter. Whatever's right."

"How about we talk it over during dinner tonight in New York?"

"You're on!" she said. "Please fasten your seat belt, now."

Chapter 52

"TURNED OUT TO be a helluva party, Jon," Tripp remarked quietly.

"Yeah," Jonathan Valley said, a terse expression hardening his matinee-idol features. "The little viper knows how to market himself."

The two, who invariably made a point of avoiding each other in public, had found themselves standing side by side for just a minute, looking up at the stunning Aiden Jannus painting on the living room wall. All around them, Valley's magnificent white villa on the beach in Malibu was alive with reverberating rock music, free-flowing champagne, and the high-energy, high-chic aura of the *beautiful people,* the planet's glitterati.

Jon Valley's ultra-lavish unveiling gala had been suggested, read that *ordered,* by Austin Feruzzi. Valley had taken on the role of reluctant host because he still hadn't figured out how to keep Feruzzi quiet. And the Feruzzi Gallery in Beverly Hills, read that *Tripp Kendrick,* had been made to take over the party preparations, also at the directive of gallery owner Austin Feruzzi.

"Did you talk to him tonight?" Tripp asked.

"What's to talk about? I lose and he gloats. And he's sucking up the glory. Courting clients in my living room. This extravaganza is for *his* business at *my* expense."

It had all been done with lightning speed. Feruzzi had shipped the enormous Aiden Jannus painting that Jonathan Valley had commissioned, and along with the painting came Feruzzi's proviso to throw this "party of the year." And the sooner the better, he'd said. Feruzzi's intent was to maximize to his advantage the massive press coverage surrounding Jannus's death while it was still hot news.

"Aiden Jannus was to America what Princess Diana was to England," Feruzzi had told Tripp.

"Hardly," Tripp had responded dryly.

"Well, to the art world, then," Feruzzi had countered. "And that's the world that supports my livelihood. Yours, too," he reminded Tripp. In any case, his boss had demanded the party, Valley would get the bill, and Tripp had to make it happen.

They'd picked this Saturday night because Jon had to be in New York on Monday morning to start shooting his new movie, *Dead Right*, and he wouldn't be back for weeks. With no time to send out proper invitations, Tripp had hired five temps and put them on cell phones and fax machines for days, in a coordinated effort to get the word out to the best and the brightest. The response, as evidenced all around them now, had been massive.

Since his death, now confirmed to have been caused by a drug overdose, Aiden Jannus's likeness had been splashed on the covers of countless magazines, and the artist was the subject of news stories throughout the media. Valley's painting, being shown off tonight, was billed as the last major work that Jannus had completed before his sudden and untimely death.

"It *is* extraordinary, though, isn't it?" Jon allowed, still gazing up at the riotously hued painting.

"It is arguably the most coveted piece of artwork in the country right now," Tripp agreed.

Jon smiled. He knew that Tripp Kendrick's was an educated assessment. It was a gigantic canvas. Twelve feet across by nine feet high, it stretched magnificently across the west wall of what Valley's architect had called the "great room," with its spectacular movable wall of glass that looked out on the dark Pacific.

It seemed that every blazing color in the spectrum and every variation thereof was represented in the mammoth painting, which depicted colossal sunflowers bordering a rambling field of perennials—multicolored asters with pert yellow centers, dazzling goldenrod next to handsome azalea clusters of every hue, stately calla lilies with tall golden spikes, willowy delphinium in royal blues and purples, and delicate sea hollies everywhere, all in riotous bloom in sunny midday.

The painting, as well as movie star Jonathan Valley's star-studded gala tonight to unveil it, had been the ongoing subjects of national and world publicity. As Valley's dramatic glass palace on the beach teemed with movie stars, writers, art patrons, socialites, and all manner of celebrities, reporters from the networks and the local stations, along with *Entertainment Tonight, Extra, Access Hollywood,* the cable shows, and many more, were elbowing each other to grab the hottest celebs for their interviews.

Oprah was there as a guest, looking svelte in a silvery-black knit pantsuit, sipping champagne and chatting with fellow stars, all the while keeping an eye on her crew to make sure that they got everyone who counts on tape. No problem there—her shooters were the ones in the bright, citrus-colored "Oprah" T-shirts, and the savvy celebs actually lined up to perform for them. Everyone knew that a single sound bite on Oprah could get you noticed for another plum role.

Arnold and Maria had driven out from the Palisades. Rita Wilson and Tom Hanks had arrived from just down the beach. Sylvester Stallone, who was a friend of Valley's and a major art collector, kept telling Jon how lucky he was to have acquired this painting. And Sharon Stone looked radiant in a white satin slip dress, with her new San Francisco journalist husband. She had starred in a recent movie with Valley, and she said glowing things to the press about him, and about the painting.

But Jonathan Valley was not a happy host tonight. When it came to Austin Feruzzi, he was a man who had no options. Not only had he been constrained to fund this flashy bash at Feruzzi's behest, even worse, he had to suffer the snake as a guest in his home. Never had Valley felt so impotent, and the man's extortion ploys looked to be limitless. The tighter Feruzzi turned the screws, the deeper Jon Valley's rage intensified.

"Oh, oh, I think he's coming over here," Tripp whispered to Jon, rolling his eyes toward Austin Feruzzi. "Shall we move away?"

"No. Don't give him that power."

As Feruzzi made his way through the crowd toward the two of them, Tripp looked the other way, while Valley, arms folded, rocked on his heels.

"By the way, his wife got out of the hospital yesterday," Tripp said in a low voice. "The word is she's divorcing him."

"Any truth to the rumor that she and Byron Lassen are an item?" Jon asked.

"I know Lassen," Tripp said, "and I happen to know that he's crazy about Kate. He went over to Cedars to see her several times. But she's a married woman, and he is the soul of propriety. So we'll see."

"Didn't I see his name on the guest list tonight?" Valley asked.

"Yes, Byron is an art collector, as you know. He RSVP'd for tonight, but I haven't seen him yet."

"Heads up," Valley warned then. "Satan is definitely slithering this way—we can't avoid him."

Austin Feruzzi was disengaging himself from a group of young people standing close by. They didn't look like potential art clients to Tripp. The tall, lanky blonde they were calling Ricki, in a strapless, shimmering bronze-sequined mini-dress, was running her hands over Feruzzi's Armani jacket. He gave her a condescending pat on the rear, then glided across the parquet floor to Jon and Tripp.

"Hi, guys," he said, all oily tan and bright white teeth. "Great party, Jon. Thanks for having me."

"Fuck off, Feruzzi," Jon floated past him, albeit with a smile.

"Charming," Feruzzi responded.

"How long will you be in town, Austin?" Tripp asked him, glossing over Valley's double-edged animus. Tripp Kendrick found himself in an untenable position, working for Austin Feruzzi while the man held the sword of Damocles over Jonathan Valley's head. Having to deal with Feruzzi in the workaday world had never really been comfortable, but it was now surreal, like trying to do business in the sepia-toned gravity of a borrowed dream. He knew he would have to leave the gallery, and soon, but Jon wanted him to hang in there until they could figure out how to neutralize his boss. Being on the inside could prove useful, Valley maintained.

"I'm planning to go back to New York in the morning," Feruzzi said to Tripp.

"Too bad," Jon jumped in. "I thought maybe you could hang out here by the pool tomorrow. Bring some of your friends," he said, gesturing with his head toward Ricki and the gang.

"You know, speaking of hanging out, maybe you two guys shouldn't be hanging out *together,*" Feruzzi slapped back. "Who knows, it might give people the wrong idea."

With that, he started to move away, when suddenly Jon Valley grasped him by the arm.

"Wait just a second, Austin," he said, looking past him toward the doorway. "Here comes somebody you ought to meet."

Valley raised his hand and beckoned a newly arrived guest over to them, a tall, trim man with even features and a wealth of blond, curly hair slightly edged with gray. He caught his host's wave and started toward their group.

"Great place, Jon!" he enthused when he caught up with them, looking around with an appreciative smile.

"And how are *you,* Tripp?" he asked, offering his hand all around. That's when he noticed that Austin Feruzzi was standing with them.

"Austin," Jon chimed in then, a mischievous smirk playing on the corners of his famous mouth, "say hello to Byron Lassen!"

THAT'S ANOTHER ONE I owe you, asshole, Feruzzi griped silently as he pushed through the crowd, moving away from Valley, Tripp, and Byron Fucking Lassen. I owe you, and it'll cost you, you can trust me on that, big Bardo! he inwardly fumed. Billy Bardo was the name of a superhero character that Jonathan Valley had played in several movies.

Feruzzi was less than thrilled to meet Byron Lassen. He had run a check on Lassen, found out who he was. A member in high standing of Forbes' 400, *that's* who he was. One of the four hundred richest Americans, according to the list put out annually by *Forbes* magazine. *Forbes* put Lassen's net worth at 1.2 billion dollars. Feruzzi had had to adjust his glasses and check the small type again. Yes, that was billion, with a *b.* Feruzzi didn't care that the man was taller, leaner, better-looking, younger than him. But the billion with a *b* is what made him crazy.

Still, possession was nine-tenths of the law, and Kate was his wife. He would turn her around. He always did. He would even convince her that the baby was not meant to be—as he'd always told her, their future together would be much better without a child. They would spend more time together, travel more, see the world. And Mr. Billion with a *B* would be left holding his dick.

Kate was out of the hospital now, recovering at home. He had hoped that she would come to the party tonight. Make this gala at Jon Valley's her first outing since the accident. He had left several messages asking her to please come tonight, telling her repeatedly that he wanted, needed, to see her. Kate had not responded to any of his messages. She was still angry, he knew, but as always, she would thaw.

Geoff and Lane Hamilton were at the party. Feruzzi had put them on the guest list because Lane was so close to Kate. Lane had Katie's ear; Kate listened to her. Also, Lane was still in town, doing last-minute things to get Katie settled in at home. Feruzzi had handwritten a special note to Mrs. Hamilton, and had it messengered over to his own house, asking Lane to please come to the party, and bring Kate with her, because he wanted so much just to see his wife.

L ANE LOOKED UP to see Austin Feruzzi making his way across Jon Valley's expansive living room. She watched as he stopped to schmooze with guests, lifting a glass of champagne from a passing waiter's tray.

"Oily bastard," Lane remarked, turning her eyes back to her group. She and Geoff were standing in a corner with Trish and Peter Newman. The Newmans had come out to the coast for Jonathan Valley's party, at Peter's insistence. He owed it to Jon Valley, he'd said. Peter Newman's Global network had recently aired its retrospective of Jonathan Valley films, and the ratings had gone through the roof. And after all, he'd told his wife, it was going to be the social event of the year.

He was right about that. Movie star Jonathan Valley was on the cover of this week's *People* magazine, standing in front of his huge Aiden Jannus painting. Although Trisha hated to be part of anything that had the smell of Austin Feruzzi on it, she had agreed to come out to L.A. with her husband so that they could go to Valley's party. But most of all, because it would give her a chance to spend some time with Kate and Lane.

When Austin Feruzzi's note had been delivered to the house, Lane and Trish were in the master suite with Kate. The patient was sitting up in bed, propped up on a pile of lacy, down-filled pillows. Christina had carried the envelope into the bedroom, holding it warily between her thumb and forefinger. From the look on her face, she might as well have been holding her nose with the other hand. Kate's longtime housekeeper had recognized her employer's handwriting, of course.

Lane took the envelope and ripped it open, and read it aloud to her pals. They actually laughed uproariously—it was the first time Trish and Lane had seen Katie genuinely break up with laughter in a long, long time. The three of them had collapsed in a group hug on Katie's bed—they might have been back in college.

Of course Kate wouldn't dream of going to the party, even if she'd been able, Lane knew. Funny, she thought, but in the old days Kate would probably have found a way to drag herself out of a sickbed and struggle with makeup, even with her arm in a cast. She would knock herself out to make an appearance at Austin's side if that was what he wanted.

No more. *Really,* no more. Kate had assured them that she had no desire to go *anyplace* where she would have to look upon the slick countenance of her estranged, soon-to-be-divorced husband. And there was something about the way she said it this time, something in the look on her face, that let Lane and Trisha know that their beloved Kate, as weak as she was, had never been stronger. And that finally, mercifully, she had had enough.

With Trish and Peter in town, Geoff had flown down from Carmel so that the four of them could make an appearance at the party. Lane wanted to get a feel for the evening and report to Kate. Kate was half-owner of the Feruzzi Galleries, but now, at least until their assets were settled, Austin would probably keep her out of the loop on the business, even though it was her money that kept it going.

Lane looked up at the painting again. She had been inexplicably drawn back to it all evening. As her eyes roamed the perimeter of the huge Jannus canvas, then dropped to explore the dazzling panoply of color, she scrunched up her brow in a puzzled look.

"Don't *do* that, Lane!" Trisha exclaimed.

"Do what?" she asked, not taking her eyes away from the painting.

"Don't squeeze your forehead together like that—you're making wrinkles."

"Oh, right," Lane said distractedly, softening her look as she continued to gaze at the massive canvas.

"Lanie, you've been staring at the Jannus all night. I wish I'd bought it for *you*," Geoff laughed.

"Yes, you could have propped it up on the sidewalk outside Hamilton House," Trisha giggled. None of them had walls that would accommodate a piece of artwork that size.

Lane just kept staring at the painting. "There's something about it . . ." she was mumbling now.

"What?" the other three echoed in unison, which caused them all to burst out laughing. But Lane ignored them.

"Darling, can you get Lane another drink?" Trisha asked her husband. "She is currently on some other planet, and we should really try to get her back to earth."

Peter took Lane's empty glass out of her upraised hand, as she kept her eyes riveted to the painting.

"I don't know, I can't put my finger on it," Lane said again, half to herself, "but there's something about that Jannus . . ."

Chapter 53

MOLLY LOOKED UP at the enormous old Bulova wall clock hanging in her studio. A collectible from the twenties, advertising a shop on Second Avenue. Van Ness Jewelers, long since closed down. She'd paid forty dollars for the big clock at a flea market sale when she first moved to the city—a find! Also a time-consuming project, it turned out, but worth every minute of it.

She thought about how she had run around the city, lugging it here, lugging it there. She'd had the dents in the heavy aluminum case pounded out, the bold black lettering on the face restored, a new round neon bulb installed to light it up, its frayed wiring replaced so she wouldn't get electrocuted, and the clockworks repaired so that it kept perfect time.

Most of all, thinking back, she could still remember the feelings of accomplishment and sheer *joie de vivre* she'd felt on that day fifteen years ago when the world was young, and Kate helped her hang it up. She had stood on a ladder and hammered the butterfly hook into the wall, then Katie carefully handed up the bulky clock. And when it was hung and they plugged it in, it lit up, it worked, and it looked spectacular.

Now that clock said that it was midnight in Manhattan. On Saturday night, in the most exciting city in America. And it was Molly's birthday. *Had* been Molly's birthday, up until one minute ago. Her *fortieth* birthday. And she'd spent it right here in her small apartment, alone.

She looked around. Once, not even that long ago, she had thought the place so New York hip, so creatively artistic. Now it looked tiny, dingy, cramped, depressing, bleak. And most of all, empty. Forty years old, and exactly where was she? No funds, no future, no friends, and a job that was tearing her insides out every day.

Across the country, the huge gala to unveil Aiden Jannus's last painting was going full tilt right now at actor Jonathan Valley's splendid mansion on Malibu beach. Aiden's last hurrah. Or not, if Austin Feruzzi could in any way sustain the hype, the clamor, and the cash flow that issued from the deceased artist's celebrated name and work.

She'd gotten a glimpse of the festivities earlier, live on the eleven o'clock news. Saw the people. And saw the painting. The enormous painting that had been done so fast. A magnificent piece—Molly knew every brushstroke.

The last time she had seen Aiden Jannus was three weeks ago, when Jannus had blustered into the gallery on that Saturday afternoon. Patrons browsing about on the floor were astounded, as they always were when the famous Aiden Jannus came in. A couple of them took out cameras and snapped pictures of him. Aiden didn't seem to notice. He wanted to see his paintings, he'd told Molly, every damn one of them that the gallery had.

Austin had warned her that the artist was going to come in, so she was ready for him. She had seven of his pieces standing against the wall behind her desk. She was hoping that he wouldn't act up, wouldn't cause his usual commotion. He surprised her by looking long and thoughtfully at each of the paintings, one after another, saying nothing.

"Any more?" he asked, when he'd finished studying the last of them.

"That's all we have right now, Aiden," she'd told him. "We sold *Three Chairs* on Tuesday, remember?"

"Are you sure these are all you have?" he persisted.

"That's all. Do you want to see the books? See when they came in, what went out, the recent activity?"

He'd looked at her hard. Which had been a bit unsettling, Molly remembered now. She wasn't used to a cold-sober Aiden Jannus. "No, Molly, I don't want to look at the books," he'd said, and with that, he'd left.

A cold-sober Aiden Jannus. What had caused him to take that deadly leap off the program just one week later? Or was it as Austin said? Almost inevitable.

Austin had come east to meet with Jannus on the very day that they'd found the artist dead. Feruzzi hadn't let his New York staff know in advance that he was coming. He'd said it was a spur-of-the-moment trip. After the fact, though, he'd told Molly that he wanted to talk to Jannus about the public appearances the artist was making all over the media, commenting that he couldn't even remember a lot of his own work. Austin said he wanted to explain to Aiden that that looked bad for him, and bad for his work, and he had to stop saying things like that. He'd thought he might be able to reason with him now that the man was sober. He never got the chance, he said.

Molly loathed Austin Feruzzi. Still, it would have been nice to be celebrating her birthday at Jonathan Valley's party tonight, with beautiful, accomplished people who were spirited and having fun. But Austin didn't invite Molly to be there, and in truth, she knew that she couldn't have handled it anyway.

On the television news pictures tonight, she had caught a glimpse of Lane, who happened to be standing in front of the painting, looking up at it. And Trisha was standing next to her, along with both their husbands. Seeing her two friends had felt like a stab in the heart. She missed them terribly.

And Katie. Kate would be at home tonight. Molly had read in the *New York Post* that Kate had taken a terrible fall. During a fight with her husband, the column said. Tripp Kendrick had filled her in on the details. Devastating injuries, but not life-threatening, he'd said. Kate was out of the hospital, now, recovering at home.

When she'd heard about Kate's disastrous fall, she had so much wanted to call her, but hadn't dared. Kate would hang up on her, she knew. Worse, she was afraid she would just upset Katie more if she called her at a time when she was obviously in pain, struggling to recuperate. Tripp kept Molly updated. He said that Kate was fast improving. And that she had thrown her husband out for good.

Molly never spoke to Austin anymore about anything that didn't have to do with business, but she knew that he had been staying in New York this past week. And that he had gone back to California just for the party. If Tripp was right, their boss would be staying at the Peninsula Hotel tonight, instead of at his beautiful home on Lexington Road in Beverly Hills.

She looked up at the clock again. Seven minutes after midnight.

Just after nine o'clock in California. A couple of tears inched down her cheeks. She had managed to restore the big Bulova on the wall, she smiled to herself. She *had* to repair the monumental mess she'd made of her life. Or try, at least.

She picked up the phone, and dialed Kate's number.

Chapter 54

"THE <u>WORLD</u> WAS THERE!" Trisha gushed. "Mel *Gibson* was there! Oh, those eyes!"

"Fabulous looking, but short," Lane observed. "It surprised me how short he is, because he plays so tall on the screen."

"How short? Is he as tall as me, at least?" Kate asked, standing to demonstrate her five foot seven inches.

"You're *standing up,* Kate!" Trisha gushed.

"Of *course* I'm standing up," Kate assured her two friends. "And the doctors *want* me to stand . . . and walk, and run if I can. They don't baby you anymore."

"You're amazing, Katie," Lane chimed in. "I'll bet you *could* have gone to the party last night if you'd wanted to."

"Yes, I could have," Kate mused. "But this cast on my arm is ghastly—and my soon-to-be-ex-husband is ghastlier. Two good reasons to stay home, don't you think?"

"Speaking of your husband," Lane offered, a mischievous grin playing on her sunny Irish face, "one of the highlights of the evening, I must say, was when Jonathan Valley dragged Byron Lassen over to meet Austin."

"He *didn't!*" Kate exclaimed, reddening, her good hand flying to her face.

"Oh yes, he did," Lane assured her.

"So what exactly *is* it with you and this Byron Lassen?" Trisha demanded to know. "Peter says he's loaded, by the way."

"Not to mention divinely handsome," Lane put in. "He looked like a *GQ* cover last night! And loads of women were making moves on him, Katie."

It was the morning after Jonathan Valley's gala at the beach, and the three women were sitting in Kate's lavish living room in Beverly Hills, drinking coffee and dishing the party.

"So what *gives* with you and Mr. Gorgeous Moneybags?" Lane asked, narrowing her eyes on Kate now.

"No comment!" Kate said, turning up the palms of her hands toward the two of them. "Oooh, I shouldn't do that," she whimpered then, gently rubbing her left hand with her right.

"Does it hurt?" Trisha asked solicitously.

"The cast cuts into my hand when I move my wrist too fast."

"Poor Katie," Trisha soothed.

"Not so poor," Kate laughed. "Just inconvenienced. The doctors say I'm going to be a hundred percent, and it's happening faster than any of them predicted."

"Thank heaven and your guardian angels," Lane said. "So what *is* the deal with you and Byron Lassen?"

"Yeah, give it up, Kate," Trisha insisted with a wicked smile.

"You *guys!* I said, '*no comment.*' "

"Since when do we give each other 'no comment'?" Lane demanded incredulously.

"Come on, give me a little time. The body isn't cold, yet. On my *marriage*, I mean."

"*Other* people can give you time. We don't have *time* to give you time!" Trisha complained, with such seriousness that the other two burst out laughing.

"I promise that you two will be the first to know, right after *I* know," Kate put in, with a finality that signaled she was not about to say anything at all about Byron Lassen.

"Now," she went on, "guess who called me last night? Guess who left a long, lovely message?"

"Hmmm . . . guess it wasn't Byron Lassen," Lane laughed. "You wouldn't tell us if—"

"It was Molly," Kate cut her off. "I listened, but I didn't pick up." The other two sobered.

"And?" Trisha inquired.

"And . . . do you want to hear it?"

Kate led the other two out of the living room and into her small sitting room. Dropping into the tall-backed English Sheraton chair behind her desk, she pressed the REWIND button on her answering machine.

"Make yourselves comfortable, ladies," she said, indicating the pair of exquisite silk-covered beechwood chairs on the other side of the desk as they listened to the tape whir.

This was the first communication any of them had had with Molly Adams since her big blow-up at Trisha's dinner party in New York nearly three months ago. An uninvited communication, but nonetheless, Lane and Trisha were curious. Kate found the beginning of Molly's message and pushed the PLAY button.

"Kate, dear Katie . . . it's Molly. I was so sorry to hear about your frightening fall. Tripp Kendrick tells me that you're home from the hospital now, and mending fast, and you're going to be fine, thank God.

"I don't know where to begin, Kate, except to say that I am so, so sorry. I'm sad, I'm hurting, and most of all, I'm ashamed. I'm terribly ashamed of what I did with Austin. I know that the three of you . . . my best, my only friends in the world . . . my sisters . . . will probably never again have anything to do with me. That's what I deserve.

"Kate, I don't know what possessed me get involved with your husband, except to say that he initiated it. Not that it's any excuse . . . I'm just trying to make some sense out of it. Thinking back, I guess I was lonely . . . again, no excuse. I never felt so strongly for any man. That's no excuse, either, but now I know that the man I fell so much in love with doesn't exist . . . it was just one big acting job for Austin. I'm sorry, Kate, but he's so full of shit . . . he lies about everything . . . well, that's another conversation, if we ever have it.

"Anyway, when Austin came on to me repeatedly, I did protest . . . I did say no, many times over the years . . . but he kept on coming. Why didn't I tell you? Because I was your friend, but he was your husband. I thought it would only hurt you.

"He escalated. He wouldn't take no for an answer. He told me that your marriage wasn't happy . . . that you two were going to get a divorce anyway. He even said that he knew you wanted a baby, Kate, and that he'd told you before you got married that he

didn't want any more children, and you'd agreed. He said that you weren't happy with that decision now.

"Austin knew that I wanted marriage, and he said he wanted to marry me. He said he would take care of the divorce, then we would get married quietly. He assured me that you wanted the divorce as much as he did. I should have realized that married men who cheat always say that to women. Lying goes hand in hand with cheating. But Kate, I had *heard* you say, many times, that you'd like to have another child, and I guess I made the leap that you would have to divorce Austin to do that.

"Katie, I'm not trying to excuse my behavior, but I really thought that he was telling me the truth, and that I wasn't hurting you. That maybe I was even helping you. I knew that you would never cheat on him . . . I know that's not in your nature. And we all saw that you couldn't seem to leave him. I really thought if my affair with Austin triggered him to push for a divorce, you would finally have the freedom you wanted.

"I know what you're probably saying, Kate . . . that I'm rationalizing . . . and maybe I am. But even if none of you ever speaks to me again, I want you and Lane and Trisha to know this . . . I never, never wanted to hurt you, Kate. And I love all of you. I always will.

"I also want to tell you that I meant what I said in anger that night at Trisha's. Austin is no good, Kate . . . you should get rid of him. Austin Feruzzi is an evil, lying, womanizing, egomaniacal sociopath . . . I saw much more of that than you ever did, because I work for him. I saw what went on. And you deserve much better.

"Maybe something good will come out of what I did. You didn't leave him then, but now this awful fall down the stairs . . . maybe it will open your eyes, and finally you'll be able to get yourself away from him. I hope so, for your sake, Kate.

"That's all I have to say. Maybe right now you think that I'm not much better than he is, and I wouldn't blame you. Maybe you and I will never talk again . . . but I needed to say this to you . . . I am so sorry, you'll never know how sorry, that this ever happened. Because in the end, Katie, your life is going to be much better from this day forward, but my life is ruined.

"I love you, and I mean that. Goodbye." BEEP. SATURDAY, 9:12 P.M.

"Pure, unmitigated bullshit!" Trisha bellowed when the tape stopped.

"If she thinks Austin is such a wholesale monster, why is she still working for the man?" Lane asked.

"That's always been a mystery," Trisha said, and Kate nodded in agreement.

"And what does she mean, her life is ruined?" Lane asked thoughtfully.

"Oh, please . . . who cares. Should I erase it, girls, or do you want to hear it again?"

"God, no, I don't want to hear it again," Trisha grumbled.

Kate raised her good arm and put her hand up to her still-bandaged head. The bruising on her face had faded, but she was still sore all over, especially when she moved, and the cast on her arm was sweaty, cumbersome, and itchy. Suddenly, she threw back her aching head and started laughing.

"Excuse me—I don't get the joke," Lane said dryly.

"Molly's right, don't you see?" Kate exclaimed, as if hearing Molly's message again was a revelation. "You two tried so hard to make me see the light, but Molly is the one who actually did the job, by jumping into bed with my husband."

"Oh, wonderful," Trisha piped up. "We should take her to lunch! Come to New York, you two, we'll take her to the Carlyle. And buy her a nice gift—"

"Funny, Trish," Kate returned, looking in decidedly better cheer now. "But, Lane, just so you don't think it was a total waste, a lot of what I heard in therapy in Carmel *did* make sense—I just wasn't open to it then. I guess I needed a direct hit from a good, old-fashioned home-wrecker."

"Better it would have been a good, old-fashioned hooker than Molly Adams," Lane tossed out.

"No," Kate said, "Austin would have been able to explain away a hooker. Or a bimbo, or even somebody I didn't know. But what better way to blow you out of a bad marriage than your husband having an affair with one of your best friends?"

"But you went running right *back* to him after that," Trisha protested.

"Ahh, but it was never the same. Never. I was always on my guard, always waiting for the next thing to happen. Even through my pregnancy . . ." Kate's face saddened at that.

"Too bad the 'next thing' had to be a scuffle that could have killed you," Lane said tersely.

"Yes, but believe me, what Molly did was the *beginning* of the end. And," Kate leveled, "it's what opened my eyes and my mind to the fact that there are *other* men, *good* men—"

"Like Byron Lassen!" Trisha pronounced with a triumphant grin.

"Stop it!" Kate jumped in, refusing to go there. "Anyway, this 'accident,' " she went on, looking down at the bulky cast on her arm, "was just the *end* of the end. And if all's well that ends well, this ended well, because I'm going to be okay. But if it hadn't been for the nasty 'Molly' business, I might have stayed with him even now."

"I'm sorry, but I am beyond steamed at Molly Adams," Trisha said dourly. "I hope to hell you're not for a minute thinking of forgiving her, Kate."

"No . . . I can't forgive her. But the fact is, she did me a favor."

"Does that mean that you are really, *really* finished with Austin this time?" Lane asked, still more than a little dubious.

"Forever," Kate said with finality.

"But do you still love him?" Lane persisted.

"Absolutely not. The love I whined to you about, Lanie . . . it wasn't love. That's something else I learned in my concentrated day of therapy. It was codependency."

"So you can *definitely* leave him—"

"I can, Lane, and I will. I already have, really. And by the way, didn't I mention, Trish? I *am* going to New York. Tomorrow."

"Tomorrow!" the other two wailed in unison.

Kate laughed. "My father wants me to get the divorce started with his lawyers as soon as I can travel."

"But you can't travel *tomorrow*," Lane protested.

"Really, there's no reason why I can't. I can heal *there* just as well as *here*. Maybe better. I know I'll *feel* a lot better when I get things moving."

"Where are you staying?" Trisha asked.

"With Mom and Dad. Poor Daddy—he can't *wait* for me to leave Austin. I think *he's* afraid that I'll change my mind again too."

"You won't, Katie," Lane said, looking at her friend thoughtfully now. "This time you won't. I can see a strength that you never showed before."

"And I'm telling you girls," Kate said, "I got that strength from what *Molly* did. She's a—"

"She's a *bitch*!" Trisha interjected. "Molly is a world-class *bitch*, and I never want to see her again. Please erase her self-serving message, and let's erase her from our lives."

"No!" Lane jumped up and grabbed Kate's hand before she hit the ERASE button. "Save it," she said. "Put in a new tape."

"For God's sake, why?" Trisha demanded.

"I don't know," Lane submitted. "Just a feeling. I guess it comes from being married to a police detective. Just save it for the time being, okay, Katie?"

Kate shrugged, and flipped the tape out of the answering machine. Picking up a pen from the desktop, she started to write on the label, then hesitated. She looked up at her two friends.

"What'll I call it?" she queried.

" 'Molly's Alibi,' " Lane said.

"How about 'My Ticket to Freedom,' " Kate offered with a smile.

"Make it 'The Bitch's Lament,' " Trisha overruled.

Resolutely, Kate dated and labeled the microcassette, just "Molly." She pulled open one of her desk drawers and tossed it inside. In the same motion, she took out a fresh tape, removed the cellophane packaging, lifted it from its mini plastic box, fitted it into position in her answering machine, and clicked the cover shut.

"I'm going to New York tomorrow, girls," she said then, "to get a divorce."

Chapter 55

"I WASN'T EVEN GONE two weeks, and I swear the boys each grew an inch," Lane complained to Liz.

"And how is Kate?"

"Much, much better," Lane said. "It was terrifying when we didn't know the extent of her injuries, but she's rallied really fast—her arm's in a cast, but she's up and mobile and actually feeling good, and she's going to New York today."

"That's wonderful. By the way, I saw you on the news! I tell you, Lane, I'd have given a month's pay to have been a guest at Jonathan Valley's party."

"It was spectacular! Even Geoff had a good time. And we had a mini honeymoon," Lane smiled.

It was back-to-work-Monday at Hamilton House for Lane. After the gala in Malibu, she and Geoff had spent her last night there at the beautiful Bel Air Hotel. Trish and Peter stayed there too, and while the women spent Sunday morning with Kate, their husbands played a round of golf at the Bel Air Country Club.

On Sunday afternoon, the Newmans flew back to New York, while Lane and Geoff drove leisurely up the coast to Carmel, stopping and shopping along the way. It couldn't have worked out better, Lane was telling Liz, when the two were distracted by the musical tinkling of the old English silver bell above the door, announcing a customer. They looked up to see Lane's father-in-law coming into Hamilton House.

"Greg! Hi!" Lane exclaimed. "What brings you here?"

"Hello, Lane, hi, Lizzie," Gregory Hamilton returned, making his way over to them at the front desk.

"I'll bet I know why you're here, Dad," Lane beamed at the elder Hamilton. "You need a gift for Maggie, and you're clueless!"

Gregory had told Lane and Geoff the week before about his budding relationship with Maggie Carlson, and they were thrilled for both of them.

"No . . . no—" he started now, and he reddened perceptibly.

Lane smiled broadly. Both the Hamilton men tended to blush when they were uncomfortable. Lane kidded father and son about that, but in fact, she found the thought of a couple of big, tough, very physically fit top cops blushing to be enormously endearing. But her smile faded as she realized that Gregory Hamilton was not smiling back. It was obvious that he had something serious on his mind.

"What's wrong, Greg?" she asked, suddenly feeling her heart sink. "Geoff? The kids?"

"Nothing's wrong," he quickly assured her. "Well, nothing having to do with *your* family."

Lane's face registered some relief. "What, then?" she asked.

"In fact I have some *good* news for *you*. Come outside with me for a minute."

Lane scooted around the counter and followed her father-in-law out the front door of the shop. Gregory Hamilton's big white Chevy Suburban was parked at the curb, directly in front of Hamilton House.

"Unbelievable parking spot!" Lane congratulated him with a smile.

Without responding, he walked, rather grimly, Lane thought, to the back of his truck, and stood peering inside the rear windows.

"Come over here," he said, beckoning to Lane then, his eyes still riveted to the windows. "Take a look."

Lane walked to the back of the truck as he opened up the big double doors. When she saw what was inside, she let out a gasp and clasped her hand to her mouth. There, tightly packed in, was a cache of the treasures that had been stolen from Hamilton House over the past months. Before she could reach in to retrieve any of the things, Gregory quickly shut the back doors and turned his key in the lock.

"Get in, Lane," he said. "We need to go somewhere and talk."

"Uh . . . where?" she stammered.

"Someplace private."

"Hold on a minute," she said, touching his arm. She went back to the shop, opened the door, and put her head inside.

"Lizzie," she called. "I have to leave for a while."

"What's going on?" Liz queried.

Lane just shrugged, waved goodbye, and went back outside. She climbed into the huge SUV with her father-in-law. Before she had completely settled into the seat, he gunned the motor and roared off.

"Where are you abducting me to?" she asked him.

"Who's home at your house?"

"Nobody," she said. "Geoff is at work, and the kids are in school."

Gregory headed north on Ocean Avenue. Along the way, he astounded his captive passenger with his disturbing story of discovery and realization while he was a dinner guest at Maggie's house that first night. He spoke haltingly, his gravelly voice cracking.

It was Maggie Carlson who had stolen Lane's things, he said, systematically, piece by piece, over time. Gregory avowed that he was no shrink, but all of it seemed linked somehow to her overwhelming feelings of emptiness and loss after her husband was killed.

Maggie told him that she had intended to return everything, Gregory said—she had been trying to come up with a way to get the things back into Hamilton House without being detected. And now she was in therapy. She was getting help.

Lane sat quietly, dumbfounded. And she could see that her father-in-law, gripping the wheel beside her, was stricken.

"Dad," she said kindly, "I'm sure that you are the best possible therapy that Maggie could have."

"I don't know, Lane. I'm not sure about anything—"

Lane saw a tear rolling down his tanned, handsome face, and it broke her heart.

"Shhh," she soothed, putting a hand on his arm to stop him. "Don't even think about it now, until you've had time to sort it all out. With Maggie," she added meaningfully.

"I just don't know, Lane."

Gregory rounded the corner onto Casanova Drive. "I haven't told Geoff," he said then.

Lane understood his implication. Involving her husband, Carmel's police chief, would mean taking all the booty in to police headquarters where it would be processed as evidence, and taking

Mrs. Carlson into custody. "I wanted to hear how you feel about it first," he said.

When they pulled up in front of Lane and Geoff's English brick-and-stone cottage, Lane jumped out of the vehicle and unlatched the iron gate. She pushed it open for Gregory, and stood aside as the truck lumbered onto her cobblestone driveway.

Gregory leaned out the driver's window. "Close the gate behind us, Lane," he called back to her. As she did, she watched the proud older man, the father-in-law she loved, climb out of his vehicle, walk around to the back, and wordlessly open up the rear doors. She had never seen him like this before—he had the look of a man who was defeated.

Lane was breathless. She was not believing this! Gingerly, as if they would disappear again were she not careful, she started sorting through her returned treasures, looking affectionately at the pieces like so many prodigal children. There were even a few things that she and Liz hadn't realized were gone.

Slowly then, she turned to her father-in-law, whose face revealed the pain he was wrestling with. Shaking her head back and forth, she murmured no, no, she did *not* want criminal charges brought against Maggie Carlson.

Lane and Maggie had been friends and business neighbors for almost fifteen years. She had frequented Manderley, Maggie's small bookshop, even before she opened Hamilton House right next door. And she had *seen* the deep depression that had gripped Maggie for the better part of two years, since Whitney Carlson was killed.

No, Maggie was no criminal, Lane assured her father-in-law. And, she urged, it would be best if neither one of them said a word about this unpleasant business to anyone. Ever. And she would tell Maggie immediately that it would be their secret. They would put it behind them, and forget about it.

"What about Geoff?" Gregory asked her.

"Don't tell Geoff."

"But—"

"Why, Dad? Why tell Geoff? Why make it a problem for him to even have to think about? This is *my* property, and let's you and I just figure I loaned it all to Maggie for a while, to cheer her up when she needed it. Now she doesn't need this stuff anymore. Now she has you."

Gregory was looking at Lane like she was making no sense. "But she—"

"Stop it, Dad. I'm sure that every last piece is here, and in fact it's apparent that Maggie took excellent care of all of it. Everything is polished, gleaming," she enthused, looking over her newly found possessions.

Then she saw it! There among the returned artifacts, the little painting that Molly had done for her years ago when she first opened Hamilton House. Lane picked it up in both hands and stared at it.

Her feelings mirrored her father-in-law's at that moment, she was sure. Sorely torn in two. On the one hand, she had always loved that painting, and all that it evoked for her—the unique closeness that four best friends had shared at Briarcliff. On the other hand, holding that jewel of a painting again seared her hand with the pain that Molly, the artist, had caused them all.

Staring at the piece, she tried to hold her emotions in check for Gregory's sake. He knew nothing about the rent in her longtime cherished group. Gregory Hamilton had his own ration of pain over all of this to deal with. Still, she seemed powerless to move. She simply stood there on her driveway and continued to stare at the sweet depiction of the idyllic white campus chapel that she had known so well.

Suddenly, it hit her, and the effect was as stunning as if a hand had reached out from the painting and slapped her in the face. Molly's hand.

Suddenly she understood what it was that had been bothering her about the Aiden Jannus painting at Jonathan Valley's house!

Chapter 56

─────────────────────────────

You DOING OKAY, Katie?" Henry Spenser asked.

"I'm fine, Dad," she said.

Kate was stirring restlessly in the plush black leather club chair, gazing down at bustling midtown Manhattan from the windows of the sixty-fourth-floor law offices. Twelve and a half years ago she had married Austin Feruzzi in the state of New York, and she had come to the city to start the wretched business of untangling her affairs with him.

She was in a meeting with her father, powerful New York publisher Henry Spenser, and their longtime family attorney, Irving Feintech. The two men were poring over mounds of legal documents. Under discussion: how best to handle Kate's divorce from Austin Feruzzi; specifically, what lawyers they should hire to do the divorce, and what steps they should take to begin to sort out the couple's complex business interests in New York, Beverly Hills, and London.

"Alright, let's talk timing," Feintech said. "When would it be propitious to serve Feruzzi with divorce papers and get this thing rolling?"

"Right away!" Kate piped up. "Today!"

"Well, let me ask you something, Kathryn," the attorney said. "Since your husband is firmly ensconced in your apartment here in New York right now, do you have anything there that is yours alone, and is of significant value, or can't be replaced?"

"Um . . . I'd have to think—"

"The Utrillo is hanging in the living room," her father reminded her.

"Oh, yes," Kate concurred, "my wonderful *Montmartre* by Maurice

Utrillo. Mom and Dad gave me that painting when I graduated from Briarcliff, long before I met Austin."

"Okay," Feintech said, making a note. "Anything else?"

"Well, all of Grandmother Spenser's jewelry is there, in my dressing room—we can't replace that."

"I'll need you to make a list of the pieces," the attorney told her. "What else?"

"I'll have to think about it, but yes, there are some other valuable things at the apartment that belong just to me. Why do you need to know that *now*, Irving?"

"Because we know how unscrupulous Austin Feruzzi can be," he said, looking at Henry for confirmation.

"Honey," her father elaborated, "as long as Austin thinks he still has a chance of getting you back, he'll be Mr. Nice Guy."

"But as soon as he knows with certainty that you are really going through with the divorce this time," Feintech picked it up, "he's liable to take your valuables and hide them, or even sell them."

"And the man has plenty of outlets to do either, as you well know," her father finished. The two had obviously gone over all of this.

"Oh, Daddy," Kate sighed.

"He's right, Kathryn," Feintech said. "So if you want those things back, you're going to have to go over there and get them."

"*Me?*" she shrieked. "I can't go there! I don't want to see him!"

"Pick a time when you know that he won't be there," the lawyer said.

"And take somebody with you, dear," her father put in. "I'll go with you if you'd like."

"Get your list together first," Feintech counseled. "That will save you time. Once you're there, you'll see other things that you'd forgotten about—that's why no one else can do this for you, Kathryn. But make your list as thorough as you can before you go."

"And be sure that Irving has a copy of it," Henry Spenser said.

"Oh dear . . . should I call ahead and let him know that we're coming?" Kate asked.

"Absolutely not," the attorney said. "Just take a car over there, a *big* car to haul away your valuables, let yourself in with your own key, preferably when Austin is not there, as I said, and just quietly remove anything that is clearly yours."

"Hah! Easy for *you* two to say," Kate laughed nervously. "Maybe I ought to bring some New York cops with me."

"Well, be thinking about how and when you want to do it, and let me know, soon," Feintech told her. "Then, once you've taken care of that, we'll have Feruzzi served with divorce papers."

"Kate, Irving and I are going to go over the structure of the business now," Henry said. "You can take a break, and come back in . . . what, about an hour, Irv?"

"About that. Then brace yourself, my girl—I'm going to bring Nate in, and we're going to have a lot of questions for you." One of his partners, Nathan Fields, specialized in corporate law.

Kate got up and went over to the small conference table where the two were working, and kissed both of them on the tops of their heads.

"What would I do without the two of you?" she asked, and she meant it. This was her second divorce, this one was far more complicated than the first, but both of them had given her the self-same depressing feelings of failure.

"When does that cast come off your arm, Kathryn?" Irving asked. She'd known him all her life, and he never called her anything but her given name.

"In three weeks, Uncle Irving. God, can I still call you Uncle Irving?" she asked wistfully.

"Kathryn, all the Spensers are family to me, and you have grown up to be easily the most beautiful woman in New York, so I am very honored to be your Uncle Irving."

Kate laughed and gave him a hug. "I can use some air, clear my head. I'll take a walk," she said. "Want sandwiches?"

"We'll have the chef prepare some lunch when you get back, dear. Be careful."

"I will, Uncle Irv," she said with a lingering smile. "Bye Daddy."

"See you in a bit, honey."

Kate felt lucky. Depressed, and achy still, but so lucky to have good friends and a loving family to help get her through this. Because she was, indeed, going to go through with this. She had never been more sure of anything in her life.

Riding the elevator down to street level on Park Avenue, oddly enough she found herself thinking about her *first* divorce. She had not been as sure about *that* one. She loved Elgin, but his drug use was turning his once-promising life to ashes, and was making *her* life with him unbearable. Her family had pushed divorce, and sweet baby Shawn was caught in the fallout.

It had taken Elgin Horner ten years to hit bottom and finally seek help, and now he walked a somewhat shaky and definitely impoverished line. He had never been able to glue the pieces of his once-charmed life back together, and Kate knew that he never would. Never could. It was too late. But Elgin Horner had always lived in a fantasy world, and from what Kate could see, he still did, no matter that he had bumped solidly up against gritty reality for more than a decade, and had been exposed to heavy Twelve Step therapy.

He'd visited Kate in the hospital every day. Sometimes he brought Shawn. And she let him drive her home on the day that she was released, in his old, grimy, beat-up Ford Taurus. Shawn came too, and the two of them helped her up the front steps, and stood by while Lane and Christina got her into the big king-sized four-poster and propped her up on the lush down pillows.

After she was settled, Lane drove Shawn to soccer practice, Christina went about tending to dinner, and Elgin hung back to talk to her alone. And their conversation was the saddest that Kate had ever remembered having, with him, or with anyone.

"Kate," he'd said. "My Katie. Are you really going to leave Austin now?"

"Yes, Elgin, I'm going to leave him."

"Finally. I've been waiting for this for so long."

"You've been waiting—?"

"Yes, Kate. We'll be together again. The three of us. You, me, and Shawn. As a family."

"Elgin, what are you *saying?*"

"I'm saying that I want you to marry me again. You know I love you, Kate. You know that I never once stopped loving you, I never even *thought* about marrying anyone else—"

"But—"

"Don't stop me, Kate," he went on. "I know I ruined our marriage with the drugs, and the booze, and my arrogance. You couldn't tell me that I needed help, I wouldn't listen. Nobody could tell Elgin

Horner. But I'm clean now, I'm sober, straight, and I'll never fall back. And I love you so much, Kate. Now we'll have another chance."

With that, he'd astounded Kate by reaching into his pocket and pulling out a small white box. A nondescript paper box like the ones they gave out at the wholesale jewelry mart in downtown Los Angeles, Kate noted. Elgin proudly opened up the box and revealed its contents—a diamond ring! A small solitaire diamond, set in a plain gold band.

Kate had looked down, averting her eyes, trying to think. Her glance had settled on her left hand. She'd experienced a flash of relief because, just out of the hospital, and with that arm in a cast, she was not wearing her rings. Her Harry Winston gold-and-platinum emerald-and-diamond rings that were worth about a quarter of a million dollars.

Elgin extended the ring he was holding to her. "It's your size," he said. "It's small, I know, but I'll get there again. I've got a job . . ."

He was sitting on an antique straight-backed chair by her bed, and for just a moment she could see through the wrinkles and the bloat and the receding hairline to the bright, handsome, forceful football hero that she had adored so long ago. She hesitated, choosing her words very carefully.

"Elgin, we had our chance . . . and . . . and we did good," she finally got out. "We created the most wonderful son on earth. Shawn loves you. And he loves me. We did good, Elgin."

"But we were *magic* together! Don't you remember, Katie? Do you remember how much we loved each other?"

"Of course I do, Elgin."

"You were homecoming queen . . . I was your king—"

"That was a long, long time ago, Elgin," she'd said.

"But we can have it all again! With Austin gone, we can—"

"No, Elgin, we can't," she'd pronounced, as gently as she could.

She would never forget the look on his crestfallen face when she'd said that. My God, she'd thought, he really *does* believe that we could be together again. Could he be *that* alienated from reality? Couldn't he see that, even though back in college the two had been on relatively equal footing, now their lives were on opposite poles? Was he the only person on the planet who didn't recognize that?

No, there was someone else who didn't see that. Shawn didn't see it. Shawn would love nothing more in life than to have his mom and dad back together. As would almost all young children of divorced parents, she knew. That was their dream.

Elgin's innocent, sincere, heartfelt, and confident proposal had taken Kate totally by surprise. It had come bouncing right out of left field, and smacked her in the head. She'd had no idea that he entertained even a notion that she would ever go back to him, marry him again, at this juncture in both their lives.

Yes, he had been living in a dream, and she had been completely unaware. Had she encouraged him? Led him to think that his fantasy could become reality? She had always tried to be as nice to him as possible, for Shawn's sake. And for his. She felt sorry for him. And yes, for the sake of what she and Elgin once had, what they once were. King and queen in a fairy tale. It was a lovely memory, but it was only a memory.

And now she was left with a profound sadness in the knowledge that she had evidently hurt him so much. As she strolled down Park Avenue in the crisp autumn air, she could still see Elgin's tired face as he'd pulled himself up out of that chair by her bed two weeks ago. He didn't even say goodbye. Just stood and turned, shoulders bent, dropped the ring back into his jacket pocket, and left the room. And left her house. She'd asked herself then, as she did now, what on earth could she do to make him feel better? Nothing.

Mitigating her compassion for him was anger that he had made Shawn a part of it. That he had snared Shawn into believing that he was going to pull it off, make it happen for them. Shawn was a kid. He couldn't yet see what Elgin was, in the world's harsh terms. To him, Elgin was his dad, and he was some kind of hero.

Austin was something else. Kate had given the lawyers her tape of Molly's apology, to show that he was a cheat, and Lane's tape warning Trisha about her battered face, to show that he was a wife beater. Kate didn't know anyone on God's earth who thought Austin Feruzzi was a hero.

Chapter 57

"Monsieur Feruzzi . . . this is Charles DeFarge . . . I am in New York, and I'm told that you are in this city as well. I must see you tonight, sir . . . it is of utmost importance. I am also given to understand that you are dining out this evening. Therefore, please be expecting my arrival at your building at precisely ten o'clock.

"I shall ask Mr. Luis Fortunas to ring your apartment. If you are not yet at home at that time, you will find me in the vestibule awaiting your return. Much will depend on a positive and successful meeting between the two of us tonight. I look forward to seeing you soon." BEEP. TUESDAY, 9:06 P.M. END OF FINAL MESSAGE.

"Shit!" Feruzzi muttered, staring at the answering machine. *"Dining out?"* Where did the creep get his intelligence? On his way home from the gallery, he had stopped off at The Brasserie on 53rd, wolfed down a greasy steak and a plate of fried potatoes, and washed it down with a couple of beers. Some kind of fancy dining out! Now, sitting at his desk at home, his stomach was churning and his head was aching.

He had finally caught up with Kate today. Christina told him that she was in New York, staying with the Spensers on Sutton Place. He'd called over there, and Kate had inadvertently picked up the phone. Before he could even launch into his usual litany of sincere apologies, undying love, and eternal devotion, she had clipped him with a cool, civil, "Austin, I'm filing for divorce."

Something about the way she'd said it was different this time. It wasn't her usual *Austin, maybe we should separate.* Or *Austin, I'm thinking about divorce.* She had flat out said to him, "Austin, I'm filing for divorce." It had the shrill ring of legalese. Like she was already doing it.

And when he got to thinking about it, what the hell else would she be doing in New York, just four days out of the hospital with a broken arm, broken ribs, and a laundry list of injuries? But for all her pain and trauma, she had actually sounded strong.

So he *gave* it to her strong, just in case she *did* really intend to go through with a divorce this time. You'd be making a huge mistake, he'd told her. Your timing couldn't be worse. Don't even *try* to look for assets. There *are* none. We're operating the business at a colossal loss. Won't be in the black for two or three years. You ought to wait awhile, Kate, if you want your dad to see penny one on his investment.

He'd lightened up then. Made a little joke. Told her that she should *really* wait until he was dead. She'd be much better off a widow than a divorcee. She wasn't amused. Threw a few ice cubes his way and hung up the phone. Now this was all he needed to cap off a crummy day—DeFarge about to land on him in the flesh to shake him down.

He looked at his watch. Almost ten o'clock. He still had Peter Newman's million, intact. And most of Jonathan Valley's payments. He could give it all to DeFarge. But who was he kidding? Even if he sold all the Rhajis he had left, including the one that he damn near got himself killed over, and even if he turned all the rubies around in sales, and dipped into his capital besides, and paid DeFarge everything he was demanding now, it still wouldn't pry the man off his back.

No, even after he ceased all dealings with him, DeFarge would be back for more. The whole DeFarge debacle had been nothing more than a slick extortion plan from the get-go, and it would only escalate, he knew that now. Charles DeFarge was not looking for legitimate payment for legitimate goods—he meant to put a hook into the Feruzzi Galleries for *life*. The man had intended from the outset to bleed Feruzzi and his business, that had been his game from the beginning. Gemstones embedded in the paintings had been just the exotic come-on.

Feruzzi sighed. Blackmail rarely stopped, he knew, until somebody went to prison or somebody died. Nor did he miss the irony—this is exactly what *he* had been doing, and intended to continue doing, to Jonathan Valley.

He kept a gun in the desk drawer in his office. It occurred to him that maybe he ought to haul it out and scare DeFarge off with his .22 caliber Ruger Bearcat. His phone rang, cutting short his reverie. Reaching across his desk, he snatched it up.

"Hello?"

"Hello, Mr. Feruzzi, it's Luis. A Mr. Charles DeFarge is here in the lobby. He says he's expected."

Damn, Feruzzi thought, but he put a smile in his voice for the doorman's benefit. "Would you put him on the phone, please, Luis?"

"Certainly sir . . . just one moment."

There was a shuffling on the other end, then the man's unmistakable, gritty voice came on the line. "Hello, Austin, this is Charles De-Farge."

"Dammit, DeFarge, what do you mean coming to my home at this hour?" Feruzzi spat into the phone.

"You owe me money, sir, and I must have it."

"Look, I don't want to have this conversation in front of Luis, if you don't mind. Call me at the gallery tomorrow and we'll talk."

"We must talk tonight," DeFarge countered, a hint of menace edging his thick Indian accent. "We must talk now."

"Put Luis back on."

There was a brief pause, then, "Yes, hello, Mr. Feruzzi, this is Luis."

"Luis, please send Mr. DeFarge up to the apartment."

"Very well, sir."

Feruzzi slammed down the receiver. He was seething. The bastard's scam was a variation on the ages-old come-on, *the first one's free!* First DeFarge had billed him for paintings at better than reasonable prices. Then his invoices reflected higher prices, because they included the cost of the contraband rubies. Feruzzi had been glad to pay—monies rendered for goods received, at fair prices. But now those prices were increasing by tens. The man who was in the elevator on his way up to his apartment right now was an experienced international con man who set up his marks, then boxed them in.

Dammit, he was not going to take it! He hadn't paid any of URA's astronomical bills for the past ninety days, and he wasn't about to start tonight.

But what were the risks? Would DeFarge dare to inform on him, blow the whistle to the feds about the Moroccan ruby smuggling operation? Maybe so, if the Rhajis really couldn't be traced back to him in Delhi. Certainly this was not the first illegal scheme DeFarge had ever run, and obviously he was one shrewd mechanic, or he'd be in prison by now.

Mr. Tokumatsu had given Feruzzi a heads-up on DeFarge in Tokyo. If the sleaze-bag really did intend to rat him out to Customs, he would have some third party drop the dime. However the man intended to bring him down, DeFarge surely had to be a master at maintaining his own slick coat of Teflon.

Ahh, but could anybody really trace the rubies back to Feruzzi? After all, he could claim that he'd had no idea that there were gemstones embedded in those paintings, and the burden of proof would rest with the government. He had been very careful. Nobody could prove that he'd dug the stones out, or that they were ever in the paintings at all, for that matter. Nor had he paid any of DeFarge's blackmail, so they couldn't nail him that way.

But why did he continue to pay those soaring prices for the Rhajis? they would ask. Simple. Feruzzi saw great potential in this young artist, he would say, and in fact it was now beginning to pay off in escalated prices in the marketplace. It would be his word against the word of a shady Indian grifter, if they could ever pin DeFarge down, and that was doubtful.

And what about the artifacts encrusted with Moroccan rubies that Feruzzi had commissioned and put out there, in Beverly Hills, New York, and London? They were practically mass-marketed. Were the rubies properly laundered, or did they have big, bold arrows on them pointing right back to the Feruzzi Galleries, then to Morocco and beyond? DeFarge knew nothing of the ruby pieces. Or did he?

Feruzzi had never known anything about the origin of the rubies, hadn't wanted to know. But he *did* know that they were not your everyday, run-of-the-mill cut gemstones. Those rubies were bright, uniform, of great purity, and very old. They had to have a story and a provenance. With modern carbon testing, they probably could be positively identified. They belonged somewhere, to someone. And Feruzzi was quite certain that the someone had never been Charles DeFarge.

The buzzer sounded. Feruzzi froze for a beat, then he opened his middle desk drawer and felt around under some papers. His hand closed on the Ruger. He took it out of the drawer, checked to see that it was loaded, and slipped it into the pocket of his sport coat.

He got up and walked to the front door of his apartment. Yes, De-Farge could probably ruin him. He had to put a stop to this treacherous Eastern juggernaut.

_____

Chapter 58

G OOD MORNING, LANE," Trisha greeted her houseguest warmly. "Sleep well, darling?"

"No. Too much on my mind," Lane offered, stifling a yawn. She sat down at the kitchen table and poured herself a cup of coffee. Bright light at the windows suddenly lit up the kitchen, and it was followed in a beat by a sharp crack of thunder. High up at the penthouse level they could hear it, could almost *feel* it, heavy, driving rain pounding relentlessly on the roof.

Trisha joined Lane at the table. "Whoa! I hate the thought of going *out* in this," she said.

"Kate's probably having a hard time getting a cab—"

"She's coming in a limousine," Trisha said.

"Really! To *your* place? For breakfast with *us*?"

"Uh-huh. We have a little surprise for you, too, Lane."

"Oh God. And I haven't slept for days! Where are we going? Do I need makeup? And when you hear *my* news, you're not going to want to go anywhere until we figure out what to do about it."

"Well, we *do* have an agenda, I'm afraid. We're going over to Kate's apartment," Trisha said. "The three of us. And the stretch limo is for hauling away her things."

Trisha explained how the lawyers had instructed Kate to get all of her valuables out of the apartment before Austin could be served with divorce papers. Since the three of them would be together today, it was a perfect opportunity to do it, Kate had figured. Austin would be at work, and they didn't have full-time help at the apartment, so the place should be empty.

"God, I hope so," Lane said. "I'm not in the mood to run up against Austin!"

"No, but what can he do? With the three of us, we've got safety in numbers, and it's not as if Kate's doing anything illegal."

"Still, I wish we had a man going with us. I wish Geoff were here."

"Her dad offered to go, but Kate said that Henry would just grab her painting, grab her jewelry, and whisk her out of there. Katie says she wants to take a good look around, so she won't overlook anything and regret it later. Like a little ceramic vase with daisies on it that Shawn made for her in sixth grade. She's got a list."

"Well, we'll just get it done then. *After* we talk about what I came here to tell you."

"Okay, enough with the teasing," Trisha breathed. "What the hell is so important that you couldn't tell Kate and me on the answering machines?"

"Trust me, Trish, you'll see why I couldn't talk about this on the phone."

"*What?* for God's sake. *Tell* me, Lane!"

"Wait till Kate gets here."

"*Laaay-nee!*" Trisha wailed. "You're making me crazy! Tell me, then you can tell Katie when Her Lateness arrives." Kate was *always* late.

"Cut her some slack, Trish—she just got out of the hospital."

"I know, I know, it's amazing she's even out of bed. But she is *so* determined to get this divorce done, Lane. She met with the lawyers all day yesterday, right through dinner."

"I think our friend has *really* seen the light this time."

"Finally! Okay, now spill it, Lane. What made you leave 'paradise' and come all the way to New York?"

"And right on the heels of spending almost two weeks with Katie in L.A.! Geoff is not thrilled. But the boys are. They get away with murder when I'm—"

"Dammit, you're *not* going to tell me, are you?" Trisha cut in.

"Not until Katie gets here. I can't do this twice, Trish."

"Can I have a hint?"

"Can I have some nonfat milk for my coffee?"

Laughing, Trisha gave it up. The two sat at the table, sipping coffee and perusing the morning newspapers, waiting for the arrival of the third arm of their triumvirate. Which used to be a quartet, Lane mused.

Ever since Monday afternoon, when her father-in-law had brought back the missing Hamilton House pieces—she refused to think of them as *stolen* pieces—Lane's mind had been in turmoil. She'd stumbled upon a startling revelation, and she had to share it with her sisters. But it had to be in person. And it had to include Molly.

She'd alerted Trisha that she was coming east, then tied up some loose ends at home, which included helping Gregory and Liz unload the Suburban at Hamilton House, inventorying the newly found pieces, and putting them back out on display. Then she went home, shared dinner with Geoff and the boys, then shared her story with her husband when they were alone. Geoff agreed with her, she had to go to New York and deal with it.

She'd flown out from San Francisco at noon the day before. Passing up lunch, passing up the movie, passing up dinner, she simply sat there in the jetliner seat, thinking about what she had learned, sifting the evidence backward and forward in her mind, trying to assess exactly what it meant, and what the potential consequences could be.

After landing at JFK and taxiing into midtown, she'd presented herself, with her one bag, at the door of the Newmans' penthouse. It was after ten o'clock, and she was totally exhausted. Trisha gave her a huge hug and led her right into the guest suite.

Her hostess had helped her settle in, all the while demanding, then begging to know what the big mystery was. Lane managed to hold her at bay. There was no way that she could muddle through it all tonight, she'd told her. Finally, with a resigned sigh, Trisha planted a kiss on her forehead and left her to get some much-needed rest. Lane immediately showered and crawled into bed. And lay there with her eyes open for most of the night.

Early morning had brought the deluge. Gloomy day for a gloomy business, Lane observed to herself. The sound of the doorbell broke into her thoughts.

"It's Katie," Trisha said, leaping for the intercom to clear her in.

"She's really holding up okay?" Lane asked.

"Wait'll you see her, Lanie! She's Wonder Woman!"

The two of them went to the front door and opened it wide before Kate had a chance to press the buzzer. Kate stood on the threshold, looking radiant in a black sweater and tights and a bright yellow rain slicker, with a dazzling smile that lit up her beautiful face. She was glowing. The three women collapsed into a huge group hug.

"Come in, come in, get dry, darling," Trisha fussed.

"Trish, I've got a limousine downstairs, which I stepped out of under your canopy," Kate laughed. "Not one raindrop has touched my body!"

"Katie, you are an Amazon!" Lane marveled, thrilled that her friend looked so much stronger than when she'd last seen her just days ago. She and Trisha helped slide Kate's raincoat over the bulky cast on her arm. Trisha hung it in the entry coat closet, then led the way into her office.

"So, tell Lane," she said to Kate. "It's over with Austin, right? For sure, right?"

"Girls, please, stop worrying! It is definitely, irrefutably, forever finished with me and Austin," Kate assured them. "Over! Done! This time you can go to the bank on it."

"Speaking about the bank, you'll come out okay, won't you, Kate?" Lane asked.

"Well, I *thought* so, but already he's starting. Yesterday he told me the only way I'd see a penny is if he's dead."

"Hmmm . . . that's code for he's hidden everything." Trisha ventured.

"Irv Feintech says the business is a rat's nest. But what can I do?"

"You could kill him," Lane laughed.

"Don't tempt me," Kate responded dryly.

They settled themselves into the two comfortable love seats in Trisha's office. Gigi brought in coffee, tea, orange juice, and cinnamon-raisin bagels with small bowls of cream cheese.

"Is this nonfat cream cheese?" Lane asked.

"Come on, Lane, this is New York," Trisha laughed. "We don't believe in eating stuff that tastes like Styrofoam."

Kate dove into the bagels. Trisha sat back and folded her arms. "Okay, Lane. Shoot," she demanded.

Lane had been carrying a tote bag. She reached into it now and pulled out a small painting, and held it out for the other two to see. "Do you remember this?" she asked. "Molly painted it for me when I first opened Hamilton House."

"Yes, of course," Trisha said.

"It's an impression of the chapel on the Briarcliff campus," Kate put in.

Lane set the painting down on the coffee table between them, facing it toward Kate and Trisha. She proceeded to explain to them, in measured tones, what she had seen in Jonathan Valley's huge Aiden Jannus painting. What had bothered her so much, though she didn't know why at the time.

There was an exotic bird, she said, painted in the lower right-hand corner of the lush landscape scene, very close to the AJANNUS signature. It was a special, very distinctive multicolored mythical bird, exactly like the one depicted in stained glass on the big, ornate rose window in that very chapel on the Briarcliff campus. A coincidence? She thought not.

"Do you remember that bird?" Kate asked the women.

"Of course," Trisha responded. "We used to stare at it when we were bored in chapel. It was about twenty shades of reds, golds, oranges—that one?"

"That's the one," Lane said breathlessly. "And that exact bird is in Jon Valley's Jannus."

Kate and Trisha looked from Lane to the painting and back again, perplexed.

"Don't you see what this means?" Lane asked impatiently. "It means that *Molly has been forging the Aiden Jannus paintings!* It means that Jannus never *did* turn out that huge body of phenomenal work when he was a falling-down, drugged-out alcoholic! It was *Molly!* Molly Adams has been painting the Jannuses! Or at least *doctoring* them."

Lane paused, letting her incredible revelation sink in. The three sat without moving, until finally, Trisha broke the silence.

"My God, Lane—you're saying that Molly was doing art forgeries . . . but why? For Austin? It's illegal. She would risk going to *prison* for him?" she asked incredulously.

"Yes. I believe that Molly was involved in some very dangerous criminal activity for Austin Feruzzi," Lane concurred.

"For *what?*" Kate gasped.

"For love, or for money, or for who knows what. And she's going to get caught—"

"Worse," Trisha cut her off. *"She's going to get killed!"*

"What do you mean?" Kate and Lane asked in unison.

Trisha was quiet for a minute, stunned by the realization she'd just had. Thinking it out as she spoke, she laid out her thoughts.

"Look, if this is true," she said, "if there really was art forgery going on at the Feruzzi Galleries, then Aiden Jannus was on to it."

"On to it—?" Lane started.

"Yes. Remember when Jannus got sober?" Trisha went on. "And he was protesting publicly, to anyone who would listen, that he never painted a lot of the work out there that had his name on it? And everybody thought he was crazy, that his brain was fried from too many drugs?"

"Of course," Lane said, beginning to see where she was going with this.

"Well, if there actually *was* forgery going on," Trisha continued, "and Aiden Jannus knew that something was rotten, and he was talking about it, then he had become a dangerous liability to Austin, don't you see? A sober, angry, and very vocal threat to expose the scam."

Trisha looked over at Kate with narrowed eyes, trying to assess how she was taking this, wondering if she would jump to her husband's defense. Kate appeared to be deep in thought. Then quietly, as if to herself, she murmured, "Austin was incensed that Jannus was saying those things. I remember when Aiden was on the Leeza Gibbons show . . . he kept cursing, muttering that he was going to have to straighten Aiden out—"

"You know," Trisha chimed in pointedly, "I watched Austin deliberately try to push Aiden off his recovery program. More than once. I couldn't for the life of me understand why he would do that . . . Aiden was not only his friend, he was the gallery's cash cow—"

"You talked to me about it," Lane remembered.

"Well," Trisha responded evenly, "Maybe Aiden Jannus did *not* die of an accidental drug overdose after all. Maybe Austin Feruzzi killed him."

"Trisha, *really!*" Kate exploded.

"Think about it, Kate," Trisha cut her off. "Why would Austin offer the man drinks at a dinner party, when everyone knew that one sip of alcohol could knock Aiden right off the program and plunge him back into drugs and alcohol? That's what I could never figure out."

"She's right, Katie," Lane put in. "Austin isn't dumb. He *had* to know what he was doing."

"Hey, once, maybe, you could say he forgot. But I saw him do it several times—"

Their conversation effectively slowed to a halt, as the horrific scope of the implications began to sink in, and the women realized what this could mean. Kate's husband, Austin Feruzzi, might be much worse than an unscrupulous businessman, much worse even than a wife beater. He might actually be a murderer—he might have killed Aiden Jannus.

"No," Kate slowly shook her head back and forth. "Not possible."

"Kate, where was Austin on the day they found Jannus dead, do you remember?" Lane asked, her voice quavering a little.

Kate thought for a minute, then she blanched. "Austin was here. He was in New York," she said.

Trisha went on with her scenario. "Well, maybe when Austin saw that Jannus wasn't going to fall off his drug rehab, or be coaxed off," she proposed, "just maybe he found a way to get a drug overdose into him . . . to silence him for good."

"To protect this supposed moneymaking art-forgery scheme?" Kate asked dubiously.

"Not just that, Kate. To save himself from scandal, professional ruin, and prison!" Trisha allowed. "Because Aiden Jannus was sober, he was catching on to something, and he was talking."

Subdued, the women started discussing their erstwhile friend Molly Adams and her part in all of this. They speculated again on what would make her do something so reckless. And tossed around some possible answers. Money? Her love, or whatever it was, for Austin? Just total naive insanity? Or all of the above.

Kate was holding her head in her hands as Trisha completed her thoughts. "If Austin *did* kill Aiden Jannus," she reasoned, "then Molly's life is in danger too."

"My God, you're right," Lane whispered. "If it's true that Molly has been forging Aiden Jannus paintings, and I'm sure it is, Molly could certainly expose Austin."

"And don't forget, she despises him now, and he knows it," Lane said. "He knows he can't count on her loyalty anymore."

"And that's got to be why she didn't quit her job!" Trisha exclaimed. "Because Austin could expose *her* as well. She's up to her eyeballs in this!"

Finally, Kate weighed in. She flat out did not believe it, she told the others. It was too far-fetched. Molly was around Aiden Jannus a lot, she said. The Feruzzi Galleries represented the artist, and since he lived and worked in New York, all of his paintings were delivered to the New York gallery.

And Jannus was in the gallery often, Kate said, for one reason or another. Maybe Molly showed Aiden some pictures from college, she reasoned. Jannus was probably taken by the odd shape and colors of that bird. That's what artists do, Kate pointed out—they take their inspiration where they find it.

Also, Kate maintained, Molly wasn't that *talented*. Not *Aiden Jannus* talented, for heaven's sake. She insisted that there was no way that her husband and Molly Adams could get away with a flagrant scheme of that magnitude without being found out.

"Look, we have to confront Molly," Lane said. "Trust me, I saw Molly's handiwork in Jonathan Valley's Jannus, a painting that has been seen all over the world press. A painting that is signed by Aiden Jannus."

"To hell with her!" Kate fumed.

"Katie, listen to me," Lane implored. "You are half-owner of the Feruzzi Galleries. You're *exposed* on this. This kind of scandal would wipe out your business!"

Kate's beautiful face darkened. She knew Lane was right. If indeed there were such a villainous, corrupt, and deadly operation going on within the business, it would certainly sink the Feruzzi Galleries. And put people in prison. And ruin her.

"We have to sit Molly down and get it out of her," Lane said again. "That's why I came three thousand miles to tell you this in person. This is dangerous information. It could be deadly."

Trisha threw out the sobering warning that they were *all* involved now, simply because they *knew* about it. It wasn't just *Molly's* life— *all* of their lives could be in danger.

"Okay," Trisha submitted. "Who's going to call Molly?"

"All of us," Lane said. "We'll conference her."

The women fanned out through the apartment and got on three different extension phones. And Trisha dialed Molly's number at the Feruzzi Gallery.

O KAY, RUN THIS past me again, will you?" Lane urged. "What exactly is the plan?"

The three friends were huddled in the passenger compartment of the sleek black stretch limo, headed for the Feruzzi apartment on Fifth. Kate had called before they left to see if Austin would answer. As expected, he didn't. The machine picked up, with her own voice on it. She'd slammed down the phone before the beep sounded.

Minutes before, they had reached Molly at the gallery. Their four-way conversation was short and to the point. Molly, sounding more than a little abashed, had agreed to meet them tomorrow night at Trisha's office at Global after her radio show. Neutral territory, the three had decided beforehand.

"The plan," Kate reiterated now, "is to get to my apartment, get ourselves inside, gather up my stuff, and get the hell out of there before lunchtime, on the off chance that Austin comes home."

She inadvertently shuddered at her own mention of Austin. Austin a forger? A killer? She didn't believe it.

"And what if Austin *does* come home? *Is* home? Then what?" Lane, the practical one, wanted to know.

"Easy," Trisha tossed out. "We are a united front! We'll beat the sonofabitch to the ground if he gives us any shit. What do you say, Katie?"

"I like it," Kate said, albeit grimly. "You two can hold him down while I gather up whatever I can find."

"Then we'll take the car and go to lunch," Trisha said with a satisfied smile. "La Grenouille. The rack of lamb is terrific on Wednesdays."

They had pulled up in front of the distinctive prewar building. "God, my heart is pounding out of my chest," Kate whimpered.

"Get over it," Trisha tossed out with bravado. "This is going to be a piece of cake."

"Got your list?" Lane asked.

"Yup."

"Got your key?" From Trisha.

"Yup."

"Good," Trisha said. "Let's go."

The three women trooped up the slick marble steps in the driving rain and scooted into the lobby, leaving the car and driver waiting at the curb.

"Good morning, Donaldo," Kate said to the doorman, ushering Trisha and Lane toward the elevators.

"Good morning, Mrs. Feruzzi," the man responded with a smile, then turned his attention back to his newspaper.

They rode silently and not a little nervously up to the eighteenth floor, then padded down the hall to the Feruzzis' unit. Kate fished in her shoulder bag and came up with a key. Tossing a brief glance at her two friends for moral support, she put the key in the lock, turned it, and opened the front door a crack.

"The alarm isn't set," she whispered.

"Dammit, he must be here," Trisha whispered back.

Kate opened the door the rest of the way and the three stepped inside. They walked gingerly through the entryway and around the corner into the large, well-ordered living room. It was empty. Trisha let out her breath in relief. Kate turned to the other two and patted her throat with her good hand, signaling to them that she couldn't find her voice.

Lane stepped into the breach. *"Austin, are you here?"* she called out. There was silence.

Led by Kate, they walked across the living room, past the game room, and down the hall to Austin's office. Empty. Then through the dining room to the bright kitchen and breakfast area. Those rooms were also empty. Noiselessly, they headed back in the opposite direction toward the master bedroom suite.

The door to the suite was closed, but not locked. Kate slowly opened it a bit and peered into the room. Then she swung it open wide and walked inside, followed by Lane and Trisha. The bed was made, and no one was there.

"Maybe he slept with one of his little Chiclets last night," Kate said.

"Oh, you don't think, do you?" Lane asked.

"Who the hell knows?" Kate threw back. "The great thing is, I don't care!"

"Whatever, let's get cracking," Trisha decreed. "I'd just as soon not see the bastard."

"Right," Kate responded, and sprang into action.

She went into a closet and hauled out four matching Louis Vuitton cases, and arranged them open on the bed. Then she scooped up armfuls of her belongings—clothes, shoes, purses, jewelry, and various incidentals. She handed them off to Lane and Trisha, who folded and stuffed them quickly into bags. Satisfied that she'd covered the drawers, the closets, and the dressing room, she disappeared into the big master bath.

Lane and Trisha were busying themselves tamping down the suitcases when they heard Kate scream. They rushed into the bathroom, then stopped short.

They had found Austin Feruzzi. Dressed in flannel slacks and a gray tweed sport coat, and sprawled facedown over the side of the black marble Jacuzzi tub. A thick stream of puddled, drying blood tracked over the marble and down to the drain.

And on the floor outside the tub lay an antique brass dagger, its handle encrusted with Moroccan rubies, and its blade encrusted with blood.

Chapter 59

FULL NAME, Augustine Dante Feruzzi," Lane could hear Kate reciting to the detective who was taking notes. "Austin always carried his passport and driver's license with him. His birth certificate, Social Security papers, and the rest of it are probably in California . . ."

The three women were still in the master suite. The body was still in the bathroom. Upon discovering it, Kate had let out a piercing scream, Trisha threw up in the sink, and Lane had pounced on the bathroom phone and dialed 911. Tiers of authorities had been arriving at the scene. She and Trisha had been interrogated. Kate had just identified the body.

Looking over at Katie now, Lane could not believe the way she was handling this. She was not at all the newly grieving widow. Not even registering the *shock* one would expect from a woman who had just discovered the hacked-up body of her murdered husband, albeit a wife beater who had victimized her for years. This was a woman who, just last week, was flat on her back in the hospital under heavy sedation. Now she was the definition of strength. Lane knew that she was still in quite a bit of physical pain, but you certainly wouldn't know it from her behavior right now.

In fact, it occurred to Lane that maybe she *should* present as just a bit weaker. Show *something* of the grieving widow, play the sympathy card a *little*. Even that cast on her arm didn't look like an impediment—instead, you got the feeling it was something she just might whack you with if you messed with her.

Before anybody got there, Lane rang up her husband at the Carmel Police Department, told him the whole grim story, and put him on speakerphone so the other two could hear him. He told the women not to touch a thing, not to move stuff around, not to put their fingers anywhere. He briefed them on who they could expect to be arriving. The uniformed officers, a couple of NYPD homicide detectives, photographers, forensics people, a medical examiner from the coroner's office, probably some higher-up officials, maybe even the feds, because Feruzzi's business was international.

They were still pouring in through the front door, singly, in pairs, in groups, carrying all manner of lights, cameras, equipment, gadgets, a gurney. In the midst of all the commotion, Kate seemed strangely emotionless. Businesslike, even. Yes, she had gone on record to her women friends, saying that she was totally and forevermore finished with Austin Feruzzi. She had been downright ebullient this morning, Lane recalled, even after hearing that her husband had probably put the reputation of her company, her family's jumbo investment, and her own fiscal future in severe jeopardy.

No, Katie was never going to go hungry, and yes, Austin Feruzzi was a quintessential creep, but still, Lane reflected, decorum would seem to dictate an air of restraint when one's husband of twelve years was lying carved up and bloody in his Hugo Boss jacket, slumped over the bathtub in the very next room.

Kate's words this morning, though said in jest, kept tap-dancing around Lane's sleep-deprived brain. "He says I won't find any assets as long as he's alive—none at all," she'd said. For a fleeting moment—no doubt, she was sure, because she was married to a police chief—Lane wondered darkly if Kate could have actually gone home and killed her husband last night, then planned to have her two friends come over to the apartment with her this morning to "discover" the body.

Or . . . could *Molly* have done this? she asked herself. She was being ridiculous now, she knew, but Geoff had taught her to consider all possibilities in any given situation, business or personal. Certainly that would apply to murder, she thought with a frown. And she couldn't begin to know what was motivating Molly Adams's heinous behavior of late. If Molly was reckless enough to have had an affair with Kate's husband, if she was villainous enough to engage in some kind of art forgery, then could she be desperate enough to kill the man who had snared her into this dangerous business, then played her for a fool in love? Hell hath no fury . . .

TRISHA WATCHED THE crime-scene activity with professional detachment. She was sure that the story was already on the news. You don't get a crowd like this in an upscale Fifth Avenue apartment, with a high-profile businessman murdered in the bathroom, without word of it leaking out to the press. She would be talking about it on her radio show this afternoon. That is, if they let her out of here by three o'clock.

It was all too surreal. And grisly. She was still reeling over the concept that Austin Feruzzi could actually have murdered Aiden Jannus, when they'd stumbled on the man's body in the Jacuzzi. So who killed *him*? It occurred to Trisha that Austin Feruzzi moved in a world of dark and unsavory shadows, despite his veneer of respectability. She had never known how sunny, beautiful Kathryn Spenser could have spent so many years in that dismal relationship. And she took upon herself a measure of guilt for it, because it was *her husband* who had introduced them.

Peter was working at home when Lane and Kate were meeting with her this morning. She had taken a few minutes to duck into his den and bounce Lane's startling theory off him. When she'd suggested to her husband that Molly Adams might have painted the Jannuses, or altered them, his response was that it sounded preposterous. And of course it did.

And when she threw out her own thoughts that, *if* it were true, maybe Austin Feruzzi actually killed Aiden Jannus with a drug overdose to protect his forgery scam, Peter had stood up, come out from behind his desk, and put his arms around her. He told her that he fully understood why she and her friends would be furious with Molly, and enraged with Austin, but overactive imaginations were probably at play here, and Trisha should just stay out of this. Trisha was torn—maybe Peter was right.

Now the investigators were asking the three of them to volunteer to have their fingerprints taken by one of the forensics technicians. To be able to rule theirs out when they chose what prints they would run through AFIS, the Automated Fingerprint Identification System, they said.

ALL OF NEW YORK seemed to know about Austin Feruzzi's murder already. Marcus, Kate's limo driver, told her that while he was waiting for the women downstairs with the car, he had heard all about it on the radio news. And, of course, he saw the police vehicles and ambulance pulling up, and the officials streaming into the building. He offered Kate his condolences. She told him to take her to the Feruzzi Gallery at 65th and Madison.

When the police had finally released her, long after they had let Lane and Trisha go, she'd felt drawn to the gallery. She was now the sole owner of the business. She felt enormously energized, physically and emotionally, despite all of her still-raw breaks and bruises.

And oddly, she felt an absence of grief for her dead husband. Someone had suggested that she was in shock, that the horror and the grief would set in later. She *did* feel sadness for what she once *thought* they had together. Funny, that's how Molly had put it. Austin was a classic sociopath—he made you *think* that what you saw was what you got.

But she *was* grieving on this day, as she had been since her tragic fall down the stairs. She was grieving the loss of her innocent baby girl. And feeling a profound sense of guilt. She would always feel that she had failed her.

Failed to protect her baby from Austin! He killed her. And she had let it happen by not removing her from harm's way. Child endangerment, they called it. Oh, it was not technically murder, she knew, but it might as well be. Her baby had died because of his violence! That's what had triggered her turnaround. That's what had made her strong. That was what had awakened her to what so many had tried to tell her, including the therapists and session leaders in Carmel. It was too late to save her baby now, but she knew that if she didn't get out, *she* would probably be next.

Maybe her dispassion over Austin's death was not so odd. Her displeasure with him, her constant disappointment in him, her fear of his rages, her humiliation over his cheating, her pain and embarrassment when she was battered and bruised, her consummate disillusionment in what their life had become—all of that in combination had turned into a blazing firebrand of searing hatred when he murdered her baby girl. She couldn't possibly grieve for him.

The detectives had asked her how she felt. Terribly upset, she'd told them. Horrified. Now she asked herself how she *really* felt, because it was nothing *close* to terribly upset. In fact, she felt empowered. Stronger than she had in years. And liberated. Free! *That* was her key emotion. She felt as if she had just been let out of prison. Delivered of her demons. No more Prozac and Valium with white wine chasers. She had a future now. She would run the Feruzzi Galleries.

As she cast her eyes out the window of the limousine, the streets of New York looked washed down and clean. The rain had let up, and the sun had come out, and her life seemed suddenly uplifted now. Worth living, finally.

Looking ahead on Madison Avenue now, Kate could see that a sizable crowd had gathered on the sidewalk, and was spilling out onto the street. With a start, she realized that it was media who had set up cameras, and lookie-loos who had stopped to watch, and the focus of their interest was the Feruzzi Gallery. It didn't take the newshounds long to sniff out a juicy story, she noted to herself with a grimace.

As the big car glided to a stop at the corner, she jumped out before Marcus could come around and open the door. Almost before her feet hit the pavement, the newsies closed in on her, minicams rolling, still-cameras flashing in her eyes, men and women shouting questions:

"How do you feel about your husband's murder, Mrs. Feruzzi?"

"Who was with you when you found the body?"

"What happened to your arm?"

"Is it true that your husband pushed you down the stairs?"

"Did you kill him, Kate?"

Putting her head down, Kate moved briskly and resolutely toward the gallery door, saying nothing, pushing through the accretion of people blocking her way. Marcus had leaped out of the car and bolted in front of her, doing his best to clear a path. Kate felt spirited, in control. Glancing up at the sign over the gallery doorway, her agenda began to take shape. She made a mental note that her first order of business would be to have her lawyers change the name of the business to the *Spenser* Galleries. A fresh start.

Well, not her *first* order of business, she amended. Her second. First she intended to deal with Molly! Pushing the heavy glass-and-brass door open, she felt herself taking on the mantle of an avenging angel. She had never before felt this kind of adrenaline rush. Marcus managed to keep the press outside, she noted with satisfaction. Closing the door behind her, she strode directly over to Molly, who was sitting at her desk.

Molly looked clearly startled to see her. Kate didn't know if it was because she had so much guilt in her heart, on every score. Or was it that Kate presented such a strange and offbeat image at that moment, a startling contrast to her former soft, serene, pulled-together self. Kate was a tower of strength, with tousled hair and ruined makeup, in black tights and ribbed-knit sweater, brandishing a clumsy cast on her arm that went from her elbow down to her knuckles.

"Oh, Kate, I'm so sorry—" Molly blurted out.

"Sorry that my husband is dead, or sorry that you slept with him?" Kate snapped back like a whip at Molly.

"Kate, please—"

"You're fired, Molly," Kate said. "Now, leave."

"But . . . who's going to run the gallery?" Molly stammered. "Howard's making a delivery—"

"That's not your concern, Molly," Kate fired back at her. "Just get out!"

"But, Austin—"

"Austin's dead."

"I know—"

"Goodbye, Molly."

Stunned, Molly picked up her purse. "My things—" she started.

"I'll have them sent to you," Kate threw back coldly.

Kate looked after Molly's departing figure and seethed. Let *her* deal with the damned press, she groused to herself. Maybe they would yell at her, *"Is it true that you were sleeping with the dead man?"* God knows, they seemed to know everything.

Molly hurried sheepishly out the door—quite a different exit from the dramatic retreat she'd made from Trisha's dinner party the last time they were together, Kate reflected. The next time would be tomorrow night, at the meeting that Lane had insisted on, to confront her about forging paintings. Kate didn't believe it for a minute, but what the hell, she thought, let Molly squirm. Her former good friend and college roommate Molly Adams infuriated and sickened her.

Kate took a deep breath, making a conscious effort to calm herself. She walked into Austin's spacious office in the back of the gallery, and tentatively looked around. She had been there many times before, of course, but now it looked different. It was *her* office now.

She opened up the file drawers, pulled out some entries, then sat down at the desk and started leafing through the gallery's books. She was not even sure what she was looking at, but she intended to learn. Putting the files aside, she slid open the desk drawers, one by one. In the bottom, left-hand drawer she saw a key, with a plastic label attached to the key chain. The label read STOREROOM.

Picking up the key, she went to the small room behind the office. She had never been inside the storeroom. She'd once asked Austin about it. Just useless inventory and assorted junk in there, he'd told her. She inserted the key, and turned the lock.

Hitting the light switch, she gasped! A treasure-trove! On tables, on chairs, stacked up against the walls, scores of paintings—all of them with the familiar signature in the lower right corner, AJANNUS!

She knelt down and started to pore through them, looking carefully at each one. And almost immediately, she saw them. Clues in the canvases of Molly Adams's handiwork. Subtly planted in different spots on each of the paintings were assorted small impressionist images—images that were lifted right out of the four friends' college years at Briarcliff!

"Dear God," she breathed, half aloud. "Oh my God, Lane was right!"

All of the paintings were signed AJANNUS. But it was obvious to her that Molly had painted them, or at least had doctored them, then left her own inventive "signature" on them. It was a "signature" that, in all the world, only Lane, Trisha, and herself would recognize.

Kate moved in to take a closer look at one of the paintings, which seemed to glisten curiously in the light. Broad, grainy strokes portrayed an ancient, charming country inn, with muted terra-cotta stucco walls, faded blue shutters, and a red tiled roof, shaded by giant poplar trees in bloom.

She bent down to scrutinize the canvas. Gingerly, she touched her finger to the paint. And recoiled! Her heart nearly failed her! Aiden Jannus was long dead—*and the paint was wet!*

Chapter 60

"Yo, Tripp! Ding, dong, the sonofabitch is dead! Is this his karma for the rotten things he did, or is it me getting my prayers answered? It's all over the news here, Tripp—out there, too, I'm sure. We've been shooting on the streets in midtown all day . . . up and down Third Avenue in the Sixties. Pete Samuels, my cinematographer, told me about it between setups. He said 'Jon, isn't Austin Feruzzi your art dealer? Well, they just found him whacked in his own bathroom!'

"We've got a technical adviser on the movie from the NYPD, a homicide detective, Joe Grasso, great guy. Anyway, I asked him if he could get me any information . . . you know, inside stuff that's not on the news. Here's what he found out . . . seems there was a steady stream of visitors to Feruzzi's apartment yesterday. A team from a housecleaning agency, a dry-cleaning delivery guy, some art dealer—Eastern looking with a heavy accent, according to the doorman—and a couple others. He also said Feruzzi's wife went in for a while, then left. And, get this, Tripp . . . Byron Lassen! Billionaire Byron Lassen paid a visit to Austin Feruzzi at home last night. Late! Now, those two apparently had never met until I introduced them at the party Saturday night, remember? I did it just to tweak Feruzzi, as you know.

"Well, I'm sure Lassen didn't kill the bastard—I mean, if he wanted Feruzzi out of the way to make sure his wife didn't go running back to him again, he could have hired the entire New York Mafia to do the job for him, right? Yeah, yeah, I know . . . I see too many movies.

"All I can say, Tripp, is that New York's finest are going to find out that there's a long, long list of people who had an interest in seeing Feruzzi dead!

"We're shooting late . . . till about seven. Then I'm going right home. Call me later at the apartment. Bye." BEEP. WEDNES-DAY, 2:46 P.M. *END OF FINAL MESSAGE.*

"Yes, Jon," Tripp mouthed with a frown, "there's a long list of people who wanted Feruzzi dead—*including you!*"

Jon Valley had been raging more and more vehemently to Tripp about Austin Feruzzi escalating the pressure on him, and now Feruzzi was dead. According to the news reports, Feruzzi was stabbed to death—hacked up, the lead detective said, with this odd-looking, old, ornate knife, brass, set with rubies. Tripp squeezed his eyes tight, try-ing to obliterate the image of the night when he gave Jon Valley the ruby-handled letter opener. Could Valley have been one of the "cou-ple of others" the doorman had mentioned obliquely? Tripp had known the movie star to grease the palms of certain doormen, limo drivers, etc., with hundred-dollar bills to "forget" his name.

Valley's words reverberated in his mind now: *"I swear to you, I'm going to find a way to kill him."* Though Tripp had never known Jon Valley to be a violent man, he remembered the chilling feeling he got when Jon had said those words—he remembered getting the distinct impression at the time that his friend was not joking.

Clearing the phone messages on his cellular, Tripp tried to think things through. He had heard about Austin's murder just an hour ago, while having lunch with an artist's agent at The Grill, a popular restaurant on Dayton Way, just around the corner from the gallery. It was *the* Beverly Hills power-lunch spot at the moment, and several people in the crowded restaurant had stopped by his table to ask if he had heard the news.

Tripp had actually reeled with shock. He excused himself to his lunch partner and hurried back to the gallery. Pouncing on the phone machine, he checked the messages. There were several inquiries, friends, clients, asking about what had happened to Austin, but noth-ing from New York, nobody in authority calling with any real informa-tion, or instructions on how he should handle things. Of course, the person who always dictated policy was Austin, and Austin was dead.

Briefly explaining the situation to several browsing patrons, he thanked them for understanding, and asked them to leave because the gallery was closing. Then he sent the rest of the staff home. Walking to the entry with the last of them, he locked up the doors and put the CLOSED sign in the window.

And not a minute too soon. Sitting at his desk in the niche along the back wall, he had an unobstructed view of the front windows and the glass entry doors. Media people had begun to gather outside. Some of the more aggressive were ringing the bell and banging on the doors. All of the phone lines were lit up. Tripp wanted to get out of there, but he didn't want to deal with the press. He decided to stay put until they all got tired of waiting.

He tried calling Kate Feruzzi at Austin's house in Beverly Hills. Christina, the housekeeper, answered, and told him that Mrs. Feruzzi was in New York. So he called the Feruzzi apartment in New York. A silly idea, he realized, as he listened to the ring—that was the *crime scene*. There had to be colossal pandemonium going on there. He was amazed when a man with a crusty voice picked up the phone.

"Yeah?"

"Hello . . . ahh, is Mrs. Feruzzi there?" Tripp had asked.

"She's gone."

"Do you know where I can find her—?"

"Whoozzis?"

"Well . . . who's *this?*"

At that, the line went dead. Guess the guy didn't want to play guessing games, Tripp figured. He considered calling back and identifying himself as Austin Feruzzi's gallery director on the West Coast. Then he decided there was no point, he certainly couldn't help.

Next, he tried calling Jonathan at his place. No answer. No surprise—they had started shooting his movie this week, and Jon's message had said that he'd be home sometime after seven. He accessed his personal messages, first at home, then on his cell phone service. Then he turned on a small transistor radio that he kept on his desk, and tuned it to KNX, L.A.'s top all-news station, to listen for updates on the story.

All the while, the noisy press were literally camped on the gallery doorstep, and just as *he* could see *them*, he suddenly realized that they could also see him. And much to his chagrin, one of the television news crews was actually pointing a camera through the glass at the inside of the gallery now. He wasn't sure where the legality lay—he knew that it was against the law for them to photograph on private property without permission, but they were standing outside, on a public sidewalk.

Deciding to remove himself from the line of sight, Tripp got up from his desk and disappeared into Feruzzi's back office. He dropped into one of the chairs at the long teak table that they used to lay out artwork for clients. It was strewn with books; papers; pens; measuring tapes and rulers; open magazines; frame corners of varying materials, styles, and colors; pieces of art; and all manner of odds and ends.

Tripp just sat there, not sure what to do. He gazed idly around the crowded space, looking at nothing. His eyes skimmed over the walls, with their floor-to-ceiling shelves packed with reference books and supplies, then settled on the locked door to the private anteroom off Feruzzi's office—the room that Austin had always told him never to go into. Not that he could have—Austin had always kept a heavy padlock on the door, and he retained the only keys. It occurred to Tripp that if he had a gun, he'd shoot the damn lock off and see what was inside. Which gave him an idea.

There was a fully equipped red metal tool chest up on one of the shelves, which they kept on hand to deal with housekeeping chores, like straightening frames and hanging artwork. Tripp got up, hauled the heavy box down, fished through the contents, and pulled out the heaviest claw hammer. It took just three whacks to crack the padlock open. Easy, he thought—locks were only for honest people. Anybody could get into any of them if they were determined to do it. Carefully, he lifted the shackle out of the link, and pushed the door to the storeroom open.

What caught his eye immediately, leaning up against the far wall, was the immense Rhaji sun painting that Jon Valley had originally bought, the one that Austin Feruzzi had flown across country and made that fateful pilgrimage to Valley's Malibu house just to retrieve.

Tripp was stunned. Feruzzi's excuse for his outlandish behavior that morning was that he'd promised the painting to someone, someone he dared not renege on. Mafia, he'd suggested, though Tripp had taken that with a grain of salt. No paperwork had ever turned up on the painting, but that didn't mean that it never got sold—Tripp knew that Feruzzi played fast and loose with the books. Still and all, it was *his* candy store, so Tripp rarely asked questions. He didn't want to know.

Feruzzi had never said another word about that Rhaji, and neither did Tripp. Wherever it went, Tripp had assumed that it was definitely gone, history. Why else would Austin have gone ballistic over it if he hadn't needed to deliver it to someone? But no, it hadn't gone anywhere at all, legally or otherwise. Here it stood, in Austin's locked storeroom!

Tripp walked across the room to get a closer look at it. Instantly, he recognized a flagrant change in the painting. It was the sun figure. That giant painted sun up in the top right corner. When last he'd seen it, the big rolling ball on this particular Rhaji appeared to be done with a built-up impasto of acrylics or resins, or some type of polymer that produced a glossy surface in low relief. Now the sun was set down flat to the canvas, and it looked to Tripp as if the giant orb had been liberally brushed over with oil paint.

Tripp remembered that when this Rhaji had come in from Delhi, it was markedly different from all the sun series paintings that they had received before, because of the artist's robust, dazzling new treatment of the sun image. He had thought at the time that Rhaji Mentour had simply come up with a bold new technique, and it was awesome. But now this painting looked exactly like all the others that had been sold out of the gallery, only bigger.

Now Tripp realized that not just this one, but *all* of the paintings in the sun series had likely been shipped with that solid buildup on the sun icon, and for some reason, Feruzzi had tinkered with them in this private storeroom before he put them out for sale. It appeared to Tripp that his boss had broken down all the raised sun images, then brushed over the remaining flat circles with oils.

But why? Why would Austin change those lustrous, glowing sun symbols on the Rhajis? Tripp asked himself. He was mystified. It made no sense. He remembered Jonathan's mandate to him. *"Find out, Tripp,"* he'd said. *"You're close to him . . . you're plugged in to his world. Find out what the hell is up with that fucking painting!"* Tripp felt certain that the answer lay somewhere in this room.

He was distracted by more doorbell clanging from outside the gallery, the press demanding entree. Well, they would have to break the doors down, Tripp vowed—he was not about to go out there. Still, he felt like a prisoner in a preposterous situation. Alone in a posh Beverly Hills art gallery, with no escape until there was an all-clear outside on Rodeo Drive. But even news vultures had to go home *sometime*, he reasoned. Then he sobered. It occurred to him with a sinking heart that maybe they just kept replenishing their ranks with fresh troops!

He watched the phone lines in the storeroom flashing, as the answering machine out on his desk in the niche, and the one on Austin's desk in his office, kept spewing dueling messages, which clashed with the ongoing radio news.

Closing the outer door to blunt the din, Tripp turned his attention to the narrow work station that ran down the middle of the storeroom, bolted to the concrete floor. Moving a couple of stools aside, he opened up drawers and cabinets, and perused the built-in shelves. All were crammed with tools and supplies, familiar materials consistent with the work they did. Except for one item. From a cabinet, Tripp pulled out a high-voltage heat lamp. Why would Feruzzi need a heating element? Next to it was a frayed cardboard box filled with scissors, wire cutters, picks, a brandawl, a high-powered magnifying glass, several palette knives, and tweezer sets in varying sizes and configurations, along with assorted bits of rags, their fabric stained with bright yellow paint. Tripp pinched off some of the thick paint and rolled it around between his thumb and forefinger. It was slick, waxy.

Moving the tools around in the box then, he caught sight of a small, dust-covered particle embedded in a corner. With one of the tweezers, he carefully picked it up. Opening a drawer, he took out a piece of clean, soft cotton chamois cloth. Dropping the particle from the tweezers into the cloth, he wiped it clean, then opened up the chamois to see what he had. It was a ruby! A small, dark red antique-cut ruby, exactly like the stones that were set into the hafts of the short brass daggers that the Feruzzi Galleries sold.

Tripp put it together. Here was the answer to Jonathan's repeated question, "What *was* it about the painting?" It was about smuggling gemstones!

The heat lamp, and the consistency of the yellow paint on the rags, told him that the process used on the sun images back in India was not acrylics or resins, as he had first thought. Rather, it was the ancient process of *encaustic,* one of the oldest forms of creating art, still to be found in two-thousand-year-old masterworks.

It was all done with beeswax, raw powdered pigment, and dammar varnish, heated together, then applied with a brush right from the hot pan. Each brushstroke would cool immediately, drying fast on the canvas. Jasper Johns used encaustic to burn in the delicate, tissue-like layers of color on his world-famous images—his numbers, giant maps and targets, his doughty American flags. And unlike hard plastic resins and acrylics that would set up rock solid, and would have to be pulverized somehow to yield the gemstones, encaustic was essentially wax. It could be broken down with . . . a heat lamp! Feruzzi had actually been *melting* the sun symbols on the Rhajis, and using tweezers to pick contraband rubies out of the residue!

So this was why DeFarge was into Feruzzi for so much money, Tripp reasoned, still cradling the little gemstone in the palm of his hand. Rubies embedded in the Rhaji sun paintings! Tripp dealt with the books—he knew that Austin was not paying up. And from the New York detective's description, it had to be DeFarge that the doorman had let up to Feruzzi's apartment last night. Did DeFarge kill Austin? If so, the man had left big tracks. DeFarge was wily, but he was certainly not invisible in the worldwide art market. It might take a while, but they would surely catch up with him, and he had to know that.

Picking up the wall phone, Tripp punched up Jonathan Valley's number in New York. It rang a couple of times, then Valley's voice came on the line.

"Hello?"

"Hello, Jon," Tripp said. "The good news is you can have your Rhaji now."

"What?"

"The big Rhaji sun painting that you paid for, the one that Austin grabbed back. I just found it. It's here in the storeroom—"

"Whatever, that's not the good news, Tripp! The *good* news is—"

"Yeah, yeah, I know," Tripp cut in. "Just tell me, Jon, where is your ruby-handled knife?"

Chapter 61

MOLLY ADAMS WAS terrified. She had made so many mistakes. Five days ago she had turned forty, a major milestone. At this juncture, she should have her life together, but instead, it was crumbling around her. Sitting alone now in the tiny studio in her Chelsea flat, perched on a stool in front of an easel, there was no way that she could bring herself to put brush to paint and canvas.

So many mistakes, she lamented, the litany cycling again across her mind's tumultuous terrain. Her affair with Austin. A gargantuan mistake. Then further compromising her principles for him, compounding that mistake. And then, believing that Austin Feruzzi would ensure her career as an artist. Taking him at his word, even after he'd dumped her, humiliated her. And even more significantly, after she'd come to know the very worst about him.

Not the least of which was the Aiden Jannus mess. She should have gone to the authorities with her suspicions about Austin's connection to the artist's drug overdose, but she had been too frightened. Too afraid that in the course of their investigation they would insert *her* into the picture. So she kept quiet, did nothing. Another mistake.

Now she had made the biggest mistake of all. And they would find her fingerprints in Austin's apartment. But could they trace them back to her? She'd had her prints taken in the past. Once when she was bonded for insurance purposes. Did those prints go into some kind of crime-data computer file? She had no idea, but probably not. And she'd had her thumbprint taken for her old New Jersey driver's license, but that was years ago. Would they find it, and make a match? Again, she had no idea, but certainly it was possible.

But this was all useless speculation, she agonized—they always found *something*. It could be traces of wool from the teal-green sweater she'd worn, or a couple of strands of her long red hair. What should she do? What *could* she do? Nothing.

She couldn't even call her "sisters," the women to whom she had turned for help and solace throughout her entire adult life. Mentally, she flashed on an image of the three of them, sitting in front-row seats, cheering at her execution.

Trisha, Lane, and Kate. Dear Katie. She had so grievously wronged Katie. She would never in her life forget the hardened glint of steel fury in Kate's brown eyes when she'd confronted her in the gallery this afternoon. And fired her. Soft, sweet-natured Kate Spenser, who was always the first to think the best of anyone, who always gave people the benefit of the doubt. Now Kate was intensely bitter, totally unyielding where Molly was concerned, and she was well aware that she deserved no better.

This morning, the three had scheduled a meeting with her for tomorrow night. *Demanded* it. And that was *before* they knew that Austin had been murdered. They'd known *something*. That's why Lane had come into New York, she'd said. Yes, it was certain that they knew something, and maybe they knew everything.

Their phone call had ripped her heart out. Cold, brief, and to the point, the three had conferenced her on separate lines, probably from Trisha's apartment. They needed to see her, Lane said. Tomorrow night at Trisha's office at Global, six o'clock. They needed to talk to her about something very serious. Very seriously illegal, Lane had elaborated. And if she didn't show up, Trisha had alluded that they might be inclined to take the matter up with the police.

Oddly, after verifying that she was there on the phone with the other two, Kate had said nothing. She was probably too white-hot angry with Molly to even speak. But she had let her know by her presence on the line that she was part of this. Part of whatever it was they knew, or thought they knew.

Now the whole world knew that Austin Feruzzi was dead, and Molly didn't dare avoid that meeting with the women. Which, to her amazement, was still on for tomorrow night. Trisha had called late this afternoon and left a message that the meeting *place* had been changed. And again, to Molly's great amazement, Trisha had gone on to say that their meeting would be at Kate's apartment. *In the apart-*

ment where Austin's body was found this morning! Was Kate going to *stay* there, she wondered? It was her apartment, after all. But *now?* And still weakened from her recent injuries? If so, there was nothing at all weak about Kathryn Spenser—she was a whole lot stronger than she'd ever appeared to be. If so, then Kate Spenser was a rock.

In fact, Molly knew that all three of them were strong, and always had been. Even beautiful, sensuous Kate, strong in her own way. She was a survivor. Austin was dead, and Kate had survived. But Molly had always thought of herself as stronger even than the other three, because she had never had their money, she'd had to work and scrap for everything she had. Even for the academic scholarship to go to Briarcliff. Molly had always been the very embodiment of fortitude. Now she wondered if *she* would survive.

Trisha's last words on the answering machine reverberated in her consciousness now. *"We'll meet at Kate's apartment,"* she'd said. *"On Fifth. I don't have to give you the address, Molly. You know where it is."* With that, a clatter suggested that she had slammed down the phone.

Yes, Molly knew where the Feruzzi apartment was. She'd been there many times when the friends were close, and again, of course, when they were not. And she dreaded going back there. But she had no choice. She had to find out what the three of them knew, and perhaps explain herself, defend herself. Maybe beg for their mercy. Ah, but there was little chance of any mercy from their camp, she knew.

Looking up, for a few long moments she studied the painting that was set up on the easel in front of her. She loathed it, and everything it stood for.

From the ledge of the easel, she picked up a small, sharp knife that she used to make fine corrections. Standing up, she grasped the painting firmly by its kiln-dried doorskin frame, and with one vicious swipe of the knife, she slashed the canvas down the middle.

Having done that, she whirled around, and with eyes narrowed, she took stock of the rest of the paintings in her studio. Then suddenly, like some kind of frenzied dervish, breathing heavily, she attacked each one of them with the knife, chopping, slashing, rending them to ruins. Until there was not one painting left intact. Only then did she stop. And look about her studio in horror at what she'd done.

Slowly, she opened her sweaty hand, and let the knife drop to the floor.

Chapter 62

I HAVEN'T TALKED TO Shawn since Austin . . . since we found . . ."

Kate was using her good hand to fidget with a lock of her dark auburn hair. "He's at his dad's," she went on, "but nobody's answering there."

"Have you left messages?" Trisha asked.

"Of course. I've been calling Elgin's apartment since yesterday afternoon. As soon as I could, after—"

Lane jumped in this time. "Did you call Shawn's school?"

"Yes—they told me he wasn't there today!"

Trisha and Lane could see that Kate was borderline frantic. Because she couldn't find her son? Or because her husband had been murdered. Stabbed to death in this very apartment. Which meant that there was a killer on the loose. Someone who'd apparently had no trouble getting past security and getting in here. Did Kate know who did it? Was it someone they all knew? Or was it possible that Kate was jittery because *she* was the one who hacked her husband from behind with a deadly-sharp letter opener?

The morning papers reported that the doorman had seen Mrs. Feruzzi go into the building at about nine o'clock on Tuesday night, then leave a short time later. The next morning, the three women found Austin's body. Kate had said nothing to her two friends about having gone to see Austin the night before, and now they didn't dare ask.

The women were sitting in the living room of the Feruzzi apartment. They looked like they belonged in three different worlds. Trisha, in trim charcoal pin-striped business suit with dark hose and high heels, had come directly from her radio show. Lane, in faded stone-washed denim jeans, yellow-and-white striped cotton shirt, and Reeboks, was living out of a suitcase. And Kate, who had hardly slept at all in the last forty-eight hours, looked tired and disheveled in oversized gray cotton sweats and bare feet, with a bulky cast on her arm.

The apartment had about it an unsettling air of unfinished business. Order had been somewhat restored, most of the things had been put back close to where they belonged, but there were yellowish ninhydrin stains in spots, and a residue of glinty gray-black dusting powder smudging nearly every surface and countertop. Reminders that a murder had taken place here.

"Promise me that you're not going to sleep here tonight," Lane demanded of Kate, looking around at the sooty mess.

"No, I'll stay at Mom and Dad's until I can get a cleaning crew in here. But I couldn't have this meeting at *their* place, and I just wasn't up to going in to Global. Besides, now we can observe Molly at the scene of the crime."

"Oh, *please,* Kate," Trisha breathed.

"Well, why *not* Molly?" Kate threw back. "I'm quite sure that the orange-headed she-devil is capable of anything! Aren't you?"

"But . . . *murder?*" Trisha persisted dubiously. "And why would she kill Austin?"

"Why would she *sleep* with him? Would you have believed *that* six months ago?"

"Hmm . . . good point. And it's certainly true that she had reason to hate him—"

"Let's table this, can we?" Lane interjected. She'd been cautioning all morning that they try to keep cool heads.

The doorbell rang, and the three of them jumped. Kate sprang out of her chair and grabbed the intercom receiver.

"Hello, who's there?" she said into the speaker.

"It's Luis, Mrs. Feruzzi. Ms. Adams to see you."

"Send her up, Luis."

Kate opened the front door and left it ajar a couple of inches, then hustled back into the living room and rejoined the others. She didn't have regular help at the apartment, and she did *not* want to open the door for Molly. Much too hospitable a gesture. Let the bitch come on her turf without any kind of greeting.

She sat down next to the other two on one of the white-on-white silk couches, deliberately leaving the facing couch empty for Molly to sit alone. The women waited in edgy silence, three pairs of wary eyes turned toward the entryway. Now thick tension hung on the tenebrous dust in the air.

Wordlessly, Molly materialized in the archway that led from the entry into the living room. She stopped there, and for a long moment, nobody spoke.

"Sit down, Molly," Trisha finally uttered, breaking the silence. She and Lane were watching her curiously; Kate was blatantly staring her down. Molly stood her ground in the foyer.

"Why did you call me here?" she asked then, aiming her question at Lane.

"Sit down," Trisha directed again. Molly walked into the room and sat on the couch opposite the other three, looking unequivocally self-conscious.

"I'm really glad to see all of you—" she started.

"Cut the crap, Molly," Kate snapped. "Lane, tell her what you found out."

"What I found out," Lane said, looking hard at Molly, "is that you have been forging Aiden Jannus artwork."

"That's ridiculous!" Molly said.

"We've seen your so-called signatures on the paintings," Lane persisted. "Your subtle subtext, all those painted images from Briarcliff."

"I don't know what you're talking about," Molly replied evenly.

"Then where did the dozens of Aiden Jannus canvases in the gallery storeroom come from?" Kate demanded.

"Austin was holding them for the next show—"

"Oh, really," Kate stopped her. "On one of them, the paint's still wet!"

"This is insane—I never touched Aiden's work," Molly insisted. "It's against the *law*, for God's sake."

"No kidding!" Kate spit out.

"You have paint under your fingernails, Molly," Trisha observed coldly.

Molly looked down at her hands self-consciously. "Of course I have," she said. "I'm an artist."

"Molly," Lane stated flatly, "you're *lying*." The quiet way in which she'd said those words stopped the conversation cold. All three women looked at Lane. Pulling the little Briarcliff chapel painting out of her tote bag now, she held it out toward Molly. Exhibit A. With all eyes on the painting, Lane explained to Molly in slow, deliberate tones how she had recognized the stylized painted bird in Jonathan Valley's Jannus, the very same bird that was depicted in stained glass in the Briarcliff chapel's rose window.

Kate picked up the thread, citing several of the specific telltale images, other Briarcliff College "signatures" that she had seen painted on A JANNUS-signed canvases in the New York gallery storeroom. The three-tiered fountain on the campus quad. The braided shafts of wheat that were depicted in relief on the Briarcliff seal. Even the lopsided terra-cotta-colored water pitcher that Lane had made when she'd tried her hand at potting in their sophomore year—all four of them had laughed at it back then. Its peculiar shape and distinctive coloring were unmistakable now, portrayed on a small pine table in an Aiden Jannus painting.

"Alright . . . stop!" Molly blurted, dropping her head into her hands. In hushed tones, she confessed that she *had* worked on the Aiden Jannus paintings. And, she admitted, Kate was right—she had painted new ones even after Jannus was dead.

"What the *hell* were you thinking?" Trisha threw out, truly stunned.

"Believe me, I've asked myself that a hundred times," Molly whispered.

"Who knows about this?" Lane asked her.

"Just you girls," she said, looking from one to the other. "No one else. Aiden is dead. Now Austin is dead. And only you three would understand those symbols."

Trisha, Lane, and Kate exchanged looks. It was true, they were the only people on earth whom Molly couldn't scam about this, the only ones who could "read" her misty Briarcliff images. Teary-eyed, Molly said it had never occurred to her that the three would ever be in a position to scrutinize the paintings, since her small Briarcliff impressions were so subtle, and the Jannuses always sold so quickly.

Kate was studying her now from under narrowed lids. "So how much money did you take out of my business?" she asked, shaking her head in disgust.

"None at all," Molly returned.

"*Oh, right,*" Kate tossed back at her derisively. "You did it for *love!*"

"Yes, love," Molly put in, "but not for love of Austin, if *that's* what you think. I did it for love of art."

She explained to them that finally, her art was appreciated. People were paying big money for it. And she "signed" the pieces with the Briarcliff likenesses, she told the women, so that at least *she* could see a little bit of herself in the high-priced paintings for which she got no credit and no money.

"What do you mean, *no money!*" Kate demanded again. "Surely you got your cut, like any criminal does—"

"Not a nickel!" Molly had found some strength. "I thought that if I didn't profit from this, if I just fixed up the paintings a little bit, everyone would benefit, and I wouldn't really be doing anything wrong."

She told them how it started, innocently, small at first. Austin was alarmed because Jannus was habitually drunk or drugged out, and the artist was turning out increasingly substandard work. Their reputation would be shot, he'd said, if the Feruzzi Galleries put out this garbage with Aiden Jannus's name on it.

It was Molly who'd had the idea, she said. She offered to do a little work on one of Aiden's particularly slipshod canvases to see if she could improve it. Austin knew that she was good. "Why not?" he'd said. He couldn't sell it as it was, and she certainly couldn't make it any worse. That's how it started. Then it escalated, Molly told the women. Soon, she was doctoring most of Jannus's work, and even creating "AJANNUS" art from scratch. And it was selling, big time. And she found herself irrevocably locked in.

"What do you mean, *locked in?*" Trisha wanted to know.

Trying hard to disregard the disdainful looks coming at her from the others, Molly attempted to explain. "As the volume swelled, I got more and more uncomfortable, but Austin urged me on. Then, when we started our affair, I . . . I became blind to everything else," she stammered, avoiding Kate's burning glare.

"Were you so blind that you couldn't see how he operated?" Kate seethed.

Recovering, Molly tossed back evenly, "Not as blind as you, Kate— you couldn't see through him for thirteen years."

"Stop it, both of you," Lane put in.

"So why didn't you quit when you got your *'eyesight'* back at my dinner party that night?" Trisha inquired in acid tones.

"After our breakup, I *did* quit the gallery," Molly said, "but Austin threatened me—he told me to come back to work, and to keep on painting, or he'd go to the police."

"That's crazy," Lane jumped on it. "If Austin had gone to the police with this, *he* would have gone to prison."

To that, Molly told them that Austin had threatened to turn it all back on her. He would tell the authorities, and the press, that because Aiden Jannus was a drug addict and could no longer work effectively, Feruzzi's New York gallery director, Molly Adams, an artist herself, went into collusion with Jannus for money. For cash on the line, she was "fixing" his work, and even doing entire paintings and signing his name to them. And that he, Austin Feruzzi, had never been aware that much of the artwork was actually Molly Adams's work, not Aiden Jannus's. When he found out about it, he went right to the police, he'd say. This was major art forgery, and his clients had been duped.

"But Aiden would have said he was lying!" Lane protested.

"At that time, Aiden was usually drugged to incoherence, and he had his own troubles with the law. Austin said that nobody would believe him. That he was a drunken, drugged-out reprobate, and he'd probably turn up dead one day, kill himself with an overdose."

"And you *fell for this?*" Trisha asked dubiously.

"I didn't know *what* to think," Molly said. "I was scared, I was devastated by Austin, I knew by then that he was capable of anything, and . . . and I had no friends to turn to for advice." That was why, Molly said, even after their final blow-up, Austin was able to get her to come back to work, and to keep her painting the forged Jannuses.

Then, when Aiden Jannus died, Austin insisted that she squeeze out a few more fakes. "We'll call them Jannus's last works," he'd said. "They'll be worth a fortune!" Austin wanted to get every last bit of mileage that he could out of the Aiden Jannus name and mystique, Molly said, and he knew that collectors would be clamoring to get their hands on the artist's "last paintings."

By that time, anything that was signed AJANNUS was going for about half a million dollars. And God knows how much he got for that huge Jannus landscape that he sold to Jonathan Valley, Molly remarked.

"Three million," Kate breathed, as if to herself. "He bragged about it."

Then Austin deepened his hooks into her, Molly told the women. When they had exhausted the Jannus mother lode, he promised, they would sell *her* work. Very soon, she would be painting out in the open, under her own name, and he would support her work by having the Feruzzi Galleries represent her exclusively. He *created* Jannus, he'd reminded her, and he would make Molly Adams the *next* Aiden Jannus. That was simply good business for both of them, he said. So she stayed.

"Charming," Kate put in dryly. "Of course he promised you the moon. He needed you to break the law for him, keep those sleazy forgeries of yours coming. And I don't believe for a minute that you weren't taking home tons of money."

"Look, you three know how I live," Molly countered, with a passion that surprised the others. "Look at my apartment, look at my clothes. Look at my bank accounts. What do you see? Someone who's raking in big bucks? No, you see a person who makes sixty-two thousand dollars a year, who pays her taxes, and who barely scrapes by in the most expensive city in America."

Then she amended her colloquy: "Someone who *made* sixty-two thousand a year, that is, before she got fired."

"If you're looking for sympathy, you're in the wrong place!" Kate actually barked at Molly.

"*Aiden Jannus* deserves the sympathy," Lane murmured, almost to herself. "Austin was right, the man *did* eventually kill himself."

With that, Molly stunned the other three. "I think *Austin* killed Aiden Jannus," she said.

She went on to expound that when Jannus got sober and started speaking out publicly, alluding to *forgery,* Austin became threatened, desperate. He deliberately tried to knock the artist off the Twelve Step program. She had seen him offer alcohol and God knows what else to Aiden, she said, even in the gallery.

Aiden had been calling the gallery constantly, she told them, asking about this piece or that piece with his name on it. Demanding that she take Polaroids for him. He was becoming increasingly suspicious. And when he called the gallery on that Monday afternoon to ask questions about three more of his paintings, he said he had to have the information right away because Austin was on his way out to Sag Harbor, and they were going to have it out. That night, they found Aiden Jannus with an overdose of drugs in him.

"Aiden was doing great on his program," Molly said. "Then Austin went to see him. And then Aiden was dead. Think about it," she concluded quietly.

Trisha and Lane exchanged glances. So their theory was not so far-fetched after all. Austin was in Sag Harbor that day! It was dangerous information, but it was moot now, because Austin Feruzzi was dead. You can't charge a person with murder posthumously. Nor could you ever prove such a thing in a civil case. But if speculation arose that Austin Feruzzi had actually caused Aiden Jannus to OD, the Feruzzi Galleries, soon to be the Spenser Galleries, would be forever tainted. And irrefutably ruined.

"Can you prove that?" Lane threw out the question anyway, studying Molly's resolute expression as she faced the others down.

"Of course not," Molly said. "Austin never let me know that he was in New York that day. He never showed up at the gallery. It was Aiden who told me that he was going out to Sag Harbor. At the time, I thought it was very strange that Austin had kept his whereabouts secret that day."

"What are you trying to say, Molly? That Austin tied the man down and drugged him?" Kate challenged.

"No," Molly said, "I'm saying that Aiden was vulnerable. Any addict is. And I'm convinced that Austin found a way to get him to shoot up heroin, or whatever it was that they found in his body. And it was enough to kill him."

"That's a big accusation, Molly," Kate said, but the others could see that she was disturbed.

"Look," Molly said again, "Austin was rotten. He was evil to the core. And in the end, I saw that."

Kate leaned forward on the couch then, favoring her injured left arm. Looking squarely at Molly, she posed the question that had been burning in her for months. "So tell me, Molly," she uttered with low-level vitriol, "since you hated my husband so much, why the *hell* did you sleep with him? After all that we four had been to each other, how *could* you do that to me?"

Fishing a wad of tissues out of her purse, Molly said that she had been trying to make some sense of it. It went back to their college days, she said. She was the misfit, and she wanted so much to be like them. Especially, like Kate. She wanted to *be* Kate, she cried now. Beautiful, cool, rich. Everybody in love with her. And somehow she had the misguided notion that if she had Kate's husband, if she had Kate's life, it would be the next best thing. "And most of all," she said, choking up, "at the time, I thought . . . I thought I was in love with him."

The others were decidedly unmoved. Kate had fixed Molly with a frigid stare. Interrupting her weepy monologue now, she threw out in measured tones, icicles dripping from her words, "Well, Molly, you are going to prison—for a long, long time."

The doorbell rang then, slicing through the tension in the room, causing all four of the women to start. Kate leaped off the couch and raced across the floor to the intercom in the entry.

"Who is it, please?" she demanded. The women could hear only her side of the conversation.

"Good Lord . . . ahh . . . put him on the phone, Luis.

"Elgin, what are you doing here?

"No, it is *not* convenient right now. I have people here—

"You . . . what?

"Oh my God! Put the doorman back on.

"Luis, please send them right up."

Kate slammed the receiver into its cradle, and announced to the room at large, or to no one, "Dear God, it's Elgin! He has Shawn with him!"

She paced a bit in the entryway then, seeming to forget that the others were there, or that she wasn't nearly finished with Molly Adams. But she didn't open the door this time. Instead, she peered through the one-way peephole, to make sure that her ex-husband did indeed have her son with him. And she was livid.

When the two appeared outside her door, Elgin with a big grin and a bouquet of convenience-store flowers, and Shawn looking sheepish, uneasy, Kate swung the door open and fell on her son, gathering him into her arms.

"Shawn, darling, are you alright?"

"I'm okay, Mom."

"Oh, my baby, I love you, honey, I love you so much . . ." Kate held him close, rocked him in her arms as best she could with the cumbersome cast.

"I love you too, Mom," he squeaked.

Ignoring Elgin, Kate held Shawn at arm's length then and said, "But what are you *doing* here? You weren't in school today!"

Shawn looked over at his father for support. Kate finally pulled herself together enough to stand aside and tacitly usher the two inside. Closing the door behind them, she directed her attention to Elgin.

"Well?" she asked.

"Well, we both love you," Elgin said, the wide grin still lighting up his puffy face. "We love you, and now we can all be a family again," he declared, extending the cellophane-wrapped flowers to Kate.

Kate was totally nonplussed. She couldn't scream at Elgin. Shawn was already uncomfortable enough. What had Elgin filled the boy's head with? she raged inwardly, but she contained her anger, for her son's sake.

"Come, Shawn," she said, putting her good arm around him and guiding him into the living room.

Elgin followed, still clutching the tired bouquet. That's when Kate remembered the three women, who were all, even Molly, sitting in place, expressionless, trying hard to be invisible.

"Hi, Lane," Elgin said cheerfully. "Hi, Trisha, Molly. This is a great place, Katie," he offered, looking around at the spacious living room.

"Elgin, we have to talk," Kate pronounced, darting a grim look his way. "Honey," she said to Shawn, "have you had dinner?"

"No—"

"Really!" Kate let out, throwing another nasty look at Elgin.

Lane sprang to her feet. "I'll fix him something," she said. "Come on, Shawn, let's go in the kitchen and get you fed."

"Darling, tomorrow's Friday," Kate said to her son then as Lane came toward them. "You can't get back home in time for school tomorrow, so you'll stay with me at Gram and Gramps' for the weekend, and I'll put you on a plane on Sunday afternoon."

"He's staying with me," Elgin said. "We're at the Blenhope." When Kate looked at him perplexed, he added, "It's on West Thirty-seventh Street, just off Broadway. His clothes are there."

"Elgin, he is *not* staying with you down there. And we don't need his clothes. He has enough here." It was patently apparent that she was trying to control her anger. "Come into the den with me, Elgin. We have to talk privately."

Shawn, seeming enormously grateful to escape from the room, allowed Lane to usher him into the kitchen. Kate fairly marched herself into her late husband's office, with Elgin right behind her, leaving Trisha and Molly still sitting awkwardly on opposite couches. With her son showing up out of the night, the "Molly" situation had ceased to be priority with Kate.

Once in Austin's den, Kate wordlessly indicated a chair to Elgin, then closed the door. "Why did you take Shawn out of school?" she demanded then, still standing. "Why didn't you ask me? What is this about?"

"It's about us, Kate," Elgin answered, laying the flowers on Austin's desk. "It's just a few days out of school for Shawn, but it's the rest of our lives for us as a family."

"What are you *talking* about, Elgin?"

"You'll never go back to Austin now. The evil hold he had on you is finally broken. You're free. And Shawn wants his mom and dad to be together."

Without taking her eyes off him, Kate lowered herself into the chair behind the desk. She was clearly flabbergasted, and trying staunchly to keep a lid on things, to stay cool.

"I know that you were confused when I offered you this before," Elgin went on, reaching into his pocket and pulling out the now familiar white box that she knew held his diamond ring. "You were badly injured, you were upset. But now Austin is dead, and we can be married again—"

"What do you mean a *few* days out of school for Shawn?" Kate interrupted. "How long have you had him in New York?"

"We got here Tuesday night. We wanted to surprise you. Shawn begged Christina not to say anything. We were going to come over yesterday, but then Austin—"

"Elgin, you *can't* just take him out of school. Listen to me," she said earnestly. "I have custody, Elgin. But Shawn is fourteen, and he loves you, so I've allowed him to be with you when he wants to be, because he was never comfortable around Austin. But you *cannot* take him out of school. You *cannot* take him *anywhere* without asking me. You—"

The shrill ring of the telephone on Austin's desk stopped her. She looked down at the phone, but didn't pick it up. The ringing tripped the answering machine, and they both listened.

> *"Mrs. Feruzzi, are you there? Mrs. Feruzzi, pick up the phone if you're there. This is Detective Watson . . ."*

Kate and Elgin sat motionless, both of them staring at the combination telephone and answering machine that had come alive on Austin's desk.

> *"Mrs. Feruzzi, we have to talk to you. Detective Mora and myself. Call as soon as you get this—"*

Kate snatched up the phone. "Yes, Officer Watson," she said breathlessly. "I'm here—"

"Oh, good. We're coming over there to talk to you, Mrs. Feruzzi. Okay? This can't wait."

"I . . . yes . . . I guess so—"

"We'll be right there."

"Did . . . did you find anything?"

"We'll talk when we get there, Mrs. Feruzzi."

"Alright," Kate said, but even before she got the word out, she heard a click on the other end of the line. She put down the phone. Then looked up at Elgin, fixing him hard with her eyes.

"From now on," she said, "we're going to stick to the judge's ruling. You'll get every other weekend, and four weeks in the summer. Shawn will not be coming to you in between those times anymore. And you are *not* to pick him up from school, *ever*, or—"

"What did he say?" Horner cut her off.

"What did *who* say?"

"That cop . . . the one on the phone."

"He and his partner are coming over here."

"When?"

"Now, I guess."

"Kate, I want you to come with me and Shawn—"

"Elgin," Kate said, making no attempt to mask the exasperation in her tone, "aren't you hearing me? Shawn is not going with you. I can't believe that you took him out of school, took him across state lines, took him all the way across the country without even *telling* me, let alone asking me . . . it is totally unacceptable, and if you ever do anything even faintly resembling that again, I'll take you right back to court . . ."

Elgin wasn't listening. His eyes were cast down, fixed on the accoutrements that were arranged on Austin Feruzzi's desktop. "I thought the police had that," he said.

"Had what?"

Elgin picked up a pen, and with it, he moved a jewel-handled letter opener which had been partially hidden beneath some papers. "This," he said. "Isn't this the murder weapon, for God's sake?"

"Uhh . . . how did you know that?" she asked.

"I don't know—I heard it on the news, or I read it somewhere. I can't remember. Maybe Shawn told me."

Kate knew that she hadn't told Shawn about the murder weapon. And she thought that the police had withheld the description of the antique-looking brass, ruby-handled knife. Still, she certainly hadn't seen or heard all of the worldwide press—the knife had probably been described somewhere, maybe even in the tabloids. These days, leaking information for money was a cottage industry.

"This is another one," she told Elgin, indicating the jeweled knife.

"There were *two* of them?"

"There were a lot of them. Austin sold them in the galleries. They're reproductions of antique knives. People use them for letter openers. The police *do* have the one that killed Austin," she said.

"It looks dangerous," Elgin remarked, picking up the blade. "Why would you keep one in your bathroom?"

"I . . . I sometimes go through the mail at my vanity table—" she started. Then, staring at him, she asked, "How did you know there was a letter opener in my bathroom?"

"It was in the reports . . ." Elgin was running the blade idly across his thumb. Was it in the reports? she asked herself. It could have been.

"Look, Elgin," she said, "you have to leave, but first I need to know that you understand me about Shawn. From now on—"

"I *do* understand, Katie," he put in, smiling now. He put down the letter opener, and picked up the box that held the ring. Carefully removing the diamond from its case, he held it in his right hand, and with the other, he reached across the desk for her hand. Kate pulled back, staring at him in disbelief.

"What I understand is there's nothing standing in our way now," Elgin went on. "All those old problems are solved, Katie, because we'll be together now. You, me, and Shawn."

He sat there, a benign smile on his face, holding the ring out to her. Kate closed her eyes. She tried to sort things out. Elgin was delusional, and somehow, he had sucked her son into his fantasy world. Shawn was here, and the boy was more than likely terribly frightened. Certainly confused. Molly Adams was just beyond this door, actually sitting in her living room. The detectives were on their way to interrogate her again about her husband's murder. Fingering the cast on her arm, she opened her eyes and fixed her gaze on the man sitting across from her, her first love, the father of her child. She felt dizzy.

"Elgin," she said quietly, in even tones, as if talking to a child, "you have to leave now. We'll talk about everything later."

"Alright. We'll stay at the hotel tonight, Shawn and me. Then tomorrow—"

"*No!*" Kate shrieked. "No! What's *wrong* with you? You're *not* taking Shawn! Just go, Elgin. Get out of my apartment."

"You know," Elgin said, as if he hadn't heard her, "you won't have to give up anything, Katie . . . your beautiful house back home . . . this place . . . all your pretty things—"

"Pretty things?" Kate echoed, watching him with narrowed eyes.

"Such pretty things," he went on. "You even kept the little silver frame I gave you with Shawn's baby picture . . ."

"Wh . . . what?"

"That little flower frame that I had Altobelli Jewelers engrave with Shawn's name and birth date."

Kate felt her head reeling. The miniature silver frame in the shape of a rose that held a picture of Shawn as a baby—she had forgotten where it came from so many years ago, but obviously Elgin hadn't. It was . . . in the master bathroom down the hall . . . *on her vanity table!*

"Elgin," she said guardedly, "you've never been in this apartment before tonight, have you?"

"No, of course not. You know that."

"But you *have* been here, haven't you? You left Shawn alone at that hotel and came in here on Tuesday night, didn't you?" She heard her voice cracking. With sickening certainty now, the pieces had fallen into place. "*You* did it," she leveled in a monotone, her eyes still fixed on Elgin's.

"Katie, what are you talking about? You're tired—"

"You killed Austin. Didn't you." It was more a statement than a question. "You killed Austin," she repeated, in a whisper this time.

After a long pause, Horner, still smiling, said, "I did it for you, Katie. Don't you see? Austin would have killed *you* eventually. He almost *did*. Now you're free. I did it for *us*!"

"How . . . how did you get in here?" She was stalling him.

"I said I was someone else. I told Austin I needed to talk to him about you. He let me in."

"You told him you were . . . *who*?" she asked, trying to keep him talking until the police got there.

"It doesn't matter," he said. "Somebody. Shawn tells me things, you know."

Kate had no idea what he was talking about, but it was clear to her now that he had an agenda, and that it wasn't sane.

"Now come on, Katie girl, we've gotta get out of here," he was saying now. "We have to get the boy and scram before they find me. I didn't come here that night to *kill* him, you know. I came here to *talk* to him. To tell him that he had to leave you alone now, he had to stay away from you this time, or I'd have to hurt him. I was just threatening him. Just trying to scare him. But he pulled a gun out of his pocket—"

Kate could see reckless hysteria glint in his eyes as the horror of what he was telling her registered. Feeling panic turn her stomach over, she started up out of the chair, eying the door. Elgin fished into his coat pocket again, and this time he came up with a gun.

"This is it, this is his gun," he rambled on, looking at Feruzzi's small Ruger Bearcat, then pointing it at her.

"I'm a lot bigger than Austin," he went on. "I wrestled him for it. I got it away from him, pointed it at him, and he started running . . . ran down the hall and into the bathroom, and tried to close the door—he was gonna lock it, I guess, and use the phone in there to call the cops . . . but I forced the door open. He started fighting me. And there was this letter opener sitting on the vanity table . . . *your* vanity table, I guess, Katie. I'd show you," he said, tilting his head in the direction of the master suite, "but we don't have time."

"No, Elgin, please don't—"

"Be quiet, honey . . . we're leaving now. You, me, and Shawn. We have to hurry. I have money. We won't even go back to the hotel for our stuff. Get a coat, that's all. We'll go right to the airport, fly to Miami. From there, we'll go to—"

Kate could contain herself no longer. She opened her mouth and let out a long, piercing scream that brought Trisha and Molly running to the den. Trisha pushed the door open.

"What's wro—*Elgin!*" she shrieked, seeing the gun in his hand and pulling up short.

"Don't come in here," Elgin said to the two horrified women in the doorway, not taking his eyes or the gun off Kate. "Now come on, Kate, right this second, or I'm gonna have to kill you, too, and kill myself. The police are coming!"

Suddenly Molly broke from the doorway and bounded in front of Elgin. "You're *crazy*, Elgin Horner," she shouted, and she pounced on the gun.

The sound of a gunshot cracked through the room, and Molly and Elgin seemed to collapse on each other. Kate thought that she was going to faint, as, with glazed eyes, she watched a stream of bright red blood dripping copiously down onto the French Aubusson carpet. Then Elgin pushed his chair back, and Molly crumpled to the floor.

Elgin stood up, still holding the gun. And the doorbell rang.

"The *detectives*—" Kate breathed.

With that, Elgin Horner put the gun to his head, and put a bullet through his brain.

Chapter 63

Have you heard anything from Kate Spenser?" Jonathan Valley asked Tripp.

"No, and I haven't called her. I'm sure she's completely unstrung over this. Her fourteen-year-old boy was in the next room when his father killed himself."

It was nearly midnight. The two men were sitting on the leather couch in Valley's wood-paneled office in his house in Beverly Hills. Earlier, Valley had signed himself off his movie shoot tomorrow, and had grabbed a plane for the coast. They could easily shoot around him, he knew, and taking Friday off would give him the weekend. He needed to get out of New York. And he wanted to talk to Tripp.

Armand, his chef, had left a niçoise salad in the fridge and stuffed butterfly shrimp in the oven before he'd gone home for the night, but food was the last thing either of them wanted. Jon had given the rest of the staff the night off as well. As always, when Tripp Kendrick came over, Jonathan Valley made sure that the two of them would be alone.

"Everything I know, I heard on the news," Tripp said soberly now. "Kate is truly a wonderful woman. I know she'll weather this latest horror, but it won't be easy."

"She's been through a lot," Valley agreed. "You're working for her now, Tripp—can she handle the business, do you think?"

"Yes, I think she can, Jon. She's been around it all these years, and what she doesn't know, she'll learn. It's a huge job, but she's very motivated to take it on. I have every confidence that she'll succeed."

"Well, I hope she can handle what happened tonight—her son . . . that's awful."

"I know. But she's strong. She was *Gibraltar* after Austin's murder. It almost made me think she *did* it!" Tripp threw out with a chuckle.

"I thought you'd pegged that Indian art dealer for the murder before Elgin Horner closed the case tonight—DeFarge, wasn't it?"

"Well, yes, Charles DeFarge was in the apartment that night. At least I'm pretty sure it was him, by the police description. Austin owed him money. And I'm absolutely *certain* that the man is capable of murder. But I don't know, the MO just didn't seem to be his style."

"Meaning . . . ?"

"Meaning that DeFarge would find a way to do his mayhem somewhere off the urbane track, I think. In a secret chamber in a casbah in Algiers, maybe, but not in a tony apartment with a doorman on New York's Upper East Side."

"Did anyone suspect *this* guy, do you think?"

"Horner? Who knows. Austin always put him down. Called him 'the beefeater.' "

"Austin put everybody down."

Tripp looked thoughtful. "For a while," he said after a long moment, "I thought *you* did it, Jon."

"You . . . whaaaa—?"

"You swore that you were going to kill him. More than once."

"Well sure, I might have *said* that, but—"

"I thought maybe you'd just snapped. That you went up to Austin's apartment, got into a knock-down brawl with the man, and did him with that ruby knife I gave you."

"You can't be serious!" Jon said, flashing a wide, bemused grin.

"I'm dead serious. Wait—scratch the *dead*," Tripp said, beginning to see the humor in his theory.

Jonathan Valley was laughing uproariously now. "You thought *I* did it? *Really*? Now it's *you* who've seen too many movies!"

"Yeah, *your* movies. Don't you remember telling me that if this was one of your *movies*, you'd kill him?" Tripp was laughing now, too.

"Yes, but *pleeeeeze*, Tripp! This isn't a movie. This is real *life*! And I have a *great* life. The greatest! Why would I want to screw it up?"

"You were pretty damned angry—"

"That's true, and I had every right to be. The man was scum. But I'm no killer."

"I know, I know—it's just . . . the knife—"

"It turns out his wife had one of those ruby-handled knives, too."

"Yes, and Horner got ahold of it."

"You know, I remember him in his glory days. Elgin Horner! We're the same age. I was a struggling actor living in a dowdy studio apartment in West Hollywood at the time, and Horner had the world by the tail. He was great-looking, charismatic, a professional football hero—he was lionized. I remember when he married gorgeous Kathryn Spenser. And I remember when their son was born—it was all over the news."

"Was it the drugs that brought him down, do you think?"

"My dime store analysis? I think the drug abuse was an effect, not a cause. In my opinion, weak character made him respond to his problems with drugs. *You* wouldn't do that—I know you, Tripp. And *I* wouldn't do that. Just as," Jonathan pronounced pointedly, "I wouldn't *kill* anyone."

"I know you wouldn't," Tripp said. "I never seriously—"

"You know what?" Jonathan stopped him. "Let's assume for just a minute that I *were* capable of murder. That I *did* have the soul of a criminal. That Feruzzi had pushed me to the limit with his threats to blow the whistle, his threats to flat-out kill my career. And suppose I actually found an opportunity to whack the guy. Even if I *were* inherently evil, I *still* wouldn't do it."

"Your reasoning?"

"Just this—*life* is what's important. And look at my life! Look at this place," he said, casting his eyes about the spacious mahogany-lined office. "And my Malibu house. And my New York digs. I drive the best cars made. I wear Armani suits. And these are hundred-dollar socks from Bijan, that robber!" Valley said, laughing. "Really, Tripp—I'm forty-two years old, I have a shitload of money, and I'm healthy. My dad's proud of me; my mom loves me. I have great friends. And best of all, Tripp," he said, his eyes softening, "best of all . . . I have *you* in my life. They can't take *that* away from me. On the other hand, how do you think I'd do in San Quentin?"

"A rhetorical question, right?" Tripp laughed. He could not imagine Jonathan Valley flourishing in a prison cell.

"Well, you get the picture, Tripp. Much better to live my life as a wealthy, happy, outed gay man in New York, Beverly Hills, and Malibu, than to spend my life in prison, huh? I actually thought about that—"

"Whoa! I thought you said that there was no *way* that you could kill a person—"

"No, no, I mean I actually thought about what my life would be like if Austin Feruzzi actually did nail me in the press, and the industry found out that I was gay. What would be the worst that could happen to me? Tony Perkins was a leading man, and most people in the business knew that he was gay. I loved that guy. He was a prince of a human being—intelligent, kind, decent to the core, a truly brilliant actor. And he had a good life. If Feruzzi *had* hauled me out, Tripp," he said softly, "it wouldn't have been so bad."

Neither of them spoke for a few minutes. Tripp found himself staring into the sputtering flames that were dancing on the hearth of the huge marble fireplace.

"No," he said finally. "It wouldn't have been so bad."

Chapter 64

Y GOD, SHE took a bullet for me!" Kate exclaimed again, shaking her head in wonder mixed with consternation. "Elgin was going to kill me!"

Molly had been in surgery for more than eight hours. Now Kate, Lane, and Trisha sat on straight-backed chairs by the side of her narrow bed in the ICU at New York's Lenox Hill hospital, waiting for her to regain consciousness. She had sustained a profoundly severe chest wound, frighteningly close to the heart, and her doctors could not assure the three women that she would recover from it.

"Elgin would have killed me," Kate murmured, a refrain she couldn't seem to stop repeating over the last hours. "I see that now. If he couldn't have me, he was going to kill me, he said so. And Molly took a bullet for me."

"He was insane," Trisha said quietly.

"I know," Kate whispered. "I know—"

"Elgin had explosive traits even back in college," Lane recalled. "That harsh aggression may have worked for him on the football field, but I remember how he used to fly into a rage when the least little thing went wrong . . . when he couldn't get a beer keg open . . ."

"It's true," Kate said. "That's really why I left him. Everybody thought it was because my parents didn't approve of him, but that wasn't it at all. His bouts of fury terrified me, especially after we had Shawn."

"You never told us—" Lane started.

"No," Kate said. "I could never tell anyone. I was young, confused, scared. Embarrassed, even, for making such a horrible mistake, and now there was a child . . . I worried that maybe it was my fault. I didn't know *what* to think. Finally, I got the strength to take Shawn and leave him."

"But Elgin was a good father to Shawn, wasn't he?" Trisha wondered.

"Just in the last couple of years, really. He seemed so much better after he got off the drugs that I trusted him with Shawn."

"And Shawn certainly loved *him*," Lane reflected. "When I took care of him while you were in the hospital, Kate, he talked about his dad all the time. He seemed to love being with Elgin."

"That's because he didn't like Austin," Kate responded. "Because Austin didn't like *him*, really—never wanted him around. Shawn would escape to his dad's, and I thought that was probably the best solution. He's fourteen now—I had no reason to believe that Elgin wasn't capable of taking care of him."

"And boys need their dads," Lane offered. "You can't blame yourself for not knowing that Elgin was dangerous."

"But I *do* blame myself," Kate said sadly. "I *should* have known. People don't change."

"You weren't one of his therapists," Trisha protested. "I'm sure that he had *them* fooled too. And maybe even himself."

Kate sighed. "I just know that it tore me apart to watch how Austin treated Shawn," she said, "and there seemed to be nothing I could do to soothe his hurt. So when Shawn was old enough, a teenager, and I really believed that Elgin had pulled his life together, I allowed him to stay with his father as often as he wanted to. Which was any time that *Austin* was home," she added, her beautiful face shaded with pain.

"Elgin always seemed to be larger than life," Trisha added. "People, football fans all over the country, still think of Elgin Horner as a hero."

"It's true," Kate affirmed. "Some of Shawn's friends collect his old football cards. And you should have seen how the parents would gather around him at PTA events, or parents' nights at school. They would pay more attention to *Elgin* than to their children's schoolwork."

"So Elgin became some kind of hero to Shawn," Lane summed up.

"A *huge* hero," Kate agreed. "Which is what Shawn *needed* him to be. And look how terribly he's hurt him now, putting him through this—" She dropped her head in her hands, and the other two were quiet, watching tears run through her fingers and down over the crusty, yellowing cast on her arm. Lane and Trisha each put an arm around her, trying to comfort her.

"I've made such a mess of things," Kate wept openly now.

"No you haven't," Trisha differed.

"It's not your fault," Lane put in.

"Of course it's my fault. I've brought Shawn into a world inhabited by two men who were not fit—"

"Stop it, Kate," Trisha urged. "You can't blame yourself."

"I *have* to blame myself. And my pitiful choice of husbands. What does that say about *me*?"

The other two became thoughtful. Both knew that it *did* say something about Kate. Lane remembered how back in college, when the four girls would sit around their dorm rooms discussing men, they used to tell Kate that she was much more interested in having a flashy escort than a caring soul mate. And that's exactly what she married in Elgin Horner and Austin Feruzzi, while the other two had truly found soul mates.

And that was not lost on Kate. Last night, Peter Newman had rushed to Kate's apartment the minute that Trisha was able to call him with the gruesome news. He assisted the paramedics with Molly, then, as soon as the police were finished talking to Shawn, he got the boy out of there, took him to the Spensers' on Sutton Place, and stayed with them until they were able to get him to sleep. Then he came back to Kate's to be there for the women all through the long and grueling police investigation, their second in just days. And when that was finally over early this morning, Peter called for a car, and brought the women to the hospital to be with Molly.

And Geoff Hamilton was on the phone with Lane half a dozen times during the night, supporting her through the whole ordeal. Now he was on a red-eye, flying out from California to be with his wife, and to take her back home when she was ready to go.

Kate broke the silence. "Shawn's going to need a lot of help to get through this," she breathed, almost to herself. "To survive this frightening ordeal . . . being right in the next room when his father committed suicide! It's horrible . . . horrible . . ."

"You're right, Kate, Shawn is going to need professional help, counseling," Lane agreed. "And you know that we'll do everything we can to help him too."

"I lost my daughter, but I won't lose my son," Kate vowed. "Shawn will get the best of care. And no more 'fathers' in his life to sabotage him. I'm through with men."

"Oh, Katie, you can't say that," Trisha exclaimed.

"You *bet* I can say that," Kate returned, with a surprising rush of strength. "I'm done with them! I obviously cannot be trusted to pick a decent man, a suitable partner—"

"We're hearing that Byron Lassen is a decent man," Lane smiled a little. "Are we ever going to meet him?"

"I can't think about that now," Kate said, not unexpectedly. She always cut off talk about the mysterious Byron Lassen.

The detectives who responded last night, Watson and Mora, the same two who were investigating the related Austin Feruzzi murder, had told Kate that Byron Lassen had *not* come to the apartment on the night of Austin's murder after all. The man who had identified himself as Byron Lassen to the doorman, and to Austin Feruzzi on the telephone, was not Byron Lassen at all.

They had talked to Lassen yesterday, Watson said. He had dined with friends at Spago in Beverly Hills on Tuesday night, then went home and, according to his houseman, retired to his bedroom suite shortly after midnight. Which was after three o'clock in the morning on New York's Fifth Avenue, where Austin Feruzzi lay dead in his black marble bathroom. The coroner had put the time of death at somewhere between midnight and 2 A.M.

When the doorman was questioned further last night, it turned out that the man who had identified himself as Byron Lassen fit the description of Elgin Horner.

The thought of Byron Lassen's involvement, or lack of it as it turned out, triggered another thought in Lane. "Kate, you never told us that *you* were in the apartment on the night that Austin was killed," she said. "We had to read it in the papers."

"I know," Kate responded, visibly reddening. "It was innocent, but I was terrified about how it would look. I didn't think that they'd find out. But of course, Luis—"

"What were you *doing* there?" Trisha demanded. "The next morning you took us there for moral support. So what on earth made you go over there *alone* the night before?"

"I'd spent that whole day with Daddy and the lawyers," Kate recounted. "One of the things they told me to do was to get a detailed list together before I went over there to pick up my things. They stressed that I would probably have just one chance at it, so I thought it would help if I could take some inventory in advance, before we did our morning raid.

"Irving Feintech had an early dinner brought in to the office, and we finished up at about eight o'clock. It was early. Too early for Austin to be home from dinner, I knew. He never cooked. He always went out. I called first to make sure that he wasn't home, and the machine answered. So I walked the few blocks over there from the attorneys' offices.

"I asked Luis if Mr. Feruzzi was in. He said he didn't think so, he hadn't seen him. So I took a chance. I went upstairs and took a quick look around, refreshed my memory, made some notes, and hustled out of there before Austin got home."

"So why didn't you mention that before we all made the trek over there in the limousine?" Lane asked her.

"Because we three were hip deep in so much *meshugas* that morning," Kate rejoined. "Your art-forgery theory, Lane. Setting up a meeting with Molly. Trisha's hunch that Austin caused Aiden Jannus's death. My head was spinning. I just didn't think of it. Then after we found Austin dead, I was just hoping that nobody would find out that I was there. What a joke. Those detectives know when you brushed your teeth!"

Molly stirred then, and moaned a little, but she didn't open her eyes. A pretty, frosted-blond nurse who tended toward plump hurried into the room and felt her forehead, then checked her pulse. Moving down to the foot of the bed, she glanced over the medical chart that was posted on a clipboard. The three friends watched expectantly.

"There's no change," she said kindly. "Are you all going to stay?"

"Yes," they confirmed in unison.

"Well, I'll be back in fifteen minutes or so. If she wakes up in the meantime, be sure to ring this bell," she instructed them again, and softly padded out of the room.

Kate dug a tissue out of her purse and dabbed at her eyes. "Molly took a bullet for me," she sniffled. "Why would she do that for *me*? I called her everything, I fired her—"

"We have to believe her, that she truly *is* sorry, that she really *does* love you, Kate—" Lane started.

"The Bible says, 'Greater love hath no man than to lay down his life for a friend,' " Trisha quoted.

"And, 'To err is human, to forgive is divine,'" Lane added. "We haven't talked about it, but if we weren't ready to forgive Molly, we wouldn't be here, would we?" she asked the others. "But it's all up to you, Katie," she added. "Do *you* forgive her?"

"Molly took a bullet for me," Kate murmured again. "And now she may die."

That signaled that the answer was yes, Kate forgave her. They all forgave her. Molly had come full circle. Austin Feruzzi had bedeviled her life, just as he had Kate's. She had finally seen that clearly, she had completely denounced him, she was deeply sorry for hurting Kate, and now she would pay a huge price, maybe even her life, for her transgressions. In the eyes of the group, their prodigal sister was back.

"Now we can only hope and pray that she'll come through this," Trisha said, looking down at Molly's small form huddled under crumpled hospital sheets.

"Kate, the last thing you said to Molly last night was that she was going to go to prison," Lane said then. "For a long time. Do you remember?"

"I remember."

"You could *put* her in prison, Kate," Lane added somberly.

"Why would I put her in prison?" Kate demanded. "She saved my life."

"Then how do we handle it that she broke the law? That a lot of people have paid a lot of money for artwork that they think was done by the great Aiden Jannus?" Trisha questioned, picking up Lane's train of thought, albeit quietly, lest someone should come into the room.

The women were silent for some moments as they pondered that moral dilemma. Into the silence, Molly moaned lightly, as if she, too, wanted to get in on the discussion, as the four of them had always done. Now the four were the only people alive who knew about the forgeries.

Lane, Kate, and Trisha looked down at Molly. Hooked up to numerous tubes and monitoring devices, with a mask over her face, she looked weak, vulnerable, and very small. The three women found themselves leaning on each other for support, as they did when back in college. Molly could die. She had thrown herself in front of a madman with a loaded gun for Kate, and probably saved her life. Molly was irrefutably redeemed now with the other three.

Still, the women wrestled with the ethics of the situation. Molly broke the law. If she were found out, she was looking at nationwide scandal, the least of it, and at worst, she faced hard prison time. Either way, her life would truly be ruined, and the career as an artist that she hoped for, in fact any career at all in the art world, would be hereinafter impossible. That is, *if* she even recovered.

"She made *no money*," Kate reminded them, "and those doctored Jannus pieces sold for hundreds of thousands of dollars."

Watching Molly's labored breathing, the women talked it out. No one but the four of them could ever prove that Molly Adams forged the Jannuses. Without any of their testimony, no charges could be brought. And after all, they reasoned, for the hundreds of hours of work that she'd put in, Molly Adams had never made a dime—why should she take a fall? The three then made a pact to keep Molly's secret forever.

"Still, what about all that artwork that's out there?" Kate asked then. "Paintings that came out of the Feruzzi Galleries, *my* galleries now, that have Aiden Jannus's name on them but were largely done by Molly Adams? Millions of dollars' worth of art!"

The women exchanged glances. Then Lane said quietly, "Who's going to know? And who's going to be hurt?"

"But money that the galleries made from these paintings was . . . ill-gotten," Kate labored over it. "Shouldn't I somehow make restitution? Even anonymously? But how—"

"Kate, you told us that your father and his lawyers said the business is deeply in the red," Trisha said.

"Yes, he and Irv did a comprehensive study of the business with Nathan Fields. They found that the tri-city galleries were losing money in buckets, and without major reorganization we're facing bankruptcy, largely because Austin seemed to be getting more and more reckless with his risky business ventures."

"And they don't know the *half* of it," Lane breathed, making a veiled reference to the forgeries.

"Yeah, well listen to *this* one," Kate fairly whispered, and she went on to tell a story that had the others wide-eyed with astonishment. It revolved around the harebrained ruby scam that Tripp Kendrick had called her about on the day that they'd found Austin Feruzzi dead. Tripp thought that the Indian art dealer, whom Luis, the doorman, had described as one of Austin's late-night visitors, might have killed him. Kate said Tripp was agonizing over whether he should go to the police with everything he knew about the man and his shady dealings, even though the scandal concerning smuggled gemstones would most likely put the Feruzzi Galleries out of business.

She and Tripp had decided to forget that they'd ever gotten wind of the scam, she said. Who would ever believe it, anyway? And with Austin dead, whether he was the one who killed him or not, Tripp was quite sure that Charles DeFarge would not dare to rear up from his netherworld.

"Do your dad and the lawyers know about *that* one?" Trisha asked incredulously.

"God, no! Only Tripp knows, and he stumbled on it in his gallery's back room, just as I stumbled on the forgeries in the storage room on Madison. And," she added, "we three are not even *having* this conversation right now, okay?"

Kate smiled. Somehow, now that Molly was back in the fold, Kate had the complete and fullest sense of trust again in her Briarcliff group.

"What in God's name was Austin thinking of?" Lane wondered now.

Kate reflected for a minute on Austin and his outrageous business escapades that were just now coming to light. And those were just the ones that she *knew* about! Dumb, high-risk capers that enormously and dangerously exposed the business, and at the same time yielded no hugely lucrative returns, judging by the books. It was pathetic, she thought, that for all of his highly placed connections, his moneyed friends, his wealthy in-laws, his knowledge of art, his oily charm, Austin Feruzzi was really at the heart of it just a small-timer, not terribly astute, as reckless and out of control in business as he was in his personal life, and not much more than a petty con man.

And further, he lived on the edge, so arrogant that he'd always thought he was above the law, that he could get away with anything. He had very little integrity, no scruples at all, and he was so greedy that he would do almost anything for a pay-off. What was Austin thinking of? "Think O.J.," Kate told them, "and you'll understand Austin."

To herself, she acknowledged that the *real* question was, what was *she* thinking of? That's the query that resonated with her. How could she have made a *life* partner, not to mention a business partner, of a man like Austin Feruzzi? But she had learned. Her amazing progress was hard won. All of her old, mistaken notions would be shed forever with the cast on her arm. She considered this truly the beginning of the rest of her life.

The women talked some more, softly, then they made a decision. They agreed that they would destroy all of the unsold canvases that still existed with the AJANNUS signature, and keep mum about the rest of them that were already out in the world.

"Let the collectors enjoy their Jannuses with nobody the wiser, and nobody hurt," Kate said. "But there will definitely be no more of them."

The three clasped hands on their pact, just as they did back in their college days. It felt right.

Suddenly, their attention was diverted to Molly. She was stirring. They watched her eyes flutter. As she slowly got her bearings in the room, the other three moved in closer. Hovering over her, they saw recognition glint in the green of her eyes.

Closing her heavy lids again, a smile flickered briefly at the corners of her mouth. She'd heard them. In a feeble voice she mouthed the words, "I love you all, so much. And," she whispered, "I already slashed the paintings."

HELLO, MY WONDERFUL, brilliant, sweet darling Katie," Byron Lassen said to his wife. "Are you happy, Mrs. Lassen?"

"If this is a dream, you must never wake me, Mr. Lassen," Kate said, looking up into his lapis-blue eyes.

"Mmm . . . I'm the envy of every man in the room," he murmured, pulling her closer to him as they danced. "I'm the envy of every man in the *world*!"

"But I can't cook!" Kate wailed, laughing. She could not remember ever before being quite this happy.

"I don't *want* you to cook! You won't have *time* to cook! Every spare minute you have, Mrs. L., I'll need you to be locked in my arms like this," he breathed, kissing her on the neck.

"Wonderful," she sighed. "We'll never eat. We'll live on love."

"That, and the fabulous cuisine of Franklin and Dee."

Franklin was Byron's chef. Dee was Kate's chef. Kate and Byron had put their respective houses up for sale, and they were in the process of purchasing together a magnificent estate high up on Tower Grove Road in Beverly Hills. They were melding their two separate households, and their household staffs.

"Christina is crazy about Franklin," Kate giggled.

"And Franklin has a crush on Dee!"

"But Dee doesn't want Franklin using her soufflé dishes . . . what are we going to do about all of them?" Kate asked.

"Leave them alone," Byron laughed. "They'll work it out. Or not. Who cares? I just want everybody to be happy."

It was one of those exquisite days in Carmel—sunny, salty, and slightly breezy, with big, puffy clouds hovering over the ocean, a day that could have been painted by Georges Seurat, and presented as a wedding gift for Kathryn Spenser and Byron Lassen.

Two hours earlier, the two had held hands and exchanged vows at the little Carmel Chapel-by-the-Sea, to the intoxicating sounds of the surf splashing hard upon jagged rocks. Now they were at the legendary Highlands Inn in Big Sur, just five minutes away, dancing at their wedding reception, Byron in formal gray morning coat and ascot, with striped gray trousers, and Kate in a silver-gray silk pongee slip-dress that shimmered down over her slender body to the floor.

Part of her had felt that she should wait a decent interval to get married, but she was so very much in love with Byron, and she wanted to have a child. Or maybe two. Byron kept telling her that he just wanted to marry her. That's all. "Now, later, next Christmas, next year, this week, tonight, whenever you want, my sweet Kate, is what we'll do," he'd said. So she chose today. Thanksgiving Day. Because she was very, very thankful.

They had agreed on Carmel as the perfect setting. Lane and Geoff played official host and hostess. Henry Spenser gave his daughter away, gladly this time. Kate's son Shawn was Byron's best man, handsome in gray cutaway coat and tails that exactly matched the groom's formalwear. Lane, Trisha and Molly were a triad, all three serving as Kate's maid- and matrons-of-honor, because there was no way that she could choose between them. And the menu, of course, was Thanksgiving turkey with all the trimmings. And a four-foot-tall wedding cake, for the guests to take home to sleep on, and dream.

Kate had traveled light-years ahead on all fronts since the dismal days surrounding her last husband's murder. On a personal level, she was no longer the weak, dependent, prescription drug- and alcohol-addicted woman that she had become as the used, abused, and unappreciated wife of Austin Feruzzi. She was in therapy for real, and getting stronger every day. No more pills washed down with wine. And no more anguish. For the first time since she'd left Briarcliff, Kate had finally found fulfillment in every way. She was happy, healthy, and strong again, and very much loved.

On the business front, with Tripp and Molly at the helms on both coasts, and with a new team of solid key people in London, thanks to Byron's connections, she was learning fast, and very effectively running the tri-city Spenser Galleries. And she was systematically cleansing the entire operation. Out with the DeFarge business, out with the forgeries, out with everything shady, risky, or suspect, Austin Feruzzi's legacy. Kathryn Spenser, of the newly renamed Spenser Galleries, was cleaning house.

Worry over any negative impact that might be caused by the scandalous murder of Austin Feruzzi and the subsequent suicide of Elgin Horner proved to be needless. The art world being quirky, it turned out that the aftermath of the murder of the wealthy gallery owner by his beautiful wife's jealous ex-husband, which had been all over the news, with pictures of the principals, and intriguing new details surfacing continuously, had actually focused attention on the galleries and brought new business into the houses.

Kate rested her head on Byron's shoulder as the two glided across the dance floor. After years in an abusive marriage, she had almost forgotten how real love really felt. Glorious. Exhilarating. And safe! Her new husband was looking down at her with such love and tenderness that it made her heart melt. He was everything that Austin Feruzzi was not—kind, loving, caring, and good. A *good* man. How grateful she was for that. She was quite simply mad about Byron Lassen, and it was enormously apparent that he was head over heels in love with her.

MOLLY WAS DANCING with a ruggedly handsome quasi-stranger, who made her feel as if she had known him all her life.

"I'm so glad that you could come to the wedding," she murmured. His response was a wide, closed-mouthed smile of genuine contentment that spread across his well-tanned features.

"Your friend makes a breathtaking bride," he said to Molly.

"She's been my college roommate and longtime dear friend, and now she's my boss," Molly returned, "and Kate is *always* breathtaking."

Molly was radiant in a floor-length sheer silk dress of many diaphanous layers, all in subtle shades of celadon green that seemed to take their cue from her own multihued sea-green eyes. This was her first significant trip since the night that she was nearly killed—she was still tender in spots, and she still tired easily, but now, finally, she had found peace of mind, and a profound sense of well-being.

With a substantial raise in pay, a newly hired assistant, and plenty of freedom to pursue her painting, she had resumed the directorship of the New York gallery. The arrangement was a perfect fit—Kate, who was based in Beverly Hills and learning the business, needed Molly's gallery experience, and Molly needed a salary while she was building up her art sales.

And Kate had come up with an extraordinary idea. They had cleared out a wide area right in the middle of the gallery floor to make a space where Molly could actually perch on a stool and paint. Larger and better lit than the cramped, cluttered studio in her Chelsea apartment, the environment was conducive to spirited creativity. Molly had set up her easels, canvases, tubes of paints, and pots of brushes, and when she was not overseeing a sale, or tending to the display or the books, clients would find artist Molly Adams at work, the centerpiece of the famous Spenser Gallery on Madison.

The unique set-up had turned out to be a boon for everyone. The recent sensational news stories surrounding the Feruzzi Galleries read like a novel. Word had spread that its director, Molly Adams, had thrown herself in the path of a bullet to save the life of the gallery's owner, beautiful Kathryn Spenser. Molly Adams at her easel, working on her vibrant canvases on the gallery floor, had in a short time become something of a New York attraction. Customers and tourists alike were coming in to watch her work, and they were ordering.

And, as Molly Adams's exclusive representative, Kate had started shipping her paintings across country to Lane at Hamilton House. Lane showed them around to business associates in Carmel, and Molly got her start on the West Coast, selling to prestigious galleries in the art-conscious little resort town.

Now she was on a much-needed vacation. For the past week, she had allowed herself to be deliciously pampered at Geoff and Lane's house. She'd come for Kate's wedding, of course, but the trip had also given her a chance to meet her very first clients, the merchants in Carmel who were selling her artwork.

And she was enormously attracted to one of them—Jackson Burke, a Carmel gallery owner and an artist in his own right, who sculpted dramatic, Henry Moore–like bronzes. Always, there was more demand for his wonderful pieces than he was able to create.

Carmel was a very small town, and Jackson was one of its own—a treasured, very talented and successful citizen. On the day that Molly had stopped in at his gallery to say hello, and to see the two pieces of hers that he had purchased for resale, he'd invited her to lunch. Two days later it was dinner at Carmel's cozy Fireside Inn. Next, she invited him to be her escort at the wedding today, and now it was clear to anyone who noticed that something sweetly romantic was happening between them.

She had never in her life felt this close to having it all. Finally, Molly was getting her piece of the good life, but she was not stealing it from anybody, she was not inheriting it, she was not marrying it. She was securing it in her own name, with her own talent, and by her own work. She had a life now, an identity. No longer did she feel that she was outside, pressing her nose against the glass—she was *in*.

And she had come to the realization that it was never about money after all. It was about having respect for herself, being at peace with who she was, doing what she had always yearned to do professionally, and being happy. And being open to *real* love, for the *right* reasons.

She and Jackson had not stopped dancing since they had arrived at the reception. Add to that the fact that she had been up since dawn, participating in the excitement of this day. She was determined to keep up, even though her body was beginning to feel the toll. Inwardly, she embraced the soreness in her chest and the shortness of breath that came with too much exertion these days, because it was her close brush with death that in the end had liberated her. It was the moment when the bullet hit that her world had changed, but for better, not for worse. It was then that Kate, Lane, and Trisha had forgiven her. Ironic, but she looked upon her near-fatal injuries as having made her whole again.

And it was on that night when the bullet hit that Austin Feruzzi's murderer had revealed himself, freeing Molly from gnawing worry about strands of red hair, fingerprints, traces of wool from a teal-green sweater, and such.

Yes, she had been in the Feruzzi apartment, but not on that night. It was two nights before, on the Sunday evening that Austin had come back to New York from Jonathan Valley's party in Malibu. The night of Molly's fortieth birthday, which she'd spent at home in her small apartment, alone. Soul searching. The night she had put in a call to Kate, and had poured out her heart on the phone machine. She remembered being relieved that Kate had not picked up. She wasn't sure she'd have had the fortitude to say everything she wanted to in person. She didn't know if Kate would believe her. In fact, she doubted it. But still, that call had strengthened her resolve.

The next evening, she'd found herself taxiing uptown to the Feruzzi apartment, bent on telling Austin that she had made up her mind, she was not going to do any more forgeries. She knew that she couldn't have that discussion with him on the phone, or in the gallery—it was too risky. So she had determined to simply drop in on him. They had a cool but professional relationship now, and when she announced to him on the phone in the lobby that she had to talk to him about business, he had cleared her to come upstairs.

She didn't go into the apartment, she didn't sit down, she stood in the entryway and got right to it, told Austin that she was through creating fraudulent artwork for him, she simply could not continue with the subterfuge.

Austin became livid. He grabbed her, shook her, threatened her, terrified her with his brutality and his rage. She'd fallen back against a wrought-iron bookrack in the entry, caught her hair, caught her sweater. Now Molly had a small taste of what Kate had been going through for years. She'd rushed out of the apartment, escaping into the New York night with a rapidly beating heart and hot tears of fright and fury.

No, of course she didn't kill him, but she had been racked with worry and guilt. Guilt for having had an affair with Kate's husband, guilt for doing illegal forgeries, and worry that when the police found trace-evidence at the murder scene that pointed to her, Kate, Lane, and Trisha would be more than happy to provide them with plenty of reasons why she could have done it.

She'd been liberated from all of that on the night that a bullet went through her chest.

J ONATHAN VALLEY was enjoying the wedding. A friend of both the bride and the groom, and a valued client of the Spenser Galleries, he was delighted to be here today. The wedding was beautiful. *Life* was beautiful! *Dead Right* was in postproduction. The movie was set to premiere simultaneously in Los Angeles and New York during the Christmas season, and it was getting some very good early press. Meanwhile, Jon had a few weeks off, and he was loving doing nothing. And Austin Feruzzi was off his back—for good.

On the other side of the room, Tripp Kendrick was sipping champagne with Trisha and Peter Newman. They were talking about all of the new and exciting plans in the works for the Spenser Galleries. Kate's new businessman-husband was helping with an innovative business plan, which included expansion of the New York gallery, an exuberant international advertising campaign, and the prospect of taking the business public down the road. Tripp had been given a lot of added responsibility on the West Coast while Kate was getting up to speed, and she had rewarded him with a hefty pay increase, along with a promise of lucrative stock options.

Peter Newman had a great interest in what Tripp had to say about plans for the Spenser Galleries. The reason, as he had finally told Trisha after Austin Feruzzi's murder, was that from the start-up of the business, he had been its silent partner. And *that*, he'd also told his wife, was why he had always been so tolerant of Austin Feruzzi over the years.

Peter was at Columbia when Augustine Feruzzi was studying art at Rutgers. They'd met at a college mixer. It was before Gus had become Austin, and Peter had found him bright, articulate, funny, sophisticated, and charming. One night, at a fraternity party where some of the students were using drugs, Peter suddenly felt a strong hand on his shoulder. Turning quickly, he was nose-to-nose with Gus Feruzzi, who whispered in his ear, "Come with me, right now—don't ask questions." Feruzzi hustled him out the back door of the fraternity house, while campus police were storming in through the front. Most of the Delta Chi's in the room that night were either suspended or expelled. At that time, Peter was very close to getting his MBA. He wouldn't have, if Feruzzi hadn't pulled him out of the house that night. And he had always felt that he owed him.

Some years after Peter had created Global and was doing phenomenally well, and before he had met Patricia Carroll, his old friend Gus, who was Austin Feruzzi by then, had asked him to back a venture that involved opening art galleries on both coasts, in New York and California. Peter felt that Feruzzi really knew the art world, and his business plan looked sound. And besides, he owed him. So he loaned Austin Feruzzi twenty million dollars in seed money to rent space, buy inventory, and get the first two galleries up and running.

What he hadn't realized, but came to know over the years, was that Austin Feruzzi was a shady character who walked both sides of the law, and an ineffectual bumbler besides, who had big ideas, but couldn't seem to keep the business in the black. Still, Peter Newman kept trying to help—he was protecting his investment. The recent million dollars that he'd loaned the man was simply more good money after what he kept hoping wasn't bad.

When Kate's father and the lawyers were digging deep into the business files to prepare for the divorce, they'd found out that Peter Newman held the huge note. Kate was astounded. She'd had no idea. She'd called a private meeting with Peter, and told him that although it was *her* money that had been keeping the business afloat for years, she had just now learned that it was *his* money that had got Austin started before she was in the picture. Peter told her not to worry about it, she would pay it off when she could.

But she *did* worry about it, she said. She wasn't sure that she could pay it off in this *lifetime*! He learned that Kate had confided to Byron Lassen that she was staggered by the amount of debt. Bad enough that the business was barely keeping afloat, she'd said, but she didn't see how she could ever pay the Newmans off, with the accrued interest. And even though Peter had assured her that there was no hurry, she felt that she was taking advantage of friends. A bank would have foreclosed years ago.

Last week Peter got a fax saying that funds were being wired to his account to cover the note, but asking him to please keep it a secret. Then, just a while ago, Kate took Peter aside, and with a dazzling smile she told him about her new husband's colossal surprise. Last night, after the rehearsal dinner and then champagne at Lane's house, when the two were back in their room here at the Highlands Inn, happily tired, standing arm-in-arm, watching the ocean roil from their balcony, Byron had presented Kate with a long, flat, black velvet box. "Your wedding present, darling," he'd said. Inside was a gorgeous diamond necklace, and under it was the note that had been held by Peter Newman and Global against the Feruzzi, now Spenser, Galleries, stamped PAID IN FULL.

TRISHA NEWMAN was still doing her network radio show, but her horizons were expanding. The scandal surrounding the Spenser Galleries, and her exclusive inside look at it, had made her ratings soar, and she had found herself invited to be a guest on all the talk shows. She had a book deal as well, on which she planned to collaborate with Kate, who felt that the project would be cathartic. And Trisha Newman, radio talk show host, was now in negotiations to do a *television* talk show, not on her husband's Global network, but on *NBC*! Peter was very proud of his wife.

LANE WAS STANDING alone on the sweeping balcony outside the beautiful Pacific's Edge dining room at the Highlands Inn, high atop the bluffs, fifteen hundred feet above the pounding surf. She looked down at the thundering whitecaps, breathing the wet, salt-laden air, drinking in the majesty of the roaring sea that had ever been her constant source of invigorating renewal. She felt great peace, back home in her idyllic Carmel, safe again in her enchanting English cottage with her wonderful Geoff, their children, and Beowulf, and back to business-as-usual at her beloved Hamilton House.

Turning, she looked in through one of the several pairs of open double doors to the festive scene inside. The bride and groom were dancing, laughing, greeting friends, greatly enjoying the moment and each other. And, Lane reflected as she watched the newlyweds glide across the floor, Kate had never been more beautiful. It wasn't very long ago when she was a beaten-down and battered wife. Now Katie had sprouted her full and glorious wings, and she was soaring.

She watched Molly dancing with brilliant sculptor Jackson

Burke—the two had eyes only for each other. Lane smiled, and silently predicted that she and Geoff would be seeing a lot of Molly Adams in Carmel, on trips to visit the gallery owners who were selling her artwork. Including Jackson. Especially Jackson. Lane approved.

Her eyes clouded for a moment as she noticed Molly favoring her left side. Molly would always have terrible scars, on her chest, and on her back where the bullet exited. Well, they would all have scars. They would never be the same after what happened at the end of the summer of '98. But they would always be there for each other.

Lane's eyes were drawn to a bright light at the front of the spacious room. Trisha was being interviewed by a correspondent from MSNBC's *Hollywood Interactive,* who was in Carmel to cover the society wedding and the merging of two great fortunes, Lassen money and Spenser money. And now the reporter was grabbing an interview with matron-of-honor Trisha Newman, who was definitely a rising media star.

Back out on the dance floor, Kate's mother was dancing with her father. Lane could tell that they were feeling good about their daughter. Finally. And Geoff's dad, Gregory Hamilton, was dancing with Maggie Carlson. They, too, had been through a very rough period. Now they were past it. On Maggie's left hand, which was resting on Greg's shoulder, Lane caught the sparkle of her brilliant diamond engagement ring. Lane was happy for them.

She saw her two sons then, looking so grown-up and handsome across the room, talking to Kate's son Shawn, and Trisha's Jason and winsome Alison. And she looked over at her Geoff, tall, handsome, smiling, chatting with wedding guests and several of their Carmel friends. As always, her heart raced a bit as she watched him. Geoffrey Hamilton, her husband. She reflected that Geoff had never possessed great wealth, power, prominence, or celebrity status. Her Geoffrey was a public servant who worked hard, who earned the salary of a small-town police chief, who had great integrity, and who was totally dedicated to his family and to the people of the community he served. How lucky she was!

Before joining her husband inside, Lane took another moment to savor this very special time. Two decades after college, her group, her sisters, her Briarcliff four, all together in the same room, and each of them doing exceedingly well. Last night, after the rehearsal dinner in town, they'd stopped for champagne at her house and the four of them had talked for a bit, privately and intimately. They took great comfort in being together, more so than ever before, because their longtime friendship had weathered a severe test, and the battle had been hard won. They had made it through—betrayal, battering, adultery, the loss of a child, treachery, divorce, threat to their lives, suicide, murder, all of it—and they had come through it together.

Today, the sun shone brightly on their future, both together and in each of their personal lives. Today was a day of great celebration. Today they knew that their bond, their very special longtime sisterhood, really was forever.

Acknowledgments

THEY SAY THAT YOUR SECOND NOVEL IS HARDER TO WRITE THAN YOUR FIRST. IT WAS, BUT THE PROCESS WAS EVEN MORE GRATIFYING. AND AGAIN, THE PEOPLE I LEANED ON FOR HELP ARE LEGION. LANE, TRISHA, KATE, AND MOLLY, THE FOUR BEST FRIENDS WHOM I INVENTED FOR GOSSIP, AND WHO HAVE NOW BECOME MY IMAGINARY FRIENDS (DON'T ASK!), JOIN ME IN THANKING THE FOLLOWING PROFESSIONALS AND GOOD FRIENDS OF OURS:

Charlie Fine, Ed Ruscha, Sonnai Frock, and **Kenneth Noland,** great American contemporary artists all, who walked me through the exotic art world, teaching me what I needed to know; and **Lance Leon,** who continues to create fantasy for me with his magical paintbrushes, just as he inspired the fanciful fictional paintings in *Gossip*.

Barbara DeVorzon, owner of the DeVorzon Gallery in Beverly Hills, who helped me set up *Gossip*'s Feruzzi Galleries, and showed me how to run the complex gallery business.

Wonderful **Charlotte Garey,** who, with her equally wonderful late husband, **Murray,** owned the fabulous Antiques Exchange in Orange County, where my character Lane Hamilton shops for choice merchandise.

Laurie Bernstein, my talented, hard-working Simon & Schuster editor, who nagged me just as much on this book as the last, thank God, and **Annie Hughes, Julie Black,** and **Brenda Copeland,** her industrious, creative, and quite adorable assistants; S&S production editor **Edith Baltazar,** for making the dreaded copy-editing process as painless as possible, and S&S Editor in Chief/author **Michael Korda,** for believing.

Thanks to my treasured friend, literary agent **Owen Laster,** for getting *Gossip* off the ground; to my publicist **Linda Palmer,** successful screenwriter and published novelist in her own right, who kept the story on track while taking on the role of social conscience for *Gossip* (e.g.: "Kelly, you have Kate drinking *champagne* to celebrate her pregnancy? Horrors! *Perrier water,* please!"); to **Shawn Kendrick** of Borders Books, for walking behind me for the last two years with a wheelbarrow full of my books, a cash box, and a credit card machine—the characters **Shawn** (Horner) and (Tripp) **Kendrick** in *Gossip* are both for you; to actor/screenwriter **Bob Factor,** for helping me out of a few deadline jams; to **Mark Gray** in NBC Reprographics, for getting me out of a couple of other deadline jams; and to brilliant agent **Nick Ellison,** who brought *Gossip* in for a landing, and who is up close and personally guiding my next three novels.

I owe great chunks of my life to both my longtime friend and NBC-4 News producer **Wendy Harris,** and my longtime friend and manager **Duncan Smith**—each was invaluable with plot points, and they both play themselves in *Gossip*.

And after playing herself in *Trophy Wife*, **Joni Lawrence,** head of makeup for NBC-4 News, took on for *Gossip* the roles of tour guide through her favorite vacation spot, Carmel-by-the-Sea, and enterprising creator of story ideas, and she still had time to do my makeup for the news every day.

And what would I do without my dear **Vera Brown,** owner of Vera's Retreat in the Glen, facialist to L.A.'s most glamorous movie stars, and a true saint among us—she played herself in *Trophy Wife,* and was the spiritual voice of *Gossip*.

I am indebted to Carmel Business Association Executive Director **Debby Alexander,** who taught me about the workings of that beautiful resort town, and provided constant support. I can't wait to drive up the coast to Carmel for a week, sign *Gossip* in its picturesque bookshops, then relax on the beach at Carmel Bay and work on *Angel!*

Gale Hayman, co-founder of Giorgio, Beverly Hills, and author of *How Do I Look?* gave fashion and beauty tips to my four fabulous women of *Gossip*; and **Paige Rense,** Editor in Chief of *Architectural Digest,* furnished and decorated their several tasteful homes.

Hamilton House, Lane's unique antiques and bakery shop in Carmel, actually exists and thrives—it is modeled upon the enchanting shop owned by my oldest (she hates that, but you know what I mean) friend **Terry Bagley,** called Bagley Home, on Sag Harbor's Main Street in the Hamptons.

Special thanks to LAPD Commander **Dan Watson,** who kept me straight on police procedure and cop-talk; to film maker **Verna Harrah,** owner of Middle Fork Productions, for coming through yet again with story help; to NBC-4 News editor **Bart Cannistra,** my once and present computer guru; to my favorite uncle, **Arthur Reason,** for his thoughtful read-throughs and cogent comments; and to my good friends **Sherry and Buddy Hackett,** for lending my Kate in *Gossip* their exquisite painting, *Montmartre,* by Maurice Utrillo.

Thank you **Michaela Hamilton,** Vice President and Associate Publisher of Dutton NAL, for publishing *Trophy Wife* in paperback, and for inspiring my character Lane Hamilton in *Gossip*.

And to the "gals"—award-winning comedy writer **Gail Parent,** my partner on the TV show *Kelly & Gail,* who inspires the humor in everything I write; brilliant novelist **Olivia Goldsmith,** who continually teaches me about life in the publishing business; and literary critic **Dorothy Sinclair,** who approached her assignment to review *Trophy Wife* with great skepticism, and ended up being my most vocal cheerleader, calling me weekly to demand that I hurry up with *Gossip*—she will forever be my friend.

And the "guys"—movie producer **Daniel Melnick,** who had brilliant answers to every large life question I put to him; NBC-4's multi-talented weather reporter **Fritz Coleman,** writer, actor, and my buddy at work, who was a great sounding-board all through *Gossip;* and restaurateur **Emilio Baglione,** who can't do enough to help with my books, and who feeds me, besides.

Thanks to NBC Executive Vice President **John Rohrbeck,** and **Leonard Rabinowitz,** co-Chairman of Carole Little, Inc., for putting me on to New York's coolest neighborhoods, shops, restaurants, and night spots, where my *Gossip* characters live and play.

My everlasting gratitude to **Steve Pass, Barbara Jean Thomas,** and **Tony Tang,** for keeping me sane at home, and to NBC-4's President and General Manager **Carole Black,** and News Director **Nancy Bauer,** for supporting my fiction-writing efforts even as we pound out the day's news in a highly charged, impossibly busy newsroom.

Heartfelt thanks to a literary giant, novelist **William Peter Blatty,** my hero and longtime friend, for always being available to read my stuff, and always being eager to cheer me on.

Thanks to my friend **Leeza Gibbons,** who graciously shared her talk show stage with my eccentric artist Aiden Jannus in *Gossip.*

Big thanks to the gang at the **Manhattan Club,** my permanent home in New York, for always taking such good care of me when I'm there doing battle in the canyons of publishing.

Always and forever my profound gratitude to **Alice Scafard,** my terrific and quite simply incredible mom, for having me, and to **Kelly Lansford,** my totally perfect, ray-of-sunshine, princess daughter, thank God I had her!

I am eternally grateful to my "brother," writer, celebrity hair stylist, and resident genius **David Blair,** who does a zillion things for my books, including setting up my webpage—you can visit me at **http://www.kellylange.com**—I'd love your comments.

AND LAST BUT NOT LEAST, BUT CERTAINLY LITTLEST, MY THANKS TO BABY BEN ROSEN, WHO WAS THERE FROM THE INCEPTION OF THE IDEA TO THE FINAL EDIT OF GOSSIP, BOTH IN AND OUT OF HIS MOTHER'S WOMB, MAKING SURE THAT NONE OF US EVER FORGOT WHAT IS REALLY IMPORTANT IN LIFE. HE HAD A TOUGH FIGHT, BUT HE MADE IT HERE—AND SO DID GOSSIP!